SARAH'S MOUNTAIN

Book Three

Bronwyn Trotter

Publisher: Inspiring Publishers,
P.O. Box 159, Calwell, ACT Australia 2905
Email: publishaspg@gmail.com
http://www.inspiringpublishers.com

 A catalogue record for this
book is available from the
National Library of Australia

National Library of Australia The Prepublication Data Service

Author: Bronwyn Trotter
Title: Sarah's Mountain
Genre: Fiction
ISBN: 978-0-6450780-1-5

Acknowledgments

A huge thank you to my family and circle of friends who have praised me with encouragement during my writing 'The Trappers Promise' trilogy, and to 'Inspiring Publishers' – whom I also extend my gratitude to for imparting your knowledge of publishing on to me, and for your support all through this journey. Thank You All.

Bronwyn

Forward

On Sarah's mountain, when a trapper makes a promise, it is made to last a life time! The night Sarah's father, Calahan Cole asked four trappers to make their promise to watch out for her should anything happen to him, Sarah was barely three years old. At seven, Sarah was used to living in the Rockies amongst men who hunt wolves for their skins. By the time she was fifteen, she had as it were, 'mastered the art of trapping,' and skinning had become second nature to her.

In Cedar Creek, where the trappers went to escape the winter blast coming over the mountains, a man used greed to cheat Sarah out of her home Mountain View Lodge, and cunning as his weapon to kill her father.

It was at her father's burial, where wealthy cattle and horse rancher Major Hardy's son Frank fell in love with her. Major Hardy's past where Sarah's father was concerned, was not one of friendship, and so Frank and Sarah's union had him threatening to make Sarah ugly with a whipping if she didn't stay away from his son. It was Frank who bore the horrendous wound from the whip while trying to protect Sarah, which only served to bring them closer together.

Having declared their love for each other, Sarah became pregnant, but before their baby could be born, Frank ventured to the High Country where he came under attack from wolves and ended his life. Franks untimely death left four trappers the only help Sarah had when she gave birth to Franks son Thomas. Blaming the trappers for not protecting Frank, Sarah told them she no longer wanted anything to do with them, and although their promise could not be broken, the men stepped back to allow her to raise her son.

When Frank fell in love with Sarah, Millicent Crawley, the daughter of the owner of Cedar Creeks general store lost her chance to marry him, so along with her father, she decided she would marry Christian Morgan, a bounty hunter who became Cedar Creek's sheriff instead. But when Sarah came to town and they fell in love, she had to get Sarah out of the way. Millicent's attempt to kill Sarah however, ended in her own death. That same day, Millicent's father lost his life in a shootout with Christian, but not before it was proven he cheated Sarah's father out of Mountain View Lodge.

The four trappers weren't the only ones watching over Sarah. Major Hardy's gun-hand Foley Andrews is in love with her and has become her friend in the hope of getting her to marry him. Having learnt Frank was dead, he began a long process of marriage proposals that Sarah constantly rejected, which left him disappointed and angry when she married Christian and is expecting his child.

Satisfied their promise was at an end, the trappers returned to the mountain for another year of trapping, leaving Sarah and Thomas living happily in town with Christian awaiting the birth of their new addition to their family.

Now sworn in as Christian's deputy, Foley is forced to watch the woman he is in love with from afar. But Foley hasn't given up hope of gaining Sarah's love. He has vowed to stick around to see where Sarah's marriage will take her...

Chapter One

ajor Hardy did not take lightly to Sarah warning him she would skin him if he should ever harm Thomas. At the close of Sarah and Christian's wedding, he returned to his ranch to ponder exactly what her threat meant, and decided to keep his new gun-hands close by in case she tried to carry out her threat, even so, he vowed he would do everything in his power to mend the rift that had come between himself and Sarah.

Cedar Creek has become relatively peaceful under Sheriff Christian Morgan's, and his deputy Foley Andrews control. Sarah was due to have her second baby any day and Christian was especially excited about the impending birth. His family has grown from one to almost four in a matter of months, making Brother Abrahams prediction of 'Three will become Four' soon to be fulfilled, and Christian couldn't be more pleased.

Summer was in full bloom, and Sarah's belongings she used for trapping had been packed away. Her heavy skinning knife in its sheath, along with her pistol and hat with the split brim were stored away in a trunk in the bottom of the pantry in the kitchen of the lodge. Her shirt with the pretty blue/grey flowers and lace collar and cuffs, her tight-fitting trousers and fur vest were packed away in the bottom drawer of her dresser in her and Christian's bedroom. Now that Thomas attends school more often, his circle of friends has grown. After Christian gave Jamie Finch and Daniel Connell a good talking to about tormenting the other children, they have become friends with Thomas and his friend Billy Henderson. Thomas and Christian spend many summer days together, fishing for trout while a heavily pregnant Sarah sits on a blanket on the riverbank and watches. Town folk continue to attend church every

Sunday, and once a month Preacher Barnes holds a church picnic. The Town Hall has become a regular meeting place, and at the end of each month women folk organize a supper and dance.

Sarah refuses to attend church, or go on church picnics. She feels she cannot attend, not after what she did in the church, the day she frightened everyone in attendance. She only meant to scare those responsible for stealing Thomas away from her, but instead succeeded in scaring the whole town, besides, Preacher Barnes would not allow her to attend. He told her she had committed a crime of sacrilege against the church, and he would not have anyone attend his church that did not respect what he stood for. Therefore, Sarah informed Christian, she was ineligible to attend any of the church picnics either. Anyway! she told him, she would rather spend her picnics with her family. Nor would she go to the dances at the Town Hall.

Sarah and Christian didn't argue, instead they had what they called 'vigorous discussions' where he insisted on taking her dancing and she insisted on not going. Sarah said she was too pregnant to learn to dance, but her real reason was her memory of the dance just a short while ago where she confronted Millicent Crawley with stealing her locket that her father gave her for her tenth birthday. That dance had been the first official dance in the newly completed hall and everyone was there, including Christian, who defended Millicent after Sarah accused her of stealing things from the lodge.

Christian loves Sarah so much he tries not to say or do anything to upset her, so has dropped asking her about going to the picnics and the dances until after she has their baby, perhaps then she will change her mind. Christian spends his free time taking Sarah on their own private picnics, where they lay on a blanket in the sun and make gentle love to each other. But Sarah is adamant she won't be changing her ways after the birth.

Christian woke early to find Sarah still asleep beside him. Reaching over and brushing her hair off her face, he kissed her on her cheek, then felt her stomach that was bulging from their baby she was carrying. Moving his hand over the bulge, he felt for the constant kicking the baby had been giving Sarah before sliding his hand under her stomach and slipping it between her legs. Feeling aroused, he wanted to have sex with her, she was already lying on her side facing away from him, all he had to do was get her ready to take him and he would push himself in from behind. But when Christian's hand felt the moist area between Sarah's legs he frowned, because Sarah seemed more wet than usual. Pulling his hand out from under the bedclothes, his eyes widened with shock at seeing it covered in blood. Throwing the bedclothes back, he saw the bed and Sarah covered in the mess.

"Sarah!" he cried in earnest while shaking her. "Sarah, wake up!" he urged. Still half asleep, Sarah rolled over to see what the fuss was about. "What? What is it Christian? What's the matter?" she asked sleepily. "Your bleeding!" he answered sounding anxious. Sarah looked at her bare legs. "Oh! it's our baby, it must be coming," she commented casually while thinking that must have been why she felt strange when she went to bed. Even though she was heavy with her pregnancy her body felt unusually light, and feeling lightheaded at the time, was glad to lay down to take the weight off her legs. As a sharp pain suddenly gripped her, she held her hand to her stomach. Wiping his hand on the bedsheet, Christian climbed over Sarah, and jumping off the bed, raced toward the door.

"Where are you going?" Sarah asked not panicking at the sight of blood. Already having had one child, Doc Harris warned her this could happen.

"I've got to get Doc!" Christian answered, wrenching open the door.

"Well you better put some pants on, I'm sure Doc or anyone else out there would just love to see you running about like that!" Sarah laughed until another pain took hold.

"You better send Thomas for Doc!" she grimaced.

While she lay back against the pillows holding onto her stomach, Christian pulled his trousers on as quickly as he could, and racing to Thomas's room, shook him hard to wake him.

"Thomas! wake up son!" he said loud enough for Thomas to open his eyes.

"What is it Pa? What's wrong?" Thomas asked through his sleepiness.

"It's your Ma! Sarah! she's having our baby!" As Christian started back toward his and Sarah's room, Thomas came wide awake.

"Now?" he yelled.

"Yes! now! Thomas, can you get Doc?" They both heard Sarah's cry of pain. "And be quick!" Christian added when he heard her.

Hearing his Ma's cry, Thomas dived out of bed, pulled his trousers on over his nightshirt and raced down the stairs two at a time. Running out the door and without stopping to speak to anyone in the street, he sprinted to Doc Harris's practice. Meanwhile Christian went back to Sarah, saw she had pulled her legs up and was now lying naked amongst their pillows.

"You better get my nightgown Christian, I can't lie here like this with everyone looking at me." Christian smiled, he didn't mind looking at Sarah lying like she was, but he got her nightgown and helped her into it. Unable to pull the gown down to cover her bent up legs, he left it covering her belly, then sat on the bed and watched as another pain gripped her.

"Oh! it's coming, I have to push!" Sarah cried, screwing up her face.

"Can you wait for Doc?" Christian asked worriedly.

"No! this baby isn't waiting for anyone!" Sarah managed to say while trying her best not to push. When the pain subsided, she lay back to wait for Doc.

"I hope Thomas doesn't take too long," she whimpered.

When he got to Doc's practice, Thomas didn't bother knocking. Bounding up the hall to the kitchen, he found Gerda and Doc seated at their table about to have breakfast.

"Thomas!" Doc exclaimed, surprised to see him so early in the morning.

"It's Ma, she's having her baby! you better come quick!" Thomas puffed.

Knowing Sarah was close to her time, Doc stood up, and while rushing off to get his bag, yelled over his shoulder, "Gerda!" When he turned to see where Gerda was, she was right behind him and almost caused him to bump into her. Unable to have children

4

herself, when Sarah was born and her mother had passed away two years later, Gerda considered Sarah her daughter, and so Sarah's family became her family.

"I'm ready Ronald, I wouldn't miss this for the world," she smiled.

Doc and Thomas raced across the street and headed toward the lodge. Gerda walked as fast as she could. She never ran, baby or no baby. Ronald would do the hard part, she would do the cleaning up.

When Thomas came rushing in followed by Doc and Gerda, Christian was still seated on the bed and all three crowded around to see what, if anything, was happening.

"Well Sarah, how are you doing?" Doc asked taking a look between her legs. When his eyes widened at what he was seeing, he quickly rolled up his sleeves and didn't bother with his bag, he didn't have time.

"I think we better get a move on, this baby is just about here, Thomas! Christian! wait outside!" he ordered, but neither Christian nor Thomas moved.

"Not on your life Doc! I'm staying right here!" Christian informed Doc while gripping Sarah's hand.

Trying to smile at him through her pain, she looked at Thomas standing beside the bed. "Thomas honey, you better wait outside," she said gritting her teeth as yet another pain overtook her. Leaving the room, but not wanting to be left out, Thomas stood just outside the door where he could look back at his Ma and Christian.

"Sarah, when you have pains, how close are they?" Doc asked just as Sarah doubled up with another pain. "Well I got my answer to that question!" he said seriously. Sarah couldn't speak, as the baby's head crowned, she pushed with all her might.

"Push Sarah, push!" Doc urged keeping his eyes fixed between Sarah's legs. Gerda quickly handed Christian a cloth to wipe perspiration from Sarah's forehead. A few anxious minutes later, when the baby slid into Doc's hands, Christian's eyes welled as he leant over and kissed Sarah passionately. Hearing the baby cry and wanting to see whether he had a brother or a sister, Thomas crept back into the room.

"You did well Sarah, congratulations Christian, you have a beautiful daughter!" Doc looked over at Thomas standing off to one side and smiled. "Come on Thomas, come and see your sister," he beckoned. While Sarah undid the top of her nightgown and let Doc lay the new born against her chest, Thomas moved to the side of the bed.

"We can't leave her too long, let Gerda clean her up and then you can nurse her," Doc said smiling at the group huddled together.

"What do you think?" Sarah asked Thomas.

Thomas had seen baby animals being born on the mountain during the spring but had never seen a human baby born before. His Ma told him about giving birth to him on the riverbank outside their cabin on the mountain, but he never imagined this was what she went through to bring her babies into the world, and he felt a lot of love for her right then.

"I love you Ma," he whispered, kneeling beside the bed as tears threatened to fall.

"I love you too Thomas," Sarah said putting her hand under his chin.

"But she looks like a skinned rabbit!" he joked, and they all laughed, all except Gerda. Tut-tutting at their making fun of the little girl, she pushed her way between Christian and Thomas. "Let me take her, she will look beautiful after I bathe her, I will make her all nice and warm, then you will see." The baby cried loudly as Gerda carried her to a table set up in a corner of the room where a dish of warm water and clothes sat ready. Thomas watched with interest as Gerda bathed then dressed his sister in a tiny calico nightgown and diaper, then wrapped her in a lace shawl and carried her back to the bed.

"Here Christian, you nurse your daughter while I see to Sarah, she needs tidying up, Thomas you want to wait downstairs? Maybe get yourself some breakfast?" Gerda ordered while ushering Thomas out the door. Doc followed Thomas downstairs and let him make them coffee.

While Gerda sorted Sarah, Christian's heart swelled with pride as he sat gazing down at his daughter nestled in his arms. After letting Gerda make Sarah comfortable, Doc came back and checked that everything was fine, and informed Sarah he would come back the next day to check on her and her baby. Once that was done, he and Gerda bid them good-day and left them to celebrate their babies birth. Pleased with how easy it had all gone, as he and Gerda made their way back to his practice, he commented on how strong a woman Sarah was and how well she coped with childbirth, putting it down to Sarah walking the mountain and trapping wolves.

With her nightdress changed and the bed freshly made, Sarah lay comfortably in bed nursing her baby. "What are we going to call her Christian?" she asked just as Thomas came in carrying mugs of coffee and a plate of hotcakes on a tray and interrupted them before Christian could answer.

"Thank you, Thomas, but I think I might have tea now while I'm feeding our baby," Sarah said smiling at his effort to get them breakfast.

"Sorry Ma, I'll go make tea," Thomas said picking up one of the mugs. Moving to the door, he stopped and turned back. "Can we call her Elizabeth, after grandma?" he asked before going out and pulling the door closed.

"Do you mind?" Sarah asked Christian gazing at the tiny bundle sleeping in her arms. "I think Elizabeth is the perfect name for her," he answered lifting his head to look at Sarah.

"When Elizabeth grows up, she is going to be as beautiful as you," he said kissing Sarah passionately while whispering lovingly in her ear. "You know I woke up this morning as randy as hell, I wanted to make love to you, but our daughter had other ideas about that!" They both laughed at his comment then kissed each other again.

When Thomas came back carrying a pot of tea, a china cup and saucer, a jug of milk and a bowl of sugar on a tray, he asked if he could nurse his sister. Gently taking her from Sarah, Christian handed her to him, and while sitting on the side of the bed, Thomas smiled down at the little girl nestled in his arms and made a promise to himself.

They were a happy family, and Thomas hoped they would live like this for the rest of their lives, but if anything should happen to Christian, or his Ma, he promised he would take care of his little sister. Smiling over at Thomas holding his sister gently, Sarah announced proudly, "her name is Elizabeth."

Chapter Two

Sarah was enjoying living in Cedar Creek but still wouldn't allow herself to relax. Although she enjoyed sunny summer days sitting on a blanket by the swimming hole with Elizabeth, whom everyone started calling Lizzy soon after she was born, and watching Christian and Thomas challenging each other with daring somersaults off boulders into the deep pool and having swimming races against each other, there were people in town she was wary of, and she refused to drop her guard. When Christian and Thomas fished for trout, once they were back at the lodge, it was up to Sarah to cook the fish while Christian and Thomas kept Lizzy occupied. Occasionally, while Thomas was in school and Christian was busy being sheriff, Sarah took Lizzy rabbit snaring on her own. Rabbit stew was always welcomed whole heartedly, especially during the cooler months.

As Lizzy grew, the family rode out to the prairie to snare rabbits together. Strapping Lizzy to the front of her the same way she did Thomas when he was a baby kept Lizzy snug so she wouldn't fall off Star as they rode along. Then waiting for rabbits to be caught, Sarah and Christian drank coffee in the shade by the ponds while they watched Thomas playing with Lizzy.

Not wanting any of Major Hardy's men coming across Sarah like he had the day he came across her at the ponds before they married, Christian would not permit Sarah to go bathing there anymore. There was no need for her to go there to wash her hair. She had a beautiful cast iron bathtub in her washroom, where, on many occasions, especially after Thomas and Lizzy had gone to bed, Christian enjoyed bathing with her. From there he carried her upstairs to their room where they fell into bed and ended the evening by making tender, and sometimes intense love to each other.

They loved visiting their many friends, often visiting Foley and Brady at their farm. The two men were always pleased to have Sarah and Christian visit. Everyone watched as months slipped by, and Lizzy went from crawling, to walking, then to running. Christian and Thomas tried their best to keep her out of mischief by chasing her everywhere she went.

Christmas became a happy affair when Sarah commenced having dinner parties like her mother used to have. Sarah thought it grand to have a large group of her and Christian's friends attend to celebrate the trappers being back in town, and it gave her an excuse to wear her mother's glamorous evening dresses. The four trappers along with Martha and Dave Henderson and their son Billy, Doc and his wife Gerda, Ham and Patrice Hammond with their two daughters Sissy and Lilly attended, as did Foley and Brady, although Sarah thought Foley could lighten up a little, he always seemed morose when around her and Christian. Patrice, Martha and Gerda were always happy to pitch in to give Sarah a helping hand in the kitchen. Everyone enjoyed the festive mood the parties brought to an otherwise gloomy winter.

Returning from the mountain each winter, Joe, Fergus, Garrett and Will, showed obvious pleasure at seeing how happy Sarah and Christian were. They enjoyed sharing Christmas dinner with them, and noted how Christian appeared to be a good husband who doted over Sarah, and he was equally good to Thomas, and of course, he adored Lizzy.

It was one night not long before Joe and the trappers were due back in town that became a turning point in Sarah's life.

Seated at their dining table having dinner with Christian and Thomas, Sarah sat nursing Lizzy on her lap feeding her when she heard footsteps hurrying along the street outside.

"Christian, can you get the door!" she demanded, not looking up while spooning food into Lizzy's mouth. Christian hadn't yet heard a knock, and frowning, looked puzzled at Sarah. The loud knock startled Lizzy causing her to open her mouth and bellow. When food fell out of her mouth all down the front of her, Christian threw down his napkin, and cursing softly, went to the door and opened it rather gruffly to find Ham standing on the porch.

"Sorry to disturb you right on dinner Chris!" Ham said apologizing, then lowering his voice, said something Sarah couldn't hear. Looking agitated when Christian ushered him in, Ham looked first at Sarah then Thomas sitting at the table in front of a glowing fire.

"Sorry for the intrusion Sarah," he said not knowing how to tell her he came bearing bad news. Sarah put down the spoon she was feeding Lizzy with and waited for him to speak.

"It's Star Sarah! he's down," Christian said in answer for Ham. When Christian said Star was down, it could only mean one thing, Star was dying. Jumping up from the table, Sarah handed Lizzy over to Christian and grabbed her coat.

"You want me to come with you?" Christian asked as she put her coat on.

"No, this is personal," she said quickly kissing him on her way out the door.

"I'm coming with you Ma!" Thomas said grabbing his coat and following her out. Left behind, Christian stood on the porch holding Lizzy and watched Sarah and Thomas follow Ham along the street and disappear around the corner.

Upon entering the livery, Sarah hurried to a stall to find Star lying on his side. "Star, oh, Star," she soothed kneeling beside him and hearing his breathing coming in short gasps.

"There's nothing I can do Sarah," Ham said quietly from just inside the stall.

"It's alright Ham, maybe he just needs to rest." Sarah dreaded this day coming. While comforting him with gentle strokes, she lay her head against him and remembered the day Frank sat on his horse outside the Ferguson House and gave him to her.

She had just lost her father and Star was a colt at the time. His coat was perfect, the star in the middle of his forehead prominent, and Sarah named him before she stepped from the porch to pat him. At first, she didn't want the horse, but Frank insisted his father was

11

going to shoot him, which she found out later to be a lie, so after riding him over the bridge and all the way along the river to the ponds, and finding him fast and sure footed, she accepted Frank's gift. Then when Frank asked her for a gift in return by saying all he wanted was a kiss, she let him kiss her. Their kiss was her first experience with a man, because Frank insisted, he was a man not a boy.

When she rode Star out of town that day, she knew he was the best horse she would ever ride, and over many years he carried her a long way from the mountain and back again. Never letting her down when taking her away from wolves and trappers alike, and when Thomas came along, he carried both of them to safety. The night Frank was whipped, when the Major's men took Star away with them, he reared savagely not wanting to go, convincing Sarah he knew the horror befalling his human friends. It was Foley Andrews, still in pain from the whiplash he received to his face that brought Star back to her days later.

A few weeks after Thomas was born, while standing in the clearing down from her cabin, Sarah introduced Star to her tiny baby. Keeping a firm grip on his lead while holding Thomas in her arms, she brought him close for the horse to smell, and after sniffing Thomas, Star nodded vigorously up and down as if to say he approved, and when Thomas was stolen from her, he carried her to the South Side Camp at the base of the mountain so she could get the wolf she used to scare the town folk into giving Thomas back. Even though he didn't like being covered in blood, he carried the dead wolf draped over his back all the way to town.

As a little boy, Thomas was able to pull Star's mane and ride him bareback around Sarah's cabin. Star never once dislodged him. When Thomas swam with him in the river, they frolicked like two children with Thomas climbing on his back and diving off. It was Star swimming around in circles looking for Thomas until he surfaced that made Sarah laugh while sitting on the riverbank holding her rifle in readiness for marauding wolves. Like he had with Thomas, Star had been introduced to Lizzy as a newborn too, and Star seemed to know she was a delicate little human not to be harmed.

On the mountain Star ran free, but he never strayed, and in Cedar Creek, after riding him out to the prairie to snare rabbits, he waited by the stand of trees near the ponds while Sarah bathed or sat at her fire drinking coffee. Whenever she left him at the livery, if she didn't tether him to a stall, he followed her down the street, making folk laugh at the silliness of the horse coming behind her, which caused Sarah to become angry at folk laughing at her, and so with her hand on her knife, she glared at them until they stopped. Star though was a smart horse. When she stopped walking, he stopped too and waited for her to set off again. But it was children joining in with laughter that made Sarah turn it into a game. Whispering a few choice words that would make a grown man's hair curl, she made him follow her all the way back to the livery, giving the children reason to laugh. With her eyes filling with tears, she smiled at the memory.

When word travelled quickly around town that Star was down, Foley stood guard at the door trying to keep the crowd that was gathering back. Patrice was there, so was Doc, made aware of the situation by Foley seeing Ham run to the lodge to get Sarah. Racing to the livery as fast as he could, he found there was nothing he could do. Christian didn't want to stay at the lodge while Sarah was with Star. Having come to like the horse too, he didn't know how Sarah would take his leaving her and wanted to be there. Dressing Lizzy in a warm coat, he headed for the livery, and standing outside the stall, watched Sarah and Thomas inside with Star.

It soon became obvious Star wasn't going to get up, and not wanting him to suffer any longer, Sarah got to her feet, and going to Christian, took his gun from his holster. Turning back, she stood over Star, and keeping her arm straight, aimed the gun toward him, but because she loved him, she couldn't handle the pain of losing Frank's precious gift, and so she hesitated.

Seeing her falter, Christian handed Lizzy to Patrice who took her into their residence, and going to Sarah, put his arm around her, then indicating for Thomas to step away, he covered her hand with his while letting her lean against him, and when Thomas stepped over to Foley standing at the entrance, he helped Sarah pull the trigger.

13

With the blast of the gun reverberating through the livery, people outside bowed their heads and knowing it was over, walked away. Realizing an important part of her life had come to an end, with her face pressed against Christians chest, Sarah wept openly. Remaining where they were, Christian let her cry.

Remembering riding Star with his Ma when he was little, then on his own when he got older, and all those times he swam with Star in the river, Thomas felt he had lost a best friend, and weeping, ran back to the lodge and raced up to his room to mourn alone.

To help Sarah over her loss, Christian took her and their children to a place by the river where they enjoyed swimming and picnics. The place he found along the road leading to Major Hardy's ranch had short grass that felt soft underfoot. The area allowed them a place to spread their blanket under stands of tall trees growing along the riverbank that afforded them shade from the hot noonday sun. While Thomas stayed on the riverbank taking care of Lizzy, Christian coaxed Sarah into the shallows where they frolicked in each other's arms.

It was several weeks later that Major Hardy pulled his surrey up outside the lodge and climbed down. With Christian out at a ranch dealing with rowdy ranch-hands, Sarah was home with just her children for company. Hearing the carriage coming down the street, and knowing it would stop in front of the lodge, Sarah waited. Major Hardy had his gun-hands with him and two horses tethered to the back of his carriage, and was halfway up the steps when the front door opened and Sarah came out carrying Lizzy.

"Hello Sarah, Thomas... hello Elizabeth," he greeted, smiling at Lizzy.

"Hello Major," Sarah said as she crossed the porch.

"Hello grandpa," Thomas greeted, following Sarah onto the porch. Unsure of the white-haired man coming up the steps, Lizzy hid her face against Sarah's shoulder.

"What are you doing here Major?" Sarah asked curiously.

"I heard about Star, and am very sorry for your loss," he said, hoping Sarah would invite him in. He and her father were never friends, so he had never set foot in the lodge, but now he thought because he and Sarah were on somewhat friendlier terms, and Thomas was calling him grandpa, he might be welcome. Sarah waited for Major Hardy to continue speaking.

"I would like you to have these horses," he said turning and going back down the steps. "I know they won't replace Star, but you need a horse to..." But Sarah didn't let him finish.

"I don't need your horse Major, I certainly don't need two of them!" She looked down at the two horses tethered at the back of the carriage.

"I brought one for Thomas, I know he rides one of your old packhorses, last time he came to visit I meant to give him a horse then, but I didn't have one ready." Major Hardy smiled up at Thomas. Since learning he was his grandfather, Thomas was a regular visitor out at his ranch, but he hadn't been out since Star died. Hearing one of the horses was for him, Thomas ran down the steps.

"Which one is mine grandpa?" he said sounding excited.

"The smaller one Thomas," Major Hardy laughed.

"You don't need another horse Thomas! you already have one!" Sarah said sternly. When Major Hardy handed Thomas the reins to the smaller horse, Thomas took them and looked up at Sarah. "But Ma!" he protested when seeing how beautiful the colt was that he was holding. The saddle was new, and he couldn't see what was wrong with taking a gift from his own grandfather.

"Please, let me do this Sarah, I know how much Star meant to you and I would like to..."

"Replace him Major?" Sarah snapped cutting him off again. "No other horse could ever replace Star!" But it wasn't so much the horse, it was the fact Frank gave him to her, and the fact Major Hardy tried taking him off her the day he threatened to whip her if she didn't stay away from Frank. She remembered him flicking his whip at her and how close it came to her face, and how it cut the brim of her father's hat she was wearing, and she could never forget the terrible whipping he gave Frank. When Sarah turned to go back inside, Lizzy smiled sweetly at Major Hardy over Sarah's shoulder.

15

"I don't want to replace him! Frank gave him to you, and I am pleased he did, Star was something you cherished from my son, and now I would like to give you something I thought you might like from me, can't we be friends Sarah?" Major Hardy knew Sarah disliked him for how he treated her and Frank, and he knew no matter how long he lived, she would never forgive him. Sarah didn't stop Thomas from visiting him, and sometimes Christian rode out to the ranch with Thomas too, but Sarah very rarely went to visit him herself.

"Ma?" Thomas called, hoping she would give in. Turning back to face them, Sarah looked at Thomas standing beside Major Hardy and took in the resemblance they had to each other. Still holding Lizzy, she walked down the steps, and going to the back of the carriage, looked more closely at two horses she could see were from exceptional stock.

It took several hours for Christian to sort out the two ranch-hands bent on killing each other over something as simple as which of them had the prettiest girl. Riding back to town, he rounded the corner near the lodge and saw Major Hardy standing with Sarah and Thomas looking at two very fine-looking horses. Getting off his horse, he tethered it to the hitching rail at the bottom of the steps, nodded to the Major's men sitting astride their horses, then said hello to the Major.

"Alright Thomas, we will keep the horses," Sarah said rubbing her hand along the taller of the two's neck. The horses coat was in excellent condition and glistened in the sun. Its white stockings reminded her of Star, except the horse didn't have any markings on its forehead. Putting its head down, the horse let Sarah rub him, which brought a smile to her face.

"You better come in Major, I have coffee brewing, I think there might be enough in the pot for three," she said turning toward the steps. Major Hardy smiled then too and followed Sarah and Christian inside. There was no mention of being friends, but this was a good start.

Thomas liked visiting his grandfather. They were getting along fine, and now he had his very own horse, he visited him more often. Although Sarah felt she wasn't ready to forget what transpired between her, Frank and the Major, she was made welcome and visited the ranch more often with Lizzy. Over the course of the next four years, Cedar Creek became a town where nothing out of the ordinary happened, or so it seemed.

After leaving school at sixteen, Daniel Connell got a job at the lumberyard with his father and was earning his own wage. Daniel soon forgot about his nasty childhood ways. After what happened with Thomas and the river rats, he gave up tormenting other children, and now considering himself a grown man, was taking an interest in a young farm girl whose family had just arrived in town. Jamie Finch, having left school too, went to work with Major Hardy as one of his cowhands and was often seen drinking with the men in the saloon. Thomas and Billy Henderson decided to stay at school for as long as they could, both hoping to further their education by going to Philadelphia to attend college. Thomas as a writer, and Billy, a lawyer.

Besides working for the Major, the four trappers enjoyed spending each winter with Sarah, Christian and Thomas, and as much as they loved Sarah and Thomas, they now had little Lizzy to dote over and entertain them. When the men greeted her by passing her back and forth between each other, Lizzy giggled when their bushy beards tickled her with their welcoming kiss, and she made them laugh with her funny little ways. Joe was happy Sarah was living in town. It took the worry of looking out for her away from him while he was trapping on the mountain. Now Christian was taking responsibility for her, Joe wondered if it was necessary for the four of them to keep their promise they made, all those years ago.

Chapter Three

Trying not to let Star's demise impact her family too much, and to return to her usual state of cheerfulness, Sarah took her family on regular visits to Foley and Brady's farm where she continually broached the subject of Foley getting married. While badgering him to marry Maria, the woman he was known to be seeing, Foley argued he wasn't ready to marry and became solemn when Sarah kept going on about it. Even though Maria satisfied him in bed, he couldn't see any reason to make her his wife, besides, he didn't want to marry needlessly because he was waiting to see how long Sarah remained with Christian. His thoughts when he saw Sarah out and about were of how he once again missed his opportunity to marry her.

He liked Christian, they worked well together, but when he learnt Sarah was pregnant and they were getting married, he rode out to the back of Major Hardy's spread to vent his anger by shooting off his gun at everything around him. Trees, logs and shrubs, birds flying overhead, and rabbits that went scurrying about in the underbrush bore the brunt of his anger. He yelled so loud his voice became hoarse. He loved Sarah, and it hurt him to think she had rejected him. Sitting in the dark that night with only a small fire for warmth, he thought about his future and believed one day Sarah would need him, and so he vowed when that day came, he would be there for her.

But Sarah and Christian appeared very much in love, and it was obvious to everyone their marriage was going to last. Two years after making his vow, Foley gave in to Sarah's demands and asked Maria to marry him.

As Deputy Sheriff, Foley earnt a reasonable living and was considered a respectable man in and around the county. After learning Sarah bought Clem's farm for him and his brother Brady, Maria wanted to marry Foley more than ever. But Maria hides a dark secret only a few men in the county know about, and Foley was not one of those men. What she wants only Foley can give her, and so while waiting for him to propose, she made sure he received special treatment whenever he visited her.

Knowing Foley loved Sarah enough to have asked her to marry him every winter right up until the winter she met Christian didn't deter Maria asking Sarah if she had feelings for Foley. Everyone in town knew of Foley's proposals, and they knew Sarah turned him down time and time again. Explaining to Maria they were just good friends, Sarah assured her she did not have romantic feelings toward Foley at all, and was adamant when saying she was very much in love with Christian. Satisfied with Sarah's answer, when Foley found his courage in a bottle of whiskey and drunkenly proposed, Maria eagerly accepted.

Even though Maria wasn't in love with Foley, she hoped once he married her, he would forget the feelings he had for Sarah. But no matter how hard Foley tried, he could not bring himself to love Maria, and although he knew he shouldn't now she was married, he still held deep feelings for Sarah, and stupidly thought by marrying Maria those feelings would disappear.

Sarah and Christian had a loving family. Thomas was doing well at school and they had their daughter Lizzy, whom everyone in Cedar Creek thought adorable. When Foley married Maria, Lizzy was a tiny two-year old with light brown curly hair who looked the image of her mother.

Foley and Maria's wedding turned out to be a huge affair. The Town Hall was overflowing with guests. Along with Major Hardy, most of his cowhands attended. To allow Sarah and Christian to attend, Thomas gladly offered to stay at the lodge and look after Lizzy. It was the only time Sarah danced. Feeling awkward on the dance floor, she sat most of the dances out while feeling contented to watch her lady friends dance with Christian.

Straight after they married, Maria continued doing housework for families around the county. She wasn't about to give up her work simply because she was married, besides, she was paid for what she did. Even though it was meagre, she had plans and needed money to carry them out. Maria didn't mind that she had to share Foley's farm with his brother. After quickly settling in, she became housekeeper to both men.

Foolishly thinking she would fall in love with Foley after she married him, Maria turned bitter when it became evident, he was still in love with Sarah. There were times while sleeping together, she became sickened to learn it wasn't her he was making love to when she unmistakably heard him call Sarah's name, and when he got drunk, he whispered Sarah's name in his drunken stupor.

Foley liked his job as deputy and continued working for Christian. It was far better than working for Major Hardy as his gun-hand, and he didn't want to be a farmer. His and Christian's partnership turned to friendship as they backed each other to keep the town safe, and over the course of their friendship, while visiting Foley and Brady's farm, Sarah and Christian enjoyed lazy afternoons sitting on the back porch of the farmhouse talking and watching the sun go down over the fields Brady, with occasional help from Foley, worked hard to plough. While Thomas and Lizzy chased pet geese around the yard, the two couples and Brady watched on laughing, as both children took tumbles on the grass. Often times Foley watched Sarah when she was with Christian, and envied Christian the love he received from her. He wanted to experience that same kind of love, but knew he would never get it from Maria.

In spite of Maria's dark secret, she was a kind, caring woman, who went out of her way to help less fortunate families around the county. Foley didn't want to hurt her by telling her he made a mistake by marrying her. By keeping their farmhouse clean and their washing done regularly, she was good to both him and Brady, and her cooking was palatable. He tried his best to make her happy but it seemed her housework was becoming more important, and she was beginning to hold back whenever he made love to her. They had, on more occasions than Foley could count, slept apart when she stayed at a farm doing housework late into the evenings.

When she arrived back at the farm after dark, she used the excuse, 'the houses were disgusting, and it took me hours to clean them.' Unaware she had been sleeping with other men beside him

21

before he married her, Foley was naive about Maria's activities. He trusted her, she was his wife, he didn't need to question her, and when she refused to let him touch her, her excuse was, 'I'm too tired from all the work I have done to be bothered with sex,' and he believed her.

The days Foley knew she would be late home, he got drunk and slept in the barn with their horses, or stayed in town and slept in the back room at the jailhouse. Not knowing the reason Maria was becoming distant, he kept up his charade of being in love with her by treating her fairly, that was the best he felt he could do. To everyone in town, they appeared happily married.

Besides the occasional church picnic, Sundays were a quiet time in Cedar Creek. After folk had been to church, they spent the rest of their day relaxing with their families. Christian allowed Foley Sundays off to spend them with Maria and Brady. Christian himself, while still on duty, spent his days either at the lodge or going on picnics with his family.

The farm was proceeding nicely. Brady finished ploughing fields ready for planting, but he didn't want to grow corn like so many other farmers, instead he ordered bean and pea seeds from Henry's Emporium. Foley spent his Sundays helping Brady plant the seeds and watering them in, then along with hired hands, helped pick the crops when they were ready for harvesting.

The next two years dragged by slowly for Foley. His and Maria's lovemaking became non-existent. Maria continued doing work around the county, spending all day, and more often than not into the evenings cleaning for others. She especially liked to take Brady's buckboard and travel to the outlying farms and ranches. One farm in particular, she made a special trip to late in the afternoons twice a week.

Bert and Ida Rankin didn't have children. Ida was poorly and couldn't conceive, she spent most of her days in bed crippled with one illness or another. Bert liked it when Maria came to their farm and offered to do their housework, her presence was like a breath of fresh air. It wasn't long before Bert and Maria began an affair. Foley was unaware of Maria's relationship to Rankin, but Rankin wasn't the only man Maria was involved with. She was steadily building a clientele to supplement her meagre income. None of the farmers or ranchers Maria was seeing spoke about the relationship they had with her. They didn't want their wives finding out they were having sex with her on the side.

Sarah heard Ida was ill again, so told Christian she would cook a stew and take it out to the Rankin's to help them out. Christian kissed Sarah and Lizzy then saw them off in Sarah's buckboard. When they pulled up at the ranch, Sarah lifted Lizzy down, and carrying her pot of stew, knocked on the front door. Ida called out and told Sarah to come in. After sitting the pot on the kitchen table, Sarah went to the bedroom where Ida lay in bed.

"Don't bring your little girl in Misses Morgan, I don't know what's wrong with me, Doc doesn't know either, you can visit with my husband if you like, he's probably in the barn... Maria is here too, she would be doing the washing if you would like to speak to her." Sarah wished Ida well, then took Lizzy to find Maria and Bert.

Maria wasn't in the washroom when Sarah looked in. The washing was still sitting in the tub waiting to be hung out, so Sarah headed over to the barn. Finding the barn dark inside, she made Lizzy wait at the door while she went to find Bert. Stepping around the opening to one of the stalls, she pulled up in shock. Bert and Maria, both in a state of undress, were lying together on the floor of the stall, and looking up suddenly, Maria saw Sarah standing in the doorway.

Becoming shocked at having been caught in a compromising situation, Maria stopped thrusting, then using her hand, hit Bert on his back to get him to stop what he was doing, but Bert was about to reach his peak and didn't want to stop. Turning his head toward Sarah and seeing her standing in the opening watching them, he grunted and kept thrusting. Turning abruptly, Sarah ran from the barn, and grabbing Lizzy's hand, hurried back to her buckboard. Pushing Bert off her, Maria dressed hurriedly and chased after Sarah. Bert pulled on his trousers and waited in the barn for Maria to have it out with Sarah. Sarah was almost at the buckboard when she saw Maria coming behind her.

"You tell Foley!" she screamed, turning and confronting Maria.

23

"I will not! and you will not either!" Maria screamed back while following Sarah all the way to her buckboard.

"How dare you do this to Foley!" Sarah cried in disgust.

"How dare I? You think when Foley fuck me, he is fucking me? He is not!... he fuck you!" Maria spat in a thick Spanish tone. Feeling completely and utterly shocked by her vile revelation, Sarah gasped.

"Foley married you because he loves you!" she answered in disgust while lifting Lizzy into the buckboard.

When Maria saw Lizzy with Sarah, she quietened but wouldn't let things go as they were. "You are wrong Misses Morgan! Foley never love me, he love you! he always love you, you think he sleep with me? He do not, he sleep in the barn with horses! that is how much he love me, so what do I do?... I find love elsewhere!"

Unable to comprehend a woman being unfaithful to her husband, or a husband being unfaithful to his wife, Sarah snapped in response to Maria suggesting Foley loved her. "Foley does not love me! he is my friend! Bert Rankin's wife is ill! it is a horrible disgusting unfair thing you are doing to Ida, and to Foley!"

"You think what I do unfair? You think housework pay? I need money! one day, I make enough from these ignorant Americano's to go back to my family!" When Maria expressed her disdain for the people she worked for, Sarah's eyes widened at the sudden realization of what Maria was saying.

"Are you seeing other men Maria?" she questioned. Maria sniggered and folded her arms.

"What do you think? Are you so naive Misses Morgan?" she almost laughed. "Some people call you a whore, but you are not, are you? You are the lucky one, you stay faithful to your men, and they stay faithful to you, no Misses Morgan, you will not tell Foley because you love him too, you will not say anything to hurt him."

Even though Sarah had been faithful to Frank when they were together, they had not been married when she fell pregnant with Thomas, and after she married Christian their daughter Elizabeth came along just five months later. The whole town was aware Sarah was pregnant before they married, it had been the talk of the town at the time. Sarah would never be unfaithful to Christian, but still she had been called a whore by a number of people for her wayward ways with the two men. But then Maria had been Christian's housekeeper before Sarah married him. Staring at Maria in disgust, Sarah suddenly had suspicions about Maria's relationship with Christian.

"What do you mean Maria when you say, my men stay faithful to me?"

Maria knew what Sarah was asking, and sniggered again. "You don't worry, your husband, he is a very stubborn man, that one! he turn me down, I try very hard to have him make love to me," she said sounding cynical.

Sarah didn't believe her. If Maria could lie about having sex with other men, she could lie about her and Christian. Sarah was going to have to confront Christian to find out what passed between him and Maria. She especially wanted to know if Christian had sex with Maria after they married. Angry and upset by what she had seen and heard, Sarah ended her confrontation with Maria by climbing into the buckboard next to Lizzy, then hitting the reins up and down on the horses back, quickly steered it away.

On her way back to town, Sarah thought about what Maria said about Foley. When Maria said she would not say anything to him because she loved him, Sarah thought Maria was right, because it was true, she did love him, but as she kept telling herself, only as a dear friend. She would never hurt him by telling him his wife was a whore. Then when Maria said Foley loved her too, Sarah tried to convince herself Maria was wrong. Believing Foley married Maria because he was in love with her, Sarah questioned as to why he would believe anything she told him about his wife? Feeling unable to confide in anyone, not even Christian, for the next few days, Sarah kept what she found out about Maria to herself.

Dinner between Sarah and Christian was strained, she had a lot on her mind since finding Maria and Bert Rankin together in his barn. She didn't hear any of the conversation that went on around the table between him and Thomas. Feeling contented and ignoring everyone, Lizzy sat quietly on her chair swinging her legs while eating her meal. Able to tell Sarah had something on her mind, every now and then Christian glanced at her from across the table.

After Sarah put Lizzy to bed and Thomas retired to his room for the night, she and Christian sat on the couch in front of the fire drinking coffee. Christian again studied Sarah sitting quietly beside him. Usually they ended the evening by talking about how their day had gone, so it was unusual to see her so quiet. Stretching his arm across the back of the couch, he put his hand on Sarah's shoulder and drew her in close.

"What is on your mind Sarah?" he asked softly.

"Nothing!" she answered a little too quickly.

"Oh yes there is! you have been far too quiet all evening, so come on, tell me, what is it that's bothering you?" When Christian kissed Sarah on her cheek she turned her face to his and kissed him fully. Liking her kiss, Christian pushed his hand into her hair and held her to him.

"What was that for?" he asked when they parted.

Sarah couldn't be sure Christian hadn't slept with anyone since marrying her. There were times during and after her pregnancy with Lizzy when she wasn't up to lovemaking. Christian had been patient by not pushing her to make love to him, so maybe those times he found love elsewhere. She hadn't thought about it until catching Maria and Bert Rankin together. Before coming straight out with what she had on her mind, she bit her bottom lip.

"Christian, have you ever slept with… Maria?" she asked almost inaudibly. Stunned by her question, Christian removed his arm from around her and sitting forward, turned sideways and looked puzzled at her.

"What reason do you have for asking me that?" he asked furrowing his brow.

"I, I just need to know, please, did you ever sleep with Maria before, or, after we married?" If Christian were to lie to her, Sarah would be able to tell, so kept her eyes on him.

Keeping his eyes focused on Sarah, Christian answered truthfully. "I have never slept with Maria or any other woman here in Cedar Creek, I had not made love to anyone for a long time before I met you, and I have not made love to anyone but you since, you know all about my past and how I lived, I was not an innocent man before you met me, besides, why should that bother you? If I had slept with her before we met, it shouldn't bother you now… there is more to your question isn't there?"

Leaning forward, Sarah suddenly kissed him and held it. She knew about his past, how he spent his life chasing outlaws, and how he drank and gambled in saloons all over the country. She knew there had been a lot of women in his life, and he swore that, after being shot in the back, he had changed his ways. Sarah had no reason not to believe him.

"I love you so much Christian," she whispered, kissing him again. Returning her kiss, then taking her by the hand, Christian led her upstairs to their room where they undressed each other and made love. His quietly spoken admissions of love for her during their lovemaking convinced Sarah he loved her and her alone. When they were done, they lay beside each other, both spent from their lovemaking, both deep in thought, Sarah with her eyes closed, Christian looking up at the red velvet canopy above them.

"Maria is sleeping with other men and I don't think Foley knows!" Christian said out of the blue. Shocked by what he said, Sarah rolled over, and lying against him, let her hand rest on his chest.

"How do you know Christian?" she asked looking confused. Covering her hand with his, he held it against him.

"I've heard some talk, just gossip really, how did you find out?" he asked gazing longingly into Sarah's eyes. As she lay back down beside him, he let go of her hand, and now they both stared up at the canopy.

"I caught her at Bert Rankin's when I took my stew out to Ida, Bert and Maria were in the barn…" Sarah went on to tell Christian what she had seen and what Maria said to her. When she finished, he sat up and leant over her.

"So that is why you asked me if I had slept with her! well let me tell you my love, I have never been interested in Maria, or any other woman before you for that matter, so you needn't worry yourself about that!" Bringing his head down to meet Sarah's, he kissed her passionately. Satisfied with his declaration, Sarah begged him to keep what he knew to himself, and Christian swore he wouldn't breathe a word, not to Foley, not to anyone.

Over the next few weeks what Sarah knew about Maria continued to bother her, so to get it off her chest she needed to confide in someone else besides Christian, someone whom she knew could keep what was told them to themselves. She headed to Doc Harris's practice.

Leaving Lizzy in the kitchen with Gerda, and seeing Sarah was agitated about something, Doc took her to the room where he saw his patients. Having sworn to uphold the oath he took as a doctor to keep patient information to himself, Doc would never divulge anything about his patients to anyone, but after hearing what Sarah had to say, he felt he could no longer keep what he knew to himself.

"She's pregnant Sarah!" Doc said breaking his oath. News of Maria being pregnant made Sarah feel sick to her stomach, and right then, she felt sorry for Foley.

"It can't be Foley's, Maria said he isn't sleeping with her," she let him know dismally.

"I don't think it is, Maria said she couldn't be sure who the father is, but said as far as she is concerned, Foley will be declared its father." When he repeated what Maria confided to him, Doc sounded disgusted. Sarah knew once Maria told Foley she was having his baby, Foley would believe her and Maria's deception would be complete. When Sarah looked at Doc, she had a worried look on her face.

"What do we do?" she asked.

Seeing what he already told Sarah made her upset, Doc pursed his lips for a moment, then explaining he had to keep his patient's confidence, made Sarah swear not to say anything.

"Nothing Sarah! we do nothing, especially you! don't you go getting yourself involved!" After giving his request consideration, Sarah reluctantly agreed to keep Maria's secret to herself and left Doc's practice, but with the knowledge as to the circumstances of Maria's pregnancy still eating her up inside, a week after talking with Doc, she again confronted Maria outside Henry's store, and knowing Sarah wouldn't risk losing Foley's friendship, Maria laughed in her face. It was then Sarah learnt Maria never loved Foley. All Maria wanted she informed Sarah, was what came with being a deputy sheriff's wife, and she would do anything to get what she thought she deserved.

"So, you!" Maria warned. "Had better keep your mouth shut!"

Besides, Maria reminded Sarah, whatever she told Foley he would not believe anyway, and when she said he would think her just a stinking trapper liar, Sarah believed what Maria said to be true. Foley would definitely think she was a liar, or worse, simply trying to destroy his marriage out of some sort of spite. Sarah didn't breathe a word to anyone, not even Christian.

Chapter Four

*L*izzy was sitting on Christian's desk at the Sheriff's Office swinging her legs while waiting for her Ma and Pa to finish being nice to each other. Christian had his arms around Sarah smiling down at her, and Sarah had her arms around Christian's waist, smiling up at him. Thomas was in school, and Sarah had come to the office to let Christian know she was taking Lizzy out to the prairie to catch a rabbit for dinner and to bring him his lunch. All Sarah wanted from Christian was for him to kiss her and let her get going, but the longer he held her the more amorous he began to feel.

"We could go to the back room, just for a moment," he whispered, winking at her.

"Why Sheriff Morgan, I think you are feeling randy," Sarah whispered, and smiling, remembered him introducing that word to her when they were in the throes of frenzied lovemaking. Putting his mouth to Sarah's ear, and before kissing her passionately he whispered, "you bet I am." Lizzy watched them kiss and kept swinging her legs.

"You can't possibly be, it's mid-morning," Sarah said furrowing her brow. They had made love last night, and again at daylight before getting ready for the day.

"It doesn't matter what time of day it is Sarah, when I'm with you, I want you," Christian replied while looking longingly into her eyes.

"Well, I have a rabbit to catch!" Sarah said patting his backside with her hand. Christian reluctantly let her go. "Come on Lizzy, let's go get that rabbit!" When Sarah lifted Lizzy off the desk and into her arms, Christian kissed her on her cheek then kissed Sarah again. Moving to the door, Sarah looked back at Christian and let her eyes travel down to his crotch, then looking back up, smiled at him cheekily.

"Don't come out, there are women and children out here that don't need to see... that!" Still smiling she stepped outside and closed the door behind her. Knowing he wasn't in a position to follow her out, as the door closed Christian smiled, and after straightening himself up, poured himself a mug of coffee then sat down behind his desk. There was a lot of paperwork to get through. Fines needed writing up and reports had to be written. Right there on his desk were several hours he could spend in his office.

After lifting Lizzy into her saddle, Sarah climbed up to sit behind her. "Hold on tight Lizzy," she warned while maneuvering her horse out of the livery.

"See you Ham," she called over her shoulder.

"See you Sarah, see you Lizzy," Ham called after them.

"Bye," Lizzy called in her sweetest voice.

Sarah walked her horse until she was over the bridge, then on the other side got it going at a canter. As the horse moved easily along, brisk morning air whipped Lizzy's face causing wisps of her curly hair to blow back. Lizzy loved going rabbiting with her Ma. She wanted the horse to go faster, but gripping the saddle-horn as her Ma told her to, had to be content with her Ma keeping the horse steady so she wouldn't fall off.

Once Christian finished writing out the fines, he had to deliver them to the law breakers. The fines he hastily wrote covered fist fights and damage to private property. Most fights happened in the saloon, and private property consisted of glasses and bottles, and tables and chairs destroyed in the fracas that belonged to the saloon's owner Kathleen. None of the fines were too serious, in fact, Christian thought as he strolled along the street carrying the papers, nothing too serious had happened in Cedar Creek for the past four years, not since he made Sarah his wife and his daughter Lizzy came along. Christian smiled to himself. He loved Sarah, he loved Lizzy, and he loved Thomas. Thomas would soon turn seventeen and Christian thought he had been a pretty good father to him. All in all, as he delivered the first of his fines, Christian was thinking life couldn't be better.

The young gunslinger rode in when the sun was high. It was hot and he could use a whiskey, but trying not to draw too much attention to himself, decided to forgo that because more importantly, he needed fresh supplies so he could hide out longer from the posse that was chasing him. He wasn't looking for trouble, just planning to ride out of town straight after getting his few meagre things. After tethering his horse to the hitching rail outside Henry's Emporium, he looked up and down the street, and although not surprisingly, saw a town that looked to be somewhere a drifter would think not worth hanging about in, and the young man thought, 'the sooner I get out of here the better.'

Cedar Creek was exceedingly quiet for that time of day. Most town folk had already made their way home for their midday meal, which meant not too many people were bustling about. This was the way the young man liked the towns he passed through to be. Pushing open the screen door to Henry's store, he made his way inside.

Staring at the kid sidling up to his counter, Henry noticed how his gun strapped to his hip hung low. The kid didn't look mean, just a might too young to be carrying what looked to be a gun that could be drawn from its holster fast. 'Hadn't he seen the sign on his way into town?' Henry was thinking. Having witnessed Christian drawing his gun fast the time he shot an outlaw dead that refused to surrender his gun, and again when he shot and killed Benjamin Crawley who owned the store before him, Henry was aware Christian had no reason to use his gun that fast since the town had become respectable. Except for a few rowdy cowhands deciding to fill their bellies with whiskey and ending with having a fist fight, the town was quiet most of the time. All Christian had to do was point his gun at someone and they willing went with him to the jailhouse. Even the trappers when they came to town had settled down. Henry thought that was due to the respect they all had for their sheriff, and for his deputy.

"Howdy young fella, what can I do for you?" Henry asked, addressing the kid the same as he addressed everyone that came to his store. He didn't want trouble from anyone, least of all strangers, besides Henry thought, it was Sheriff Morgan's job to tell this kid about the law regarding carrying guns in town, not his. It was Sheriff Morgan's, or Deputy Andrews job to get the gun off him.

After getting his supplies without any trouble, the kid left Henry's store quickly, and hooking the bag over his saddle-horn, lifted his foot toward the stirrup and was about to get on his horse when a deep voice bellowed from behind him. "You better hand over that gun mister!"

Sensing trouble, the kid put his foot back down and stepped away from his horse.

Having delivered most of his fines, Christian was walking back to his office and was still carrying two in his hand when he saw a stranger come out of Henry's store wearing a gun. Standing in the middle of the street facing what could only be described as an unkempt looking youth, he moved the papers to his left hand to allow him to lift his gun up and down in its holster, which he hoped would help his gun come free quickly if he needed it.

As he moved away from his horse to stand in the middle of the street, the young gunslinger turned and saw the sun bounce brilliantly off the badge pinned to Christian's shirt and could not mistake he was being confronted by the towns sheriff. Sizing Christian up, he saw a man of about forty years old, tall, broad shouldered, tin star on his chest, right about where his heart was, right-handed, gun-hand steady. The colt .45 sitting in its holster hung low, low enough for a fast draw. How fast?... The kid was about to find out!

"You're not getting my gun sheriff, but if you think you can take it, then you better try, cause I won't be handing it over!" The kid's hand was steady as he held it level with his gun.

Christian held his hand just as steady, but he was worried. The kids gun sat low on his hip, which, by any-ones reckoning, would make him fast at the draw. Having not had to draw on anyone in a long time, Christian now wished he had been out to the gulch for a practice shoot. Worried he may have slowed down some, he flexed his gun-hand.

Inside his store, Henry watched what was going on outside through the window. Out on the street town folk stopped and stared. A little further along, Doc Harris heard someone say Christian had a kid with a gun about to draw on him, and stood on the boardwalk to watch. When he saw Christian staring down a lad not much older than Thomas, he thought this was no match, Christian would take his gun easily. A crowd of men and saloon girls came out of the saloon and gathered together out the front to watch their sheriff face off with the kid. That was all Christian needed, a drunken rowdy crowd to egg him on. But no-one uttered a word.

"I don't want trouble sheriff, all I want is to ride out of here free… and easy," the kid said while thinking because he hadn't been in town long enough to cause trouble of any kind, maybe this sheriff would be decent enough to let him leave without giving him reason to cause any. But he was wrong.

This was Christian's town, he set the law here, and anyone who came to his town, no matter how long they stayed, they were going to have to abide by his law. Christian was pleased with the way his law was working. His town had become peaceable. He found his niche when he found Sarah, the woman he was going to spend the rest of his life with. He had a daughter, who could run around town without a care in the world, and there was Thomas, he was a good boy, Christian loved him like a son. Brother Abraham from the mission in Les Rios was absolutely right when he told Christian he would find what he had been searching all his life for. 'Three would become four' Brother Abraham said, and it took eight long years for Christian to understand that part of his prediction. When he met Sarah and Thomas, he figured it out after Sarah told him she was pregnant with their beautiful daughter. There were four people in his family, and he was on top of the world.

Needing to know the kids name in case he killed him instead of wounding him, because bullets sometimes had a way of going where you didn't want them to go, and he would need the kids name for his tombstone, Christian asked, "what is your name son?"

Grinning slightly, the young man turned his head and looked away, then looked back at Christian. Once he told the sheriff his name, he figured the sheriff would know he was wanted by the law, and that would lead him to regret what he was about to do, but he told him anyway.

The kid's name didn't matter really. Christian didn't know anyone by the name he told him, he was not from around Cedar Creek. At the same time as the kid told Christian his name, he drew his gun, and in that split second when the kid pulled the trigger, and Christian pulled his, time seemed to stand still. Men and women jumped at the sound of the two guns going off simultaneously.

Christian's bullet struck the kids left arm and grazed him below his shoulder. Startled, he grabbed his arm with his gun-hand and looked at Christian. Christian stared back at him, and couldn't believe it, he was sure he aimed at the kid's chest.

The pain spreading across Christian's chest was severe in its entirety. As it spread to his shoulders and down his arms, making him waver, he let go of the fines and the papers blew away in the breeze. Looking down at the spreading red fluid that was quickly covering the front of his shirt, he looked back up and uttered, "Sarah." Suddenly seeing himself a young boy back at the orphanage struggling to survive, he heard his best friend Max laughing at something mischievous they had done. Seeing the mission at Les Rios and the brothers, he remembered clearly Brother Abraham's prophecy. Brother Abraham foretold he would find what he had been looking for all his life, and he had. Sarah was whom he searched all his life for. Brother Abraham said three would become four, and they did, after marrying Sarah, she presented him with his daughter Lizzy and Thomas her son became his son. But Christian hadn't been told all of Brother Abraham's prophecy. If he had, he may have done things differently.

After seeing Christian off from the mission, Brother Abraham returned to the privacy of his alcove where he sat on a mat and closed his eyes. Hating when the brothers brought people to him to have their futures told, while rocking back and forth, Brother Abraham began chanting. Only permitted to foretell good things about their years ahead, when Christian came to him, he had already foreseen what would become of him. He told Christian his life would revolve around a bright shining star. He told him he would find the woman with the long brown hair he would spend the rest of his life with.

When he saw Christian's child that was of his making and the one not of his own blood, all he said was 'three would become four,' and when he saw how Christian's life was going to be short lived, he said nothing. As Brother Abraham rocked back and forth, he felt at pain for seeing a foreboding darkness envelope Christian. Brother Abraham saw clearly, Christian Morgan's body awash with his own blood.

As the light dimmed in his eyes, Christian saw Sarah. He loved her with all his heart, but now his heart had a hole in it, his love for her was dying with him. Falling to his knees, he teetered for a moment, then fell face down on the dusty street of his town. He had drawn fast, but the kid was faster.

Women screamed, men cursed and swore. Doc Harris ran from the boardwalk to where Christian lay. Keeping his gun in his hand, the kid quickly made for his horse and untethering it, swung himself up in his saddle. Pulling his horse around, he yelled at the crowd now gathering around Christian. "He should never have tried taking my gun!" Kicking his horse hard, he rode out fast, leaving town the same way he rode in.

When someone went running to the schoolhouse and told them there their sheriff had been shot, the school emptied quickly as kids scrambled to see what went down. With Billy running behind him, Thomas raced into the street as men carried Christian to the undertakers.

Seeing Christian's body lying on the wooden table, Doc was forced to hold Thomas back while he cried for his Pa to wake up. When Phelps the undertaker got his measuring tape out to measure Christian for his coffin, Thomas pushed him away.

"Don't you touch him you son-of-a-bitch!" he screamed hysterically through his tears. Although tightening his arms around Thomas, there was nothing Doc could do to comfort him.

"Where is Sarah?" Gerda asked standing back with her eyes brimming with tears. Hearing her asking after his Ma Thomas answered, "she's gone rabbiting! she doesn't know!" and knowing when his Ma found out Christian was dead what it was going to do to her, he cried in pain, "Ma! oh God, Ma!" Then burying his face against Doc's chest, wept openly.

Sarah and Lizzy came riding in over the bridge with one dead rabbit hooked to her saddle-horn. Taking her horse to the livery, she was surprised to see Ham wasn't there as he always was, hammering away at his forge or nailing horseshoes to horse's hooves. Lifting Lizzy down, and unhooking the rabbit, she pushed her horse into a stall. Walking down the street holding Lizzy's hand and the dead rabbit swinging in the other, she couldn't help noticing how the town seemed unusually quiet. Coming to the business end of town, she could see a crowd standing outside the undertakers and slowed when someone saw her and said something to make everyone turn to look in her direction. As she approached, she saw Ham and Patrice standing with Martha and Dave. When she saw Billy standing with his parents and they were all crying, she squeezed Lizzy's hand a little tighter. As they stepped aside to let her through, no-one uttered a word. Someone could be heard crying inside the undertakers. Having heard that cry before, it sent shivers coursing through Sarah that made her drop the rabbit. By the time she pushed her way through the crowd she was crying. Her keen sense of knowing what was to come told her she would find Christian.

With her heart threatening to explode as the scene before her almost made her pass out, she stepped through the doorway and let Lizzy's hand go. The blood curdling scream that escaped Sarah, sent shivers through men and women standing outside. Women burst into tears, men uttered curses at her sorrow and walked away.

Seeing Christian lying on the undertakers table Sarah's eyes flooded with tears. As she gasped for air, her legs threatened to go out from under her. Moving in an almost trance like state to where he lay, she could see his eyes were closed and his shirt soaked with blood where his life seeped out of him. Running her hand through his hair while sobbing uncontrollably, she bent down and kissed him. "I love you Christian," she sobbed. "I love you so much." Only a few hours before they were standing in his office. Christian wanted to make love to her right there. Here now, she wished she had let him.

Going home early to have lunch with his wife was something Foley did whenever Christian said Sarah would be bringing his lunch to the office. He would let them use the time to be alone, then ride back to town. When Foley got home, Brady was busy ploughing a field ready for planting. Sitting at the table on the back porch with Maria, Foley had a somewhat pleasant lunch until she informed him, she would be going out to do housework later that day. Today would be one of those days she wouldn't get home until late, making Foley wonder how something as simple as housework could keep Maria away late into the night, but he never questioned her about it, not even when she came home too tired to let him make love to her.

He was on his way back to town when a horse and rider went racing past him, making him somewhat surprised. Never having seen the kid in town before, he pulled his horse up and turning in his saddle, took another look as the horse disappeared along the road in a trail of dust. Foley noticed the gun-belt the kid was wearing, but that wasn't unusual, because any man, young or old was allowed to carry a gun outside town. Foley continued back to town at a leisurely pace.

"I will take Lizzy home with me," Gerda sobbed as she bent down and picked Lizzy up. Indicating he would stay with Sarah and Thomas, Doc nodded dismally to his wife. Letting go of Doc, Thomas reached for Sarah. "Ma!" he said sadly while putting his hand on her shoulder to comfort her. Ignoring him, Sarah climbed on the table, and lying beside Christian, put her arm over his chest. She didn't care about getting blood on her clothes, she got covered in blood plenty of times before, only not Christian's. She wept openly, Christian was gone, she could tell him she loved him all she wanted, but he would never now hear her words. She was glad she told him so many times. Unlike Frank who had been gone from her cabin for three weeks and was all alone on the mountain when he died, Christian knew when he died that she loved him. She still believes Frank died not knowing she had ever loved him. Sarah didn't know why she thought of Frank at that moment.

When Foley got back to town, he saw a small crowd in the street where some of the women were crying.

"What's going on Jameson?" he asked innocently of one of the men whose wife was sobbing. Shaking his head from side to side, Jameson looked bleakly up at Foley.

"He's dead!" he said thinking Foley should know who he meant. Confused by Jameson's statement, Foley glared at him.

"Who the hell are you saying is dead?" he barked.

Realizing Foley had been out of town when the gunfight happened, Jameson replied. "Sheriff Morgan, goddamn it! that's who!" Foley felt his stomach drop and his heart lurch, but stunned by what he was hearing, found it difficult to believe what Jameson was telling him.

"What do you mean, he's dead? What happened?" he asked.

"A goddamn kid! wouldn't give Morgan his gun! they had a shootout and sheriff, well, goddamn it! he winged the kid but took a bullet! died right here in the middle of the goddamn street!" Jameson shook his head again as if he couldn't believe his own words either.

Realizing the kid riding away from town in a cloud of dust must have been who shot Christian, Foley felt a shiver race up his spine, and thinking the kid would be long gone, lost in the foothills somewhere between Cedar Creek and Moreton, he thought it too late to get a posse together to chase after him.

Knowing where Christian would be, there was only one thing Foley felt he could do. Kicking his horse, he raced up the street to find another crowd milling about outside the undertakers. When he walked in and saw Sarah lying on the table beside Christian, and Thomas with his arms over her trying to coax her away, he removed his hat. Seeing Foley come in, Doc looked sadly over at him and shook his head from side to side indicating there was nothing he could do to help them.

"Come on Ma… we can't stay… he's gone," Thomas was saying.

"I'm so sorry Sarah," Foley said quietly from behind them.

Hearing what sounded like a feeble attempt at sympathy, Sarah got off the table, and swinging around suddenly, used all the strength she had left in her to hit out. *"Where were you? You son of-a-bitch! you were supposed to back Christian!"* she screamed, swinging her arms wildly as she belted her fists into him. Tears stained her face, her eyes were red rimmed from crying, blood covered the front of her blouse. Sucking in great mouthfuls of air, she sobbed uncontrollably as her chest heaved and she began to crumple. Letting go of his hat, Foley caught her as she fell.

Almost a man now, Thomas had to be strong for his Ma and for Lizzy. He would have to become the man of the house. Forcing himself to stop crying, he watched his Ma hit out at Foley and watched Foley lift her into his arms as she collapsed.

"Where do you want me to take her?" Foley asked Doc.

"Take her to the lodge," Thomas offered.

"I will go with you Foley," Doc said. "There's nothing we can do here."

As Foley carried Sarah outside, Phelps the undertaker stretched his measuring tape out and finished measuring Christian for his burial.

As Foley carried Sarah across the street and around to the lodge, Doc Harris and Thomas followed. Once inside, Foley followed Thomas upstairs to her room where he lay her gently on her bed. While Thomas covered her with a blanket, Doc felt her forehead.

"She's had quite a shock, but she should be alright, given time," Doc told them sadly. Foley had been to the lodge many times to have dinner with Sarah and Christian. Brady, and sometimes Maria attended those dinners with him, but he had never had occasion to go to the rooms upstairs, and so took a moment to look around Sarah's room.

Sarah lay on a huge four poster bed amongst layers of soft pillows. The canopy of red velvet matched the drapes covering a huge bay window. Along one wall a dresser and large closet sat side by side. An open fireplace taking pride of place on another wall had a red velvet covered chair sitting alongside it. Plush woven floor rugs covered the floor. Foley imagined Sarah and Christian making love in the huge bed amongst the pillows. He and Maria made love, when it had suited Maria, in a small wooden framed bed in a small room at his and Brady's farm. Standing in Sarah's room, he imagined lying in Sarah's bed making love to her, then cursed himself for thinking that way when she had just lost Christian.

Wanting to support Sarah in her time of need, Foley returned to the undertaker to find out when Christian's burial would take place. Phelps told him the burial would take place the very next day and handed him Christian's sheriff's badge. Foley held the shiny tin star stained with blood in his hand and studied it.

All the town folk turned out for Christian's burial. Doc Harris and Gerda were there supporting Sarah while Thomas held Lizzy. The Hammond's and the Henderson's stood behind them giving Sarah extra support. Major Hardy and those of his cowhands not tending his herd, attended too. The only people not there were the trappers. They were on the mountain trapping as they always were during the warmer months, oblivious to what happened to Christian, and unaware of the dismay Sarah was feeling.

Foley stood well back from the hole in the ground, but still in full view of Sarah. Watching her reminded him of when she buried her father. Glancing over at Calahan's grave to the headstone that had been erected, he read the inscription and the date. 'Calahan Cole, Beloved husband to Elizabeth and Father of Sarah, 1 December 1859.' Foley remembered it had been raining that day, today the sun shone brilliantly down on everyone. He wanted to comfort Sarah back then too but she had been surrounded by trappers, and being wary of the men at the time and rather shy when it came to women, he didn't have the courage to approach her. Here again he wanted to show Sarah he cared, but was disappointed he couldn't stand alongside her in her time of need. While Brady stood solemnly on one side of him, he had to be satisfied with standing with Maria on the other.

When the burial was over, Sarah took Lizzy off Thomas, and carrying her, made to leave the cemetery. As she approached Foley standing beside his wife, she stopped in front of Maria and glared at her. Because she lost her husband whom she loved and never cheated on, here was Maria, being comforted by Foley who believed Maria loved only him. Sarah could not help feeling hatred for Maria right then for her deceit, and glancing at Foley, didn't speak before walking away with Thomas.

Confused by the way Sarah looked at Maria then him, Foley remained bewildered as he watched her leaving. Knowing full well Foley would never feel for her what he felt for Sarah, Maria watched Foley watching Sarah. But Maria didn't care anymore, she had a surprise for Foley. Even though she would never divulge the child she was carrying was not his, once he knew she was pregnant, she hoped it would change the way he felt about Sarah Morgan.

Having made their way back to the lodge, Patrice, Martha and Gerda set about making supper for a few close friends of Sarah's and Christian's. Sarah didn't care for supper. After putting Lizzy down for a nap, she went straight to her room where she curled up on her bed and wept. Foley didn't attend either. He didn't want to witness Sarah's suffering, nor did he want to experience the anger she had shown him the day Christian had been shot.

It became obvious to Maria Foley was upset by the death of his friend Christian, and he was showing signs of sympathy for Sarah, so seizing her opportunity that evening, Maria told Foley she was expecting his child. Thrilled with her news, Foley forgot for a moment the sad occasion that had befallen Cedar Creek. Although he could not forget Sarah's pain at the loss of her husband, nor his feelings he had for her, he embraced Maria and said how wonderful it would be to finally be a family. Maria let Foley make love to her for the first time that night in a very long time.

Chapter Five

Foley called an urgent town meeting. Everyone interested in what he had to say was to gather at the Town Hall. Picking the sheriff's badge up off his desk, and after studying it, he gripped it in his hand while making his way across town. The hall was packed to overflowing when he arrived, making it standing room only inside. After making his way through the crowd to the back of the hall and getting up on the stage, he looked at everyone to see who was there and couldn't see Sarah or Thomas anywhere. Not that he expected to see Sarah around town for quite some time, it was far too soon for her to come from mourning the death of her husband, so it made sense that she would not attend the meeting. Holding up his hands, he called for quiet.

"I have asked you all here because we need to decide on who we want as our next sheriff!" he announced, speaking loud and clear for those standing near the entrance to hear.

"Why don't you just pin it on Foley?" a voice called from the crowd. Searching over the top of everyone, Foley found Smith standing near the doors to the hall with his back pressed against the wall and grinning. Men and women standing near Smith laughed at his comment.

"Yeah! you're our deputy! now pin it on and be our sheriff! but be careful not to stab yourself with it!" a man whom Foley recognized as Smith's friend Taylor, standing next to Smith called out. Seeming to think the meeting was a bit of fun, both men looked at each other before laughing at their own heckling. Foley ignored the laughing and continued speaking.

"Unless I'm voted for by the town, I won't be sheriff, so is there anyone wanting to take on the job?" Foley waited while he looked around the room, but no-one volunteered.

"We didn't vote Sheriff Morgan in, and he did alright by the town!" Smith called loudly.

"Didn't do him no good though did it? Got himself shot dead anyhow!" Taylor put in just as loud. While some nodded in agreement, most of the crowd became angry at Smith and Taylor for their non-caring outburst, and erupted in argumentative banter. Foley held up his hands, and yelling at them all to shut up, got the crowd to fall silent.

Standing next to the stage to be near his brother, and while listening to the heckling, Brady moved his eyes around the hall looking at everyone he was acquainted with until his eyes settled on a young fair-haired girl that he didn't know standing with a man and woman, and another much younger girl he thought must be her family. The girl and her family didn't know the sheriff that well, or Sarah his wife, they had moved to the county just a few months before Christian was shot. Seeing how pretty the fair-haired girl was, Brady couldn't take his eyes off her. When the girl suddenly looked his way and gave him a fleeting smile before turning back to watch Foley on the stage, Brady stopped listening to what Foley was talking about. Moving between the crowd, he brought himself closer to where the girl stood.

"Everyone who wants Foley to be our sheriff, raise your hand!" a man in the crowd called loudly, and every hand in the hall went up.

"Anyone who don't, raise your hand!" he called again. No-one put up their hand.

"Looks like you're our new sheriff, Foley!" the man called. Before Foley could object, the crowd erupted in applause.

Watching the girl and her family clapping at what had been said, and even though he hadn't heard what he was clapping for, Brady clapped along. The girl turned her head when she saw him approaching and smiled again.

"Seeing how you've all voted, I don't mind being sheriff," Foley said, unpinning the deputy's badge from his shirt and replacing it with the sheriff's badge. When the crowd continued clapping and followed with loud cheers, he held up his hands to quieten them.

"Now, I need a deputy!... how about you Smith?" The crowd closest to Smith roared with laughter at the irony. Smith though wasn't at all fazed by Foley's suggestion.

"How much does it pay?" he called, causing everyone in the hall to laugh much louder.

"More than what you get from the Major!" Foley called back. "And you can stay in the back room at the jailhouse if you like! you'll find it more comfortable than the bunkhouse out at the ranch." Foley knew the bunkhouse well. Having worked for Major Hardy, first as a cowhand then as his gun-hand, he lived there for more years than he cared to count.

Tired of being a cowhand, Smith had been waiting for something better to come along and now saw his chance. "I'll take it!" he called, pushing his way through the still laughing crowd. Jumping onto the stage, he let Foley pin the deputy's badge on him.

"I swear you to uphold the law, say I will," Foley said hurriedly swearing Smith in.

"I will!" Smith replied. While the crowd watched on, Foley and Smith shook hands.

"What about Taylor? Can you use him?" Smith asked. Foley looked over the crowd at Taylor waiting at the entrance for his partner to come back. Taylor was good with a gun but had a bad temper, which Foley thought could spell trouble, but also agreed it could be useful.

"Yeah! I guess I could use him, bring him to my office after the meeting and I'll swear you in properly." When Smith jumped off the stage and went back to his friend, Foley watched him telling Taylor he was going to be a deputy, then watched as they congratulated each other with laughter and slaps on the back. Before everyone could leave, Foley hushed the crowd again.

"As sheriff, my first rule of order is, I'm going to let every man have his gun back!" The hall erupted in loud cheers and back slapping from most of the men at hearing his news.

"There will be no more law about not carrying guns in town, but the law still applies to shooting them off!" he yelled above the din. Relieved after Christian removed the danger of drunken men firing at anything they tried aiming at, women folk were not happy about their men having guns in town and once again feared for their children's safety, and feeling they were taking a step backward, voiced their concerns loudly. Ignoring their concerns, the meeting ended when Foley got off the stage and made his way outside.

As a throng of noisy people began making their way outdoors, Brady found himself being shuffled along beside the blonde-haired girl, and so felt inclined to introduce himself.

"Hello, names Brady, Brady Andrews," he announced loudly with a smile.

"Ellen, Ellen Farmer," Ellen said smiling up at him while trying to make him hear her above everyone's chatter. Brady could have sworn she was telling him she was a farmer, but unable to make out clearly what Ellen was saying, yelled, "me too!" above the din.

Ellen looked at him rather strangely, then laughed at his mistake. When they got clear of the crowd, she introduced him to her family.

"This is my father Otis, my mother Isabella, and my sister Lara… Farmer." When understanding he made a mistake about her name, Brady laughed with embarrassment and bending closer to Ellen to let her hear him, apologized. "I'm sorry, I thought you said you were a farmer."

"Yes, that's right, I am!" Ellen said seriously. "But my name is Farmer too!" she added, then seeing the look on Brady's face had become serious, she and her parents burst into laughter.

"Don't worry about it Brady," Otis said still laughing. "We get that all the time." Brady was glad Ellen's family were easy going, and liked them straight away, especially Ellen.

"There is a dance at the hall this Saturday, would you like to go with me Ellen?" he asked without the slightest hesitation. Ellen smiled, then asked her father if it would be alright if she accompanied Brady to the dance. Otis said it would be fine if Ellen wanted to go. Then while trying not to sound too eager, Ellen said yes to Brady's invitation.

Cedar Creek had a new sheriff. Foley Andrews took over from his role as deputy and swore in two new deputies, Smith and Taylor. Foley was instantly pleased with the two men. They took their roles as deputy's seriously, helping him break up a fight straight after the meeting between two men who had a difference of opinion about having guns in town. Smith and Taylor hauled the two men to the jailhouse where they refused to let them go home with their wives until they agreed about the guns and shook hands. Once they accepted Foley's law, Smith and Taylor let the two men have their guns before they left.

Saturday came around quickly. Now that Foley was sheriff, he was kept busy in town and didn't spend much time at the farm. Maria was pleased Foley had become sheriff, but that did nothing to stop her from spending time going from farm to farm providing more than just housework. Foley and Maria didn't see each other at all during daylight hours, and Maria continued to return home late at night. Although Foley gave up worrying about her staying out late, he planned on putting a stop to her doing housework for other people once she got close to giving birth to their baby.

The dance was a huge success. Brady collected Ellen from her farm which he was pleased to learn was the farm adjoining his and Foley's. Brady and Ellen danced every dance with each other. They drank lemonade and sat talking with their heads close together. Brady told Ellen how he and Foley came about their farm and what crops he intended growing. Ellen told Brady they had a herd of cows they milked twice a day and that they hoped to supply the town and county with fresh milk and cream. That night Brady and Ellen fell in love and began seeing each other on a regular basis.

Ellen visited Brady and Foley's farm and was introduced to Maria as she was about to leave to go about her housework. She stayed for dinner that Maria had left prepared and afterwards when Brady took her home, he kissed her goodnight on her porch and made up his mind he was going to marry her. He waited three months before he got the courage to ask Ellen to marry him. There was a crop of beans he had to get harvested first, and new ground to plough. He became so busy he had little time to spare.

When the crop was harvested and a field ploughed, he took Ellen on a picnic and proposed to her. Ellen said she would accept his marriage proposal, only if he asked her father if he could marry her and her father said yes. When Brady took Ellen home, he didn't hesitate before asking Otis for her hand in marriage. Respecting Brady as a well-known and respected farmer and his brother Foley as the towns sheriff, Otis was happy his eldest daughter was marrying into a fine family, and gave them his blessing. Brady and Ellen decided to wait until after the birth of Foley's baby to marry.

When Sarah heard Foley had taken over the job of sheriff, she thought it only natural for him to step into the role once Christian was gone, but because she and Thomas were still mourning their loss, at the time she heard the news, she couldn't have cared less. Sarah heard too that Brady was engaged to a girl from a family that had just moved to the county, and was happy for him, but secretly hoped he had met a decent girl, and not one like Maria.

Chapter Six

*B*aking and playing with Lizzy was the only way Sarah could keep from thinking of Christian. It was at night when she felt Christian's loss the most. Lying in bed unable to hold him close, she missed him terribly, and cried herself to sleep every night for the next few months.

Working like an Amazon during the day, she managed to keep her mind occupied by scrubbing the floors of the lodge from top to bottom and washing windows and cleaning floor rugs. Late at night when Lizzy was put to bed, Sarah and Thomas sat together on the couch in front of the open fire where they talked about Christian and cried together. After retiring to their respective rooms Thomas often heard his Ma crying. Burying his head in his pillow, he cried too, not only for his own loss but for his Ma's pain. Thomas worked particularly hard to get them through the first few weeks. Lizzy didn't understand when she saw her Ma and brother crying. All she knew was, the man that let her climb all over him and cuddled her, making her feel loved, was not around anymore.

It was almost a month after Christian's burial that Thomas began to worry about school. He was almost seventeen and if he was going to take the college entry exam he had to go back.

"I can't do the test Ma!" Thomas said one morning when all three of them were sitting at the table eating breakfast.

"Why can't you Thomas?"

"It's gone Ma, everything I ever learnt, it's all gone, I can't remember any of it!" Thomas's eyes filled with tears.

"Well, you don't have to do the test because I have decided, we are going back to the mountain!" Sarah informed him.

One night while crying for Christian, Sarah made up her mind to go back to her cabin where she could always find happiness. Left in the care of Christian for a number of years, the trappers weren't around for her anymore, and she missed Joe terribly. Only he would know how to comfort her in her time of need. Sarah wished she were back on the mountain doing what she knew best how to do, and couldn't wait for the men to return to spend winter in town so they could travel back to the mountain with them in the spring. Thomas's eyes widened. That was the last thing he wanted to do.

"I don't want to go back Ma!" he cried.

"You don't have to go back Thomas, you have learnt enough," Sarah said, not understanding what he was saying.

"That's not what I meant Ma!" Thomas snapped. "I don't want to go back to the mountain, you know how much I want to go to college!"

"Well you won't be going, you will..." Knowing what Sarah was going to say before she said it, Thomas snapped at her before she could finish. "I won't be a trapper Ma! I won't be a goddamn stinking trapper!" Calmly putting down her spoon, Sarah looked at her plate of food.

"I am one of those you call, stinking trappers Thomas," she said quietly.

"Well I want to be a writer!" Thomas cried before jumping up from the table and running out the front door. Racing along the street and up the alley beside the livery, he crossed in front of the bridge and ran to the schoolhouse where he rushed inside and came to a stop behind Jonathon whom he knew would be there getting ready for the day. Jonathon turned when he heard him come in. "Hello Thomas! I'm glad you are back, but you are a little early!" he said smiling, then frowning when he saw Thomas's tear stained face. "Thomas?" he questioned. Thomas brushed a tear off his cheek.

"I won't be taking the test Mister O'Rourke, Ma's taking me back to the mountain! she wants me to be a trapper!... I... I can't remember anything anyway!" Bursting from the classroom, he ran back to the lodge, and racing inside, found Sarah clearing the table.

"I told Mister O'Rourke about going back to the mountain, I hope you're satisfied Ma!" he said before taking the stairs two at a time. Racing to his room, he slammed the door closed behind him and didn't come out all day.

Figuring he would eventually come around, Sarah stayed away from him. When Thomas didn't come down for dinner, Sarah and Lizzy ate by themselves.

Jonathon went home from school that afternoon worried his best student would miss out on his chance at becoming the best writer he could be. After telling Tilly what happened, Tilly begged Jonathon to talk to Sarah to make her see sense. Although friends with Sarah, Jonathon still felt a little afraid of her. When Sarah rode in that winter before Christian sorted her out and before Lizzy came along, Jonathon rang his school bell which caused Sarah to threaten him with a shooting and sending him off to Mexico to get her runaway horses, which had him wanting to pack up his family and go back to Philadelphia where he felt at the very least, a little safer.

With Christian gone, Sarah kept away from everyone, and no-one knew how to approach her, but Jonathon conceded he had to try to get her to see she was making a mistake. The next morning, he shook off his nervousness and went to the lodge to talk to her.

Jonathon listened patiently while Sarah told him they would go about trapping wolves with the rest of the trappers where they belonged. Sarah listened without interruption to Jonathon's argument as to why Thomas should continue his schooling.

"We are going back Jonathon, this town means nothing to me, I don't belong here, I belong on the mountain," she said when he finished.

"You belong on the mountain Sarah, but Thomas is a writer, he will never be a trapper. He writes wonderful stories, and has worked hard all these years you've been in town, please, give him a chance, don't take his dream away from him," he begged.

Sarah gave thought to what Jonathon was saying before giving him her final answer. "I know all about his stories, but Thomas is my son, he has to go with me!"

Disappointed with Sarah's decision, Jonathon tried to think of something to say that would jolt her into staying. "I hope you don't regret your decision Sarah, I would hate to think Thomas would resent you for making him do something he doesn't like doing!" Jonathon left Sarah thinking about her decision and what it would mean for Thomas to go back to the mountain.

Standing at the top of the stairs, Thomas listened to their conversation, and hoped Jonathon could talk his Ma into staying. But Sarah's parting words to Jonathon told him she stood firm by her decision. Disappointed Jonathon failed to change Sarah's mind, Thomas came downstairs with a feeling of dread at having to go back to the mountain. He didn't hate what his mother did for a living, but for himself, he couldn't justify killing the majestic wolves.

Seeing Sarah and Lizzy seated at the table, and although not hungry himself, he sat down opposite Sarah.

"I'm sorry Ma, I didn't mean to be mad at you, of course you're right, the mountain is where I belong." After looking at Sarah with tear filled eyes, he got up and went to the study so she couldn't see him crying. But Sarah saw his tears and followed him in.

"Thomas, do you think you could pass this, test?" she asked standing behind him. Drying his eyes with his sleeve, Thomas turned to face her.

"I don't know Ma, I think I could, but I feel pretty shitty right now," he answered trying to laugh. Sarah tried smiling then too.

"What will it mean if you pass?" Thomas thought carefully about what to tell her. Except for when he was taken from her as a baby, he had never been away from her longer than a day. If he went to college, she would never get to see him, but there was no other way of telling her.

"It means, I get to go to college." With that reply he knew what Sarah's next question was going to be.

"And where abouts is this... college, Thomas?"

Sarah hoped the college would be in Moreton, that way she might be able to visit him. She knew she could ride that far. It only took two weeks by horse to get to Moreton from Cedar Creek, she and Lizzy could make an adventure of it.

Thomas swallowed before giving her his answer. "Philadelphia!" he said, and because that city was all the way across the other side of the country, he was of the opinion his Ma would never let him go that far away. It certainly was not the answer Sarah was hoping for, and she took her time before answering.

"Well, you had better become, un-shitty! because you have a test to do!"

Surprised by her answer, Thomas rushed toward her, and almost knocking her backwards, threw his arms around her. "You mean it Ma? You mean we aren't going back to the mountain?"

Hoping he heard right, he studied her closely for confirmation as to what she said.

"Yes Thomas, we are not going back," Sarah answered while trying to sound convincing, but to herself said, 'at least not yet.'

"Go on, go do your test," she said, tightening her arms about him.

Thomas suddenly laughed. "It's still months away Ma! maybe my head will clear by then... thanks Ma!" he said kissing her on her cheek, and suddenly feeling hungry, went back to the table where he ate a plate of hotcakes, hugged Sarah again, kissed Lizzy on her cheek, and rushed off to school. Upon entering the classroom, Jonathon pulled him aside. When Thomas informed him, his Ma changed her mind about going back to the mountain and that he could do the test, Jonathon sat behind his desk feeling pleased with himself for thinking he helped Sarah make her decision.

After Thomas rushed off to school, Sarah stayed sitting at the table with Lizzy. She would not take Thomas's dream away from him, but silently prayed he would fail the test so he would not go all the way to Philadelphia. She was afraid she would never see him again. Not if he went that far away.

55

Days passed and weeks turned into months. Jonathon made Thomas and Billy stand in front of the whole school. Twenty-five boys and girls of differing ages sat crammed inside their small one room schoolhouse, and because he was spending so much more of his time concentrating on the older children, especially Thomas and Billy, Jonathon was hoping to extend the schoolhouse to accommodate the growing number of children attending. While Jonathon stood at the back of the room studying the papers he was holding, Thomas and Billy stood side by side waiting for him to tell them why they were standing there. Thomas smiled nervously at Billy, and Billy smiled nervously back at Thomas.

"Thomas... Billy... children!" Jonathon suddenly announced while holding sheets of paper above him for the class to see. "We are here today to give Thomas and Billy... their test results!"

Thomas and Billy's smiles faded from their faces. 'Shit,' Thomas thought. 'This is it!'

In a few minutes he would know if he was going to go to college, or if his Ma would have good reason to take him back to the mountain. Believing Sarah gave up the idea of going back to where she was happiest and taking him and Lizzy with her just so he could take the test, he hoped he passed so she would be proud of him.

Billy's face went white, he felt sick, he only took the test because Thomas had. Having spent many hours sitting in Sarah's study at the lodge with Thomas while reading all the books on law they had, Billy decided he wanted to be a lawyer. The books fascinated him so much, he soaked up all the information in them. Jonathon hadn't realized Billy was smart, not until he started spending his days with Thomas. With Thomas finding he had a passion for writing, he wanted desperately to go to college to hone his skill at story-telling.

"Thomas, how do you think you went?" Jonathon asked while looking expressionless at Thomas's test result and the letter in his hand. Thomas shrugged his shoulders.

"I hope I did alright, Mister O'Rourke," he answered, keeping his voice low.

"What about you Billy? How do you think you went?" Jonathon asked, shuffling the papers. Billy swallowed nervously.

"I reckon if Thomas did alright, then I reckon, I did alright too!... I reckon!" he replied.

When the class erupted in laughter at Billy's answer, Billy's face went bright red. "If you are going to be a lawyer Billy Henderson! you won't want to stand up in court and let your face go red like that! you will want to make people believe you when you are defending some murdering scum that slit some poor wretches throat!" Jonathon said seriously.

With the class laughing louder at Jonathon's remark, he walked along the aisle holding the documents out in front of him, while Billy stood there glaring at him. Stopping between Billy and Thomas, Jonathon turned to face the class and held the papers high.

"After these two, fine young men here took this test, I sealed their papers and sent them off to Philadelphia to be marked, and now..." No longer able to hide his excitement, with a huge grin on his face, he first looked sideways at Thomas, then turning to Billy, slapped him on his back before saying, "here they are!... back at last!"

Thomas was feeling sick, his stomach churned. The test had come around far too soon after Christian died. Seeing him lying on the undertakers table, he hadn't been able to think straight. Taking care of his Ma and Lizzy those first few weeks after the burial were the hardest. They stayed at the lodge and didn't come out for a month. When his Ma didn't want to eat, he took over doing the cooking, and gradually with his help, she began to get back to her usual self, but it still worried him about doing the test.

Jonathon was addressing the class. "Thomas, read the result on that piece of paper for the class to hear please." He handed Thomas his result. Thomas looked down at the paper and swallowed. After studying it for a moment his face broke out in a wide grin.

"I got a hundred!" he said, looking surprised at Jonathon.

"Out of what Thomas?" Jonathon asked, keeping his face to the rest of the class.

"Out of a hundred... sir!" Thomas answered smiling. Along with Jonathon, the classroom erupted in loud applause and cheering.

"Well done Thomas! that means you are going to college, you can read the letter of acceptance later when you show it to your Ma, now Billy, tell us your result please." Thomas waited for Billy to read his result. Unsmiling, Billy looked up from his paper.

"I got ninety-nine... damn!" Billy said, disappointed he didn't get the same result as Thomas.

"That is great Billy!" Thomas said smiling and clapping along with the class. Jonathon agreed with Thomas.

"That is right Billy! that is a great result, you will be going to college too!" With that, Thomas and Billy hugged each other, then laughing, gave each other congratulatory slaps on the back.

School in Cedar Creek ended that day for Thomas and Billy, but before he went home, Jonathon asked Thomas if he wouldn't mind coming back to help him with his younger students until he left for college, and Thomas agreed he would.

Both boys decided they wouldn't tell their folks they passed their college entry test, at least not yet. Worried how his Ma would take the news when he told her he passed and would be leaving her, Thomas wanted to wait for the right moment and asked Jonathon not to say anything either before he got a chance to tell her himself, and Jonathon agreed he wouldn't say a word.

Chapter Seven

*I*t was late in the afternoon, and everyone was getting ready to settle down for the evening. Except for Henry's Emporium, other businesses had already closed their doors when a stagecoach came rumbling to a stop outside. The few people still milling about inside Henry's waiting to be served, emptied out quickly and stood on the street to observe what was going on. They had never had a stagecoach in their town before, and they wanted to know why it was there now. As the driver threw two valises from the top of the coach onto the ground, Foley and Smith hurried across the street to see what the commotion was about. When two male passengers got out and stood with their bags on the boardwalk, the taller of the two men spied Foley coming toward them, and stepping out of the crowd, stuck his hand out in greeting toward Foley.

"Hello sheriff, my name is Donovan, Peter Donovan, I'm from the United Coach Company, and I've come here to your, um... lovely town, to start a coach service," Donovan said taking in the towns unusual rustic appearance. Donovan was as tall as Foley but clean shaven and well dressed in black jacket and matching trousers. After looking Donovan up and down, Foley took his hand in his and shook it.

"I'm Sheriff Andrews," he said rather curtly, and without so much as introducing his deputy, put his hands on his hips.

Donovan thought it only proper to introduce the other man with him. "This is Blake Stevens, he is with the Government Telegraph Department, and is here to bring the telegraph to your town." Foley grasped the hand Stevens offered him.

"And a U S Mail Service!" Stevens said shaking Foley's hand vigorously.

Pushing his hat back so he could get a better look at the men, Foley refrained from smiling. After all, he was sheriff and had to keep the peace, if he wasn't careful, strangers coming to town could pose a threat to the community.

Thomas was with Billy when they saw the stage come rumbling into sight. Running down the street and joining the crowd to welcome the passengers, they heard what the men were saying. Learning about stagecoaches and telegraphs, along with mail services in school, both knew they were things that brought people from far-away places together. Thomas was excited, and wanted to get home to tell his Ma what had come to town.

"See you Billy!" he called as he ran across the street. Racing home, he flew up the steps two at a time, and shoving the front door hard to open it, ran inside. Sarah was in the kitchen busy baking bread, Lizzy thought she was helping. Sarah had flour on her nose, Lizzy was eating the dough. "Stop eating it Lizzy! we won't have enough for a loaf if you keep eating it!" Sarah was saying when Thomas burst through the door excited, and talking fast told Sarah about the stagecoach and how it would take people to Moreton and beyond. Sarah replied, saying she didn't care, she didn't need to go to Moreton, there was nothing beyond Cedar Creek she wanted to know about. When he told her about the telegraph and how they could send messages to people in other cities, Sarah said she didn't care about that either. After saying she didn't know anyone in other cities, she kept kneading her dough. Thomas went on to tell her about the mail service and how they could write letters and send them off to people, and how they could get letters back. Sarah said she didn't know anyone to write to, besides she said, she couldn't write very well anyway. Thomas was still talking when there was a loud knock on the front door.

Everyone was excited about the stagecoach and telegraph coming to town. There would be something new to talk about over dinner. After the crowd departed, Donovan and Stevens were left to find themselves somewhere to stay. Having business to attend to that would take them all the next day to complete, they would not take the stage back to Moreton until the following day. Before leaving them and returning to the Sheriff's Office, Foley informed the two men, the only place in town that might accommodate them for the two nights they would be in town was the saloon. Donovan and Stevens however were city men, and because the saloon was a noisy place, they didn't want to stay there. Having blazed a trail for two solid days all the way from Moreton, they would not get much sleep. When they came in on the coach however, the two men noticed the grand house situated in the street running adjacent to the river. Left standing in Henry's Emporium, Donovan asked Henry about the lodge.

"That house isn't a boarding house, belongs to Misses Morgan, a widow woman, she's not particular about people she knows, let alone strangers! she won't have you staying there!" Henry informed them curtly. Donovan didn't let that bother him. Taking Stevens across the street and around the corner, they hurried past the Ferguson House.

"That's a big house! looks like it's all closed up though! what a waste! we could have stayed there!" Stevens said breathlessly as they arrived in the street where the lodge was.

Eyeing the lodge, Donovan made out a grand structure built entirely from cedar. A porch ran the entire length of the building and large windows looked out from every side of the upper floor. Pleased with what he was seeing, Donovan carried his bag up the half dozen steps to the front door and knocked.

Hearing the loud knock from her kitchen, Sarah wiped her hands on her apron covering her skirt, and before going to the door, looked at Thomas and he looked at her. She hadn't expected anyone, and unable to recognize their scent, couldn't tell who was standing on the other side. Opening the door cautiously, and seeing two strangers on her porch, she opened the door a little wider. Thomas stood behind her looking on in amazement when he saw the two men. Feeling his heart skip a beat when he saw Sarah, Peter Donovan removed his hat.

"Ma'am, my name is Donovan, Peter Donovan, and this is Blake Stevens." He bowed slightly as he smiled at Sarah.

"Ma! it's the men off the stagecoach!" Thomas said excitedly. Donovan smiled over Sarah's head at Thomas.

"That is right son, we are, and we are looking for somewhere we might stay for two nights, we saw...!" Before he could finish, Sarah interrupted him.

"The saloon has rooms!" she said sharply beginning to shut the door.

"Five hundred dollars for the two of us for two nights!" Donovan said quickly before the door could be closed. Sarah pulled the door back open.

"It does not cost that much to stay at the saloon! if it does, then they are robbing you!" she said sounding incredulous.

"Oh! no, ma'am! I mean, we would pay you five hundred dollars for letting us rent rooms here, in your home." Sarah glared at him. Although he looked a decent man, and quite handsome, she wasn't in the business of letting strangers stay in her house.

"I don't need your money, and I certainly don't need you staying in my house!" With that she shut the door.

"Ma! they wouldn't be any trouble, they are from the city! and five hundred dollars Ma! you know how many wolves we would have to trap to get that? Come on Ma! let them stay!" Thomas begged.

"I don't have room Thomas, I can't ask them to pay all that money to sleep on the couch!" Sarah said heading back to the kitchen and Lizzy.

"We have a guest room going to waste up there," Thomas said pointing above them. "I can sleep at Billy's, that way, they could have a room each!" he added quickly. For at least two nights his Ma would have someone to talk to other than him and Lizzy, besides, he wanted to ask the men all about the telegraph and stagecoach.

Quickly giving what Thomas was saying consideration, Sarah turned back and opened the door. Donovan and Stevens were standing at the bottom of the steps with their bags in their hands trying to figure out somewhere else to stay when Sarah walked across the porch and looked down at them. When Donovan looked up at Sarah, his heart began beating rapidly. 'She is lovely,' he thought, while also thinking, 'a beautiful woman to be way out here at the end of this god-forsaken country has to be my lucky day.'

"Alright, you can stay, but come back in two hours, I will have your rooms ready then, you can leave your bags here, if you like," Sarah said without feeling. Donovan hurried back up to the porch. "Thank you, ma'am," he said with a smile at the top of the steps. Stevens followed him up without speaking.

While sitting their bags on the floor just inside the door, Donovan took the opportunity to look around the room and was amazed at such a fine house being in such a small town. A leather couch faced the open fireplace where a fire was burning, sending a warm glow over the furnishings. A comfortable looking green winged chair that could grace any regal manor sat beside it. An elegant dining table and four tapestry covered chairs sat behind the couch, and a grand staircase led to the next floor. Looking above the fireplace, Donovan saw a painting hanging over the mantle and thought it a beautiful portrait of the woman standing in front of him, and felt he was in love already. After putting his bag down and straightening up, he looked longingly at Sarah, and knowing that look, Sarah quickly ushered the two men back out the door.

"Like I said! come back in two hours, dinner will be ready then too," she said trying to close it.

"We can eat at the saloon ma'am." Donovan offered before she could shut them out. Staring into two very dark blue eyes, Sarah didn't feel anything for Donovan.

"You are staying here, you will eat here! and stop calling me ma'am! names Morgan... Sarah Morgan," she answered sternly.

"Then we shall return in two hours, Sarah, after we look around your fine town," he said thanking her with a smile. "That won't take you two hours!" Sarah said laughing, and having said that, she closed the door.

Once Sarah finished baking her bread, she enlisted Thomas and Lizzy to help change the sheets on Thomas's bed. The guest room was opened and the bed there hastily made, then after wiping a damp cloth over furnishings, she put fresh water in jugs standing in hand-basins on dressers in both rooms. Lizzy carried towels, and Sarah put one on the end of each bed with a cloth and soap for washing. Not being a city person, she didn't know what the men expected for their five hundred dollars and hoped they found their rooms to their liking. While Sarah began preparing dinner, Thomas helped set the table in the formal dining room. He lit the fire to warm the large room making it comfortable to eat in, then racing up the street, passed the two men on his way to Billy's. After asking Martha if she didn't mind him staying there for two nights because, now they had guests he didn't have a bed, Martha reminded him he was welcome at their home anytime, so after telling Billy he would let him know what the men talked about when he came back to sleep, Thomas ran home to have dinner with two men that would play a part in changing his life forever.

Donovan and Stevens arrived back at the lodge precisely two hours later, and Thomas showed the two men in. When Sarah came out of the kitchen, the two men's eyes widened in surprise. Sarah was wearing trousers, which they hadn't seen her wearing when they first met, but it was what she was wearing with her trousers that had both of them staring as she crossed the room to greet them. Fastened around her waist and hanging from her hip was the sheath that held her skinning knife. Her pistol was fully loaded and shoved down the front of her pants. Neither man could take his eyes off her as she stopped in front of them.

Sarah liked that the two men were prompt when coming back. "Well! here we are! I will show you to your rooms," she said with a hint of a smile.

Donovan feeling surprised, and Stevens feeling overwhelmed by Sarah's appearance, picked up their bags and followed Sarah up the stairs. Watching her hips sway as she climbed the stairs to the landing, Donovan suppressed a smile as he thought his stay might prove better than expected. Coming to a stop outside Thomas's room, Sarah opened the door.

"This is your room Mister Donovan," she informed him. Dropping his valise on the floor inside the door, Donovan surveyed the room. Like the rest of the house, Thomas's room was clean and tidy. The huge cast-iron framed bed looked comfortable. The fresh towel and washcloth folded on the end of the bed was the same as he had seen in many hotels in cities around the country that he had travelled to on business. Satisfied with his accommodation he turned to Sarah.

"Please Sarah, I would very much like it if you would call me Peter," Donovan smiled. Nodding slightly in reply, Sarah left him in his room and took Stevens across the hall where he found what appeared to be a comfortable bed adorned with many pillows. Also pleased with his room, Stevens complemented Sarah on it, then having informed both men dinner would be ready as soon as they freshened up, Sarah returned to the kitchen.

At the dining table, Lizzy sat between Sarah and Thomas, which surprised Donovan to see Sarah had a small child. Remembering the store owner Henry telling him she was a widow, he wondered how long ago she lost her husband, but thought he shouldn't ask in case it wasn't too long ago. Sarah deliberately sat Donovan and Stevens opposite her so she could keep her eyes on both men. When the men had been left upstairs, each commented on the pistol and knife Sarah was carrying. Donovan didn't seem at all fazed by it, after all, he said, they were in the west where everyone carried weapons. But Stevens had never had to venture west. He instead delegated teams of men to do the work for him, but this time, it being so distant from anywhere of importance, he decided to set things up for himself, but sitting here now, he wished he had delegated the job because stories about the west scared him, and so it seemed did Sarah.

While plates of roast chicken and baked vegetables were passed back and forth, Thomas asked Donovan about the stagecoach, and Donovan, being only too pleased to talk about his venture, began a long commentary.

"Let's say we are coming from Moreton to Cedar Creek!" he stated, and everyone laughed at how silly a statement it was, because they did come from Moreton to Cedar Creek.

"We travelled a very long way in two days, but when the coach stopped to let us rest at the junction under construction halfway between Moreton and here, our horses should have been replaced with a fresh team, but alas, there weren't any to be had... horses need corralling where travelers break their journey! never-the-less, we travelled on regardless, and arrived here on dusk in your..." Unable to take his eyes off Sarah, Donovan smiled seductively at her. "Beautiful town," he said pausing for effect before going on.

"The same is done for the journey back to Moreton, what I have to do here is secure teams of horses for each trip, then our run can begin." Picking up his knife and fork, he began eating.

"You mean, it only takes two days to get here from Moreton?" Thomas asked amazed by what he was hearing.

"Absolutely!" Donovan replied. "So long as the driver keeps up the momentum and the horses are replaced with a fresh team, we can arrive comfortably on the second day."

"Woah!" Thomas said sounding excited. "It takes two weeks by horse to get from here to Moreton!"

"Ah yes!" Donovan said. "But we blazed a trail straight across the prairie, cutting off vast tracts of land and winding gorges, and going back would take the same amount of time."

While Donovan talked, Sarah's face became flushed, making her appear delicate, giving Donovan cause to think his presence may be contributing to her seemingly coy appearance. Although Sarah could feel her face burning, it was cleaning rooms, and spending so much time baking that was making her feel hot. Looking up at Donovan their eyes met across the table.

Donovan smiled again and continued. "It would be superb if there were somewhere people could stay instead of the saloon, that won't do for city folk... tell me Sarah, what is that big house at the end of the street?"

"The Ferguson House!" Thomas interjected before Sarah could answer. "The trappers own that!... but they only use it during winter!" and going on, told the men about the trappers.

"We are from the mountain too!" he ended. Donovan looked more intently at Sarah.

"You?... a trapper?" he asked Sarah while thinking, surely an attractive woman such as she would not know the first thing about trapping. Sarah was about to answer when again Thomas jumped in ahead of her.

"Yep! Ma is the best!"

"That is not true Thomas, everyone knows Joe is the best," Sarah replied looking at him. Donovan thought that explained the knife hanging from her hip and the gun in her pants, but hoping what Thomas said was a fabrication of the truth, he sought confirmation. "Are you Sarah?... a trapper I mean." Out of respect for the two being city gentlemen, and being courteous of Donovan's title, Sarah answered. "Not any more, Mister Donovan."

While Donovan commanded all the attention, Sarah looked over at Blake Stevens sitting quietly eating his meal and changed the subject. "Mister Stevens, would you tell us about your telegraph?"

Having listened to Donovan talk glowingly about his stagecoach, Steven's was pleased to be asked about his role in coming to town, and told them he was hoping to get a contract from Cedar Creek's lumberyard for poles to go all the way from town back to the halfway junction, allowing for wires to join up to poles and wires being erected along the route from Moreton.

Sarah and Thomas listened intently as he went on to explain, when mail came on the stagecoach every three weeks, a new building housing both the Telegraph and U S Mail Office would need to be built, and that he was here to organize that as well. Both Sarah and Thomas found Stevens an interesting man to listen too. With Sarah wishing him all the best for getting his contract, she turned back to Donovan.

"Major Hardy owns the biggest spread around here, he should be able to provide you with horses… given the right price." Donovan asked Sarah where he could meet Major Hardy.

"I can take you to his ranch tomorrow if you like?" Looking forward to spending the day alone with Sarah, Donovan smiled and accepted her offer.

Once dinner was over, Thomas left Sarah with the two men and made his way to Billy's. After pouring the men coffee and telling them to make themselves comfortable, Sarah put Lizzy to bed in her room where she could keep an eye on her. The two men were relaxing sitting on the couch in front of the fire when Sarah returned and Stevens asked her about the portrait above the mantle, saying it was a lovely painting of her. When she informed them, it was a portrait of her mother, both men stared in awe at the painting's likeness to Sarah. Then leaving the two men to finish their coffee, Sarah went through to the kitchen to clean up.

Before retiring, Stevens went to the kitchen and handed Sarah his half of their two nights stay, then excused himself for the night. Finding him a quiet, unassuming man, Sarah smiled sweetly, and thanked him for the money.

Having finished her chore, Sarah went back to the living area to find Donovan still seated in front of the fire. Withdrawing cash from his money-pouch, he handed it to Sarah who thanked him, then, having been up since daylight and wishing for an early night, she bid Donovan good night. "I will see you in the morning Mister Donovan, breakfast will be in here, after which we will head out to Major Hardy's," she announced before moving to the staircase. But Donovan wasn't ready to retire to his room just yet.

"Do you have to go Sarah? I thought we could sit and talk, maybe get to know each other a little better," he enquired in the hope of getting more from Sarah than just a kiss. For a moment Sarah looked undecidedly at him, then headed up the stairs.

"Good night Mister Donovan," she said without looking back. Watching Sarah as she climbed the stairs, and seeing her stop halfway, Donovan thought she had a change of heart about staying to get to know him.

"Oh! and Mister Donovan, I sleep with my knife, and my pistol." Donovan looked stunned, but when Sarah retired without further ado, he figured she had read him like a book, and although disappointed he hadn't made headway with her, he retired to his room determined he would try again tomorrow.

The next morning, before the men finished breakfast, Sarah had her buckboard out and ready. Stevens said he would see her at dinner, but before he could go on his way, Sarah offered to take him to the lumberyard herself. Stevens was grateful for her offer, but said he didn't want to inconvenience her in any way, and that he could get a horse and ride out there himself. With that polite refusal, and thinking because of his manners he was a well-bred man, Sarah liked Blake Stevens more than she already did. On the other hand, even though Donovan was well-mannered too, Sarah thought he had another agenda where she was concerned.

Thinking he might get to put his arm around Sarah on the way out to Major Hardy's, Donovan climbed onto the buckboard and plonked himself on the seat beside her, but Sarah squeezed Lizzy in to sit between them and kept Donovan at a safe distance.

It turned out to be a pleasant ride to Major Hardy's ranch. Donovan was impressed by the many different farms they passed as Sarah explained along the way who owned them and what crops they grew. When they arrived at the ranch, he was even more impressed. Major Hardy's ranch-house was a huge hacienda type structure surrounded by tall shade trees and grassed areas. White painted fences bordered corrals running along both sides of the wagon trail. Donovan was thinking he could settle here, especially with a woman like Sarah. While entertaining that thought, he glanced sideways at Sarah and smiled. Sarah though was too busy concentrating on controlling her horse to take any notice of him. She hadn't been out to the ranch since Christian had been shot, and holding the reins tight in her out-stretched hands while steering carefully through the gates, she pulled the buckboard to a stop in front of the house. When Major Hardy was informed by one of his gun-hands someone was coming, he came out to see who it was.

"Why Sarah! Lizzy! hello!" he said surprised to see them, but when he saw the man seated beside Sarah, his smile faded to one of suspicion. After Sarah introduced Donovan and explained who he was and what he represented, and why he was in Cedar Creek, Major Hardy was delighted to meet him and shook his hand vigorously, then ushered everyone inside where he made them comfortable.

While Major Hardy and Donovan spent several hours discussing business Sarah excused herself, and taking Lizzy out to the garden, let her play on plush grass growing between shrubs and shade trees while she sat in the shade waiting patiently for the two men to finish. On the way back to town, she pulled the buckboard off the road near a clearing beside deep waterholes that made up the river to let Lizzy relieve herself. This was where Sarah spent many picnics with Christian and her children. It was the same place Christian and Thomas liked to fish for trout and she and Christian swum together.

Getting off the buckboard and after Lizzy was taken care of, Sarah let her run around for a moment so Donovan could stretch his legs and take in the scenery. Donovan liked the view, especially when he looked back at Sarah leaning against a tree twisting a long piece of grass in her fingers. He could see she was deep in thought about something that made her appear sad, so walking up to her, he put his hand on the trunk beside her head, and leant in close.

"You are a very beautiful woman Sarah, a man could decide not to go back to the city, especially if he had a woman like you to come home to." Hoping to steal a kiss, he leant further in. Thinking about the times she spent here with Christian plunged Sarah deep in thought which made her feel her loss even more. As Donovan's mouth almost touched hers, Sarah stared into his dark blue eyes.

Feeling something unusual pushing against him, Donovan frowned, and looking down, saw Sarah holding her hunting knife, the tip of which was pressed against his stomach. "Mister Donovan, I have met a lot of men like you… trappers, cowboys and ranchers, and farmers too, who have all tried talking pretty to me, now!… if you don't want my knife sticking out of your belly, you better take a step back!" Taking Sarah's warning seriously, Donovan stepped away.

"Come on Lizzy, time to go," Sarah said sheathing her knife, and glancing sideways at Donovan, found he was no longer smiling.

The two men finished their business they had in town, and after it was agreed horses would be provided from Major Hardy's stock, Donovan organized for the stagecoach run to go ahead. Running every three weeks between Moreton and Cedar Creek, the stage would stay in town one night only before picking up passengers for the return trip to Moreton. Until such time as a new boarding house could be built where travelers could stay, the stage would stop outside Henry's Emporium. Stevens secured a contract with the lumberyard to provide the poles for his telegraph. He purchased a block of land opposite the schoolhouse, and organized timber for the building of the combined Telegraph/ US Mail Office. Men assigned to do the job were happy to commence work as soon as the lumberyard had the supply of timber ready.

Donovan and Stevens left at daylight the next day for their return journey to Moreton. Sarah was there seeing both men off. She shook hands with Peter Donovan and kissed Blake Stevens on his cheek, then said she would be happy to let him stay at the lodge if ever he was to return to Cedar Creek anytime in the future.

Stevens blushed profusely when Sarah kissed him, and was only too happy to inform her he would be returning to oversee the building of the new building and the erection of the poles to the junction. Sarah wished him well and waved the men off. As the stagecoach pulled out of town, Donovan glared at Stevens.

"Why did Sarah Morgan kiss you Stevens? What on earth, could she possibly think is so special about you?" he snarled.

"Oh, I don't know, maybe it was because I didn't force myself on her, you shouldn't try so hard Donovan!" As the stage rumbled past the Andrews farm, Blake Stevens looked out the window and smiled to himself. When he left town, he was no longer scared of Sarah, and couldn't wait to return to see her again.

Chapter Eight

*H*aving Peter Donovan and Blake Stevens stay at the lodge gave Sarah something else to think about besides Foley and his problem with Maria's infidelity. It also saved her from thinking too much about Christian. Occasionally, still wanting him to hold her in his arms, Sarah cried herself to sleep. A pillow was no substitute for his warm body lying next to hers.

Autumn soon turned to winter. When the nights began to cool, Sarah thought about the trappers and the arduous journey they would be taking to get to town. Pushing open the window in her room, she stood in front of it looking out at the mountains in the distance. Snow already falling on high ground sent a cold wind blowing through her window causing a chill to come over her naked body. The trappers coming back made Sarah feel both sad and relieved. She would not have to tell the men what happened to Christian. There was no doubt they would find out as soon as they rode in. Shivering from the cold night air and feeling the lump forming in her throat, she reached out and closed the window. The drapes she left open to enable morning light to filter through so she could awake to a new day. Making her way back to her bed, she climbed in, and as she pulled the covers up, she prayed the trappers were on their way.

Up on the mountain the men woke to freezing conditions. Winter had returned with a vengeance, catching the trappers unaware at the High Ridge Camp. Snow was already coming over their boots as they trudged around, and hoping the snow wasn't as deep through the pass as it was higher up, but not holding out much hope that it wouldn't be, Joe gathered all the trappers that were at the camp together and informed them it was time to leave. Although each man was responsible for themselves and their horses, Joe knew the mountain better than all of them, and it was his responsibility to lead them to safety, but that did nothing to stop them worrying about following him and traversing the pass in deep snow.

Obeying his orders to leave, they hurriedly loading their packhorses heavily with skins and supplies and set off for Sarah's cabin where they planned to take shelter before going on to the pass and the caves.

The nights the men spent camped on their way to Sarah's cabin were far from ideal. Snow continued falling heavily. The roaring fires the men built were useless, forcing them to huddle together for warmth. After making Sarah's cabin at nightfall on their fourth day, Joe, Will, Fergus and Garrett made camp inside, while a dozen men camped in Sarah's old dirt floor cabin. At least it had walls and a roof to keep out the cold. The open stone fireplace proved a blessing. The men were now able to feel warmth emanating from their fire.

When they awoke the next morning, it had stopped snowing and the sun had come out. Everyone was in high spirits as they ate a hearty breakfast. When trappers that had been trapping along the River Flats arrived at the cabin, Joe was pleased every man had the good sense to know it was time to get going.

Arriving at the pass, Joe was relieved to find his markers still clearly visible. The trek across would have been far more difficult if the markers had been covered by snow. But snow on the ground was a lot deeper than he expected, making the journey tough going. Men pushed through snow up to their knees, and in some places, struggled to walk at all when it came up to their thighs. Pulling their horses behind them was hard work when horses became bogged down in hidden snow-drifts. Finally making it across the pass, they breathed a sigh of relief when the caves came into sight, allowing them a comfortable nights rest before the ride to the bottom of the mountain. Next morning, the men joked and laughed with each other as they loaded their rifles ready for the attack they were about to face.

When wolves came bursting from the forest to hunt the men's horses, the men rode at a gallop with their heavily laden packhorses racing along behind them. Hoping they would beat Joe to win the thousand-dollar pot, the trappers began taking down as many wolves as they could as these skins added to their total for the year. But Joe had no time to waste.

He could ride all day and all night if he had to, and he wanted to, because he was missing Sarah, and he wanted to say howdy to Christian. Missing one night's sleep wouldn't hurt him, so knowing the men would catch up, after skinning his kill, he got his group going until they made camp at the wells. Having proven himself to be a good husband and father, Joe had grown to like Christian, and thought him a decent man, and wasn't bothered when he found out he had been a bounty hunter. Most men Joe knew had something in their past they weren't proud of. He thought Sarah lucky to have met him, and he wanted to see Lizzy too, to see how much she had grown since he last saw her, and there was Thomas who was happy now he had a Pa. Joe felt pleased that Thomas had settled in to life in Cedar Creek and was doing well at school. He couldn't wait to catch up with all of them, so after settling down for an easy night at the wells, before the next part of their journey took them to Cedar Creek, he informed the men he wasn't going to stop out on the prairie. All the men agreed when saying if that was what he wanted, then they didn't mind riding hard all the next day. They would arrive in town tired, but glad to be back in civilization that afternoon.

When the trappers approached the bridge, Joe was in the lead as usual. The first thing he noticed missing from the trail was the sign Christian erected telling everyone firearms were not permitted in town. Joe frowned but kept going, and rode in over the bridge. Fergus came next, while Garrett and Will rode in further along in the group. Joe noticed something else amiss as he rode down the main street. The town seemed much quieter than when they rode in last winter. There wasn't the happy bustle of town folk from year's gone by. People standing stony faced on boardwalks and in the street, stared at the men as they rode by. No-one greeted the trappers with waves. There were no smiles, or shouts of welcome.

When he saw Foley standing outside the Sheriff's Office with two men he recognized from Major Hardy's ranch, that he worked alongside of when breaking horses, and both wearing badges, Joe furrowed his brow further. Riding past Smith and Taylor, he looked down and nodded to Foley, and when Foley nodded back up at him, he felt the solemn atmosphere emanating from the men. Something had happened, Joe was certain of it. The trappers coming behind him couldn't help noticing men walking about and those standing outside the saloon, were all packing guns.

Pulling his packhorse down the street, passing Kathleen's Saloon, Henry's Emporium, the Ferguson House and on to the Trading Post, Joe pulled his horse to a stop and got down. While muttering to each other about the tense atmosphere they felt when riding through town, other trappers pulled their horses around in a bunch and dismounted. Joe got busy unloading his skins and with Fergus, waited for Garrett and Will to catch up. When they tied their horses to the hitching rail, Joe picked up an armload of skins and carried them inside. Fess looked gloomily at Joe when he came through the door. "Howdy Joe," he said, then nodded to Fergus and Garrett when they came in behind him. Stepping inside, Will took off his hat and said howdy to Fess.

"Howdy Will, you want coffee? Where be your skin's?" Fess asked at seeing Joe the only one bringing in skins. It seemed to each of the men, Fess was a little confused, as he well knew, each man had to wait their turn at bringing their skins in to be counted.

"What's going on Fess? Why are the men wearing guns? And why, goddamn it! does everyone look so goddamn pitiful?" Joe asked throwing his skins on the table and putting his hands on his hips.

"It's bad news Joe, had a bit of trouble quite a few months ago now," Fess answered while going to his potbelly stove and holding his hands out to warm them.

"What kind of trouble?" Joe asked innocently. All four men waited with Joe for Fess to tell them what happened. Without taking his eyes off the stove, Fess broke the bad news.

"It's Sheriff Morgan Joe, he dang well went and got himself shot!" Dropping his hands off his hips in shock at what Fess said, Joe moved close to where Fess was standing.

"What do you mean shot!?" Joe exclaimed. "Is he alright?" The other men quickly gathered by the stove so they could hear better what Fess was telling them. Fess looked sadly around at each man before explaining.

"Got shot in the chest Joe... he's dead!" Just like everyone else, Fess had come to like Christian. When he broke the news, he had a tear in his eye.

The trappers sucked in their breath in shock, and while cursing, Joe felt a chill run up his spine. When Joe wheeled around, Fess was still talking.

"I'll be back Fess! let the other men go first!... come on!" he beckoned to the other three. Following Joe outside, the men walked swiftly past the other trappers still coming in with their packhorses. The late comers stared at the group as they hurried across the road. Some scratched their heads in bewilderment, others hurried inside to Fess to find out what was going on.

Half walking, half running across the road to the Ferguson House, Joe walked quickly along the street in front of it then turned into the street where the lodge was situated. Taking the steps to the porch two at a time, the other men keeping up with him did the same, then waited while Joe punched his fist on the front door.

Their horse's hooves made a lot of noise as they were ridden over the wooden bridge. Hearing the trappers coming from inside the schoolhouse, Thomas raced out without excusing himself. Knowing he was going home to tell his Ma the trappers had arrived, Jonathon let him go. Running to the bridge where the trappers were filing in, Thomas darted between their horses to get through. Seeing Joe and Fergus already further along, he turned down the alley beside the livery and raced to the lodge where he flew up the steps and went inside.

"*Ma!*" he called, running to the kitchen where Sarah and Lizzy were busy baking.

"*Ma!*" he shouted before stopping and looking at Sarah.

"The trappers are here!" he said, as if she didn't know.

Already sensing they had arrived, Sarah stopped kneading the dough she was preparing for the next loaf, and taking the uncooked dough Lizzy was busy playing with off her, wiped her hands on her apron. Leaving everything as it was, and with Thomas and Lizzy following, she made her way to the living area to stand in front of the open fire where she stared into the flames.

"Ma, Joe will be here soon, he will come when he hears," he said sadly, and placing his hand on Sarah's shoulder to comfort her, Sarah tried her best not to cry. She needed Joe when Christian had been shot, but he was on the mountain trapping at the time. She didn't know how she would react when she saw him. Thomas and Sarah stood together and waited while Lizzy climbed on the couch, and looking at her Ma and Thomas, still didn't understand what was going on. All she knew was her Ma cried a lot, and she missed her Pa who was no longer around.

Sarah heard the men coming up the steps, but still jumped when she heard the loud banging on her front door. Turning from the fireplace, she moved slowly toward the door, and after taking a moment to compose herself, took a deep breath and pulled the door open. Joe was the first she saw, then Fergus. Peering at her from behind them was Garrett and Will. Sarah had missed them terribly since Christian's death, and now here they were, all four, standing on her porch.

"Joe!" she said looking into his face and bursting into tears. Stepping through the door, Joe quickly wrapped his arms around her, and putting her arms around Joe, she clung to him.

"Oh! Joe!" she cried.

As her body shook from suddenly seeing him, Joe held her while taking her back to the fire. Feeling speechless to know what to say, the other men moved silently into the room. Seeing Lizzy where she was sitting, Will lifted her off the couch and into his arms.

"Hello Lizzy darlin, how you doing?" he asked not expecting an answer. Lizzy only saw these men every winter, and she studied Will carefully. His beard had grown wild and long, but remembering who Will was, she wrapped her arms about his neck and hugged him tight. Fergus and Garrett shook hands with Thomas, and hugging him, said how sorry they were to hear about Christian. When a tear ran down Thomas's cheek, he quickly swiped it away with the palm of his hand. It was a good while before Joe asked Sarah to tell them what happened.

Sitting together on the couch, they waited while the other men pulled chairs out from the table and crowded around to hear her relate the events that took place several months ago, but Sarah found it difficult to tell the men everything through her sobbing. Joe held her while Thomas, struggling through his own sorrow, filled them in on some of the details his Ma had trouble relating. The men listened patiently and after hearing what happened, Fergus and Garrett busied themselves making coffee. While Will sat nursing Lizzy, Thomas helped by getting mugs and cookies for everyone. Not wanting to leave Sarah while she was still upset, the men stayed until late into the evening. Sarah told them she would be alright, that she didn't know where her tears were coming from. But Joe had an idea Sarah would cry for a very long time.

After telling Sarah and Thomas they would see them in the morning, the four men reluctantly left the lodge and headed back to the Trading Post. Understanding it would take the men time to return from seeing Sarah, and with them still having skins to put in, Fess kept the Trading Post open. Joe won the pot again, but none of the men felt like celebrating. After getting their chits for the bank they went straight to the Ferguson House and told the rest of the trappers there what had been told to them. The men already heard from Fess that Christian had been killed by a kid that was fast becoming an outlaw. They said how sorry they were for Sarah and Thomas, and especially little Lizzy now she no longer had a Pa.

With Christian out of Sarah's life, after trying unsuccessfully once before to bed Sarah, the meanest trapper that ever trapped saw an opportunity to try again. While Logan kept his lust for Sarah hidden, he asked Joe if it meant she would be going back to the mountain now she was a widow. Joe hadn't had time to think about Sarah going back to trapping, and made a mental note to ask her if that was what she would do. He just had to pick the right time to ask.

By spending many of her days with the four men, Sarah finally had an excuse to get out of the house. Firstly, and to show their respects for Christian, the trappers accompanied her to the cemetery to visit his grave where she had to be held by Joe with her head pressed against his chest as she wept unconsolably. Once the men saw where Christian was laid to rest, none of them ventured back there. Wanting Sarah to be happy while in town, the four men organized the first of many days relaxing at a picnic with her and her children. They took Sarah's buckboard along the road toward Major Hardy's ranch and stopped by the river where they had fun fishing for trout in a shallow waterhole. Thomas and the men laughed and argued jovially over who caught the biggest and most fish. Taking their catch back to the lodge, Sarah cooked the fish for dinner while the men kept Lizzy amused with games. Lizzy's infectious giggle had the men laughing loudly. While everyone enjoyed their meal, no-one talked about Christian.

Convinced they made Sarah happy, after leaving the lodge, the men headed back to the Ferguson House in high spirits. Thomas and Lizzy were already fast asleep when Sarah retired for the night. Although happy the four men were back, and having enjoyed their company, Sarah cried herself to sleep still longing for Christian to hold her.

The trappers had been in town for a little over a month when snow began covering the ground with a good dusting. While Thomas helped Jonathon with his students at school, the trappers became busy breaking Major Hardy's horses. This particular day Sarah didn't have much to do at the lodge, so bundling Lizzy into warm clothes, she took her along to the corral's to watch the men at work, and climbing up the fence, perched herself and Lizzy on the top rail next to the corral's shelter where they could see everything that was going on.

"Hold on tight Lizzy so you won't fall off," Sarah warned, and reaching behind her, pressed her hand over Lizzy's to give her extra support.

Lizzy was tiny, and because the fence was high and felt slippery, she felt afraid. With her legs dangling over the side, she gripped the post as best as she could and watched as horses, objecting when saddle blankets were thrown over their backs, ran wildly around and bucked while trying to keep the men from getting saddles on. The twisting and turning dislodged saddles and riders, making Sarah and Lizzy laugh as men were routinely thrown into the slush. Lizzy giggled shrilly when a horse, becoming used to Garrett on its back, stopped bucking and settled down. Joe and Fergus, standing outside the fence further along from where Sarah and Lizzy were sitting could hear Lizzy's shrieks of laughter, and it made both men smile.

Not having any trouble to deal with, Foley became interested in seeing what horses the men were breaking, so walking past Sarah and Lizzy sitting on the fence, he stopped near the gate into the corral and peering through the railings, could see Will standing in the middle of the corral holding a tether attached to a stallion that was giving him a whole mess of trouble. The horse wasn't about to let Will get a saddle on him, and kicking out viciously, forced Will to let go of the rope. When the stallion bucked, coming dangerously close to the fence, Sarah pressed her hand firmly over Lizzy's and held it as the horse rushed past. Not liking Lizzy sitting high up on top of the fence, Foley glanced up at Sarah, but because he hadn't spoken to her since Christian was killed, he didn't say anything.

After two more attempts at getting a saddle on the stallion, Will had success, but immediately he climbed onto the horses back it started twisting and turning. Hanging on with one hand, his other arm flailed wildly in the air as he tried to keep his balance. As the horse kicked its way around the corral, Will was suddenly thrown off to land heavily on the ground. Now free of its rider, the horse smashed itself against the fence in a frenzy, causing the fence to shudder violently.

Shaking along with the fence, and unable to hang on, Sarah's hand slipped off the top of Lizzy's. Feeling herself falling, Lizzy opened her mouth to scream, but hit the ground before she could let out a sound. Unable to save her from falling and fearing the worst, Sarah did scream. Seeing Lizzy fall and land heavily, Foley clambered through the fence, and racing to her, managed to scoop her up just as the horse crashed into the fence beside him. Striking out wildly while snorting, the huge beast continued to kick the fence. Unable to stop herself falling, Sarah toppled off the top rail. Quickly turning his back to protect himself and shield Lizzy from danger, Foley watched Sarah land on her hands and knees on the ground next to him.

Hearing the commotion, and looking to where Sarah and Lizzy had been sitting, and seeing both gone, Joe opened the gate, and with Fergus and Garrett, raced to where Foley was holding Lizzy.

Not understanding what happened, Lizzy opened her mouth wide and bellowed. When Sarah picked herself up, Foley tried handing Lizzy to her, but Lizzy had been badly shaken and clung to him. Will and one of Major Hardy's cowhands managed to hold the stallion back while more men rushed through the gate to where everyone had gathered.

"That was a stupid thing to do Misses Morgan, letting Lizzy sit on top of the fence like that! she could have been killed! I didn't think you were that goddamn stupid!" Foley voiced fiercely, and getting Lizzy to let go, thrust her toward Sarah, then, after pushing his way through the throng of men and storming through the gate, he hurried away. Because Sarah was holding a screaming Lizzy whose face was smeared with dirt and tears and surrounded by a wall of men, she couldn't see him go.

When Foley went to the corrals, he hadn't planned on being that close to Sarah. After picking Lizzy up, he was relieved when she bellowed, because it clearly meant she hadn't been hurt, just had a bad scare, that was all. Sarah's precious little girl could have been seriously hurt and Sarah knew it, but it was the way Sarah looked at him when they were standing close to each other that made his feelings for her resurface. By the time he passed Lizzy over and their hands touched, his heart was racing, and able to see the sadness in Sarah's eyes when they were searching his face for some sort of recognition, he left the corral as quickly as he could, and still shaken by what happened, made his way back to the Sheriff's Office, where once inside, he paced the floor trying to understand the feelings that came rushing up from the very depth of his being.

Maria was due to have their baby in the spring, and here he was feeling the same way he had always felt about Sarah. He knew it was wrong to feel the way he did, but he couldn't help it. When Joe came in to thank him for getting to Lizzy as quickly as he did and for stopping the horse from trampling her, he forced himself to stop thinking about his situation with Sarah. The two men shook hands, then Joe congratulated him on his and Maria's impending birth and they talked about children. Foley was happy to talk about becoming a father, and was grateful to Joe for not berating him for calling Sarah stupid.

After taking Lizzy home and putting her to bed, Sarah sat on the side of the bed and thought about what happened at the corral. 'What was that look Foley gave me when he held Lizzy?' she asked herself, trying to understand it. Unable to get over the fact Maria was pregnant with another man's child, and hating that she had to keep Maria's deceit to herself, she studied Foley, and while feeling grateful for him being there to stop the horse trampling Lizzy, she wondered whether she should have said something to him about Maria, but once he called her stupid, and she hadn't the time to refute him about it before he stormed off, she made up her mind not to say anything.

The next day, Sarah decided it was time to hold her first dinner party of the season. Her usual group of friends such as Doc and his wife Gerda, Martha and Dave Henderson and their son Billy were invited. Ham and Patrice Hammond along with their daughters Sissy and Lilly welcomed the invitation to attend. Sarah knew Sissy was keen on Will, and she was sure Will was keen on Sissy. When the trappers were in town, she witnessed the secretive looks passing between the two, so to encourage their fondness for each other, she planned to sit them together. Sarah didn't invite Foley, nor Brady. Since knowing about Maria, and Christian's death, she avoided having them come to the lodge, and she stayed away from their farm, and so, with the four trappers being her special guests, she got busy making all the arrangements.

Taking Lizzy's hand, she walked across to Henry's Emporium to order supplies without Thomas for the first time since losing Christian. While Sarah and Henry sorted out the list of things Sarah needed for her party, Henry handed Lizzy a candy to keep her occupied. Lizzy was sitting on the counter with her legs dangling over the edge sucking on the candy when Foley entered and stood blocking the doorway. Wriggling his fingers in a wave and winking at Lizzy got Lizzy giggling. Looking around to see who she was giggling at and seeing it was Foley, Sarah abruptly ended her order.

"That will do Henry, I think I have all I need, will you deliver everything please?" After picking up her basket that held a few small items, she lifted Lizzy off the counter.

"I will have everything to you this afternoon Misses Morgan," Henry said as he watched Sarah try to get past Foley without acknowledging him. But Foley didn't budge.

"Misses Morgan," he greeted, tipping his hat.

After a moment of staring at each other in silence, he stepped aside, and with Lizzy in tow, Sarah rushed out the door. Once outside, she picked Lizzy up, and struggling with her basket, hurried across the street and back to the lodge. Standing near the window where he could see the street, Foley watched her go.

"Can I help you with something sheriff?" Henry asked from behind him.

When Foley saw Sarah and Lizzy enter Henry's store, he came to confront her about the look she had given Maria at Christian's burial. He also wanted to ask her about the look she gave him at the corrals after Lizzy fell off the fence. Watching Sarah getting supplies, it became obvious she was organizing one of her famous dinners, so while wondering where his invitation was, he decided now was not the time to confront her, and instead kept watching as she crossed to the other side of the street and disappeared around the bend further along.

"No thanks Henry, I've changed my mind, I don't need anything," he answered before pulling the door open and walking out.

Sarah's dinner party was going along nicely. With everyone talking at once and laughing, the mood in the lodge was cheerful. Seated between Fergus and Garrett, Lizzy was amused by the two men helping her with her meal. Sissy and Will, seated beside each other for convenience, remained engrossed with each other most of the night. When talk turned to the new Stagecoach Service and combined Telegraph/U S Mail Office, Sarah informed Joe she let the men that commenced the services stay at the lodge and how successful it had been. Joe raised his eyebrows at her for letting strangers stay in her house. But when talk turned to Foley being sheriff, and Thomas brought up the fact Foley was going to be a father, Sarah went quiet. She didn't want to get into a discussion about Maria in case she said something to let everyone know Maria's secret. Sarah wished right then she didn't know anything about it. Joe said he heard and had congratulated Foley already, then noticing Sarah sitting quietly while staring down at her plate, and thinking she was missing Christian, he covered her hand with his, but didn't ask her of her thoughts.

It was Garrett who brought her out of her reverie. "Will you go back to the mountain now you are on your own Sarah?" he asked. Everyone went quiet as they turned their attention to Sarah waiting for her answer. Thomas stopped eating and looked expectantly at her. "No Garrett, we will be staying in town, Thomas has a test he needs to pass."

When Sarah mentioned the test, Thomas decided there was no better time than now to give his Ma his news. When he pushed his chair back and rose to his feet, Sarah's eyes darted from Garrett to him. Billy knew what it was Thomas was about to tell everyone, and sitting opposite, exchanged looks with him. With everyone's eyes focused on him, Thomas looked down the length of the table to where Sarah sat and cleared his throat.

"Ma," he said taking a deep breath. "I finished the test."

From outward appearances Sarah didn't waver, but while watching Thomas intently, inside, her heart was pounding. Everyone remained quiet as they listened to Thomas explain himself.

"And Ma…" Thomas swallowed. "I passed!"

Understanding what it meant for Thomas to pass the test, the four trappers stood up as one and rushing around the table, crowded around to congratulate him with pats on the back and handshakes. Sarah however, remained in her seat unable to move. This was what she had been dreading. While shaking each man's hand vigorously, Thomas studied her and could see her dismay.

With everyone showering Thomas with happiness, Billy wasn't going to let his moment of glory pass without notice, so rising from where he was sitting between his folks, he cleared his throat to get everyone's attention. When he stood, Martha looked as worried as Sarah. If Thomas passed the test, then it was more than likely her precious son passed too, and that would mean he would be going far away from her.

"I have something I would like to say," Billy said, interrupting Thomas's celebration. Everyone stopped what they were doing and looked at Billy.

"I passed too!" he beamed. *"I'm going to college!"* he announced loudly with a broad grin. Jumping to his feet, Dave hugged Billy, and told him he was proud of him. While the men slapped him on the back and shook his hand, everyone except Martha and Sarah, laughed and cheered. Joe and Thomas's smiles faded however when they saw Sarah get to her feet. Instead of congratulating Thomas, and trying not to show her dismay at his news, Sarah hurried from the room. *"Ma!"* Thomas called following her out. When Sarah turned to face him, her eyes brimmed with tears. Thomas saw her tears as he approached her. "Ma," he repeated softly. Coming into the living room behind Thomas and Sarah, Joe watched Sarah embrace her son.

"Thomas, I don't want you to go," she sobbed. "Joe! I can't bear to lose him too!" she cried seeing Joe waiting by the door. Thomas assured her his going away would in no way mean he would never see her again. "It will be fine Ma, you'll see, and I will write you lots of letters."

"You aren't losing him Sarah, he is your son, he will always return to you," Joe said from across the room. When Thomas was a baby, Joe warned her one day he would leave her to follow his own path. Sarah had hoped that time would never come, but here it was, the time had come to let him go. When Joe gave her a nod, she held Thomas at arms-length.

"I love you Thomas, we have been through so much together, and now here you are, all grown up, and going your own way." She pushed her hand through his curly hair and while straightening his cravat, smiled sadly at him. "I expect lots and lots of letters."

"I will write you often Ma," Thomas answered hugging her. Stepping up to Sarah and Thomas, Joe drew them into his arms and held them for a moment. "We better get back in there and celebrate with Billy, I hear he's going with you!" Keeping his arms around Sarah and Thomas, he led them back to Sarah's dinner guests.

Christmas was only a day away. With Sarah's dinner party relegated to everyone's memory, Joe sent Samuels to the lodge to ask Sarah to bring Thomas and Lizzy to the Ferguson House to spend Christmas Eve with them. Sarah dressed Lizzy warmly. Thomas had his coat on and was waiting for Sarah and Lizzy to come downstairs. When Sarah came down wearing a white off the shoulder peasant blouse tucked into a hip hugging long grey skirt with a pink sash tied around her waist and her gold locket about her neck, Thomas stared. Sarah looked as radiant as she did, the day she married Christian. A pink ribbon matching her sash, and tied in a bow around her head, kept her freshly washed and brushed long hair away from her face. As Thomas helped her into her fur coat, he complimented her on how she looked. Sarah thanked him and smiling, picked up the basket that held their gifts for the trappers.

Before stepping off the steps into deep snow, Thomas picked Lizzy up and carried her while Sarah bunched her coat and skirt up to keep them from getting wet, they then hurried to the Ferguson House. Hearing their knock, Samuels opened the door and let Lizzy through first. When Joe picked her up and stood her on a chair to help her out of her coat to reveal a little blue dress with lots of petticoats that made it stand out, all the men smiled. White stockings covered her legs and brown boots adorned her tiny feet. Her long curly hair tied at the back with a blue ribbon was brushed loose like Sarah's. Lizzy's eyes lit up when Joe carried her to the fireplace where she could see the Christmas tree in the corner with gifts stacked under it.

Following Lizzy in, Sarah handed her basket to Samuels who sat it aside for later. After Garrett helped her out of her coat, she brushed her hands over her skirt to straighten it, then drawing her into the room, the men fell silent as they moved aside to let her stand in front of the fire. Her feminine figure was on show and all thought Sarah an attractive woman. Garrett himself felt his heart skip a beat when seeing how pretty she looked dressed in a simple blouse and skirt.

Feeling a wanting rising in him, Logan especially thought Sarah looked desirable, and struggled to keep his lust for her hidden. Looking around the room at the men eyeing Sarah, and aware of Logan's past where Sarah was concerned, Garrett moved to stand beside him.

Last through the door was Thomas, wearing dark trousers under his coat and a tweed jacket he was going to take with him to Philadelphia. The men gathered merrily around him and while wishing him a Merry Christmas, shook his hand.

Dinner turned out to be a rowdy affair. Joe sat at the head of the table with Sarah and Fergus either side of him. While everyone talked, dishes of hot food were passed around the table. Lizzy was being doted on as usual. Thomas was asked about college. Having warned the men not to mention Christian's death before Sarah arrived, the men kept their talk away from him.

With dinner over, the men made all three guests sit on a blanket in front of the fire where they presented each with a gift. Giving Lizzy her gift first, she opened the box eagerly to find dainty china tea cups and saucers, a china jug and sugar bowl as well as a little teapot with a lid sitting neatly in the box. Lizzy was thrilled, and the men laughed when she handed Joe a little cup and poured him a pretend cup of tea. Thomas was given a new valise with the initial's TM engraved on the gold clasp to carry his clothes to college in. Thomas thanked everyone, saying the valise would be very useful and that he was pleased with his gift. Sadly, the valise reminded Sarah Thomas would soon be leaving her, but not wanting to spoil the men's evening, she swallowed the lump in her throat and opened her gift.

Sitting in a floral embossed box was enough paper for Sarah to write her letters to Thomas while he was away. The edge of the paper was bordered with pretty flowers, the envelopes too had flowers in one corner, and there was a small bottle of ink and a quill for writing. The writing set was beautiful, but Sarah couldn't help herself, while studying it, she burst into tears, and straight away apologized to the men for crying, saying simply, she didn't know why she cried a lot lately. The men were silent. They understood perfectly why she would cry, she had good reason. When Sarah dried her eyes, Thomas and Lizzy helped her hand out the men's gifts. Each man got a box of cigars and new socks, which they were all pleased to receive.

Christmas Eve at the Ferguson House ended with the presentation of the gifts. The very next day the men had horses to break, and cattle needed branding out at Major Hardy's ranch.

Major Hardy had stock he wanted to get to Moreton for sale. Neither Christmas nor snow was going to keep the men indoors this year. Bidding goodnight to their guests, the men said they had enjoyed Christmas, even if it was a day early, and silently hoped it made Sarah feel a little less unhappy.

Will and Garrett, nominated to accompany Sarah and Thomas back to the lodge eagerly accepted their task. While Joe and some of the men stood on the porch watching them trudge through the snow, Will carried Lizzy, and Thomas carried his valise with Sarah and Lizzy's gifts stored safely inside. Halfway up the street Sarah suddenly bent down, and scooping up a handful of snow, tossed it at Will who copped the freezing ball on the back of his head. When he turned to see who threw the snowball, Sarah giggled and bent down to make another. Hastily putting Lizzy down, Will scooped up a handful of loose snow, and before Sarah could throw her next ball at him, he tossed his at her. When it hit her in the face causing her to gasp, they stared wide eyed at each other for a moment, then both burst out laughing. Seeing what was happening, Thomas put down his valise and joined in. After scooping snow into his hand and pressing it into a ball, he tossed it hard at Garrett, who in turn tossed one back with equal gusto.

When she saw snow flying between her Ma and Will, Lizzy giggled, then scooping up some herself, she ran toward Sarah and threw it. Sarah tried to get out of her way, but failed and copped Lizzy's snow all over her. With everyone laughing hysterically, snowballs began to fly in all directions. Seeing the fun everyone was having, Joe and the other men came off the porch and joined in.

Snow flew thick and fast back and forth across the street covering everyone. Lizzy was laughing so hard she fell over. Garrett scooped her up, and making out he was going to throw her like a snowball, ran toward Sarah making Lizzy squeal with delight. It was late in the evening when Deputy Smith came around the corner to see what all the commotion was about only to be met by a barrage of snow thrown his way. Everyone laughed at seeing him covered in snow. Laughing too at seeing their harmless fun, Smith waved his hands at the noisy crowd then left them to continue with their snow fight.

Having worn themselves out, after hugging each other, everyone bid each other goodnight. Handing Lizzy to Sarah at the door,

Garrett kissed Sarah softly on her cheek then turning, made his way down the steps. Sarah watched him return to the Ferguson House before carrying Lizzy inside where she put her to bed. It was the first time since losing Christian Sarah didn't cry herself to sleep, but she couldn't help feeling she was losing her son. He was going all the way across the country to a place she imagined she would never see.

Over the next few weeks Joe talked at length with Sarah, convincing her she had to let Thomas be his own man, besides, Joe said, she still had friends in town as well as the trappers looking out for her each winter. Thomas was pleased his Ma finally put the idea of him going away aside. It let them enjoy the rest of winter with the trappers. But winter passed by all too quickly for Sarah.

Chapter Nine

Nineteen trappers loaded their packhorses with enough supplies to get them through another year on the mountain. Wishing Thomas all the best at college, Joe, Garrett, Will and Fergus shook his hand and said goodbye. They said goodbye to Sarah and hugged her tight. Each man held Lizzy up high while saying goodbye to her. A giggling Lizzy gave each of them a hug.

Saddened to see the men leaving, Sarah, along with her children, stood at the end of the bridge and watched them ride out. When Christian was with her, she let the trappers go without so much as a worry, now she wished she were going back to the mountain with them. The thought of Thomas leaving soon too was back in her mind. She didn't want the men to leave her here, and hated the very thought of Thomas going so far away. Lizzy waved to the men as they disappeared along the trail.

It was several days after the trappers left that Sarah took Thomas to Henry's Emporium and bought him new clothes to take to Philadelphia. Not wanting her son to look out of place, she looked through Henry's catalogues and saw what men were wearing in the city. Along with his tweed jacket and two pair of trousers, Thomas packed shirts, long johns, socks and bow ties in his new valise. Billy Henderson packed the same. Martha and Dave spent almost all of their life savings giving Billy the best that they could. They weren't going to let their son go off to college in drab clothing.

While the stagecoach sat waiting outside Henry's for its passengers, Sarah and Thomas stood in his room with his bag packed. A second bag carried his journals that held stories he had written while growing up on the mountain. Sarah couldn't understand why he would want to take those with him.

"Leave them Thomas, they may get lost," she urged. "You won't need them in the city."

After packing the last journal, Thomas closed the bag. "I may want to read them Ma, to remind me of home."

Sarah gave thought to what he said. Maybe his journals would make him homesick and he would come back to her sooner rather than later. Trying to appear happy, she held a money pouch toward him.

"What is this Ma?"

Before answering, Sarah quickly put the pouch in Thomas's inside coat pocket and patted it down. "It's money Thomas, you will need money along the way and when you get there, keep it safe." When she handed him another smaller pouch, Thomas took it.

"And this?" he asked.

Sarah smiled. "I want you to give it to Billy, I know Martha and Dave don't have much left after buying Billy his clothes, don't say anything to him about charity, just tell him it is a going away gift." Thomas hugged Sarah and thanked her.

Walking together to Henry's store, Thomas carried his two valises while Lizzy walked beside Sarah holding her hand. When they rounded the corner into the main street, a large crowd of well-wishers were gathered at the stagecoach waiting to see him and Billy off. Thomas could see Billy there already and was both nervous and excited. Thanks to Peter Donovan for commencing the stagecoach service, this would be Thomas's first ever coach ride, and it was going to take him all the way to Moreton, where he would catch another coach that would take him to another town where he would catch his first ever train and then another and another, until he got all the way to Philadelphia.

After Thomas and Billy greeted each other with hugs and excited laughter, the coach driver took their bags and loaded them on top of the coach, then saying he had a long day ahead of him, called for his passengers to get aboard. Sarah and Thomas kissed each other goodbye and held each other for the longest time.

"See you Lizzy," Thomas said, picking her up and giving her a kiss on her cheek. Lizzy put her arms around Thomas's neck and with her bottom lip curled in a pout, hugged him.

"Bye Thomas," she whimpered as he passed her to Sarah. "I don't want Thomas to go mommy," she said sadly, putting her head on Sarah's shoulder. Sarah couldn't soothe her, because she didn't want Thomas to go either.

After watching the crowd gathered around the coach from outside the Sheriff's Office, Foley stepped into the street, and crossing it, pushed his way through the crowd until he came to Thomas and Sarah. Trying to ignore Sarah, he extended his hand to Thomas.

"Good luck Thomas," he said with feeling.

"Thanks Foley," Thomas smiled, taking his hand. They held their grip for a moment, then without warning, Thomas reached out and put his arm around Foley's shoulders, surprising him.

"Thanks again Foley, and all the best to you and your new family," he said with a grin. Foley smiled and thanked him for his well wishes, then letting Thomas go, he shook hands with Billy and wished him luck before stepping back to get out of everyone's way. Bumping into Sarah accidently caused them to look at each other. With a look on his face that gave nothing away, and without any word of apology for almost stepping on her, Foley moved quickly through the crowd and made his way back to the Sheriff's Office where he stood waiting for the coach to move off. As the coach drew away, Thomas and Billy stuck their heads out the windows and smiling, waved goodbye to everyone. Sarah and Lizzy waved as the coach rounded the bend and disappeared past the Trading Post in a cloud of dust.

Outside the Sheriff's Office, Foley watched the fanfare as everyone waved the coach out of town. Seeing Sarah again in tears as she hurried back to the lodge, he figured she would cry for weeks for her son as she had for Christian. Left with only Lizzy for company, she would undoubtedly feel lonely, so as a friendly gesture, while thinking she could give Maria advice on child rearing, he decided he would invite her to his farm, after Maria had their baby.

Time in Cedar Creek passed by quickly for some folk, not so quickly for others. After the trappers left, Cedar Creek reverted back to its lawless ways before Christian became sheriff and introduced his gun law. Foley and his deputies struggled to maintain law and order when farmers and ranchers accused each other of stealing horses and cattle and fought each other over land and water. Cowhands too caused their fair share of trouble. Fights in the saloon over saloon girls and shooting their guns off in town became a regular pastime. Foley was seriously thinking of reintroducing Christian's law. It worked before, and he couldn't see how it wouldn't work again.

Even with all the trouble going on around them, people went about their business as usual. School continued for Lizzy, and Sarah kept to herself as much as possible. She missed Thomas terribly and still had a burden she was carrying. She didn't want to run into Foley anywhere.

Having insisted Maria stop travelling the county doing housework for others when she was eight months into her pregnancy, Foley returned to the farm each night to be with her while Deputy's Smith and Taylor were left to take care of things in town. Although Maria didn't want to, she gave in to Foley's demand, after all, she wanted him to believe the baby was his. After telling him she was pregnant the evening Christian had been buried, she could see his life had taken on new meaning, and she thought perhaps he was in love with her and not Sarah Morgan after all, so she thought it only natural for him to worry about her, and of course he wouldn't risk losing his baby, not now she was close to full term.

Foley was unaware that early on in Maria's pregnancy, Doc discovered her irregular heartbeat. He also had difficulty listening to her bulging stomach through his horn like listening device that made it easy for a baby's heart to be heard beating in its mother's belly. Eventually thinking he heard the echo of a beat, he was satisfied everything was as it should be, but told her not to over exert herself. Doc was pleased when she told him Foley made her give up doing housework for other families so she could concentrate on having her own.

With less than a month to go before the birth, Maria went to town for her scheduled visit with Doc, and once again Doc felt dismayed when her heart sounded erratic and her face appeared flushed. Maria breathed deeply, saying she got short of breath without having to do very much, and this worried Doc. He couldn't locate the baby's heartbeat at all when he listened to her bulging stomach. Although aware of her own ill health, when Maria asked him if everything was alright and he answered everything appeared fine, but perhaps she should come back in a few days, Maria left Doc's practice satisfied all was well and went straight to the Rankin farm to visit Bert. Having convinced Rankin the baby was his, he was ecstatic in his belief and couldn't wait for the impending birth. Bert and Maria went to his barn where they spent a long time.

Foley couldn't help feeling excited at the prospect of becoming a first-time father. His baby was due any day, and he wanted to be there when Maria gave birth, so after making arrangements with his deputies to take over most of his duties, when he rode into the barn and climbed out of the saddle, it was dark. Hearing the door to the farmhouse slamming shut, he stepped into the opening to see Brady come rushing out of the house.

"It's Maria! she's having the baby!" Brady called urgently as he raced toward the barn. Before Foley could think of unsaddling his horse, Brady made a grab for the reins, and putting his foot in the stirrup, quickly lifted himself into the saddle. *"You stay with her Foley! I'll go get Doc!"* he yelled spurring the horse out of the barn.

After watching Brady disappear along the road heading to town as fast as the horse could carry him, with his heart beating wildly with excitement at the prospect of his baby about to be born, Foley ran into the house just as Maria screamed in pain. Rushing to their bedroom, he saw blood saturating the bedclothes and Maria writhing on the bed in agony.

"Jesus Christ Maria!" he exclaimed, taking her hand and holding it tight.

"Foley... baby not..." Maria tried to speak, but her face contorted in pain as she struggled for breath.

"Shush Maria, don't talk, Brady's gone for Doc, he'll be here soon." Sitting on the edge of the bed but at a loss as to know what he could do to help her, Foley rested his hand against her forehead and decided the only thing he could do was comfort her.

95

Time seemed to pass by ever so slowly before Doc and Gerda came running in. Hurrying to the room with his bag in hand, Doc dumped the bag on the bed and looked at the mess covering Maria. Lifting the saturated bedclothes to see how far along she was, it was obvious Maria and her baby were in trouble. Dropping the sheet, he turned to Gerda. "Get me lots of hot water, I have to clean some of this mess away, Foley, go... *now!*" he yelled. Becoming angry at being told to leave, Foley wanted to stay so Maria knew he was by her side.

"I'm not leaving Doc, this is my wife and baby, you do something to help them!" he begged.

"It's not your... it's not..." Maria said squeezing Foley's hand, but there was no strength in it. Struggling to tell him what she had been keeping from him, her eyes dimmed as she took a breath.

"Not... baby..." she whispered, letting his hand go.

Shoving Foley aside so he could listen to Maria's heart, Doc could hear clearly a rapidly beating sound pounding against the inside of her chest. While thinking about what he should do to help her, Maria suddenly screamed in pain, and pushed with what little strength she had left in her.

"Push Maria! push!" Doc urged.

Agonizing minutes passed with no sign the baby would come naturally. Lying limp against the pillows, staring up at Foley, Maria knew what was about to happen. Sarah Morgan begged her to tell him he wasn't the father, but she had refused. Every Sunday she attended church faithfully, and if she wanted to be forgiven for her sins when she got to the other side, she had to make her peace before it was too late.

"You ask Doc... he knows," she gasped. "This baby... not... your baby." Unable to tell who the father was, Maria thought perhaps it was Bert Rankin's, after all, she spent more time with him than any other man she had been acquainted with. What she did know for sure was, because Foley hadn't been sleeping with her when she fell pregnant, it wasn't his.

Watching Maria's face turn as white as the sheets she lay on and her eyes grow unseeing as she stared up at him, Foley moved back to the bed and held her hand against his cheek until he felt it go limp. As Maria succumbed to her ordeal, Doc picked up his scalpel, and ignoring the bloody mess he created, took the baby from Maria.

Shocked at seeing what Doc had done, and equally shocked at what Maria said to him before she died, Foley stood up, and not wanting to remain witness to the terrible scene before him, nor wanting to believe what she told him, thinking surely she must have been delirious, he turned and rushed from the room. The entire house reeked of death, and so to escape it, he pushed past Brady and Gerda standing in the hall, then rushing through the kitchen, came to a stop on the back porch where he filled his lungs with cold night air.

There was nothing more Doc could do. After washing his hands, he left Gerda in the room to clean up and prepare Maria for Phelps the undertaker. When Doc went to the porch, Foley was staring into the dark.

"I'm sorry Foley," Doc said quietly from behind him. "Maria had a bad heart, there was nothing I could have done to save her."

Foley didn't look at Doc. "And the baby?" he asked. Doc felt sorry for the baby, but thought it must have succumbed before Maria was due to give birth. "The baby was already gone Foley… I'm terribly sorry," he repeated.

Standing side by side looking over the backyard, Foley asked Doc if what Maria said about him not being the father was true. Keeping private what his patient discussed with him no longer mattered, Foley had a right to know of Maria's deceit. Taking a deep breath, Doc told him what Maria's first visit revealed, and what she said as far as Foley was concerned. After telling him he wasn't able to divulge what he knew about Maria before because of his oath, Doc apologized for the way he handled the birth.

While Doc related what he knew, Foley kept his face turned away. Just once in his life he had been happy, and because he wanted to be a good husband to Maria and an even better father, he buried the love he had for another woman deep within him, but now he felt devastated to learn the child he thought was his was not his at all. Knowing Maria deceived him was too much for him to bear.

Keeping his face turned away, his eyes filled with tears as he went back over his and Maria's marriage.

He thought how she had wanted to continue doing housework for what he believed were less fortunate families, and how she spent long hours not coming home until well after dark, and how she pushed him away when he wanted to make love to her. He should have known then something was going on. He couldn't believe how gullible he was. Thinking Maria must not have loved him at all when they married, he thought how ironic it was, because he didn't love her either. But he had hoped with time, they may have grown to at least like each other, instead as the years progressed, they grew further apart.

Foley thought about something else too. He thought about the look Sarah had given Maria at Christian's burial, and put his question to Doc.

"Who else knows about Maria Doc?"

Not liking what he was asking, Doc remained silent for some time. When he didn't answer, Foley turned to confront him with what he believed.

"Misses Morgan! Sarah! she knows! doesn't she?" A look of anger etched his face and gripping the front of Doc's shirt in both hands, he pulled him up to face him.

"She knows, doesn't she?" he snarled through clenched teeth as he studied Doc's face for an answer. Worried Foley might hit him over his miss-handling the birth, and with his oath broken, Doc felt he had no choice but to tell. "Yes, she knows," he answered regrettably.

Shoving Doc away forcibly, Foley brushed his fingers through his hair in dismay then stepped off the porch and walked into the dark. When he was a good distance away from the house he turned.

"*Who else besides you....!*" he yelled pointing at Doc. "*And fucking Sarah Morgan knows?... who else fucking knows I'm a fucking fool?*"

Taken aback by Foley's sudden outburst, Doc answered without much thought. "No-one Foley! just me and Sarah, and I suppose the men Maria was seeing."

"Men!... men!... you mean there were more than one?" Foley replied looking horrified at Doc. When Doc didn't come back with a reply, he raised his hands in the air in disgust, and cursing, stormed off past the barn.

Walking into the field Brady had ploughed, he kept walking until he got as far away from the farmhouse as he thought fit, then falling to his knees, pushed his hands into the rich black soil and squeezing them into fists, let his tears flow. He cried because he had been happy when thinking he was about to become a father. He wanted so much to have a family and now it had been taken away from him. He cried because an innocent baby had died. He cried because he felt such a fool to be taken in by Maria's lie, and he cried because he felt disappointed and angry that Sarah felt she needed to keep what she knew about Maria to herself.

Believing Maria to be a good woman, he hadn't cared that he didn't love her, as far as he was concerned that didn't matter, once she said she was having his child he began to feel something for her. Maybe it was pride, or maybe it was love, that was something he would never know. He didn't have an inkling Maria had been deceiving him, and he couldn't believe how stupidly naive he had been. After a time, he stopped crying but stayed in the field for several hours just sitting in the dirt, and thinking.

When Christian had been killed, he figured Sarah had known then about Maria. When she walked past Maria at Christian's burial, he had seen the way she looked at her. He hadn't understood what her look meant at the time, but now he knew. It had been a look of knowing, a look of disgust. Foley hated that Sarah knew what Maria had been doing and didn't tell him. Why had she thought to keep it to herself? Why had she let him believe he was going to be a father when she could have told him and he could have ended his sham of a marriage? He had been in love with Sarah a long time and only recently admitted he still had strong feelings for her. So why couldn't she have trusted him and told him? They were friends, weren't they?

What he did for Sarah that night at Major Hardy's shack was the catalyst that brought him and Sarah closer together. When Frank got whipped across his back, and he got the tip of the whip down his face, he suffered unbearable pain so he could get her back to the safety of the trappers, and with Frank dying on the mountain a year later, they became true friends. But their friendship didn't matter now. All he could feel for Sarah now was contempt for not finding it within herself to confide in him with the truth about Maria.

While remaining in the field, Foley decided he wasn't going to let Sarah get away with keeping what she knew to herself. He was going to make damn sure she knew exactly how he felt about her keeping it from him.

Doc and Gerda finished cleaning the room where Maria lay. They told Brady to stay out of there, and that they would send Phelps the undertaker out to collect Maria when they got back to town. Phelps arrived at midnight with two other men. Carrying a wooden box into the room, and after wrapping Maria and her baby in a winding-sheet, they lifted them into it. After Phelps put the lid on, Brady sat in the kitchen fighting back tears as he listened to the two men hammering nails around the edges to seal it. He hadn't heard Maria's last words to Foley, and now Foley's wife and baby were being taken away to be buried. Phelps stopped in the kitchen on his way out. "Tell Foley I'm right sorry about his wife and baby, the burial will be tomorrow at three." Brady uttered his thanks, and after Phelps and his two helpers took the box carrying Maria and her baby back to town, he walked into the field, and kneeling in the dirt beside Foley, put his hand on Foley's shoulder to comfort him. "Phelps has been, the burials tomorrow."

Foley had stopped crying, and although still deep in thought, got to his feet. "She knew Brady, Sarah, she knew... that bitch knew!" he kept repeating angrily.

Brady was confused. Why was Foley calling Sarah a bitch? They had been friends with Sarah a long time. It was she who bought them their farm, and what was it she knew that was so bad that it made Foley resort to calling her a bitch?

"What did she know Foley?" Brady asked following him back to the house. While sitting in their kitchen talking that night, Brady was shocked to learn what Maria said on her death bed, and dismayed that Sarah kept what she knew to herself. Foley begged him not to say anything to anyone. As far as others were concerned, Maria died trying to give birth to his son.

The burial was held right on three. Foley felt numb as he held his hat in his hands and looked into the hole in the ground. Although unable to feel anything for Maria, he held sympathy for the baby. It didn't matter whose child it was, Foley thought if the boy had lived, he would have raised him as his own. Brady stood alongside Foley supporting him while his fiancé Ellen, stood with her family where she could see both men. She wanted to stand with Brady but was satisfied to let him be the one to comfort Foley, so stayed where she was.

A lot of people came to show Foley their respect. Every cowhand from Major Hardy's ranch were given time to attend. Major Hardy was there too, although he stayed in his buckboard outside the cemetery while the rest of the mourners stood around the grave inside. Farmers and ranchers mingled with town folk.

Standing toward the rear of the crowd holding Lizzy, Sarah glanced around at each man, and wondered which farmers and which ranchers Maria had been with. Feeling horrible for thinking such a thing while attending Maria's burial, she scowled when she spied Bert Rankin standing behind the first row of men with his face wet with tears, and looking the most upset. 'He has a nerve coming here,' she thought, hating the fact she knew he had sex with Maria and for thinking the baby was probably his. Rankin's wife Ida was at home too ill to attend the burial. Maria had done a lot of housework for the Rankin's, and Sarah felt disgusted that Maria had betrayed Ida's trust when she took Bert as her lover.

Everyone lowered their heads while Preacher Barnes said a prayer. Then as the grave diggers lowered the coffin into the hole, Foley put on his hat, and turning abruptly, walked away. There was no need for him to stay to see the box that held his deceitful wife's body and that of an innocent baby covered with dirt. Walking quickly past Sarah and Lizzy without so much as acknowledging they were there, he hurried out of the cemetery.

Before the burial, Sarah heard of Maria and her baby's demise, and so hurried to Doc to ask him what happened. Still very much upset and grieving the loss of his patient in such awful circumstances,

Doc told Sarah, that just before Maria's passing, she confessed to Foley that he wasn't the baby's father. Upset and feeling sorry for Foley, Sarah rushed from Doc's practice, and returned to the lodge before Doc could inform her Foley was aware she knew Maria's secret. Not knowing he knew she knew Maria had deceived him, Sarah sadly watched him go, leaving her unaware of what was to follow.

On his way back from the cemetery, Foley stopped at the saloon and bought two bottles of whiskey, then rode back to the farm where he slowly drank himself into oblivion. When darkness came, he was able to forget about Maria and her deceiving him, and he could forget about Sarah knowing about Maria's deception. At the very last moment before blackness enveloped him, he despised both women for their deceit.

Because he loved Maria, after the burial, Bert Rankin made his way home to his farm feeling distraught. She was the best thing that ever happened to him. He despised his wife lying in bed all crippled up with god knows what and demanding he wait on her. 'Get me this! get me that! take me to the outhouse! wash me! feed me!' He hated every demand his wife gave him. He was tired of it. When Maria came along offering to do their housework, he didn't waste time before approaching her saying he was in love with her. Smitten by his attention, Maria didn't hesitate to go to the barn with him to consummate their love, and he didn't mind that she demanded payment for their lovemaking. Having her love was worth every dollar.

When Maria informed Rankin she was pregnant with his baby, he wanted to start a new life by leaving Cedar Creek and taking her with him. Maria was in love with him too she lied, so they made their plans. Maria planned to have their baby at Foley's farm first, then she would wait a little longer before telling him the baby was Rankin's. Foley being the respectable man everyone knew him to be, would not want anyone knowing he had been duped by her not having his child. He would merely say she walked out on him and had taken their child with her. Therefore, she would still be considered a respectable woman, and with Rankin planning on leaving his sick wife for someone else to take care of, she and Rankin could live the life they both wanted.

That was before Maria died giving birth to the child Rankin believed was his. He was devastated that he could not be by her side in her time of need. Now they would never be together. Now he would have to stay with his sick wife.

Pulling his buckboard into the barn, Rankin unhitched the horses and left the wagon standing in the middle of the floor. With his eyes red rimmed and swollen from crying, he walked across the yard to the farmhouse, and going to the kitchen, reached up and took his rifle down from where it hung and checked it was loaded, then walking through the house to the room where his wife was lying in bed, opened the bedroom door and stood just inside.

On hearing him enter, Ida turned her head to face him. "Where have you been? I've been calling for you to take me to the outhouse! now look what I've done!... I've wet the bed!" Her eyes, still wet from crying, went wide when she saw the rifle.

Raising the gun to his shoulder, and without hesitation, Rankin pulled the trigger and released both barrels. As he walked out of the room he thought, 'now she won't have to worry about going to the outhouse anymore.' Dropping the rifle on the kitchen table, he took a handgun from a drawer, and walking out the back, crossed the yard to the barn where he made his way to an empty stall. Sitting the handgun on the ground, he stripped off all his clothes, then picking up the gun, leant his back against the wall, and after sliding to the ground, he put the barrel of the gun in his mouth, and while crying some more for Maria, ended his life.

The day after Maria's burial, out at Brady and Foley's farm, Foley could be found lying in a drunken stupor on the couch in the living room. When he woke, he saw he was still fully clothed and his gun still in its holster on his hip. Forcing himself into a sitting position and holding his head in his hands, he looked through bleary eyes at the empty whiskey bottles on the floor next to the couch. After a moment of feeling sorry for himself, he staggered to his feet and went to the washroom where he splashed cold water over his face to wake himself up. Brady was in the kitchen cooking when he entered.

"Want some greasy eggs and ham?" Brady asked as he looked at his brothers haggard face. Foley plonked himself on a chair at the table.

"Just coffee," he replied, still feeling intoxicated.

After drinking his coffee, he went to the room he shared with Maria, and pulling the blood-stained mattress off the bed, dragged it outside and threw it in the yard, then carrying each part of the wooden framed bed outside, he smashed them to pieces and piled them on top of the mattress. Gathering Maria's clothing, he threw them on the pile, then after setting it all alight, he and Brady stood on the back porch and watched everything burn.

Ellen's father Otis, supplied the whole county with milk from his cows, making deliveries of fresh milk to the many farms and ranches dotted around Cedar Creek every couple of days. Along with Lara her sister, Ellen helped milk the cows. Rising at daylight every day, they headed to the barn, then did it all again in the afternoon. It was a hectic life for the two girls but Ellen was happy. She had fallen in love with Brady Andrews, the man from the farm next to theirs and now they were betrothed. But because they were waiting until Foley's wife had her baby, they hadn't set a date for their wedding. When Ellen heard what happened with Maria and her baby, she became worried about her and Brady having children. Ellen hadn't yet been with a man, she and Brady decided to wait until they married to consummate their love for each other. Hoping what happened to Maria wasn't a family trait inherent from the Andrews family, Ellen wanted to talk to Brady about her concerns, but not knowing Maria's secret she had to wait. Brady had to have time to help his brother get over his loss.

Otis's buckboard was loaded with tin cans full of fresh milk. Having already delivered to several ranches he was now heading to the farms. The first farm on his stop was the Rankin farm.

Pulling his buckboard up at the front of the farmhouse, he climbed down and walked to the back of the wagon. Knowing Ida was crippled with illness and couldn't get out of bed, and Bert, well, he would probably be in the barn working as he often was when he called in, Otis didn't expect anyone to greet him. Pulling a large can of milk to the back of the buckboard, Otis lifted it out, and carried it to the front door.

"Hello!... Misses Rankin!" he called, then waited for an answer.

When Ida didn't answer, he called out once more, and thinking she must be asleep, which she sometimes was when he made his delivery, he put the can down and tried the door. When the door opened easily, he picked up the can and went inside. Carrying the can through to the kitchen, and after noticing the rifle laying on the table and making nothing of it, he sat the can on the table and noticed the back door was open, which wasn't unusual for that time of day, it was warm outside and a slight breeze wafted up the hall airing the house.

Otis wasn't an inquisitive man by any means. Turning to leave, he was heading back along the hall when he noticed the bedroom door was ajar. He thought to take a peek in, if Ida was asleep, he would sneak out, if she was awake, he would say hello and tell her the milk was on the table, then he would leave her to rest.

Pushing the door open, he stumbled back in shock, and felt his legs go numb. Ida lay in a blood-soaked bed, her head a mangled mess, blood had sprayed up the walls and all over the bedhead. Stumbling out of the house, Otis ran to his buckboard as fast as his numb legs would carry him. Climbing onto the seat, he hit the horse hard with the reins causing it to become spooked by the sudden lashing. As the horse jumped forward and raced away, milk cans slopped about in the back of the wagon. Once they became unsteady, several toppled over leaving a trail of spilt milk on the road. Otis headed at a cracking pace toward town. By the time he pulled his buckboard to a stop outside the Sheriff's Office most of the cans were empty and he was in a state of panic. When Deputy Smith heard the ruckus from inside the office, he came out to see what the commotion was all about.

"Come quick!" Otis called. "It's Misses Rankin!... Ida!... she's dead!"

Being a man used to things out of the ordinary happening, Smith calmly asked Otis to slow down and tell him what happened. After Otis finished telling Smith what he came across, he was still as white as a sheet.

"Did you see Rankin anywhere?" Smith enquired.

Otis shook his head vigorously from side to side. "No! no I hightailed it out of there! if he killed his wife there's no telling what he was planning on doing next! I wasn't hanging about to find out!" Seeing Deputy Taylor coming from Henry's store, Smith called him over and told him what Otis told him. "You get Foley, bring him to the Rankin farm, I'll meet you both there!" he ordered Taylor. Racing to his horse, Taylor rode fast to the Andrews farm.

Foley and Brady were watching the last of the bedroom furnishings and Maria's clothing burn to ash when Taylor arrived. After telling Foley about Otis finding Ida, Foley forgot his hangover and rode off with Taylor.

At the junction of the roads leading to outlying farms, Foley and Taylor met up with Smith, and rode on to the Rankin farm together. When Foley got to the front door of the farmhouse, he could see the door standing ajar from when Otis had been there. Leaving Taylor waiting outside with his gun drawn, Foley drew his gun and cautiously made his way inside., Holding his gun at the ready, Smith followed him in. Both men were sickened when seeing what was left of Ida. Backing out of the room, they went to the kitchen where they saw the milk can Otis left sitting beside a rifle on the table. With his gun held in readiness in case Rankin was lurking about and had an idea to shoot them, Foley walked out the backdoor. Smith and Taylor followed him to the barn.

"Rankin!" Foley called while all three men waited at the entrance for Rankin to answer.

"Rankin! you in there?" Foley called again. When he didn't get an answer, he told Smith and Taylor to wait outside while he checked inside.

To get into the barn, Foley had to walk around the buckboard standing in the middle of the floor. Walking gingerly along with his gun held ready in case Rankin tried to jump him, he saw two horses in their stalls. Moving stealthily, he passed in front of several empty stalls and peered in as he went. Coming to the last stall at the end of the row, he stepped into the entrance, and aiming his gun inside, saw he didn't need it. While straightening up and holstering it, he felt the effects from his drinking the night before making his stomach rise, from at first seeing Ida's remains, and now this. Studying Rankin's body slumped against the wall, he took in a middle-aged balding man wearing not a stitch of clothing covering his bulging stomach that rested on top of his legs hiding his manhood. Seeing Rankin's brain spattered on the wall behind his head, he called Smith and Taylor to come and take a look at what he found.

Putting their heads together, the three men figured Rankin shot his wife first, then went to the barn and shot himself. They surmised Rankin had been under a lot of stress lately, what with his wife being crippled with illness like she was. They surmised too, poor Bert Rankin couldn't take it anymore and simply wanted to end his wife's suffering, and they ended with surmising, poor Bert could not live without his dear wife, so took his own life to be with her.

That night, Sarah wrote her very first letter to Thomas. She wasn't a good writer and struggled over some of her words, but in the end, she told him about Foley losing Maria and the baby. She didn't tell him the baby wasn't Foley's, that information she thought wasn't necessary now Maria and her baby were gone. She said she missed him terribly, and told him about Brady getting engaged, and that Lizzy had started two days at school. The very next day she carried her letter over to the US Mail Office and mailed it.

That week, Phelps the undertaker was kept busy with two more burials. Foley went back to working as sheriff but remained angry with Sarah, and wasn't about to let her forget that he knew she knew about Maria.

Chapter Ten

Ellen smiled at Sarah "I would really like you to come Sarah, it would mean so much to Brady and me to have you there." Ever since Ellen had been introduced to Sarah, she had come to like her. They had spoken on several occasions, and Ellen was hoping their speaking would lead to friendship, but Ellen had an ulterior motive for asking Sarah to come to her and Brady's wedding. Sarah looked at the hand-written invitation. "When is it?" she asked without reading it.

"Saturday, at three o'clock, at the church, then there will be a celebration at the hall, please say you will come, you can bring Lizzy, we would love to have her there too."

Two months had passed since Maria's burial, and during that time Ellen could see there was something going on between Foley and Sarah, but she couldn't figure out what. When Ellen quizzed Brady for information, he told her Foley used to propose to Sarah, and that he had done so every winter since Thomas was three years old, right up until she married their sheriff.

Armed with this information Ellen was convinced Foley must again be in love with Sarah but was simply too afraid to make his feelings for her known. Ellen figured enough time had passed since Maria's burial for Foley to stop being so angry with the whole town and for him to start a new romance, so she formulated a plan to get Foley and Sarah together. But Ellen didn't realize just how much she was interfering. Sarah and Foley were not getting along at all. The looks passing between them whenever they crossed paths were obvious each were keeping something from the other.

Sarah had not been anywhere since Christian died that called for her to dress up. Getting around in worn out shirts and skirts in the lodge and trousers when out riding made life easier.

"I would love to come Ellen, thank you for inviting me, three o'clock you say?"

"Yes, Oh Sarah, thank you, everyone will be there!" Feeling pleased her plan so far was working, Ellen hugged Sarah and left her standing on the boardwalk outside Henry's store.

The day of the wedding, Sarah put Lizzy in the bath with her and washed her hair, then, while Lizzy played with the bubbles, she washed her own. "Mommy?" Lizzy questioned smiling at Sarah while she tipped a pot of warm water over her head to wash the suds off.

"Yes Lizzy, what is it?" Sarah said blinking water out of her eyes so she could see her.

"You have big titties!" Lizzy announced seriously.

When Sarah's eyes went wide after hearing her remark, Lizzy giggled. Sarah giggled then too, and splashed water at Lizzy. Lizzy giggled some more and splashed water back at Sarah. When Sarah splashed again, Lizzy returned with another splash. They kept splashing so much, water splashed over the sides of the tub wetting the floor, turning their giggles into hysterical laughter as they kept splashing each other in a frenzy.

Standing up suddenly, Sarah lifted Lizzy out of the tub and quickly wrapped her in a towel, then while wrapping herself in one too, Lizzy watched her closely.

"You have a hairy bum too mommy!" she said wiping the edge of the towel over her face.

"Lizzy!" Sarah exclaimed laughing. "That is not my bum!" Then picking a giggling Lizzy up still wrapped in a towel, carried her upstairs to get ready for Brady and Ellen's wedding.

A cream off the shoulder top with a wide lace border draped delicately across Sarah's arms, was teamed with her best grey skirt. Around her waist, separating the two was a soft pink sash tied in a bow at her back. The petticoat under her skirt kept her skirt flared, making it easy to control when she walked. Her long hair was brushed until it shone, the sides of which were secured at the back of her head with a cream ribbon. To finish her look, Sarah fastened her gold heart shaped locket around her neck. She dressed Lizzy in her dark blue dress with white lace edged neckline and puffed sleeves. Petticoats made her dress swish when she walked, and she wore white stockings with her brown boots. Her long curly hair was brushed and tied back the same as Sarah's, only her ribbon was dark blue to match her dress.

Sarah hadn't stepped foot inside the small church since threatening those few worshippers that stole Thomas from her. She and Christian married on the riverbank, at the very spot where she used to camp. Later, when Christian asked her to attend church with him, she flatly refused by saying she would not step foot in a church where people thought they had a right to take her child away from her then pray to God for forgiveness, she thought them hypocrites, and she would not be one of them.

Hoping no-one would notice her, she stood at the door for a moment to catch her breath, then holding Lizzy's hand, stepped gingerly inside. But the church was packed with guests and her high heeled lace up boots echoed on the wooden floor making everyone turn to see who had entered. When they saw Sarah making her way along a pew, they put their heads together and began whispering as to why, after all these years, had she decided to attend a church wedding.

Standing at the alter waiting for Ellen, and hearing footsteps and people murmuring, Brady and Foley turned to see Sarah seating herself at the very back of the guests. Foley's heart skipped a beat, and with his lips pursed in frustration, he turned to Brady.

"What is she doing here?" he whispered sounding angry.

Leaning forward to look around Foley, Brady saw Sarah and Lizzy and smiled. "Ellen invited them," he replied. He didn't care that Foley had issues with Sarah, he was still friends with her and wanted Ellen and Sarah to get to know each other so they could become friends. Foley though was not happy. He couldn't forget the fact Sarah had known about Maria when he hadn't, and didn't want Sarah in close proximity to him either. With his heart threatening to burst, he looked around again. Her long hair fell in soft curls over her bare shoulders. Her lace edged blouse with its wide border accentuated her figure. Sarah looked beautiful and Foley couldn't help himself. He turned to look at her once more.

Lizzy wanted to stand at the end of the pew nearest the aisle so she could see everything that was going on, but Sarah made her sit beside her. The pews were full of town folk who kept turning and looking in Sarah's direction, causing her heart to race, which caused perspiration to break out on her forehead, and what else was unnerving? There was Foley giving her looks that were making her feel even more uncomfortable. The walls of the church seemed to be closing in. Beginning to feel dizzy, and struggling for breath, Sarah grabbed Lizzy's hand, and stepping into the aisle, pushed her ahead of her and out the door. Watching them leave, Foley turned to Brady.

"I'll be back in a moment," he said before making his way quickly down the aisle. Once outside, he found Sarah and Lizzy standing under shade trees nearby. Sarah saw him come out to stand on the steps and look in her direction.

"Why don't you go home Misses Morgan? You don't need to be here!" he said with scorn. His voice sounded harsh, but not about to let him order her about, Sarah replied defiantly. "We have been invited here Sheriff Andrews, and we will be staying!"

Before Foley could retaliate with another scathing remark, Ellen's carriage carrying her and her family arrived. Climbing down, and after helping Ellen out, Otis left his wife and youngest daughter Lara to climb out unaided. Foley glanced once more at Sarah then pursing his lips, disappeared back inside.

"Sarah! Lizzy! shouldn't you be inside?" Ellen said surprised to see them outside.

"It was stuffy inside, Ellen you look lovely," Sarah complimented truthfully. Ellen's dress made of cream taffeta fell from her waist in a full skirt. It's high neckline and long puffed sleeves gave nothing of her away. Her veil covering her face stretched behind her in a long train. Sarah guessed the bouquet of mixed flowers she carried were from Martha Henderson's garden.

"You look like a fairy princess," Lizzy announced sweetly.

"Why, thank you Sarah, and thank you Lizzy, now, let's not keep everyone waiting, especially not Brady," Ellen smiled coyly. Sneaking back to her seat, Sarah let Lizzy stand in the aisle so she could see the bride in her princess dress. As Ellen walked down the aisle on the arm of her father, Brady's eyes were for her only. Guests became invisible when the only person Foley could see sitting amidst them was Sarah.

As Sarah sat through the lengthy service her chest felt tight. This was where she punished Harold Finch, the main offender in Thomas's disappearance. Roy Connell got punished too, so did their wives. Sarah didn't spare any of their friends either. Glancing around at the guests, Sarah couldn't see Finch, or Connell, nor their wives, they hadn't been invited, and Sarah was pleased about that. Brady knew only too well how much she still despised them. When Preacher Barnes announced Brady and Ellen husband and wife, Sarah felt relieved and hurried Lizzy outside to wait for everyone to come out.

As the wedding party rode away in their carriage to get their picture taken, everyone else made their way to the Town Hall. It was a beautiful day, the sun was shining, warming everyone. While Patrice and Ham followed on behind at a leisurely pace with their two daughters, Sarah walked ahead with Martha and Dave Henderson. As they walked Sarah and Martha asked each other if they had any news from Thomas or Billy. Letters often took months to come all the way from Philadelphia, so neither had any news to offer other than both Thomas and Billy had settled in to life at college.

At the Town Hall, white cloths covered tables decorated with a mixture of foliage and flowers. Place settings sat arranged in front of chairs. When Sarah asked the Henderson's and the Hammond's if they didn't mind if she and Lizzy sit with them at their table, the two couples welcomed them.

When the wedding party arrived, guests milling about outside hurriedly made their way inside so they could welcome them with a fanfare of clapping. With Lara on his arm, Foley was the first to enter. Lara was a twelve-year old girl, appearing small in comparison to Foley's tall stature. Round black framed eyeglasses, and her face covered in freckles made her the complete opposite to Ellen's blonde-hair and fair skinned complexion. Lara's dark hair set in ringlets fell to her shoulders. Her pale blue dress with long puff sleeves hung limply from under her non-existent bust. Likening her to Millicent Crawley, but feeling sure Lara was a much nicer person than Millicent had ever been, Sarah quickly pushed that thought to the back of her mind, then moved her eyes from Lara to take in Foley.

Foley's dark jacket hanging almost to his knees, made him appear taller than he already was. A matching cravat tied securely around the neck of his high collared white shirt highlighted his strong jawline. Sarah liked how he always wore his beard trimmed close to his jaw and his dark hair with its smattering of grey sitting over his collar. She liked how loose strands at his brow hung almost in his eyes.

It hadn't taken long after Christian was buried for Foley to change Christian's law about wearing guns in town, three days in fact. Foley couldn't forget for one moment he was now sheriff and wore his gun to his brother's wedding, as did every male guest. Sarah couldn't forget he didn't back Christian against an outlaw barely out of short pants. Along with knowing about Maria, that was another reason she avoided Foley. But as Foley walked past where she was sitting, Sarah felt a sudden warmth surge through her that made her blush.

As soon as he stepped through the door, the sight of Sarah seated with the Henderson's and the Hammond's made Foley's heart race. Acknowledging other guests as he and Lara made their way to the bridal table helped him ignore her. While food was being laid out on tables along one side of the hall, a makeshift bar situated near the stage where a piano and fiddle sat waiting to be played already had men crowding around it. As women formed a line at the food table, Foley made his way to the bar. By the time Sarah crossed the room to line up with the women, then carried two plates back to where Lizzy was waiting, Foley had his third drink.

At the bridal table, when Foley stood up to make a speech, he was feeling a little intoxicated. While making jokes about Brady and welcoming Ellen to their family, he could feel Sarah's eyes on him and wished she wasn't there making him feel uncomfortable. As soon as the formalities were over, tables were quickly moved aside to make way for dancing. Brady took Ellen out on the dance floor for their first dance. When Foley partnered Lara, Sarah tried her best not to stare. With Martha and Patrice dancing with their husbands, Sarah was left sitting with Lizzy watching everyone twirling to the sound of the piano and fiddle.

"Mommy, I have to go," Lizzy said tapping Sarah on her arm and jiggling on her seat. Bending to hear what Lizzy was saying, Lizzy informed her again she needed to go, and so with Lizzy in tow, Sarah made her way out the front door and down the steps. On the dance floor, Foley saw them leaving, and excusing himself from Lara, passed her over to a boy more her own age, and headed out the door after Sarah.

Sarah raced Lizzy around the side of the hall, but Lizzy wasn't going to make it to the outhouse. Quickly squatting, Sarah lifted Lizzy's dress, and pulled down her stockings.

"Don't wet on them honey," she said helping Lizzy squat.

"Outhouse is right there Misses Morgan!" A somewhat slurred voice resounded behind Sarah. Standing up quickly, she turned and tried to keep Foley from seeing Lizzy behind her.

"Lizzy couldn't make it to the outhouse, she won't hurt anything by going here." Embarrassed at being caught out in the open, Sarah's face turned pink.

"Well! we had better hope you make it, hadn't we? Or we will have a real show on our hands!" Already having had too much to drink, Foley swayed as his slurred comment and snigger made Sarah blush even more, but she refrained from offering up a retort to his remark.

"I'm finished mommy," Lizzy said standing up. Turning her back on Foley while she straightened Lizzy, then taking her hand, Sarah kept her head down as they hurried past him. Relieved to see Martha and Dave seated at their table, Sarah lifted Lizzy up to sit on the seat beside her and sat next to them where she tried to push all thought of Foley out of her mind.

After staying outside for some time to gather himself, Foley pushed his way through the throng of dancers and made his way toward the bar, but halfway across the floor he changed his mind about having another drink.

When Sarah looked up from speaking with Martha, Foley was standing silently in front of her. An awkward moment passed where Sarah and Foley stared at each other before Foley held out his hand. "Dance with me, Misses Morgan," he requested with little feeling.

Glancing around to see who was watching, and seeing most couples were, and not wanting to cause a scene, Sarah placed her hand in his. As he helped her to her feet, and she moved onto the dance-floor with him, he no longer appeared to be intoxicated.

"Just so as you know Sheriff Andrews, I don't dance very well," she informed him.

"I don't dance at all Misses Morgan, so I guess we will dance like fool's together," he replied, and slipping his hand around her waist moved her to stand against him. When their bodies touched, Foley felt a sudden rush of wanting run through him. A tingle of excitement rushed through Sarah. Taking Sarah's right hand in his left, he held it up. As Fess played a slow melody on his fiddle, they began stepping from side to side, then back and forth.

Foley said he couldn't dance, but he wasn't doing too badly. Keeping his focus on Sarah, he took in the soft wisps of hair framing her face, and the curls falling about her slender neck and over her bare shoulders. His gaze fell on her full breasts, of which he could see a hint of at the top of her blouse. The gold locket around her neck brought a frown to his brow.

Sarah tried her best not to look at Foley. They had never been this close, not even out on the prairie where they met each winter when he proposed. They never had reason to kiss. Feeling herself becoming warm at his nearness, and wanting the moment to go on, she swayed from side to side in his embrace.

"You would have thought Christian would have taught you to dance Misses Morgan, he was a good dancer, he danced all night with Millicent Crawley that night, you remember? The night this hall was first opened," Foley said breaking their silence

When Sarah didn't speak, he kept his eyes on her and went on. "You tried swiping that locket you are wearing off Millicent, didn't go so well though did it?" Bringing her eyes up to meet Foley's, Sarah remembered every detail of that night. How could she not? He had been there watching what happened along with everyone else. This time when Sarah didn't answer he bent his head toward her and brought his mouth near to her ear.

"Have you ever asked yourself, did Christian fuck Millicent? After all, they knew each other long before he fucked..." Foley didn't get to finish his smear. Stunned by his contemptable question, Sarah quickly pulled herself out of his grasp and slapped him hard across his face.

When her hand connected with his cheek, Foley staggered sideways and bumped into other dancers. Martha and Dave, watching them dance were shocked at seeing Sarah slap Foley and wondered what caused her to do it. Dancers stopped dancing to take in the altercation. Men at the bar interrupted their drinks halfway to their mouths and wondered why Sarah slapped Foley too. Not waiting for him to regain his composure to have his slur out with him, Sarah rushed to where Lizzy was sitting, and taking her hand, pulled her off her seat and hurried toward the door. But Sarah was fleeing in haste and Lizzy couldn't keep up.

Hurrying outside, Lizzy felt her legs give way, causing her to fall and land on her knees at the bottom of the steps. Quickly scooping her up and carrying her, Sarah made her escape. By the time they passed the Trading Post and the Ferguson House, Lizzy and Sarah were crying.

Blindly crossing the road and hurrying up the street to the lodge, Sarah pushed the front door open and once inside, locked it behind her.

Standing at the entrance to the hall watching Sarah carry Lizzy away, Foley felt disgusted with himself. Even though he would never harm Sarah physically, he wanted to hurt her with his venomous remark, and it seemed to have worked. Believing he and Sarah were friends, he expected her to have said something to let him know what Maria had been doing, instead she let him believe Maria was having his baby. He couldn't deny his feelings for Sarah, he was still very much in love with her, and so going back to the drinks table, he got blind drunk, and at the end of the night, he was found passed out across the very chairs Sarah and Lizzy had been sitting on.

Brady and Ellen were to spend their first night of married life together at the farm. After enlisting two male guests to help him get Foley into their buckboard, they took him home with them. When the buckboard pulled up at the front gate, Foley was still passed out. Brady looked dismally at him asleep in the back.

"I ought to leave him there," he said to Ellen in disgust. But Ellen didn't want to be responsible if anything were to happen to Foley if he were left out where wild animals lurked, and offered to help Brady get him into the house. When Brady pulled Foley by his legs to the edge of the buckboard and lifted him out, Foley opened his eyes. Although unable to see where he was through his drunken haze, he threw one arm across Brady's shoulders.

"Sarah," he muttered drunkenly as Ellen lifted his other arm and put it over her shoulders. Brady and Ellen looked at each other, then together, half dragged half walked Foley to his room where they dropped him on his bed. After Brady removed his boots, Ellen covered him with a blanket. "Sarah," Foley whispered again before rolling onto his side.

"What happened tonight Brady? Why do you suppose Sarah slapped Foley?" Ellen asked when they were in their room.

"I don't know," Brady answered as he began undressing Ellen. Ellen was deep in thought, but her thoughts weren't on what was to come of their wedding night. Not happy her plan to get Sarah and Foley together hadn't gone the way she planned, she still wanted confirmation to what she thought all along.

"He is in love with Sarah, isn't he?" she asked as she helped Brady out of his clothes.

"Maybe, I told you he was in love with her before she met Christian," Brady answered.

"Yes, but was he in love with her while she was married to Christian?... and what about when he was married to Maria?... was he in love with Sarah the whole time?" Ellen queried as she studied Brady standing naked in front of her. Solidly built, Brady's arms and legs were muscled from clearing and ploughing fields. Ellen could see he was ready to make love to her, but she couldn't let what happened at the hall go. Like everyone, she had seen Sarah slap Foley hard for something he said to her.

"Maybe he still is," Brady offered, kneeling in front of Ellen and sliding her underwear to her feet. This was the first time he had seen Ellen naked, and gazing longingly over her body became fully aroused by the sight of her. This was their wedding night and all he wanted was to make love to her.

"Can we discuss this some other time?" he said, pushing Ellen gently onto the bed and straddling her, made her giggle.

As Brady and Ellen consummated their marriage, their bedhead banged loudly against the wall separating theirs and Foley's room, but Foley didn't hear a thing. He was in a deep, dark, bottomless pit of despair, and couldn't find his way out.

As Sarah carried Lizzy to her room where she undressed her and got her ready for bed, Lizzy was still crying from falling down the steps at the hall.

"I'm so sorry baby, I didn't mean to hurt you," Sarah cried. Lizzy's stockings were dirty where she fell, so after checking her knees for scrapes and finding they were fine, Sarah tucked her into bed, then lying beside her, wrapped her in her embrace and let Lizzy nestle against her.

"I love you mommy," Lizzy sobbed.

"I love you too sweety, very much," Sarah returned.

Sarah stayed with Lizzy until she fell asleep, then going to her own room, after opening the drapes covering the window facing the mountains, she moved to her bed where she got undressed. Dropping everything in a heap at her feet left her wearing nothing but her high heeled lace up boots. Stepping over the pile of crumpled clothes, she stood in front of her full-length mirror and took a long look at herself. Her body was still conditioned, her breasts full and firm. Running her hand over her flat stomach, she moved her eyes downward to look at her crotch. Turning sideways, she looked at her profile. Her buttocks were firm, her legs long and taut. Satisfied with the way she looked, she made her way to her bed, and sitting on the edge while removing her boots, her mind was on Foley and their dance at Brady and Ellen's wedding.

Except for taking her back to the trappers the night Frank was whipped, neither had ever been that close to the other. Thinking of him holding her in his arms while they danced, a feeling of warmth overtook her. After removing each boot, she threw the covers back and climbed into bed, but instead of covering herself, she lay against the pillows and imagined Foley making love to her. She had never thought of him in a lustful way before and her face became flushed when her thoughts sent a sudden surge of heat rushing through her as she pictured him joining with her. But then he said a nasty thing to her about Christian.

Forcing herself to stop thinking about Foley in a sensual way, she pulled the covers up, then leaning over and blowing out the lamp, she turned on her side, and lying in the dark, let her thoughts return to what Foley said while they were dancing. 'They had all been friends, so why would he say such a horrible thing about Christian? Christian had never slept with Millicent. He told me he had never slept with any woman in Cedar Creek before he met me, and I believed him. Why would Foley bring such a distasteful thing up?' Sarah's gut-wrenching sobs tore tears from her at the very thought Christian may have lied about sleeping with Millicent and at Foley's nastiness toward her when confronting her with it, at of all places, Brady and Ellen's wedding.

The clash at Brady and Ellen's wedding was the first such clash between Sarah and Foley, but it would not be the last. Over the next few months, they had many more, and one of those was to prove far worse than the others.

Chapter Eleven

As word about Sarah slapping him at Brady and Ellen's wedding gathered momentum, Foley avoided talking to anyone. No-one, not even Brady knew the reason she hit him.

Having been on his feet for days, his lack of sleep was making his anger toward Sarah smoulder. Remembering what he said to her disgusted him, and even though he knew he went too far, when he was called to intervene in a brawl at the saloon between two cowhands fighting over a saloon girl, instead of breaking up the fight, he joined in. After all three men threatened to kill each other, he smashed the two men's heads together before forcing them at gunpoint to the jailhouse where he locked each in separate cells to calm them down. Then Smith came down with a fever, and Taylor broke his gun arm slipping over while carrying a load of firewood to the fire, which meant, when his two deputies couldn't back him, he had to be on duty on his own for several weeks.

When the town at last quietened down, Foley seized the opportunity to ride out to his and Brady's farm for a break. The first thing he planned on doing when he got there was using his time to take a bath so he could change into fresh clothes, then, with Ellen being a good cook and her stews a pleasure to eat, he planned on sitting down to a hearty meal.

Arriving at the farm, he saw a horse tied to the rail outside the front gate and recognized straight away whose horse it was. He didn't want to see Sarah anywhere in town let alone at the farm, besides, he wouldn't be able to strip off and have his bath while she was there. Even if she couldn't see him in the washroom, she would be right outside where it would make him feel as if she could tell he would be naked. It didn't matter that he had seen her bathing naked out at the ponds, but hey! she had never seen him that way.

Pursing his lips in frustration, after taking his horse to the barn where he fed and watered it, he decided he would just have a quick wash instead. On the table in front of Sarah and Ellen who were sitting on the back porch having afternoon tea, were freshly baked cookies in the tin Martha Henderson gave Sarah when Thomas and Billy first became friends. Walking toward the house while rolling his sleeves up ready for his wash, he could feel Sarah's eyes on him, and taking a quick step onto the porch, he grabbed the door handle and pulled the screen door open.

"What are you doing here Misses Morgan?" he queried harshly without glancing at either woman. But instead of waiting for Sarah to answer, he slammed the door closed behind him and disappeared straight into the washroom.

It was a long time after their wedding before Brady and Ellen could entice Sarah back out to the farm. After bumping into her coming from Henry's store and telling her Ellen was expecting, Sarah congratulated them wholeheartedly, then when they said the two women had something in common, and added they would like Sarah to give Ellen her knowledge on what to expect at childbirth, they begged her to come for a visit, and Sarah accepted their invitation.

As Ellen and Sarah's friendship grew, Ellen couldn't understand why Foley was treating Sarah so unfairly. Obviously, what happened when Sarah slapped him for something he said, making Sarah flee from her and Brady's wedding was his fault. By the time they got him home, he was passed out, but they both heard him call Sarah's name, twice. Ellen still doesn't know the reason for that slap. Sarah hasn't offered up anything about it, and she doesn't like to pry.

After pressing Brady into telling her about Sarah and Foley's connection, Ellen felt sure they had feelings for each other. But when Foley's anger toward Sarah didn't abate, and Sarah tried her best to avoid him, Ellen began to think she could be wrong, and hearing the way Foley spoke to Sarah just now, she was beginning to think his problem with her was far more serious.

When Foley rushed past her and went inside, Sarah stood up. "I better go," she said sadly. Ellen could see the sadness that crossed Sarah's face and stood too. "I'm sorry Sarah, he's been staying in town, I didn't expect him back today," she said trying to apologize.

"It's not your fault Ellen, we just aren't getting along." Gathering up her cookie tin, Sarah proceeded along the hall, and was heading toward the front door with Ellen following closely behind when the washroom door burst open and Foley stepped out unexpectedly and bumped into Sarah. Feeling herself being held in a crushing embrace that stopped them both crashing against the wall opposite, Sarah glanced fleetingly into his eyes. As his arms encircled her, Foley looked into hers and frowned.

"You still here Misses Morgan?" he said, trying to cover the feelings rising within him with a sarcastic remark.

"You needn't worry yourself about me staying Sheriff Andrews, I'm leaving!" Sarah answered with her own sarcasm.

"Good!" he said, removing his arms quickly from around her and making for the kitchen. Before Foley could disappear, Ellen gave him a look of disgust, then once she was outside with Sarah, she apologized again. "Please, do come back and visit, won't you?" she begged.

"I really don't think I should," Sarah answered, shoving the tin in her saddlebag and climbing into her saddle. Ellen watched from the gate as Sarah pulled her horse around and rode away. Standing in the front room of the farmhouse, Foley watched her ride away too and wished she would stop coming to the farm to torment him.

Even with Brady and Ellen apologizing to her for Foley's attitude toward her and their begging her to visit, after the way Foley spoke to her this last time, Sarah didn't have the courage to go back to the farm. Once upon a time she would not have let Foley's remarks deter her, she would have told him to go to hell, just like she would anyone, but since Christian's passing, something was happening to her she couldn't explain.

Coming out of Henry's Emporium a few weeks later, Sarah met up with Ellen coming from visiting Doc Harris at his practice. After the two women greeted each other with hugs and kisses, Ellen burst into tears.

"Ellen, what is it? What-ever is the matter?" Sarah pressed while holding her basket of supplies in one hand and Ellen's hand in the other. Drawing back a sob, Ellen could hardly speak to tell Sarah what was wrong.

"I'm, I'm having... oh, Sarah! I'm... I'm having... twins!" she cried. Sarah frowned and looked at Ellen rather strangely.

"What do you mean twins? What are twins, Ellen?" Sarah didn't know about twin babies, there were no twins in Cedar Creek. Ellen's and Brady's babies would be the first.

"Oh! I'm having two babies!" Ellen sobbed louder when she explained. "That's why I'm so big, I'm as big as a horse... and only five months gone!"

When Sarah understood having two babies at the same time meant twins, her eyes widened as she smiled. "You lucky thing, to have two babies all at once, where is Brady?" she asked looking around and unable to see him anywhere.

"He's over at the lumberyard, he wants to build a fence out the back so our baby can play outside without wandering off... oh dear!" she exclaimed. "Brady doesn't know!" and started sobbing again.

"Come on Ellen, you come with me, I'll make us both a nice cup of tea." Sarah poked her head back inside Henry's store, and after telling him to tell Brady where Ellen would be, she took Ellen by the hand and walked her to the lodge. By the time Brady came to collect Ellen, both women were talking and laughing, but when Ellen gave him her news, she burst into tears again, and because he wasn't going to be a father to just one baby, Brady's chest swelled with pride, and wrapping his arms around Ellen, he laughed really loud and said he couldn't wait to tell Foley.

Watching Brady help Ellen down the front steps and into their buckboard, the back of which was loaded with timber for their new fence, Sarah heard Ellen tell Brady they would need two of everything now and didn't know how they would manage. Sarah didn't think she would have more children, not now Christian was gone, and certainly not now she had decided she would never remarry. After they left, she went upstairs to the room that had been Lizzy's nursery, and standing beside the cradle Lizzy spent her baby years in, ran her hand over the delicate netting hanging from a hook attached to a board attached to the cradle. Touching the polished timber sides, and the soft blankets and mattress Lizzy slept on, Sarah admitted she liked Ellen very much, so decided she would let her have the cradle. Then when Henry delivered her supplies, she asked him if he could help her get the cradle into her buckboard, and Henry obliged by taking the cradle off its stand to make it easy for him to carry the two pieces downstairs and load it into Sarah's buckboard. It was too late in the day to take the cradle to Ellen, so deciding to make a quick trip out to the farm first thing the next day while Foley was still in town, after thanking Henry, Sarah covered the cradle with a blanket and left it in the buckboard overnight.

The next morning, after taking Lizzy to school, Sarah headed back to the lodge by way of the main street. Drawing level with the Sheriff's Office, she tried peering through the window to see if Foley was there, but while trying not to be too obvious, she had no luck and had to take a chance Foley would not be at the farm that time of day.

Hearing Sarah's buckboard pull up at the front of the farmhouse, Brady and Ellen came out to meet her. Having seen Sarah at the lodge only the day before, Brady greeted her merrily while Ellen, smiling widely, waddled to the gate behind him.

"Can you help me with this Brady?" Sarah asked hopping off the buckboard and going around the back where she uncovered the cradle. Seeing the two pieces of polished wood and able to see what it was and how superb it looked, Ellen and Brady stared.

"We can't possibly take this!" Ellen exclaimed.

"Yes, you can," Sarah said in protest to Ellen's refusing her offer. "I don't have any further use for it, besides, you're the one having two babies, you need two cradles." After Sarah lifted the small mattress and blankets out, Brady took the cradle to his and Ellen's bedroom and put it together. After the mattress went in and the netting hung over it, all three stood back to admire the cradle standing beside the plain one Ellen had already prepared, and didn't hear the front door open and close.

125

"Oh Sarah, it's beautiful, are you sure you want me to have it?" Ellen asked giving Sarah a hug.

"Yes, I'm sure," Sarah answered, feeling her stomach lurch as Foley poked his head through the door. Giving all three a quick look of indifference, he went to the kitchen to get himself some coffee, and Brady followed him out.

"She's not staying I hope?" Foley asked Brady over his shoulder.

"I wouldn't think of it Sheriff!" Sarah replied from the doorway.

Not having seen her come to the kitchen behind him Foley turned, and for a moment their eyes met. Turning back to the stove, he sat the coffee pot down and putting his mug to his mouth ignored her. Turning on her heel and without causing a scene, Sarah left as quickly as possible.

After she had gone, Brady and Ellen showed Foley the cradle Sarah had kindly given them, even so, he didn't show much interest, after all, how could he feel overjoyed for them having a family when having his own had been denied him so cruelly? Besides, he hated seeing Sarah in town let alone at the farm where she caused him so much grief. His feelings were taking a beating every time he saw her.

Having decided the best thing for everyone was to stay away from the farm, most days Sarah could be found visiting friends in town and seeing Lizzy safely to and from school. Other times she filled her days by taking Lizzy for rides to the ponds or the swimming hole where they enjoyed picnics on their own. When word travelled around town Ellen had delivered her two babies and all three were doing well, Sarah was relieved to hear good news.

Foley wasn't at the farm when the babies were born. He preferred to stay in town at the Sheriff's Office where, because Smith slept in the back room, he slept in one of the cells. Having made up his mind he would never put a woman through childbirth, making his chances of ever becoming a father highly unlikely, he chose not to have anything to do with either baby that Brady and Ellen named Matthew and Charlotte, then deciding he should congratulate them on the twins birth, he gave staying at the farm a chance, but after suffering several days of their constant crying, and unable to keep his head clear for any sort of trouble that might eventuate in town, he gave up staying at the farm and went back there.

Several uneventful weeks had passed when Sarah heard Foley would not be home, so she baked a cake, put Lizzy in the buckboard and took her to visit the babies. The three adults were sitting in the kitchen having coffee and cake while Matthew and Charlotte were in the front room lying on a blanket on the floor kicking their arms and legs at Lizzy, who was talking to them in her sweetest voice when Foley, having organized for his deputies to take over for him while he took the rest of the day off, came home unexpectedly. Seeing the buckboard at the front gate, he knew straight away Sarah was visiting and thought perhaps he should turn around and go back to town, but he desperately needed another bath.

Having warned her several times she wasn't welcome at the farm, Sarah's stomach dropped and her heart leapt in sudden surprise at seeing him enter the kitchen.

"What are you doing here?" Brady asked Foley after seeing the surprised and downcast look on Sarah's face when he came in.

"Unlike some people, who seem to always be here Brady! I live here!" Foley snapped while standing at the fire with his back to everyone and pouring himself a mug of coffee. Now that her visit had come to an abrupt end, Sarah just wanted to get Lizzy and go home, so when Charlotte began to cry and Ellen got up from the table to see what happened, she stood too, and made her way around the table to follow Ellen. It was when Matthew started to cry as loudly as Charlotte that things took a turn for the worse.

"Don't those children ever close their mouths Brady?" Foley thought to ask Brady as a joke. But Foley's remark gave Sarah the impression he was being nasty, and becoming furious at his attitude, didn't think before she spoke.

"You wouldn't know of such things, would you Foley Andrews? Seeing how you never had a baby of your own!" The moment her words left her mouth she knew she said a dreadful thing, and regretted straight away her cruel words, but it was too late to take them back. With her eyes wide, she looked at Foley and saw the shocked look that crossed his face.

"I'm so sorry," she said softly, trying to apologize. But Foley's retaliation happened so fast Sarah hardly had time to draw breath. Slamming his mug on the table and spilling its contents on the cloth, he grabbed Sarah by her arm, and while gripping it tight, started dragging her out of the kitchen and along the hall.

"*Get out!*" he yelled savagely, pulling her along. "*Get out of my house!*" he barked through gritted teeth.

With her eyes wide with fear, Sarah tried holding onto the wall to stop him dragging her, but her hands slid along the wooden panels. Wrenching the front door open, and still gripping her arm tight, Foley pushed her forcibly across the porch and watched her stumble down the steps. Barely managing to keep her balance, she came to a stop on the path just as he slammed the door closed behind her and locked it. Hearing the unmistakable sound of the door being latched, and realizing Lizzy was locked inside, visions of the moment Thomas had been snatched from her came flooding back. "*Lizzy!*" Sarah screamed while rushing back to the door. "*No, no! Lizzy!... no, Lizzy!*" she screamed hysterically.

Looking along the hall, Foley was stunned by what he was seeing. When Lizzy heard the commotion, she came out of the front room and ran toward the kitchen looking for her Ma. Hearing her thumping her fists wildly on the door and screaming for her from outside, Lizzy stood with her bottom lip quivering at the end of the hall, and looking at Foley whimpered, "mommy."

Unaware Lizzy only went to school two days a week, Foley hadn't realized she was there with Sarah. It was a week day, as far as he was concerned, she should have been in school.

Too young to attend school fulltime, all Tilly O'Rourke was doing was reading stories to her and helping her learn her ABC's. "*Lizzy!*" Foley heard Sarah screaming.

When Lizzy didn't come out, Sarah thought perhaps she could get to her if she went to the porch at the back of the house. Staggering backwards when her feet slipped over the steps, her legs buckled causing her to fall heavily to land on her knees on the path. The thought of never seeing her daughter again brought on a sudden tightening of her chest. Pressing her palms firmly on the ground to steady herself, she gasped for breath. The sound of terror tearing from Sarah's throat sent shivers up everyone's spine.

After the shock of what happened faded, Brady gathered himself and swung into action. "Goddamn it Foley! what have you fucking done?" he cursed, and taking Lizzy by the hand, hurried her up the hall where he quickly unlocked the door and led her outside.

Having been told Sarah lost Thomas when he was two months old, the same age her twins were now, and told how Foley helped in Thomas's rescue, Ellen couldn't understand his treating Sarah the way he was, especially with what he did just now and what it was doing to Sarah. While Matthew cried loudly on the floor in the front room, Ellen's eyes flooded with tears as she stayed back holding Charlotte. "There you go Lizzy darlin, go to mommy," Brady said nudging Lizzy forward.

Crying hysterically, Sarah's tears mixed with snot as they ran down her face. She felt sick to her stomach at what was happening. Hearing the door open she looked up to see Lizzy come out. Hurrying down the steps, Lizzy threw herself into her Ma's outstretched arms. "*Mommy!*" she cried. Clutching Lizzy tight, Sarah staggered to her feet as Brady stepped off the porch. "I'm so sorry Sarah," he said in dismay at the sight of her.

What Sarah said cut Foley deeply, but shocked by what he had done, he was sorry it had come to this. Stepping off the porch, he made to approach Sarah to try and apologize, but Sarah didn't give him the opportunity to speak. Wiping her sleeve across her face to wipe away the mess, her eyes became distant, her body began to shake, and not seeing Foley or anyone else, she turned away, and still carrying Lizzy, stumbled her way to her buckboard. Lizzy clambered onto the seat as Sarah, struggling to see through her tears, climbed up and taking hold of the reins, whipped them harshly across the horses back. Becoming alarmed, the horse shot forward, causing Sarah to pull sharply on the reins and send the buckboards wheels spinning on gravel in front of the house. Wanting to get away as fast as she could, she kept the buckboard going at a cracking pace along the road back to town. As they sped along, Sarah resolved never to set foot out at the farm ever again. Nor would she ever speak to Foley Andrews. As far as she was concerned, their friendship was at an end.

As the buckboard raced along, Lizzy bounced on the seat beside Sarah. "*Mommy!*" she cried, while hanging on the best she could. But Sarah kept the buckboard going. Unable to hang on any longer, Lizzy let go and almost fell. "*Mommy!*" she screamed. Hearing her cry and seeing her begin to fall, Sarah put her arm across her and pushed her against the back of the seat until she brought the buckboard to a standstill, then taking Lizzy in her arms, held her tight.

"Lizzy, sweetheart! oh baby, I'm so sorry!" This was the second time she almost hurt Lizzy because of Foley, and Sarah was not going to let such a thing happen again.

Standing at the farm gate, Foley watched Sarah's buckboard disappear along the road in a cloud of dust. "I'm sorry Sarah, I didn't mean to hurt you, or Lizzy… I love you," he whispered. What did it matter if Sarah knew about Maria, or what she said just now? After what he did to her and Lizzy, he realized he made a terrible mistake. A mistake he believed, that had destroyed any chance of him ever getting Sarah to love him.

After locking the front door to the lodge, Sarah decided she would keep Lizzy home with her until such time as she had no choice but to go to Henry's store for supplies. Word quickly spread about what happened out at the farm. On hearing the talk, Doc went to the lodge to speak with Sarah and see if she and Lizzy were alright. Sarah let him in and informed him, come spring, she would be leaving town with the trappers. When news Sarah would be returning to her mountain got back to Foley, he was devastated. It was all his fault. He didn't want her to go. He wanted to marry her and have her stay in town like she had with Christian, but he couldn't very well walk up to her and ask her to marry him like he used to, not after what he had done, which left him not knowing what he could do to stop her leaving.

Locking Lizzy in the farmhouse caused Sarah to vow, just like she had with Thomas, never to let Lizzy out of her sight. After marrying Christian and she had settled in town, she no longer had further use for her things she used for trapping. Except for wearing them the time she let two strangers stay at the lodge, one from the Stagecoach Company, the other from the combined Telegraph/

Mail Office, the items had been stored away a long time. She had been happy to leave her things in the trunk, because along with keeping the whole of Cedar Creek and the county safe, Christian had kept her and their children safe. He had been a good husband and sheriff. No-one had reason to fear for their safety.

Going to the supply cupboard where her wooden trunk was stored, she lifted the lid, and lifting out a long wooden box, opened it to find her silver ivy leafed pistol with its engraved ivory grip sitting on its bed of red velvet. Wanting to see if her gun still felt comfortable to hold, she gripped it tight and aimed it around the room, then loaded it with bullets. After lifting out her sheath that held her hunting knife and her father's old hat with the split brim, she carried everything upstairs and got dressed in tight fitting trousers and shirt. After braiding her hair in a single thick braid, she shoved her pistol down the front of her trousers. The strap holding her sheath she buckled at her waist before putting her fur vest on over the top of her shirt and tying a cord around it to hold it in place. Lastly, she pulled her father's old hat down on her head.

After going back downstairs, Sarah cooked strips of bacon, eggs and fried bread, and had Lizzy's clothes on the table ready to dress her. When Lizzy smelt food cooking, she went downstairs, and seeing her Ma at the fire, her eyes widened in puzzlement. She couldn't remember seeing her Ma dressed the way she was before. Sure, she wore pants when they went rabbiting, and she wore them again when two strangers stayed in their house, but this was entirely different.

"Morning Lizzy, come and eat, you can go to school today," Sarah said turning and finding Lizzy standing behind her. While Lizzy ate, she studied the strange looking hat on her Ma's head, the vest that had fur on it, the big knife she wore hanging from her waist, and the gun she had stuffed down her trousers. Several times Lizzy's eyes travelled over her Ma and back again.

After they finished eating, Lizzy was dressed in trousers and a check shirt. Her feet were pushed into her brown boots. Lifting Lizzy up to sit on the table, Sarah braided her hair in two braids and secured them with ribbons. As far as Sarah was concerned, there would be no more frilly dresses for Lizzy, she was her daughter, and she was going to look like it.

With Lizzy holding her hand, they proceeded up the main street toward the schoolhouse. Figuring if she saw Foley, she might be tempted to shoot him, Sarah and Lizzy crossed the street well before the Sheriff's Office.

A group of men milling about outside the saloon nudged each other when they saw Sarah coming towards them and the way she was dressed. Not having seen her wearing her trapping gear for a long time, to the men, this could mean only one thing. Someone was in big trouble, and they guessed after hearing talk, it would be their sheriff.

With her braid swishing across her back and the hunting knife bouncing at her side, and keeping Lizzy in step with her, Sarah walked with a determined stride. When men and women saw her coming toward them, they remembered that walk and hurried to get out of her way. As Sarah drew nearer to the Sheriff's Office, Deputy Smith, leaning casually on a post outside, rushed inside to let Foley know she was there.

"You should see Misses Morgan, she's coming up the street!" he said sounding excited. Peering through the window first, Foley saw Sarah walk past, and knowing he was the cause of the way she was dressed, stepped outside and watched until she and Lizzy turned the corner out of sight, then went back inside.

"Keep an eye on her O'Rourke, if anything happens to her, I will hold you responsible," Sarah warned when she took Lizzy into the schoolhouse.

When Calahan Cole lost Mountain View Lodge to Benjamin Crawley in a game of poker, everyone believed he signed the deed to the lodge over to Crawley, but Calahan knew Crawley cheated, because although his hands crippled him with pain, he managed to sign the lodge over to Sarah. Crawley kept hidden the fact he didn't own the lodge, and stole what he wanted from inside the house. It took Jonathon, newly arrived in town to see through Crawley's cheating, and along with Christian and the four trappers, helped get the lodge back to Sarah.

Having heard what Foley did to Lizzy, Jonathon was not surprised to see Sarah had reverted back to how she was the day he met her. He couldn't be sure what state of mind she was in, it may have had a detrimental effect on her, making her revert back to her uncivilized ways, and having had his own run in with her, he figured it would be best if he were formal when addressing her. "I will take care of her Misses Morgan," he replied nervously.

"I will come back for you Lizzy, so don't you go leaving here with anyone but me!" Sarah warned kneeling in front of her. Understanding her Ma telling her never to leave school unless she came for her, Lizzy gave her a hug. After kissing Lizzy on her cheek and straightening up, Sarah addressed Jonathon. "It's Cole, O'Rourke... Sarah Cole!"

On leaving the schoolhouse, Sarah made her way to Ham's livery where she saddled her horse. Then ignoring peoples stares, led her horse to Henry's Emporium where she tethered it to the hitching rail out front before removing her saddle-bags and going inside. Henry's back was to the door when Sarah entered. "Howdy Sarah," he greeted with a smile when he turned, but his smile faded when he took in how Sarah was dressed. "What can I um... do for you?" he asked, studying her pistol down the front of her pants and the knife at her hip.

"Three boxes of shells for my pistol, and the same for my rifle," Sarah asked approaching the counter. Looking around to see who else was there and seeing no-one, she asked Henry for two more boxes. "Put them on my account, please," she ended.

When the amount owed was written against Sarah's name in his book, he got her to sign for it, and afterwards when she picked up the boxes and shoved them in her saddle-bags, he turned the book around to see what she had written, and his eyes widened.

"Hold it Sarah! you can't sign this with Cole! you're Misses Morgan!" he called as she headed for the door. Not knowing how she would react to what he said, when she turned with her hand resting on her knife and looked at him, he swallowed nervously.

"Christian is dead Henry, I'm no longer his wife, I'm Sarah Cole!... and I always will be," she informed him.

Henry didn't want trouble, especially from Sarah. Witness to the many arguments the previous owner Benjamin Crawley had with her every time she came to the store, guaranteed the store would be left in a mess from her throwing things about. To show he understood her reasoning for the name change, he nodded and replied, "well, you better go see Morley and get him to change your name on your account, then I guess this will be fine."

Leaving Henry's store without having caused trouble, and after throwing her saddle-bags over the back of her horse, she took her horse along to Morley's bank. Morley was as shocked as Henry to see Sarah dressed as if she had just come in from trapping. Never one to argue with her, he didn't hesitate to change her name to what she demanded.

Having sorted things out with Morley, Sarah headed along the street on her way back to the lodge, and keeping her eyes straight ahead, passed by the Sheriff's Office. There was no need for Foley to go back outside. Standing at the window when he saw her go by, he took his gun from its holster and opened the chamber to check it was fully loaded, then shoved it back in its holster.

"Smith! check your weapon!" he ordered Smith who was lounging in a chair with his back against the wall.

"I checked it this morning," Smith said without moving a muscle.

"Well check it again!" Foley snapped.

"What's up?" Smith asked, standing up and pulling his gun from its holster to check it.

"Where's Taylor?" Foley asked not answering his question.

"At the saloon… why?" Smith questioned, coming to the window.

"Misses Morgan is up to something, and I want to be prepared… that's all," Foley stated while watching people moving about out on the street.

Back at the lodge, along with two empty fruit tins, Sarah packed her rucksack with her coffee pot, her mug, and her tin of cookies. Her rifle was loaded and sitting in its holster attached to her saddle. Her rucksack she hung from the other side. Putting her foot in the stirrup, she swung up into the saddle, then prodding her horse, brought it around the front of the Ferguson House where she sat facing along the street looking toward Ham's livery and the bridge. Several men passing by nudged each other and wondered why she was just sitting there, waiting.

Without warning, Sarah let out a yell, and gripping her reins tight, kicked her horse hard in the flanks and sent it jumping at being prodded violently. Taking off at a gallop, the horse raced up the street passing wagons and men on horses. Town folk scurried out of its way.

Hearing a yell and then a horse galloping by, Doc Harris with Gerda, and Henry from the store, Morley at the bank and others rushed out to stand on the boardwalk from where they could watch Sarah ride past.

Rushing from the Sheriff's Office with his deputies, Foley watched her race over the bridge and out of town. Quickly ordering the men to take charge, he ran to his horse, and jumping into the saddle, kicked it hard and raced after her. By the time he cleared the bridge, Sarah was a speck in the distance. Deciding not to catch up to her, he slowed to a canter and followed her trail of dust all the way to the dry gulch behind Major Hardy's land where he got off his horse and drew his gun in case of trouble. Creeping stealthily up a ridge, he lay on his stomach on top of the rise where he could watch Sarah without being seen. When he saw she was alone, he holstered his gun and watched her build a fire and make coffee.

While the coffee brewed, Sarah placed two tins side by side on a stump. Walking away, she turned, and drawing her pistol, fired a full round at the tins. When neither tin fell off the stump, Foley heard her curse while reloading, and this time, taking careful aim, she fired two shots and sent the tins flying to land a good way away from the stump. Shoving her gun back in her pants, she stood with her hand poised at her side, and although looking as though she were thinking about what she should do, she drew her gun, and feathering the hammer, sent the tins flying along in the dirt. Gathering the tins and sitting them back on the stump, and this time using her rifle, she sent the tins flying into the air where she shot them again. After repeating the practice twice more, and satisfied when she hit her target each time, she pulled her knife from its sheath, and letting it go swiftly, embedded the blade deep in the stump the tins had been sitting on. Foley watched intently as Sarah regained her ability to hit targets effortlessly. After repeating the throw several times, Sarah was satisfied. 'Sarah Cole, wolf trapper, was back! and she was not going to take any shit from Foley Andrews!'

Foley had seen enough. Sliding down the rise he made his way back to his horse. It had not been his intention to hurt Sarah, or Lizzy, all he wanted was for Sarah to know how he felt about her knowing about Maria. He hated that he had resorted to being nasty and it was eating him up inside, and he was thinking he should have ridden down to the gulch and shared her coffee with her. Maybe he could have apologized for shutting her out of the farmhouse, then ask her to marry him like old times. 'Ah! who the hell was he kidding?' he asked himself. If he did that, Sarah would be justified in putting a bullet in him for what he had done. He had always been in love with her and always would be, but as he rode back to town, he had himself convinced it was too late for him to do anything about it.

Sitting on a log near her fire, Sarah poured herself a mug of coffee, and while letting her eyes scan the hilltops and ridges surrounding her, she put the mug to her mouth. She had sensed Foley was up on the ridge watching her, and she sensed too when he left.

Leaving her horse at the livery for Ham to unsaddle, and carrying her rucksack on her back and her rifle over her shoulder while deep in thought about how her practice shoot had gone, she walked along the street and unwittingly passed by the Sheriff's Office. Seeing her walk by, Foley felt he had to put an end to their impasse, so coming out, he stepped off the boardwalk and into the street.

"We have to talk Misses Morgan!" he said from behind her. Sarah stopped walking, and keeping her back to him, pulled her pistol from inside her trousers, and cocking it while turning, brought it level with his face.

"It's Cole sheriff!... Sarah Cole!" she informed him curtly.

"You knew, didn't you? Why didn't you tell me?" he asked ignoring the pistol pointed at him and keeping his voice low so people passing by couldn't hear. When several men standing outside

136

the saloon let drinkers inside know Foley and Sarah were facing off, a crowd quickly gathered on the boardwalk with whiskeys in hand to watch. They hadn't been able to make out what Foley said, but seeing the gun in Sarah's hand, they quickly took bets on whether Sarah would shoot him. When she didn't answer, Foley became angry and went on.

"I helped you when Frank got whipped and I got this fucking scar on my face!" he snarled while pointing to his face. "Why couldn't you tell me?" he asked with his voice growing louder. Unsure exactly what he was asking, Sarah kept her pistol pointed at him, and still didn't answer. Looking along the barrel of her gun, Foley pursed his lips and stood his ground.

"Before you shoot me! you fucking tell me why you kept the fact you knew about Maria seeing other men to yourself!" he implored through gritted teeth.

'So that's it!' Sarah was thinking. 'He knows I knew about Maria. It could only have been Doc who told him, but how he found out isn't important, he isn't going to get away with locking Lizzy in his house.'

"Tell me goddamn it!" Foley barked savagely.

Keeping her arm straight and her gun aimed directly at his nose, Sarah became furious at him for putting her on the spot.

"What was I supposed to say to you!" she snapped loudly in retaliation. "Oh, hey! Foley! you want to know something? Your wife is fucking other men!" Gripping her gun tight, Sarah swallowed. Hearing clearly what Sarah said, the crowd peered wide eyed at each other, then with their mouths open, uttered disbelief before falling silent as Sarah went on.

"Oh! and hey! just so as you know! the baby she is having!... it isn't yours!" Hating herself for her outburst, and the look of shame on Foley's face, Sarah eased her grip on her gun. Hearing what Foley was trying to keep quiet, the crowd gasped. Feeling Sarah didn't have to put what she knew so bluntly, and for everyone hearing what she said, Foley felt anger rising in him.

"Goddamn it, Sarah! I shouldn't have done what I did at the farm, but I swear you forced my hand!" Stepping in close, and bringing

Sarah's pistol within a hairs breadth of his face, while keeping his hands by his sides, he hoped to distract her long enough to get her gun off her before she could shoot him.

"You want to shoot me?" he asked. "Go ahead! but before you do, you should know I loved you long before Frank ever did, and before Christian. We are friends, you should have trusted me enough to tell me what you knew." Foley kept his eyes fixed on Sarah. "We are friends, aren't we Sarah?" he asked keeping his voice steady.

What he was saying was true, they were friends, and she should have trusted their friendship was strong enough for them to have discussed what Maria was doing, but instead, she went along with Doc and kept it to herself. That was a mistake she had to live with, and now she had lost their friendship. Sarah's eyes though never wavered when she saw the sadness creep into his eyes as he stared into hers. She knew he was telling the truth when he said he hadn't meant to hurt her or Lizzy, but with her trappers upbringing kicking in, she was unable to back down, she had come too far.

"It's too late," she said, keeping her hand steady. As Foley and Sarah stared each other down, the crowd watched in anticipation of winning a bet.

Turning his head to take in the crowd standing outside the saloon, Foley quickly brought it back to look at Sarah, and surprised everyone including her when his hand shot upwards and grabbed her gun-hand. Forcing her hand up, the gun went off, sending people ducking for cover when they weren't sure if they were being shot at. Grabbing Sarah around her waist, and with her body pressed against his, he sent her rifle and rucksack swinging wildly to one side.

As they continued wrestling, Sarah tried to get loose of his hold, but with her rifle and rucksack getting in her way, she didn't stand a chance. Remembering what Crawley did to her father, she did the only thing she thought she could do to get Foley to let her go. Stomping her foot hard on top of his, she got him to pull his foot back, but it did nothing to make him lose his balance and let go of her. Keeping a tight grip on her gun-hand, and using all his strength, Foley jerked her pistol out of her hand and almost sent her flying. Shaking off her rifle hanging over her arm and dropping it, she tried grabbing her pistol back off him, but he held it high above his head so she couldn't get at it. Balling her hand into a fist, she swung her arm hard toward his face, and smashed it into his jaw. Shocked by the blow but unhurt, Foley kept turning in a circle away from her. The crowd watching them erupted in raucous laughter at how silly they looked as they scrambled about. When they both suddenly gave up struggling with each other, Foley emptied Sarah's gun of its bullets and handed it back to her.

"Go home!... Cole!" he ordered.

Having been made a fool of, Sarah snatched her pistol out of Foley's hand and shoved it inside the top of her trousers, then stooping down and picking up her rifle, turned on her heel and stormed off. After watching her turn the corner near the Ferguson House until she disappeared, Foley turned to the crowd, and jabbing his finger in anger at everyone, threatened them with a beating if they didn't keep their mouths shut about what they heard. Knowing how good Foley was with his fists, everyone stopped laughing and stared at him. Thinking they wouldn't talk, Foley stormed back to the Sheriff's Office satisfied, and after going inside, slammed the door closed behind him.

The men outside the saloon who bet on Sarah shooting Foley voiced their disappointment at losing the bet. The winners happily collected their money and headed back inside to buy a round of drinks. Not heeding Foley's warning about keeping their mouths shut, their talk turned to what they heard about Foley and Maria. Some talked only of Sarah, but most talked about Foley and Sarah. When someone was heard saying, "I don't know why they don't just get married!... they dang well hate each other enough to be married!" everyone laughed.

When Foley let Sarah walk away his stomach was churning and his heart racing. He had never held Sarah that close before, not even when he danced with her at Brady and Ellen's wedding. He never dared kiss her when he proposed to her out at the ponds where they shared coffee. Sarah's body pressing against his as she tried to get free of him, flooded him with feelings he never thought he had inside him, and anger rose from the pit of his stomach for causing the rift that had come between them.

139

Rushing back to the lodge with her face burning from her scuffle with Foley, Sarah's stomach fluttered, her heart pounded. His arms when he held her had been forceful, she could feel his muscles tightening when they flexed. What was she thinking aiming her gun at him like that? She could never forgive herself for calling out what she knew about Maria, now the whole town knew, and soon everyone in the county would know. She felt sorry for outing Foley's private life like it didn't matter. Sitting on the couch holding her head in her hands, she thought herself despicable, and right then hated herself.

That afternoon when Sarah went to collect Lizzy from school, she did what she thought was best to avoid another confrontation with Foley. Instead of walking along the main street and passing the Sheriff's Office, she went via the alley running beside the livery and made her way to the schoolhouse from there. After collecting Lizzy, she returned to the lodge the same way.

Having settled his nerves after his run in with Sarah, Foley went back to doing his usual checks around town. Coming along from the direction of the Ferguson House, he headed into the street where the lodge was situated. When he saw Sarah come around the corner from the direction of the livery, his heart lurched. Thinking now they were away from the glaring crowd of onlookers they could sort out what was happening between them, he kept walking toward her.

When Sarah saw him approaching, she picked Lizzy up and continued walking. When they drew level their eyes met, but neither spoke a word. Hurrying past Foley and up the steps of the lodge, Sarah rushed inside with Lizzy and quickly closed the door.

Foley stopped when Sarah hurried past him, and turning when he heard the door shut, looked sadly up at the lodge, and not having had the guts to say anything, he continued along the street where he turned into the alley and made his way back to the Sheriff's Office.

Chapter Twelve

rady watched from the porch as Foley rode his horse into the barn. His brother had become a whole lot angrier since Maria's passing, and his confrontation with Sarah in the middle of town wasn't helping. His fighting with men in the saloon or in the street was becoming a regular pastime. Not only did he break up fights, he hit out at anyone for no apparent reason. Sheriffs were supposed to uphold the law not break it, but Foley didn't let being a lawman stop him getting drunk and taking his anger out on anyone he thought was talking about what happened between him and Sarah.

When Brady found his voice Foley was pleased, but was finding it difficult to stop Brady having opinions about him. After their twins were born, Brady and Ellen were on top of the world, but Foley was making it difficult for them to be happy. A lot of his anger aimed at Sarah left Brady unable to understand his actions. The pain from the whiplash Foley suffered to his face the night they took Sarah back to the trappers had been unbearable for Brady to watch, but it confirmed Foley was in love with her, and it was obvious all these years later he was still in love with her.

Brady had wanted to return to farming like his father had done before him and was grateful to Sarah for the farm she bought them in payment for saving her life, and for giving him that chance, but now, after the way Foley had been treating her, their friendship was strained.

After much discussion, both he and Ellen came to the conclusion Foley was too afraid to tell Sarah how he felt about her in case she rejected him like she always had before, and perhaps that explained why he was acting the way he was. Ellen urged Brady to demand Foley put aside his fear and ask Sarah to marry him like he used to. After seeing Foley ride in, Brady decided there was no better time to talk to him than now, so he approached him in the barn.

Back in town, Foley's deputies were told they could find him at the farm if they needed him. In his saddlebag, he had a bottle of whiskey he was planning on drinking. Busy unsaddling his horse, his back was to the entrance, and he didn't hear Brady come in.

"Why are you being nasty to Sarah?" Brady began awkwardly, and stepping into the stall where Foley was busy with his horse, stood directly behind him and didn't leave him much room to move about. Picking up a brush, Foley began rubbing down his horse and didn't answer.

"You can't still be blaming her for knowing about Maria?" Brady questioned, but Foley remained silent. "You know you want Sarah now just as much as you did before she married Christian, so why don't you swallow your damn pride and go ask her to marry you?" Taking in Brady's remark, Foley glanced over his shoulder as he continued to rub down his horse.

Thinking he had the solution to stop Foley from being so miserable, Brady ignored that he didn't answer and went on. "Go ask her Foley, go ask Sarah to marry you, maybe now both of you are on your own she will say yes." But Foley had already given a lot of thought to the way he behaved when Sarah was around and didn't think what Brady was suggesting a good idea. What happened in town when she held her gun on him was the worst day of his life, and he felt such a fool now the whole town knew about Maria, and because he didn't want to make an even bigger fool of himself, he wasn't about to ask Sarah to marry him.

"Don't you go telling me what to do Brady!" he snapped.

"All those years I put up with your whining every time you proposed to Sarah and she turned you down, I couldn't tell you what I thought, but I'm telling you now, I saw how miserable it made you when she told you no, and I watched your drunken fighting because of it, and goddamn it! you're doing it again!" Watching Foley ignoring him, made Brady's anger rise.

"You think it didn't make me just as miserable? Well it goddamn did!" he stated angrily.

"Goddamn it Brady! I'm not going to ask her!" Foley replied just as angry.

"*You!*" Brady stressed jabbing his finger into Foley's back. "Are fucking in love with her!" That was something Foley knew already and didn't need Brady reminding him of. Besides jabbing him with his finger, the next thing Brady said made Foley explode with rage.

"Maybe all those times you asked Sarah to marry you, you just wanted to fuck her like the other men wanted to!"

Not about to let anyone talk about Sarah in such a despicable way, especially his brother, Foley turned, and throwing the brush aside while yelling in anger, made a grab for Brady.

"Maybe you're too scared to ask her again because you know she will turn your offer to fuck her down, just like she does the others!" Brady managed to say before Foley shoved him backwards out of the stall and across the barn where he slammed him against the wall.

"Shut your filthy fucking mouth!" Foley snarled. "I won't have anyone talking about Sarah that way! least of all *you!*" Feeling at last he was getting somewhere, Brady gripped Foley's hands as he held him against the wall, and wasn't about to let up.

"You were in love with Sarah while she was married to Christian and you were married to Maria! I could see it every time you fucking looked at her! it was so goddamn fucking obvious, so! go fuck her!" he sneered. It was a well-known fact Foley would never take liberties where Sarah was concerned, but Brady was still surprised by what Foley did next.

Astonished at Brady slandering Sarah's good name, Foley pulled his arm back and driving his fist into Brady's face, split his lip and made his nose bleed. With his head ringing from the blow, Brady went down, and crouching on hands and knees with his head down, wiped blood from his chin.

Never having had reason to hit Brady before, Foley stood over his brother with his hands clenched into fists. Ever since their family farm burnt down and their parents and younger sister died in the fire, they had looked out for each other. Now all Foley could feel was anger. Anger at himself for the terrible way he behaved at Brady and Ellen's wedding, and anger for the way he behaved every time Sarah visited the farm to see Ellen. When Sarah said he wouldn't know anything about children because he never had a child of his own, he was hurt by her scathing remark and he just wanted her to leave. How could he have known Lizzy was with her? It wasn't until he slammed the door shutting Sarah out, that he saw Lizzy and was horrified at what he had done. He tried apologizing, but Sarah ran. The next time he saw her she was wearing her trapping gear and had reverted to calling herself Cole, and because she made a fool of him outside the saloon, he would not waste his time trying to apologize to her again, nor would he ever ask her to marry him.

"Sometimes I think it was better when you couldn't talk," Foley said standing over Brady and unclenching his hands. Still reeling from Foley's blow, Brady staggered to his feet.

"You better ask Sarah to marry you so we can all get some peace, even if her answer is no, at least you will have an answer, and you can move on," he said sadly.

"I'm not going to ask her," Foley replied quietly, letting his anger subside. Going back to the stall, he pulled the bottle of whiskey out of his saddlebag hanging over the railing.

As Brady got up, he looked at the bottle Foley was holding. "If you're going to get drunk you get back to town and stay there, because Ellen is threatening to take my babies and go back to her folks, and goddamn it! I won't be having that!" he said, holding his chin.

"You seem to have forgotten Brady, this is my farm too," Foley said to Brady's back. "Yes, and you seem to forget who bought it for us," Brady muttered, and staggering from the barn, felt dismayed at his brother hitting him. Brady stopped outside with a final demand.

"Ask her damn it! I don't care what answer you get, but you get a goddamn answer! besides, you have nothing to lose." Wiping his sleeve across his mouth, he headed back to the farmhouse, but halfway across the yard he stopped and came back.

"And if you ever hit me again!... I will fucking hit you back!" His voice broke in an audible sob as he hurried back to the house. Foley stood in the doorway watching as Ellen opened the door and wrapped her arms around Brady, then drawing him inside, watched her close the door behind them.

Now Brady was gone, the barn was quite. Taking the top off the whiskey bottle, Foley brought it toward his mouth, but before taking a drink, he stopped and looked at the bottle before hurling it angrily at the wall where it shattered, sending whiskey and shards of glass all over the floor. While spending considerable time picking up as much glass as he could find, he thought about what Brady said and came to the conclusion he was right when he said he had nothing to lose. Brady and Ellen were in bed when they heard Foley's horse gallop along the road outside the house.

The town was bathed in darkness when Foley rode in. The only light visible was coming from the Sheriff's Office where his deputies were on duty. Riding past the Trading Post, he took his horse around the front of the Ferguson House and rode into the street where the lodge was situated. Bringing his horse to a stop at the bottom of the steps, he looked up at the house and saw light from a lamp flickering in the front window that told him Sarah was still awake.

Sarah sat in the green winged chair with her feet curled in front of her and her arms wrapped around her legs. Ever since Foley confronted her in the street, she had given him a lot of thought. Although she had been confused as to why he was treating her badly when they had been such good friends, their confrontation at the farmhouse and in the street had given her the answer. What followed was exactly what she had been trying to avoid. By keeping Maria's deceit to herself she had hoped to avoid losing their friendship, but she should have known that was what was going to happen. It had only been a matter of time before he found out she knew. She didn't hate Foley, but their friendship had suffered the consequences of her decision. Hearing hooves out on the street, she unwrapped her arms from around her legs and put her feet down.

Thomas left Cedar Creek for Philadelphia and college months ago, and Lizzy would certainly be in bed asleep. Aware Sarah

145

would be alone, Foley walked up the steps leading to the porch and crossed to the front door. With his hand poised to knock, he hesitated for a moment and wondered if he was doing the right thing by being there. Knowing Sarah as much as he did, he thought when she realizes who it was at her door, she would open it with a gun in her hand and shoot him simply for being on her doorstep. But if he didn't go through with this, he would never know what may come of it, so taking a deep breath, he removed his hat and knocked, then, waiting for Sarah to open the door, thought back to a time when he was standing in the rain beside a hole in the ground at the cemetery.

A wooden coffin held the body of Sarah's father, Calahan Cole. Watching Sarah crying for her father while he stood alongside Major Hardy protecting him from trouble, Foley wanted to put his arms around her, but being shy, he didn't want to make a fool of himself in front of the trappers if she pushed him away. Neither Joe or Fergus, nor Garrett or Will, whom that very day became Sarah's guardians embraced her to show they cared how she was feeling. When he learnt Frank Mason sat in the rain with her after the burial and fell in love with her, he knew he lost his chance of getting to know her, and because Frank got to be alone with her on her mountain, there was no way he could stop them getting together.

He wasn't happy when he found her and Frank at Major Hardy's shack where they had been making love. It was the first time he saw Sarah as the beautiful woman she was, but because trappers protected her, he resolved never to touch her without her inviting him to do so, and he has kept his word to this day.

It was an unthinkable act, to leave a young girl naked and vulnerable out in a storm without her clothes and no way of getting back in the shack to get them after it had been sealed up. Taking her horse and leaving her unable to get back to town was something Foley wanted no part of, and he appreciated the fact he saved Sarah from the whipping Major Hardy was going to unleash on her, but didn't appreciate the disfiguring scar he received because of it. He felt it made him repulsive to women and was self-conscious about his looks. If Major Hardy had whipped Sarah that night, he would not have hesitated to shoot him dead.

It left him feeling disappointed, but not surprised, when on the ride back to town he learnt Sarah was having Frank's baby. He loved Sarah deeply even then, and Brady was right when he said he had to listen to him complaining about losing his chance with her. Complaining got him no sympathy from anyone.

When word spread like wildfire that Frank had been killed hunting wolves and Sarah gave birth to his son Thomas, everyone thought it only natural for Major Hardy to be devastated when he heard the news, but blaming Sarah for his son's death, and denying Thomas being his grandson was wrong.

Standing on Sarah's porch, Foley remembered how Major Hardy's hatred for Sarah became evident when he organized to have Thomas taken from her. With Thomas gone, Sarah became a shadow of the woman he loved as she battled the town to get her son back, and he worried for her health. Even though she didn't trust anyone, and threatened those that came near her, he wanted to comfort her, but knew if he tried, she would more than likely shoot him for interfering, so like every other coward, he stayed away.

He thought there was nothing he could do to help her, but found his chance to make things right when he helped the four trappers dispatch Major Hardy's expensive longhorn bull. He would never divulge it was them that did it, because it was him who showed the men where they could find it. It was a cruel thing to do, but it worked when Major Hardy gave in and returned Thomas to Sarah.

Unlike everyone else, Foley looked forward to winter when Sarah returned to town from her mountain. With Frank gone, he thought he stood a better chance of getting to know her.

It had been while riding the boundaries on Major Hardy's land that he accidently came across her at the ponds. There she was, sitting in front of a small waterfall with Thomas, a tiny one-year old chubby baby, sitting between her legs letting her wash him. Hiding behind trees growing around the edge of the ponds, he watched the two of them giggling, and when she leant back to rinse suds from her hair after washing it under the waterfall, he became mesmerized and kept watching until she looked up and almost caught him spying on her. Riding away from the ponds that day left him enthralled by what he had seen.

The following winter, when he came across her out on the prairie snaring rabbits, Thomas had turned two, and was running everywhere. After offering him coffee, they sat talking as friends would, and because her hair was damp, he could tell she had been bathing in the ponds.

It was the year Thomas turned three that he found the courage to declare his love for her and asked her to marry him for the first time. Saying they were friends and she wanted it to stay that way, was the first time Sarah turned him down. Then when he said he would ask her again the following winter they laughed about it, but he was serious, and vowed to himself he would ask her every winter, if he had to, until she agreed to marry him.

Having taken up asking her, he became the butt of everyone's jokes when cowhands especially didn't let him forget the rejections he got. There are men that wanted Sarah for themselves, and he worry's now she is a widow that she may accept another man's proposal. One such man is the meanest trapper that ever lived, and Foley remembers how angry he became when Logan tried forcing himself on Sarah when Thomas was a baby. He wanted to kill Logan for trying to take something not offered him. But he needn't worry about Sarah liking Logan. Sarah hates him like she hates no other man. Each winter, when she turned every man's proposals down, Foley was relieved. Until she met and fell in love with Christian Morgan.

Foley remained deep in thought. He wasn't in town the day Sarah was almost killed by Millicent Crawley, work at Major Hardy's ranch kept him busy, but he heard both women had been standing on the cliff above the river where Sarah let Christian know she was expecting his child just before she and Millicent plunged over the edge. Having survived the fall and the rapids, Christian proposed to Sarah and her acceptance shocked Foley, forcing him to hide his feelings he had for her from everyone again.

When Christian was killed, folk said Sarah would go back to her mountain once the trappers came to put their skins in, but she proved them wrong by staying to let Thomas finish school, and Foley was glad she did. When she came out of mourning, although to his dismay, he often found her visiting Ellen at the farm.

It was at the insistence of Sarah that he married Maria because she convinced him Maria was a decent woman. But cheating on him and having someone else's baby was not something that could be forgiven. If he had known what Maria had been doing, he would never have married her, and because his feelings for Sarah ran deep, he couldn't understand why she didn't trust their friendship enough to tell him what she knew. So here he was now, standing on her doorstep ready to find out.

He knocked again but when Sarah didn't open the door, he pursed his lips in disappointment at not being able to talk to her, and putting his hat on, crossed the porch and made to leave. Foley's foot was on the top step when the door opened.

Sensing someone coming up the steps, Sarah unfolded herself from the green winged chair and tiptoed quietly to the door. When out trapping her instinct was sharp, and she knew when trappers were near. Learning from her father and the four trappers where to hide and how to mask her own scent, helped her hide easily from them, but none of the trappers could hide from her. Not having lost her sense of sniffing out the peculiar smells people gave off, she stood with her nose pressed against the door, and knew straight away it was Foley standing there.

"Why are you here Sheriff Andrews?" Sarah asked opening the door and wondering what possible reason he had for being on her porch.

With his heart beginning to pound, Foley had to say what he wanted to say quickly before she slammed the door shut on him. Removing his hat, he crossed the porch and stood in front of her.

"I haven't come here to cause you any trouble Sarah, I came to say I'm sorry for what I said about Christian, and for shutting the door on you and Lizzy out at the farm." He paused for a moment to gather his thoughts. "I swear I didn't know Lizzy was with you, it was never my intention to hurt her, or you, you must believe that, but when you said I never had a child of my own, that hurt me, and I was angry because you knew what Maria had been doing and didn't feel I had a right to know." Looking into Sarah's eyes, he could see how they appeared sad when she looked into his.

"Why did you let me go on believing Maria was having my child? We are... were friends Sarah, and friends don't keep secrets from each other." Feeling a lump rising in his throat at seeing the pain in Sarah's eyes, he didn't want to hurt her by speaking angrily so lowered his voice. "Why couldn't you have trusted me to tell me?" he asked waiting for her answer. "Have you ever trusted me?" he said, sounding annoyed when she didn't reply.

Not wanting him to become angry, Sarah finally replied. "I wanted to tell you Foley, but I didn't know how to go about it without hurting you, I begged Maria to tell you herself but she refused, and when she said you wouldn't believe me if I told you, I knew that would be the case, I knew our friendship was at stake, but I thought, if I kept it to myself, I wouldn't hurt anyone... least of all you." Sarah drew back a sob that threatened to break. "I am truly sorry," she ended.

Foley kept silent while trying to absorb what Sarah was saying. What she was telling him made sense. Had she told him earlier, he may not have believed her and their friendship would have been destroyed anyway. Foley turned his thoughts to what Brady said in the barn, about him not having anything to lose.

"Everyone hated winter, but not me, I liked it, because it meant you were coming off that mountain of yours and I would get to see you... every time we met at the ponds I prayed this winter would be the one where you would say yes to my proposal." He looked away then back again. "I have always loved you Sarah, you must know it wasn't a game we were playing, for me, it was real." Thinking he had nothing to lose by going on, he went on. "Brady had this crazy notion that I should come here and ask you to marry me like I used to, but then why would I ask you when all you would do is push me away?" He stopped to swallow the lump in his throat. "Visit Ellen any time you like, I won't be around to bother you." Afraid of Sarah's rejection to come straight out and ask her to marry him, he stopped himself saying more.

Confused with him saying he wouldn't be around, Sarah thought perhaps he meant he would stay in town when she visited. "Where will you be?" she asked to confirm what she thought. Foley hadn't given much thought to saying he wouldn't be around before he said it.

Putting his hat on, he answered, "I don't know, I may head over to Moreton, or go further, there are a lot of places out there still waiting to be discovered." Tipping his hat, he bid Sarah goodbye, then retraced his steps back across the porch.

Having lost her father, whom she adored to Crawley and a game of cards, then losing Frank, her first love to wolves, and Christian whom she had been married to for four wonderful years to an outlaw, and with Thomas gone to Philadelphia, Sarah regretted keeping Maria's secret. Foley was her dearest friend, and over the last few days she thought long and hard about her relationship with him, and thought if she were to take another husband, he would be the only man she would ever consider for that role. Realizing she was losing everyone she loved, and how lonely she was, she couldn't bear to lose him too.

"Yes, Foley!" she said, her voice barely audible. But with his foot hovering above the top step, it was loud enough for Foley to hear, and pulling his foot back, he turned to face her. Standing in the doorway watching him standing where he was, Sarah thought perhaps he didn't understand what she was saying.

"If you were to ask me Foley, my answer would be yes!" she repeated clearly.

After taking a moment to digest what Sarah was saying, Foley crossed the porch in a few quick strides and brought himself to a stop in front of her. Removing his hat again, he clenched it in both hands as he looked down at her, and for a soul-searching moment, gazed into her eyes.

Unsure of what he was about to do when he came striding toward her, Sarah stepped back. Being a tall man with broad shoulders, Foley filled her doorway. With his heart threatened to burst from his chest, Foley thought of what Brady said to him.

"Marry me Sarah!" he asked softly, hoping he wouldn't be rejected.

Sarah's eyes brimmed with tears. Tilting her head to look into his, she placed both hands gently on his chest, and having said yes twice already, with a whisper, repeated it twice more.

"Yes Foley, yes!"

Throwing his hat aside, he reached out, and slipping both hands around Sarah's waist, bent his head close to hers. As his arms encircled her, he lifted her against him, causing her feet to almost come off the floor. He waited a long time for his first kiss with Sarah and when his mouth covered hers, he wasn't disappointed. Their kiss was passionate, and they held it for the longest time. After easing her down gently, he lifted her back up to him.

"Marry me," he asked again to be sure of her answer. Standing on her toes, Sarah slid her hands over his shoulders and clasped them behind his head.

"Yes," she repeated. Their next kiss was gentle, more loving. When a tear ran down Sarah's cheek, Foley wiped it away with his finger.

Sarah hadn't understood the feelings she had for Foley. When he started proposing to her out at the ponds, they had simply become friends, so she had, as he explained, thought it was a game they were playing. Even if she had known Foley loved her more than just as a friend, she couldn't help falling in love with Christian. Their love was like it was meant to be. When Christian told her of Brother Abraham's prediction, neither could have known their love would not be forever. When Foley started treating her badly at Brady and Ellen's wedding and at the farm, she hadn't thought he could be in love with her, but when he said he had always loved her, it confirmed he had never stopped loving her.

"We need to talk Sarah," he said, moving them away from the doorway.

"Close the door Foley," she said up to him.

Keeping Sarah in his arms, he glanced over his shoulder, and stretching his leg back, kicked the door closed behind him. Looking up at him, Sarah lowered her arms down his chest. "Would you like some coffee? I have enough in the pot for two." Having welcomed him out on the prairie by saying she had enough coffee for both of them, and even though he wanted Sarah more than he wanted coffee, as yet he wasn't sure if he was able to have his way with her, so while gazing lovingly at her, he gave considerable thought to his answer before answering, "yeah, coffee would be welcome."

Taking him by his hand, Sarah led him to the fire where he waited while she went to the kitchen. When she came back carrying two mugs, he noticed her bare feet and a hint of a smile crossed his face.

Sitting side by side on the couch in front of a blazing fire with their mugs of steaming coffee, they talked long into the night. They sorted out what Sarah had known about Maria and how she found out. Sitting forward with his arms resting on top of his legs, Foley kept his head bowed as he listened to Sarah recount what she knew. When Sarah mentioned it was Rankins farm where she caught Maria out, Foley had the truth about Bert Rankin and his wife's death. Foley remembered seeing Rankin at Maria's burial and how he seemed the most upset person there, but hadn't been wise to his deceit at the time. Rankin left the burial and went home and shot his wife then himself, and all because of Maria.

Foley was no longer angry at Sarah for knowing about Maria. He was sorry she carried the burden with her for so long, and said once more how sorry he was for the way he treated her and for scaring both her and Lizzy when he shut Lizzy in the farmhouse. Sarah told him Lizzy was fine and she accepted his apology. Foley would never take liberties with Sarah, but now she agreed to marry him, he thought it ok to kiss her without her permission. Reaching out suddenly, he pushed his fingers into Sarah's hair, and pulling her toward him, kissed her longingly, leaving her no choice but to hold his kiss until he let her go. "That's for not telling me sooner," he said as they looked into each other's eyes.

Sarah blushed, Foley's kiss left her feeling breathless. Aware he always took things seriously, she knew he would never touch her without her say so, but she thought it ok if he wanted to kiss her, now they were spoken for. When Sarah didn't slap him for his action, Foley breathed a sigh of relief then sat back. They still needed to discuss their wedding.

"I will make arrangements with Preacher Barnes for us to be married right away, but I suppose we should let Thomas know, do you think he will accept me Sarah?" Foley asked sounding concerned. Although he wouldn't have to worry too much about being a father to Thomas now that he had moved to Philadelphia,

Thomas had loved his stepfather Christian, and Foley stood witness to him suffering the loss of the only father he knew.

"Thomas has always accepted you Foley," Sarah answered truthfully. Accepting Sarah's answer to be true, both Sarah and Foley sat in silence while contemplating their own thoughts.

Sarah had only set foot in the church once since cutting up a wolf inside, and that was when Brady wed Ellen. "I don't want to get married in the church," she said breaking their silence.

"Where do you want to be married?" Foley asked thinking she might like to be married on the riverbank like she had with Christian.

"Here in the lodge would do, wouldn't it? I don't want a huge fuss, just a few of our close friends."

Foley nodded in agreement. "Yes, here would be perfect, I will talk to Barnes, he can come here." Then standing up to go, he took Sarah's empty mug from her and sat it on the table next to his, then reaching for her hands, pulled her off the couch and into his arms.

"I love you Sarah," he said holding her in a warm embrace. Sarah hadn't been with anyone since losing Christian, and her body ached to be loved. Resting her head against Foley's chest, she decided she wouldn't mind if he wanted to stay.

"Do you want to stay?" she enquired softly.

Wanting to spend every night with her, Foley closed his eyes for a moment before answering just as softly. "Yes Sarah, very much so… but I won't, not until we are married." Sarah looked up at him. "I've been lonely Foley, if you want to stay, I will allow it."

Kissing Sarah passionately, Foley held their kiss for a moment, then let her go. If Sarah had asked him to sleep with her when they met out on the prairie, he would not have hesitated to do so, but now he wanted to do everything the right way. Sarah had been with Frank and had his child out of wedlock, then fell pregnant to Christian before they married, causing the whole town to talk about her loose ways with the men she got involved with, and because he listened to the gossip, Foley would not give the town anything more to talk about. As far as he was concerned, what was between him and Sarah would remain between him and Sarah until such time as he saw fit to tell everyone they were married. He waited a long time to be with Sarah and he decided he could wait a little longer until they were legally wed for him to bed her. Bending his head again, he kissed her softly. Sarah had never kissed Foley before tonight and was surprised at how nice his kissing her made her feel.

"Am I dreaming Sarah?" Foley asked when they stopped.

"If you are, then I must be dreaming too," Sarah answered tilting her head up to his and letting him kiss her goodnight.

After seeing him out, Sarah stood on the porch with her arms folded around her against the chill of the night and watched him get on his horse. Looking up at her standing in the shadows, Foley tipped his hat before riding to the end of the street and turning the corner in front of the Ferguson House. Sarah listened to the echo of his horses' hooves pounding on the road until she couldn't hear them anymore, then going back inside to the fire, she stirred the coals and placed several logs of wood on it to keep the lodge warm. After placing the grill in front to stop wood or ash falling on the floor, she checked in on Lizzy, and finding her fast asleep, bent down and kissed her on her cheek, then retired to her own room.

While undressing and getting into bed, Sarah's thoughts turned to Foley and what just happened between them. Deep inside she knew she loved him, perhaps she always had, and it made her happy to know he loved her. She once loved Christian with a passion unlike any she had ever known before, and would not take the love they felt for each other for granted. She would never forget Christian, or Frank, but now she had to move on. Now she had to let Foley know how much she loved him.

Sarah couldn't wait for Foley to come visiting so he could tell her when they were getting married. Giving in to thoughts about his kissing her, and how his kisses made her body warm all over, she remembered when he proposed to her out on the prairie, and how there wasn't any reason for them to kiss, after all, she always turned his proposals down. Now all she could think about were those kisses they exchanged tonight, after she accepted his proposal, before he had even asked her. Sarah smiled, then turning on her side and pulling the blankets over her head, went to sleep thinking about Foley in a sensual way.

After Foley left Sarah, he rode back to the farm feeling happier than he had ever felt before. A while back he thought he could never be happier when told he was going to be a father, but now, marrying Sarah was what he had always wanted, and he thought how he had gone to the lodge to ask her to marry him because Brady said he had nothing to lose, but fearing she would turn him down like she always had, he had been too afraid to ask her. Adding he was leaving town was a thought he was just toying with, but he didn't care if that was why Sarah stopped him going. He didn't need her rejection, and hadn't expected she would accept his proposal before he had even asked her. Overjoyed at Sarah saying yes, he smiled broadly, but he hadn't bought her a ring, so as his horse galloped along, he decided he would go to Henry's Emporium first thing in the morning and buy one for her. Now though, all he wanted was to get back to the farm as quickly as possible to let Brady know Sarah had accepted him. Riding along, his mind was on how soft Sarah's mouth felt when he kissed her, and how her body felt warm when he held her in his arms. When he arrived back at the ranch, he was in high spirits.

Brady and Ellen were sound asleep when Foley's horse came galloping along the road in front of the farmhouse. Foley didn't waste time unsaddling his horse before charging into the house where he banged on Brady and Ellen's door to give them the good news and startled Charlotte and Matthew awake, and setting them both off to cry loudly. Waking when he heard Foley's loud banging, Brady dived out of bed, and reaching for his trousers, pulled them on before grabbing his gun and yanking the door open. "Goddamn it, Foley! are you drunk?" he snapped when seeing Foley at his door. "You woke the goddamn babies! now we won't get them back to sleep!" he said putting his gun back in its holster as Foley came right into the room. Waking sleepily, Ellen's eyes went wide when she saw him come in, and pulling the covers over herself quickly, hoped he hadn't seen her nakedness.

Ignoring Brady's outburst and Ellen's bashfulness, Foley went to one of the cribs, and lifting out a baby, held it in his arms and began rocking it.

"Shush," he said to the crying baby. "Which one have I got Brady?" he asked with a silly grin on his face.

Brady had never seen Foley attempt to pick either one of the twins up. With his eyes wide, he made to take the baby from Foley, only Foley turned away so he couldn't take it. "It's Charlotte! don't you dare drop her Foley, or so god help me I'll..." Brady stated angrily. "Don't worry, I won't drop her," Foley cut in looking down at Charlotte as he rocked her. Feeling warm and secure in his arms, Charlotte stopped crying and closed her eyes.

"She said yes," Foley said suddenly. When he saw Brady's confused look, a smile spread across his face.

"What? Why?... Who said yes?" Brady said confused with what Foley said.

"Sarah, she said yes, she's going to marry me." Foley laughed at Brady's open mouth. Having gone to sleep in his arms, Charlotte was put back in her cradle and tucked in. Matthew had a full belly and went straight back to sleep. When Foley went to the kitchen, Brady went along too. His mouth still hurt where Foley hit him but that no longer mattered, he wanted details. "You asked her?" he asked frowning.

"Not at first," Foley answered frowning at Brady's look of confusion. "She said yes before I asked her, then she said if I were to ask her, she would say yes, so I asked her and she said yes, then I asked her again and, well, she said yes again, then... I think I may have asked her one more time, and she may have said yes... one more time."

Hearing yes said so many times, Brady was confused, but figuring what it meant that Foley was telling him, he threw his arms over Foley's shoulders and hugged him. Foley hugged him back and apologized for hitting him, and Brady accepted his apology by saying don't do it again, they then hugged each other some more and laughing, patted each other on the back.

Upon hearing what Foley told Brady, and now decently covered in a lace robe, Ellen came out of the bedroom, and without saying a word, rummaged around in a cupboard until she found a bottle of wine and handed the bottle to Brady. While Brady pulled the cork, Foley grabbed three glasses and Brady poured each of them a drink.

"To Foley and Sarah," Ellen said holding up her glass.

When Ellen made the toast, she could not have been more pleased. Her plan to have Sarah and Foley marry had come to fruition.

Chapter Thirteen

*P*reacher Barnes had only just got out of bed when Foley pounded on his door and tried telling Foley it would take him two weeks to organize for him to marry Sarah. But Foley wanted to marry Sarah now, not in two weeks. Standing over Preacher Barnes he got it down to three days.

It was Wednesday, he and Sarah would be married on Saturday at four o'clock. Foley swore Preacher Barnes into keeping quiet, saying if he told anyone, he would find out and would lock him up for a week with nothing to eat but bread and water for breaking an oath. Preacher Barnes was a man of the cloth and wasn't concerned by Foley's threat, but said he wouldn't breathe a word. After inviting Ham and Patrice to come along with Martha and Dave Henderson, Foley swore them to secrecy too when he told them he and Sarah didn't want the town talking about them, and that they would let the town know they were married in their own good time. When both Sarah and Foley lost their partners, the two couples had been confused by what was happening between them, and were happy now they had sorted out their differences and were getting married, but that didn't stop them worrying Foley's plan not to say anything might backfire. Still, no-one breathed a word.

At the Telegraph Office, even though the operator knew the story behind Sarah and Foley as well as any other town folk, when Foley swore him to secrecy, he said the telegram he was about to send was private and if he were to spread the contents around, he would lose his job. Foley informed him he would not only lose his job but his life, and the man nodded vigorously to show he understood his meaning. Satisfied the news would not be leaked, the telegraph operator then informed Foley it would take longer than a week for him to get a reply. Not happy with this information, but knowing Thomas would understand his meaning and to save on cost, Foley sent him a simple message.

'Ma said yes - Stop

Married Saturday- Stop

Foley - Stop'

When the telegram arrived, Thomas was sitting at a table in his hotels restaurant with Billy and Gabrielle, a young woman he met in his writing class. Thomas read the message to himself first, just in case it was bad news concerning him or Billy. Sitting opposite Thomas, Billy watched Thomas's face change from an expression of concern to one of surprise. Passing the telegram to Billy, Thomas watched Billy read the message, then grinning at each other they jumped up, and shouting with glee, hugged each other excitedly while ignoring discerning looks from other diners. Thomas always thought since Christian died Foley should marry his Ma.

"Heavens," he said to Billy. "He asked her often enough." Besides, he said, when his Ma and Lizzy saw him off to college, Foley shook hands with him to wish him luck, then before disappearing straight back to the Sheriff's Office, he gave his Ma a fleeting look that couldn't be mistaken for anything other than love. But Foley was married to Maria at the time and was expecting his first child, and Thomas said it hadn't made sense that Foley still had feelings for his Ma. After receiving his Ma's first ever hand-written letter, he was saddened to learn Foley had lost Maria and his baby, but Foley's telegram carried the best news ever, and so knowing by the time Foley received his reply he and his Ma would be married, Thomas didn't spare the expensive when he replied.

'Happy to have you as family – Stop

Congratulations Foley and Ma - Stop

Thomas - Stop'

After speaking with Preacher Barnes and inviting Sarah's friends to their wedding, Foley rushed off to Henry's Emporium where he was shown in private, an assortment of rings. With Sarah left to invite Doc Harris and Gerda, it was hoped Doc would agree to escort Sarah to the fireplace in her formal dining room where the ceremony would take place. After choosing a single diamond set on a gold band, two wedding bands were put aside for Foley to collect later. It was midday by the time he organized everything for his part of the wedding.

After swearing Henry to secrecy and with the ring in his pocket, Foley smiled to himself as he made his way to the lodge. Walking slowly onto the porch, and although he could see the front door standing open as if Sarah was expecting him, he knocked, but when there was no reply, he stepped inside.

He was in the living area when he heard an almighty crash then a loud splash followed by loud cursing coming from somewhere in the house. Drawing his gun, he held it ready as he walked gingerly from room to room. Coming to the washroom, he saw Sarah with her back to the door, and drenched from head to foot with a metal tub tipped on its side next to her. Water covered the floor and what looked like bedsheets lay sodden and tangled around her feet. Standing with her arms outstretched, Sarah let water drip from her forehead and run down her arms. Holstering his gun, and looking serious, Foley could see she wasn't hurt, just soaking wet.

"What happened here Sarah?" he asked leaning against the doorpost and folding his arms. When Sarah turned to face him, he couldn't help noticing how her shirt made her visible through the wet material. Unfolding his arms, and trying not to stare, he hurried over to the tub, and bending down, pushed it upright, then with Sarah's help, lifted the soggy bedsheets back into it.

"As you can see, I was doing the washing and dropped the sheet, water went all over me!" Water was still dripping off Sarah's hair. After straightened up, they stood facing each other.

"You want a hand to get these on the line?" Foley asked, focusing on Sarah's face.

Sarah could tell she was visible through her shirt and could see Foley looking, but there was nothing she could do about it, she had to get the sheets outside to dry.

"That would be good, thank you, but we have to wring the water out of them first."

Taking hold of an end of the sheets each, they twisted them until no more water ran out, then stooping down, Foley picked up the heavy tub and followed Sarah outside where he helped her hang them on the line. When the last one was almost hung, she turned to him and smiled. He was so much taller than her, and his shoulders and arms seemed huge against hers. When he stretched up to hang the sheet, his muscles flexed making his arms look solid.

"Did you speak to Barnes?" she asked as a feeling of warmth enveloped her.

"Yeah, I did, he said he can marry us on Saturday, at four o'clock."

Sarah stopped smiling. Saturday was only two days away, she would have a lot to do. "This Saturday?" she asked quizzically. When the smile left Sarah's face it bothered Foley that she might change her mind about him before he had a chance to marry her.

"Yes, is that a problem?" he queried.

"No... no that's fine," she answered, hesitating slightly when she saw him trying his best not to look at her chest.

"I can't help being wet Foley, just look at them if you want, it wouldn't be the first time you've seen them." Sarah didn't think he was the kind of man to blush at a little thing like looking at a woman's breasts, and almost laughed at the look that crossed his face when she said he could look at her.

Foley though did feel embarrassed. Although he had seen them once before, while he was hiding in a stand of trees across from the ponds where she was bathing, he was a good distance away from her when he saw them. Trying to ignore what she said, he reached into his pocket, and feeling around until he found the ring, held it up for Sarah to see.

"I got you this Sarah, it is rather plain, but I thought you might like to wear it." As the sun danced off the diamond, Sarah studied it, then holding up her left hand, let Foley slip the ring on her finger.

"It's beautiful," she said smiling. Then without warning, she stood on tiptoe and flung her arms around his neck. Pushing her fingers into his hair, she brought her face up to meet his and kissed him passionately.

For a moment Foley was taken by surprise, then quickly wrapping his arms about her waist, lifted her off her feet and held her against him. When Sarah's breasts pressed against his, a feeling of arousal rushed through him as their coolness consumed him. Letting her go, Sarah giggled like a young girl at seeing his shirt wet down the front. Foley looked down then too, and laughed. After telling him to sit at a table in the sun to let his shirt dry, Sarah went inside and brought them coffee. While enjoying sitting together, they discussed the rest of the details for their wedding.

It was to be a small wedding. Doc Harris agreed to give Sarah away, and while Ellen would attend Sarah, Brady was to be Foley's best man. Lewis and Esther Morley were invited as was Jonathon and Tilly O'Rourke. Sarah asked Fess from the Trading Post if he wouldn't mind attending and would he bring his fiddle, after all, he played at Brady and Ellen's wedding and proved very entertaining. Sarah made him swear he wouldn't say anything to anyone. Aware it would take Thomas far too long to travel across the country to attend, Sarah felt saddened he wouldn't be with them to celebrate their day.

The night before the wedding, Brady brought Ellen and the twins to the lodge to stay with Sarah. Lizzy was thrilled to have the twins stay overnight so she could play with them. At dinner, while Sarah and Ellen sat with a baby each on their laps feeding them, Ellen smiled over at Sarah holding Matthew. "Will you and Foley have babies?" she asked suddenly.

Sarah stopped feeding Matthew and became lost in her thoughts. It wasn't the first time she thought about her and Foley. The day Foley helped her hang her bedsheets on the line, they sat in the sun talking comfortably with each other like they used to when they met out on the prairie. After putting Lizzy to bed that night, she lay awake in her own bed going over what it would be like when she and Foley were finally husband and wife. 'Would he be like Frank, or Christian when he made love to her?' she had wondered. She wondered too what Foley would look like naked, and tried her best to picture him without his shirt and trousers. Her face burnt red when thinking of him that way, making her giggle so loud she had to bury her head under the covers so she wouldn't wake Lizzy. Sarah had never seen Foley without his shirt, and right then, couldn't wait to see him without being clothed at all.

Sarah had given up thinking about having more children, but she wasn't too old to have another baby, and with Foley suffering a terrible loss at not becoming a father when Maria deceived him, he deserved a child of his own, and Sarah hoped she would give him one, or perhaps two. Sitting there at the dinner table, she wondered again what it would be like to have sex with him. With her face becoming flushed at the very thought of them lying naked together, she smiled coyly at Ellen. "I hope we will," she managed to say.

After dinner, when the children were put to bed, the two women had fun selecting their dresses they would wear for the wedding from Sarah's many dresses she inherited from her mother Elizabeth. Foley and Brady were to get dressed out at the farm. The two men would come to town in Brady's buckboard so Ellen and the twins could be taken home after the wedding was over.

It rained overnight and along with Cedar Creek, the whole county was waterlogged. Hitching up their dresses to avoid the mud, Patrice, Martha and Gerda went to the lodge Saturday morning to help Sarah and Ellen prepare the wedding feast and decorate the dining hall where the nuptials and dinner would be held, then returned home to get dressed in evening clothes ready for the celebration.

Everything was ready. Sarah, Ellen and Lizzy dressed upstairs in Sarah's room. The lace bodice of the long cream dress Sarah chose showed off her curves. The lace sleeves she wore off her shoulders. Falling gently from her hips in a mass of fine lace and tule, the skirt spread out in a small train at the back. Curls Ellen helped Sarah do, held to one side by a diamond encrusted comb, sat delicately over one shoulder. Ellen's dress of soft yellow silk with its shirred bodice and small puff sleeves that she refused to wear off her shoulders, suited Ellen's pale complexion. Sarah gave up tugging the sleeves down when Ellen kept pulling them back up. To allow the dress to sit smoothly against her bare skin however, she refused to let Ellen wear underwear. Ellen was beside herself when explaining she would feel naked, and that everyone would be able to tell. But when Sarah said, 'when Brady takes one look at his wife, he would never look at her the same innocent way again,' Ellen's face burnt bright red, which sent both women into hysterical giggling. Lizzy's yellow dress with its mass of petticoats under it was perfect, teamed with white stockings and little white boots.

It was fast approaching four o'clock when Preacher Barnes stood in the dining hall waiting patiently for the proceedings to begin. With all the guests gathered, Sarah stayed upstairs in her room with Ellen and Lizzy awaiting the arrival of Foley and Brady. Out at the farm, Foley and Brady took their time hitching a horse to Brady's buckboard so as not to get their fancy wedding apparel they so carefully dressed in soiled.

Racing the buckboard along the rain-soaked road toward town, one of the back wheels hit a hole in the middle of the road causing the wagon to suddenly pitch to one side. Having become spooked, the horse dragged the careening wagon across the road and back again. Pulling on the reins hard, Brady tried bringing the wagon under control, but the already loose wheel bouncing on the edge of the roadway came adrift, and rolling past the wagon, disappeared over the side.

Now lopsided, the wagons axle dug into the mud-soaked gravel verge, causing the wagon to tip sideways and for Foley and Brady to be flung into a waterlogged ditch beside the road before it toppled into the ditch where it became bogged down in thick mud further along. The horse tried to keep going, but the more it struggled, the more trouble it found itself in. When Foley and Brady gathered themselves, they were covered in mud but relieved to find they were unhurt. Shaking mud off his boots, and while wiping his hands over his clothes trying to get them clean, Foley cursed loudly and excessively. He didn't want to keep Sarah waiting, not now, not when he had waited so long to marry her.

Meanwhile back at the lodge, Sarah sat by her window looking out at the distant mountains. Foley hadn't arrived at four o'clock, and when the time approached five and he still hadn't arrived, she was of the belief he had changed his mind about marrying her and made the remark to Ellen and Doc, saying maybe he planned the whole thing as an elaborate scheme to get back at her for knowing about Maria and saying she would never forgive him if he made her go through all of this then not make her his wife. Ellen was appalled by what she said, and tried to convince her Brady would never let her take part in something so cruel. Doc agreed with Ellen, saying Foley was not the type of man to be that cruel. When he offered to send someone out to look for the men, Sarah told him to wait. Looking sadly at the ring on her finger, she thought surely Foley would not have given her the elegant ring if he didn't intend marrying her. Slipping the ring off, she sat it on her dresser, and waited.

It was five o'clock by the time Foley and Brady got the buckboard back on the road and managed to get the wheel back on. After spending precious time searching along the road for the pin that held the wheel in place, Brady located it, and while Foley put his back against the wagon and lifted it, Brady shoved the wheel back on. Quickly bashing the pin with a rock, they hoped it would stay in place until they got to town. The sun was setting when the mud-caked horse and buckboard went bouncing around the corner into the street passing by the Ferguson House in a rush. People wandering about wondered what was going on when they saw Foley and Brady dressed up but filthy dirty and heading to the lodge. Assuming Sarah must be having one of her dinner parties, they shrugged their shoulders then went back to minding their own business.

Jumping out of the buckboard, both men ran up the steps to the porch, and racing inside, met Doc coming down the stairs from Sarah's room.

Foley could see Doc wasn't impressed with their state of dress and thought because he was late arriving, Sarah had changed her mind about marrying him after all. "We lost a wheel and went into a ditch!" he announced as he stood at the bottom of the stairs. "Is Sarah alright Doc? Go tell her what happened! let her know I'm here!" he begged sounding urgent.

"She knows you're here Foley, she got a little upset when you hadn't turned up on time, give her a few minutes to compose herself while you get cleaned up, then go to the dining room… Sarah will be along shortly," Doc replied. Seeing a faint smile cross Doc's face, Foley felt certain everything was alright. With a sigh of relief, he dragged Brady behind him and headed to the washroom to freshen up.

It had been an agonizing wait for Sarah before Foley arrived. When Doc knocked on her door and told her the buckboard lost a wheel and that it had taken the two men a long time to fix, she accepted accidents happen, and was grateful neither man was hurt. She failed though at wiping her tears away so she didn't look like she had been crying. Her eyes were still red rimmed when she hooked her arm in Doc's and made her way downstairs.

A fire burning in the grate sent a warm glow throughout the dining hall. Candles inside tins with holes in them placed on shelving around the room had been lit, sending what appeared to be stars sparkling over the ceiling and walls. A stand of flowers from Martha's garden stood either side of Preacher Barnes.

Entering the dining room first, Ellen saw Brady standing beside Foley in front of the ornate fireplace. Stepping forward so he could see Ellen looking stunning in her soft yellow dress, the sleeves of which were now sitting off her shoulders, Brady couldn't take his eyes off his wife. As she walked toward him, the dress brushed against her body, and when she stopped opposite, he smiled, sending Ellen's face blushing pink. Figuring she wasn't wearing anything under her dress, he raised his eyebrows and let his eyes wander over her. Ellen raised her eyebrows too, and smiling back, confirmed what Brady was thinking.

With her dress swishing from all the petticoats she wore under it and carrying a small basket filled with flower petals, Lizzy came through the door next, and taking dainty steps, dropped the petals on the floor making everyone smile. As she approached Foley, she crinkled her eyes in a smile, and looking up at him, stopped next to Ellen.

When Sarah entered, Foley's heart leapt. Now he knew how Christian felt when he married her. Sarah looked beautiful then, she looked stunning now. Moving gracefully toward him on Doc's arm, her delicate lace dress glistened in the light from the candles, her hair looked as soft as silk. The single white flower she carried was a delicate bloom from Martha's garden.

Dressed in dark trousers now stained with mud, Foley wore a once white shirt and a black mud-spattered jacket he tried to clean. At least the cravat tied at the collar under his neatly trimmed beard had been spared. Sarah was pleased he hadn't trimmed his long hair, and liked the way strands with its smattering of grey fell over his forehead. He was a handsome man, even with his scar, and Sarah felt her heart leap when she saw him waiting for her. As Foley and Sarah faced each other, Foley could see Sarah had been crying and leant forward.

"I'm sorry Sarah, the wagon…" he started to say. Putting her finger to his lips, Sarah stopped him speaking. Taking her hand in his, they turned to face Preacher Barnes and said their vows. While promising to love one and other, Foley thought he didn't need to make that promise because he had always loved Sarah, and he would keep on loving her for as long as he lived. When Preacher Barnes announced they were husband and wife, Foley didn't wait to be told to kiss the bride, he swept Sarah into his arms and they kissed each other passionately.

Bottles of wine were opened and everyone drank a toast to Sarah and Foley. Almost five years old now, and feeling very grown up, Lizzy drank lemonade Sarah made from a wine glass. With the ceremony over, Preacher Barnes gathered his things and made to leave.

"Where are you going?" Sarah asked walking towards him.

Preacher Barnes took his hand off the doorknob and looked around. "My job is over, Misses Andrews, I should go and leave you to celebrate," he answered sounding sad. Twice now Sarah had married, and twice she had not married in his church. He had not liked telling her she could not come to church, and felt it not very godly to have denied her the opportunity to worship.

"Please stay, I would like you to celebrate with us," Sarah said quietly. Surprised at her invitation, Preacher Barnes gathered himself.

"I would like that very much, Sarah, thank you." Taking his hand in hers, Sarah led him back to the table.

"Would you like some wine?" she asked, holding up a glass.

"I don't mind if I do," he said taking the glass Sarah offered and taking a drink. When he raised his eyebrows at the sweet taste and smacked his lips together, Sarah and he laughed.

Everyone enjoyed the banquet that followed the ceremony. When Foley and Brady described in comical form how the buckboard went off the road and how it sent them flying through the air to land in the ditch, and how they struggled to get the wagon back on the road and the wheel back on, everyone joined in with laughter. When their talk quietened, Fess, seated between Morley and Preacher Barnes, got up and played his fiddle. With a serious look crossing his face, Foley got to his feet and held out his hand to Sarah.

"Dance with me, Misses Andrews," he requested softly. Waiting for her to take his hand, he remembered the night at Brady and Ellen's wedding where he caused Sarah anguish with his drunken foolishness and for a moment felt saddened. Sarah too remembered where she danced with him only to have him say something to offend her about Christian, causing her to slap him. Foley had since apologized for the hurt he caused. They had passed that point in time, so putting her hand in his, she let him lead her away from the table.

With neither paying any attention to those around them when they got up and joined in, they held each other in a warm embrace, and began to move from side to side then back and forth. When Fess stopped playing, everyone gave Sarah and Foley a round of applause while watching them bring the celebration to a close with a loving kiss. Standing arm in arm on the porch, Foley and Sarah bid goodnight to their guests.

Leaving their damaged buckboard behind, Brady and Ellen put their twins in Sarah's buckboard and headed off. Feeling grateful to Sarah for letting Brady take her buckboard and relieved at knowing they and their babies would get home safely, Foley relaxed.

When everyone was gone, Foley lifted Lizzy off the couch where she had fallen asleep, and after carrying her to her room, waited in Sarah's room while Sarah put her to bed.

Facing each other in Sarah's room, neither knew what they should do next. Foley dreamt many times of the moment he would make love to Sarah, but now he didn't want to seem over-zealous. He didn't want to scare her by rushing her, and then there was Sarah watching him watching her. Was he going to undress her?

Or should she undress him? Sarah didn't want to act like she was over sexed, but she was his wife now and wanted him to make love to her.

It was Sarah making the first move that broke their tension by reaching up and untying the cravat around Foley's neck, then letting her unbutton his shirt, he came alive and helped push it over his shoulders and remove it. The fact both Frank and Christian were hair free surprised Sarah pleasantly to see hair on Foley's chest. Reaching out, she moved her fingers gently over his soft down. When her fingers slid over his nipples, excitement swelled in both of them.

Moving her hands over his arms and back over his chest caused Foley's muscles to flex involuntarily. Becoming aroused at her continual touching him, Foley loosened his trousers to expose a mat of hair at the opening. Seeing him almost naked and knowing what was to come caused Sarah's arousal to rise further, but stepping away, she turned her back on him.

"Please, Foley, help me with my dress," she whispered while looking over her shoulder. As Foley untied the ties holding her dress in place, she pulled her arms free of the sleeves, and to keep her bust covered, held it against her. With her back exposed to her buttocks, Foley rested his hand against her warm skin and felt the impact of his touch course through him. Sliding his fingers downwards, he moved to stand in close, and placing his hands inside Sarah's dress, brought them around her waist to rest against her stomach where he could feel her warmth emanating from her. Bringing her back to lean against him, he let her warmth engulf him.

Feeling desire coursing through her and still holding her dress in front of her, Sarah turned to face him, and slipping her dress to her waist, let it fall to the floor. Watching it fall, then bringing his eyes back over her, Foley became aroused at seeing her wearing nothing but thigh high white stockings and high heeled lace up boots. Stepping over her dress lying bunched at her feet, Sarah stood facing him so he could take in all of her.

With both eager to consummate their marriage, Foley removed his boots quickly and dropped them at his feet, all the while keeping his eyes on Sarah and she him. Taking hold of his trousers and working fast, he pushed them down his legs, and after stepping out of them, kicked them aside, then straightening up, yielded to Sarah. Foley's muscles rippled when he moved, and he was ready to take her, but still he waited while she moved to her bed.

Sarah was pleased at the sight standing before her and for the fact she could still make a man feel aroused when looking at her. Pulling the covers back, she sat on the edge of the bed, and keeping her stockings and boots on, lifted her legs and lay back against the pillows. "You are my husband Foley, come, make love to me," she whispered seductively.

Foley didn't need telling twice. While his eyes took in the silkiness of Sarah's body, he climbed on the bed, and straddling her, leant forward. When his tongue brushed across her teeth, a soft moan of desire escaped him. Sliding one hand over her breasts and down her stomach, he brushed it through the soft hair between her legs before moving to the foot of the bed where he sat at her feet. Lifting her leg and working methodically, he unlaced a boot, then rolled her stocking down her leg and removed it. Watching her nipples harden as he worked, he removed the other the same way. Taking both Sarah's legs in his hands, he lifted them apart, and knowing where he wanted to be, brought himself back over her. As he lowered himself onto her, Sarah moved her legs further apart so he could take her easily.

When they began, their lovemaking was slow and deliberate, but it soon became unrestrained lustful wanting. Foley took Sarah knowing she was everything he had ever dreamt she would be. But before their wedding, he vowed to himself never to put her through what Maria had gone through. While consummating his and Sarah's marriage, he tried not to penetrate too deeply, but gave in when the moment got the better of him.

As the new day dawned, they made love again, but not wanting to risk Sarah getting pregnant, when Foley reached his peak, he pulled back.

When Foley suddenly stopped making love to her, Sarah frowned. This was different to when they consummated their marriage, but she let it go when he kissed her longingly and told her he loved her before falling asleep with their arms and legs tangled together. When the sun rose fully, they awoke again to caress each other with their kisses.

"There is something I need to say Sarah," Foley said holding her in his arms when they were done. Sarah knew when Foley had something to say he spoke seriously and came straight to the point. "I don't want us to have children, Thomas and Lizzy are enough for me."

Taken aback by him saying he didn't want children, Sarah frowned, and looking up at the red velvet canopy above her, thought of Maria deceiving him. Thinking he couldn't be serious, and that he would want her to have his children, she didn't take what he said seriously. There was no way she wouldn't get pregnant! not if he made love to her again the way he had the first time, besides, she already planned on giving him two children. But Sarah also had something she was holding back on.

Having told Frank and Christian she loved them at every opportunity, she naively believed she lost both men far too soon because of that reason. Determined not to lose Foley the same way, she thought it would be enough if every time they made love, she let her body show him how much she loved him, and so decided he didn't need to hear those words.

When Lizzy came bounding into Sarah's room and jumped on the bed, Foley was mortified. He was naked under the blankets and so was Sarah. Sarah laughed when Lizzy tried to push her way under the covers to get between her and Foley.

"Goddamn it Sarah! does she do this every morning?" he asked, holding the covers tight so Lizzy couldn't get in.

"Most mornings, if I'm still in bed," Sarah said laughing at seeing his bashfulness. Sarah didn't hide her body from Lizzy and couldn't understand why he felt uncomfortable, still, she made Lizzy leave the room while they got dressed.

"She is not to see me naked Sarah, she is a little girl, and I won't have her looking at a grown man," Foley said seriously while pulling on his trousers.

Sarah agreed what he was saying was right. She had never seen her Pa naked, or any of the trappers for that matter, they would never let her see them, and all except Joe seeing her at the ponds with Christian that one time, she was of the belief they had never seen her.

"Alright, I will talk to her so she will understand why she can't come to my bed anymore." Foley didn't want to come between Sarah and Lizzy, but felt it was the decent thing to do.

Chapter Fourteen

Three uneventful weeks passed where Sarah and Foley's lovemaking, was at most times satisfying, but Sarah felt Foley could do more to make her feel fulfilled, she was sure he wasn't being fulfilled either. The morning after their wedding Foley told her he didn't want to get her pregnant, but she still wanted him to make love to her the way a man should, by having them finish together.

After many years of burning over open fires, Sarah's old pot had finally worn out. When she filled it with water, it poured straight back out a small hole in the bottom, so she needed a new pot for making her stews. She didn't want a pot that was already too heavy to lift, so while standing behind the shelves in Henry's Emporium looking at heavy based cast iron pots and tin pots, she was moving a tin pot up and down feeling its weight when she heard a group of men come into the store laughing and talking animatedly. One of the men Sarah recognized was Pike, a loud-mouthed cowhand of Major Hardy's who had been at the shack the night Frank was whipped and who at the best of times had nothing nice to say about anyone. None of the men saw Sarah standing at the pots and pans.

"Goes without sayin' don't it?" Pike said sniggering. "We all knew it wouldn't be long before she put her legs in the air again." When Sarah heard his remark, her ears pricked.

"Put em up for Mason! stuck em up for Morgan! now it seems she's puttin' 'em up for Andrews! saw him comin' out of the lodge a couple of times real early! makes you wonder just who the next lucky son-of-a-bitch is goin' to be to fuck Misses Morgan!" Pike laughed uproariously at his own crude comments. The two men

175

laughing with him stopped laughing when they saw Sarah come out from behind the shelves carrying the pot.

"It won't be you, you son-of-a-bitch!" Sarah snarled as she swung her arm back, then bringing it forward with force, sent the pot smashing into the side of Pike's head. Pike didn't know what hit him, and his two friends eyes went wide as they knelt over him where he fell.

"You've killed him!" one of the men yelled up at Sarah. Seeing Pike wasn't moving, Sarah dropped the pot, and as it clattered on the floor, she stepped wide eyed toward the door.

"He's fucking dead!" the other man yelled. With Lizzy being with Tilly O'Rourke, Sarah didn't have to worry about her for the moment, so knowing if Pike was dead, she would be in serious trouble, she made her escape along the street to the livery.

After one of the men ran to the Sheriff's Office to get Foley, Foley raced across the street to the store where he found Pike sitting up holding his head and Henry leaning over him trying to see what damage Sarah had done. The lump on the side of Pike's head they could all see was enormous.

"Where did she go?" Foley asked the man that got him.

"I think she headed for the livery," he answered.

Leaving the men with Pike, Foley rushed out and made to run to the livery, but stopped when he saw Sarah come charging out of there on her horse. Running to where his horse was tethered outside his office, he jumped into the saddle and went after her.

Wanting to get as far away from town as possible to think what to do, Sarah kicked her horse hard and sent it racing over the bridge at full gallop. As the horse raced past the ponds it quickly lathered but didn't slow its stride.

Feeling the sharp spike of Foley's spurs, Foley's horse stretched its legs further and began catching up to Sarah. Reaching over when he came alongside her, he grabbed Sarah's horse by its bridle and slowed her down. But Sheriff Foley Andrews, her husband of just three weeks, was not going to take her off to jail just for killing a slimy river scum like Pike, not if she could help it. Taking her feet out of her stirrups, she looked across at Foley, then swinging her leg over the horses neck, she dropped out of her saddle and hit the ground running.

Stunned by her action, Foley jumped from his horse, and while stumbling to gain his footing, gave chase. As well as having to hold his gun as it bounced against his hip, he had to run with his holster strapped to his leg. Sarah though wasn't carrying a gun and it was much easier for her to get away.

Running as fast as she could, she rounded a bend in the river, and running along the muddy riverbank, headed for the ridges behind Major Hardy's land. Seeing this as his chance to head her off, Foley ran straight up and over a rise beside the river and came hurtling down the other side, and keeping up his momentum, tackled Sarah as she came running around the bend.

Soaring through the air, they both landed in an explosion of water in the river. Still not a very good swimmer, Sarah thought herself lucky this part of the river wasn't deep. Landing with Foley on top of her in just enough water to get soaking wet, she scrambled to get up as a wave came crashing back over them making them both gasp for breath. Desperately trying to get away, Sarah kicked and flailed wildly. Getting out of his grasp, and seeing another chance to escape, she scrambled toward the opposite bank. Foley scrambled to his feet, and gathering all his strength, tackled her around her legs and brought her to a stop in the dirt. Unable to shake him off, Sarah gave him several punches to his head as she kept trying to escape his clutches.

"Sarah! Stop!" he yelled trying to ward off her blows.

"I killed him!" she cried loudly. "I didn't mean to kill Pike, but I killed him!"

"You didn't kill him, all he has is a nasty bump on his head," Foley tried explaining, but Sarah's arms continued to flail. Grabbing her wrists, he pinned her arms above her head, and using his size and weight, kept his body over hers as they both slowed their breathing.

"I didn't kill him?" she questioned while her chest heaved as she looked up at him.

"No, you knocked him out that's all, why did you run from me?" Foley asked keeping himself on top of her.

"You are a lawman Foley, I thought if I killed Pike you would take me to jail," Sarah answered sounding concerned. Understanding her concern, Foley looked seriously into her eyes.

"If you had killed him Sarah, I would have had no choice but to lock you up... and keep the key close to my heart." Lowering his head suddenly, he kissed her, then running his hands down her arms, brought them to rest on the front of her. Wrapping her arms about his neck she returned his kiss. When they stopped, Foley let his gaze go over her. Sarah was as wet as he, but her breasts once again could be seen clearly through her shirt. Foley's face was close to Sarah's when he smiled.

"I wanted to do that every time I proposed to you out on the prairie," he informed her. Smiling up at him, Sarah lifted her head and gave him a quick peck.

"What stopped you?" she asked seductively. Instead of answering right away, Foley sat up, and Sarah sat up next to him.

"I was afraid you would knife me with that knife you always carried," he said looking at the river. "Besides, you never invited me to kiss you." Sarah knew he would never take something that wasn't offered him. Then before she could say anything, he changed the subject.

"Tell me, why did you hit Pike with that pot?" When Sarah leant back on her hands to let the sun dry her shirt, her nipples poked out visibly, but it didn't matter, Foley had seen them plenty of times now they were married.

"He was saying things about me, it wouldn't have mattered if I hadn't heard him, but I heard every word... he was damn lucky it was a tin pot and not one of those heavy iron ones!" she said sounding angry. While they both sat contemplating what Sarah said, their clothes dried.

"What did he say exactly?" Foley asked standing up and brushing dirt off the back of his trousers.

"It doesn't matter." Sarah didn't want to repeat what Pike said. "You know you wouldn't have caught me if I had been on Star," she added. She missed Star, he had been a good horse, fast and sure footed, no other horse could outrun him. They both looked at their horses grazing while waiting for their riders.

"I would have caught you sooner or later, besides, you would never leave town without Lizzy," Foley said matter-of-factly. Sarah had to agree, no matter what happened, she would never leave Lizzy. Foley went back to what happened with Pike.

"I want to know what Pike said, and I want it word for word!" Holding out his hands, Sarah took hold of them and let him pull her to her feet, then repeated Pike's exact words.

When Foley strode angrily back to where his and Sarah's horses were grazing, Sarah had to hurry to keep up with him. As they rode silently side by side back to town, she kept glancing at him and could see by his face his anger was building. By the time they rode over the bridge and into town, Foley was furious, and Pike was in big trouble.

Tethering their horses to the hitching rail outside the Sheriff's Office, Foley took Sarah's hand in his, and pulling her along behind him, stormed across to Henry's store where he shoved the door open so hard it slammed against the wall and almost came off its hinges. The store though was empty except for Henry.

"Where is he?" Foley asked Henry angrily. Henry didn't like the look on Foley's face, nor having his door broken, but he wasn't about to say something to rile him more.

"He's up at Doc's getting his head looked at," he answered.

Keeping a firm grip on Sarah's hand, Foley forced her to follow him as they hurried along the boardwalk to Doc's where rushing inside, they were greeted by Gerda coming along the hall.

"Where is he Gerda?" Foley snapped. Hearing the anger in Foley's voice and not mistaking the look on his face, it was all Gerda could do to point to the front room. Doc was just finishing with bandaging Pike's head when Foley burst through the door.

Pushing Doc aside, Foley grabbed Pike by the front of his shirt and lifted him out of the chair he was sitting in, then driving his fist into his face, smashed Pike's nose and mouth and sent blood pouring all over his chin. While Doc cursed Foley for creating more damage he had to fix, Pike fell back in the chair with a surprised look in his eyes. Standing wide eyed in the doorway, Sarah watched Foley smash his fist into Pike's face.

"Next time you say something about my wife, you asshole! it won't be my fist you will feel, it will be my fucking bullet!" Foley didn't wait around for Pike to say anything about them being married. Grabbing Sarah's hand, he rushed her back outside, and only stopped pulling her along once he got to the middle of the street opposite the saloon where he could see some of Major Hardy's men milling about with drinks in their hands. The last time the drinkers saw Sarah and Foley standing outside the saloon like this was when Sarah threatened to shoot Foley after outing Maria's dark past. Hearing Foley and Sarah were outside and something was about to go down, more men rushed from inside and stood with the already large crowd. To avoid running into Foley and Sarah as they stood facing each other, horses with riders, and wagons loaded with goods quickly made their way around them.

It was no surprise to Doc that Sarah and Foley were married, he was there giving Sarah away and kept it quiet as they wanted. But it was the first time Pike heard they were married.

With his face busted and in agony, Pike pushed Doc aside, and rushing into the street, charged toward the saloon where he could see Sarah and Foley were standing.

"You fucking belly crawling sidewinder Andrews!" he bellowed as he kept coming toward them. "She could have killed me with that fucking pot! and *you!*" he cursed, jabbing his finger toward Foley. "You broke my fucking nose!"

Looking over Sarah's head, Foley watched Pike marching toward them in an agitated state, and moving Sarah to stand behind him, levelled his hand with his gun. When Pike saw Foley's stance, he stopped walking, and spreading his legs, brought his hand level with his gun.

"Sarah had cause to hit you! you ignorant fuck! I hit you because you were spreading tales about my wife!" Foley barked savagely.

News Foley and Sarah were married brought surprised gasps from onlookers gathered on either side of the street.

180

"I didn't know you were fucking married!" Pike yelled.

"Doesn't matter, you shouldn't have been talking about Sarah like you was anyhow!"

"Well it's true! ain't it? She is putting her legs up for you?" Pike questioned.

"Goddamn it!... *she!... is my wife!*" Foley yelled as if to justify Sarah having sex with him. Then figuring Pike was just an arrogant cowboy, he went for his gun, but he wasn't going to kill him, just teach him a lesson.

The thought that Foley wouldn't take it upon himself to put a bullet in him just for a comment that was the truth disappeared from Pikes mind when Foley's hand hit leather. Drawing his gun too, Pike got it out of his holster, but Foley's draw was faster, which made Pike think he was a dead man for sure.

As a warning to Pike to keep his mouth shut about Sarah, Foley's bullet slammed into his arm. When Pike dropped his gun and grabbed his arm, the crowd standing outside the saloon let out an astonished gasp as they watched him stagger backwards. After watching what happened, Doc ran to Pike who was kneeling and clutching his arm trying to stem the flow of blood quickly soaking his sleeve. The cowboys in the crowd who thought Foley wouldn't shoot one of their own, poised their hands over their guns. Knowing Pike was a friend to most of the men watching, Foley levelled his gun at the crowd.

"Don't any of you think about doing something stupid," he warned. Even if they could take Foley down, no-one wanted to be the one wearing Foley's bullet. Everyone moved their hands away from their guns.

Because Lizzy was just a little girl, and little girls were sometimes prone to telling tales, no-one believed her when she told everyone she had a new Pa. It also seemed Sarah and Foley had a few real friends in Cedar Creek after all, because no-one gave up their secret.

"Sarah and I were married a couple of weeks ago, we didn't tell you because we wanted time for ourselves without all your fussing and talking, I guess we should have said something sooner," Foley said holstering his gun. Holding his hand out to Sarah who had been watching him, she took it and let him draw her into his arms. Clasping her hands about his neck and standing on her toes, his passionate kiss sent a feeling of arousal coursing through her. With his arms about her waist, a sudden rush of wanting surged upwards through Foley. When they finally stopped kissing, and while the large crowd of men, and women that had joined them continued to stare, they found it necessary to keep their arms around each other.

"Don't any of you forget what I said, you say anything about my wife, you will be dealt the same as what Pike got!" Foley inclined his head to where Doc was helping Pike get to his feet. With blood staining the sleeve of Pikes shirt, his busted nose and two of his front teeth now loose were the least of his worries. Everyone staring at Pike thought it best to heed Foley's warning.

Turning his back on the crowd and holding Sarah's hand, Foley walked her quickly to the lodge where, while rushing up the steps, he untied the cord holding his holster to his leg. Quickly unbuckling his gun-belt, he dropped it on the floor inside and pulled her through the door behind him. Neither got very far inside before their lust for each other had them tearing at each other's clothes. Quickly lifting Sarah's shirt out of her trousers, instead of undoing buttons, he pulled it over her head, then throwing it aside, cupped her breasts and gave them a squeeze. But they weren't going to make it upstairs to the bedroom.

As Sarah got busy with his trousers, he pushed her hands out of the way and lowered her onto the rug in front of the fireplace where he pulled her boots off her and quickly stripped her trousers from her, then taking hold of her legs, spread them wide.

Unable to contain himself and kneeling between her legs, he hurriedly pulled his shirt over his head and dropped it as Sarah sat up and helped pull his trousers to his knees, then keeping her legs spread and leaning back on her elbows, she looked up at him kneeling in front of her with his trousers bunched around his ankles. But this wouldn't do. While Foley's eyes trailed over Sarah, he sat back, and yanking his boots off, pulled his legs free of his trousers. Then hovering between her legs and kissing her, he gave her breasts a good rub before running his hand down her stomach and bringing it between her legs. At the same time as feeling her womanhood swelling, Sarah ran her hands over Foley's chest and down his stomach. Circling her fingers around his manhood, she worked him for a moment while his fingers worked at getting her ready to take him. Sliding her arms around him, she brought him down to lie on top of her.

Having worked themselves into a lather, and ending in a frenzied climax, they lay panting beside each other on the rug.

After staying where they were for a few minutes to catch their breath, they gathered their clothes from where they tossed them, and went together to the washroom. Using cold water and washcloths, they freshened each other up before getting dressed, then with a feeling of satisfaction in him, Foley let Sarah do up the buttons on his shirt while he did up his trousers.

"I better get back before my deputies wonder where I am," he said smiling at her. Sarah's cheeks remained flushed pink from their union as she smiled at him.

"You do know we just did what Pike was saying, don't you Foley? I think everyone in town might know where you are right now, and they probably have guessed what we have been up to." Foley fastened his gun-belt around his hips and when they got to the front door, he embraced Sarah.

"I don't care what they say about me Sarah, but I won't have them talking about you, you're my wife, it's nobody's business what we do." He kissed her softly, pulled his hat on and opened the door.

"Do you think shooting Pike will stop them talking about me?" Sarah asked.

"It better, or there will be more men out there with bullets in them... I'll see you tonight," he said seriously before Sarah closed the door behind him.

Sarah hoped his shooting Pike would work in her favour, if it didn't, she thought it might help if she continued carrying her knife and pistol. Leaning back on the door, her thoughts turned to the sex they just had and she smiled. That was the first time she felt fulfilled since they married. Foley made deep, penetrating love to her like he did on their wedding night, and she enjoyed every minute of it.

Still without a pot to cook her stews in, after collecting Lizzy from school, she took her to Henry's store and purchased a new tin pot. While there she didn't much care for the stares some women folk were giving her, and given she knew what they were thinking, decided she definitely would carry her knife and pistol, that way, it would at the most, stop them staring at her.

When Sarah and Foley made love again, Foley reverted to being careful by withdrawing before he came. Thinking everything was alright between them, after kissing Sarah lovingly and telling her he loved her, he went to sleep holding her in his arms, but when he rolled over at daylight, he woke to find the bed beside him empty. Looking around the room, he found Sarah standing in front of the open window facing the mountains. The room felt cold from early morning mist wafting through the window, and when he got out of bed he shivered before striding over to stand behind her. Wrapping his arms about her, he brought her back to lean against him and felt how cool her bare skin was to his touch.

"Aren't you cold?" he whispered putting his mouth close to her ear and hearing her subdued sobbing. "What is it Sarah? What's wrong?" he asked thinking it may be his lovemaking making her cry. Of course, he wanted to make love to her the way he did on the floor in front of their fire, but he didn't want to risk getting her pregnant. Fearing he would lose her the way Maria had gone, he knew he wouldn't be able to satisfy her all of the time.

"I want to go home," Sarah sobbed.

She missed her mountain, and she missed the trappers, especially Joe. She hated Cedar Creek, she hated the stares and the whispering that went on behind her back. Looking over the top of Sarah's head to the mountains in the distance, Foley didn't question as to why she wanted to go home. Since Christian had been killed, she hadn't been happy living in Cedar Creek, and he hadn't made it easy for her.

"If that is what you want, then I will take you," he answered.

Closing her eyes, and feeling secure in his arms, she covered his hands with hers and held them against her. "Could you live there, where it is wild? What about your farm and being sheriff?" she asked.

"So long as I am with you Sarah, I can live anywhere, I don't love being sheriff, it's you I love, and Brady already takes care of the farm." Foley's answers to her questions came without the slightest hesitation, and they were all Sarah needed to hear. With a tear balanced on her lashes, she turned to face him.

"I want to sell the lodge."

Cupping Sarah's face in his hands, and using his thumb, he wiped her tears away before kissing her softly. "Why would you want to do that? Won't we need a place to stay when we come back to spend our winters here?"

Sarah closed her eyes, then opened them to gaze into his. Living at the lodge was fine when Christian was alive. They made memories that would stay with her forever. But with Foley, she wanted to start afresh, to forge new memories somewhere other than the lodge.

"We could stay with Brady and Ellen," she answered softly.

After making love earlier, Sarah lay awake thinking, and had it all figured out. But Foley didn't like the idea of selling the lodge. It was a grand house, and although Benjamin Crawley kept it from Sarah for a time, it had been her home since birth. "Come back to bed Sarah, we can work it all out later." Leading her back to their bed and after caressing each other gently, they managed to get some sleep before bathing and dressing for the day.

At breakfast they discussed leaving town, and both agreed it was too late to leave right then, winter would soon be upon them and they would just have to turn around and come back. Besides, they needed safe passage to Sarah's cabin, so they agreed to wait so they could travel back with Joe and the other trappers in the spring. Foley talked Sarah into renting the lodge to visitor's that would come to town while they were on the mountain, after all, he reminded her, she let rooms to the men from the Stage-coach Service and the Telegraph Office and that had been successful. Sarah remembered the two men well. She hadn't liked Peter Donovan because he came across as being rather forward in his approach to her, whereas Blake Stevens was a quite unassuming man, whom respected her position as a widow and didn't come on to her at all.

Blake Stevens came back to Cedar Creek to oversee the completion of the building for the Telegraph/ U S Mail Office. When he returned, he was filled with intentions of marriage and wanted to re-acquaint himself with Sarah, but as things turned out, the trappers were back in town and Sarah was spending all of her time with them. Stevens was more than a little afraid of the wild looking trappers that frequented the saloon to drink and gamble, and who spent their time upstairs in rooms adjoining his doing lord knows what. Once the Telegraph/US Mail Service was up and running, he never returned to Cedar Creek.

With the town becoming known to outsiders, men came regularly to look at starting businesses, and they needed somewhere better to stay instead of in rooms at the saloon, which at the best of times, were being frequented by sex starved cowhands and percentage girls. Mountain View Lodge was the grandest building in the County of Cedar Creek and possibly all of Wyoming. It was the only place in town for anyone of social standing to stay.

Sarah agreed with Foley that it was a good idea to rent out the lodge. They still had a month to go before Joe and the trappers would return, which gave Sarah plenty of time to organize with Morley at the bank to draw up a contract, putting him in charge of the lettings while she was back on the mountain.

Chapter Fifteen

Sarah was excited to be going back to the mountain. Having been gone so long she wondered if her cabin was still livable, and she missed the four men terribly and couldn't wait for them to return to tell them about being married to Foley.

A rider coming over the bridge at full gallop raced down the street waving his hat in the air while yelling excitedly at the top of his voice, *"the trappers are coming! the trappers are coming!"* then pulling his horse to a sudden stop outside the saloon, he jumped down, and running inside, let everyone know there the trappers were on their way. On hearing the news, the saloon emptied quickly. Crowds of people gathered on boardwalks on either side of the street, waiting for the trappers to come over the bridge and into town.

It would be months before Sarah and Foley left town, but Foley wasn't leaving anything until the last minute. While he was out at the farm helping Brady before he and Sarah made the journey to Sarah's mountain, his deputies, who he left in charge, came out of the Sheriff's Office to see what was going on. Sarah and Lizzy were visiting Gerda when the rider went racing past, and they hurried outside and stood with Gerda on the boardwalk. Unable to hear what he was saying, Sarah left Lizzy with Gerda and hurried to the saloon, and pushing through the crowd, raced inside. "How far away are they?" she asked the man leaning on the bar with a whiskey in front of him. "Almost past the ponds," the man said excitedly, then swallowing his drink in one gulp, ordered another. Rushing back outside, Sarah hurried back along the boardwalk to Gerda.

"I'm going to wait for Joe at the bridge, see you later Gerda." Taking Lizzy by the hand, they hurried to the bridge where they could see along the trail.

Even before he came over the bridge and rode down the street, Joe could see Sarah and Lizzy standing off to one side. A long line of tired and bedraggled trappers, pulling their heavily laden packhorses, and riding as if they were returning from war, came behind him.

"Hey Sarah! hey Lizzy!" Joe called, pleased to see them. Even though he slowed his horse, Sarah had to keep moving to keep up with him.

"Hello Joe," she called. "Will you come to the lodge tonight?' she asked before he could get ahead of her. Holding Lizzy up so she could see Joe and he her, made it difficult for Sarah to keep level with Joe's horse.

"Once I get everything stowed away, I'll be there," Joe called as he got further away. Letting him go and after watching some of the other men pass, and still carrying Lizzy, Sarah raced back to the lodge. There was a lot to do, Joe would bring the other three men with him, and they would be hungry, food needed preparing.

As the trappers made their way down the street, town folk waved and cheered. To the trappers, Cedar Creek's folk appeared happy as they smiled and greeted them in return. When Joe rode in last winter, the town was mourning the loss of its sheriff, but none more so than Sarah and Thomas. When Thomas left to attend college, Sarah was left with just Lizzy for company, and for a time, Joe worried about her being on her own, but as the year progressed and trapping became serious business, he didn't have time to dwell on her. The promise he made though was never far from his thoughts, and he felt bad for not being able to keep her close, but looking at her now, he felt pleased she seemed happy once more.

Before making his way to the Ferguson House to get settled, Joe put his skins in, then waited for the rest of the trappers skins to be counted and written on the board. He was surprised to learn Samuels got one skin more than him and was declared the winner. After forcing Fess to do a recount and the result confirmed he got beaten for the pot, Joe didn't mind. Samuels was a good trapper, and except for the fact he hadn't been on the mountain nearly as long as them, the four men didn't hold anything against him.

After helping Brady all day out at the farm, when Foley rode back to town, he was feeling tired and just wanted to relax with a good meal and make slow love to Sarah. Passing by the Trading Post he saw the trappers had arrived, so instead of going straight to the lodge, he stopped at the Sheriff's Office where he spent several hours talking with his deputies and sorting out a roster for each man to take over extra duties while he spent time with Sarah and the four men. It was dark when he made his way to the lodge to find Sarah had dinner ready. When he saw seven place-settings around the table, he was surprised when told the trappers were coming for dinner their first night in town, and because there was no way of telling how long they would stay with Sarah, he thought it best to get a kiss from her before they arrived.

"I better go wash then," he said after kissing her passionately before disappearing into the washroom.

A fire blazing in the open fireplace, and the aroma of cooked food wafting throughout the lodge made the lodge comfortable. After the four trappers greeted Sarah with warm hugs and kisses, each man hugged and kissed Lizzy, causing her to giggle when their bushy beards from almost a year's growth tickled her face. When Foley unexpectedly came out of the washroom, Will was still holding Lizzy and was as surprised as the other men at seeing how at home he appeared to be.

"What is he doing here Sarah?" Joe asked, narrowing his eyes with suspicion while watching Foley roll his sleeves down as he came around the table to greet each man with handshakes.

"Foley lives here Joe," Sarah informed him as if he should already know. When Foley put his arm around Sarah and she him, the men sucked in their breath, because to them, living didn't mean touching.

"Foley is my husband," she announced casually as an awkward silence descended over the room.

"We are married Joe," Foley said as if Joe hadn't heard her.

Furrowing his brow in confusion, Joe wanted to know what was going on. Because when he left town last spring, Foley was married to Maria and was excited to be expecting his first child. Now here he was saying he was married to Sarah.

"Somebody tell me what the... hell, is going on here?" he said feeling a curse coming on, but although he was angry at this new event, Lizzy was with them, so he held his tongue.

"Sit down Joe, I will bring the food and we will talk." Sarah took her arm from around Foley and hurried to the kitchen.

As tension filled the room, the men pulled chairs out from the table, and sitting down, didn't utter a word to Foley. Joe didn't hate Foley, in fact he liked him, but he didn't think Sarah would have reason to marry him. Wanting to know what happened for them to be wed, and wondering where Maria and Foley's baby was, Joe waited on tenterhooks for Sarah to come back. Along with Fergus, Garrett and Will equally thought Foley a decent man, but while wondering how come he was married to Sarah, all eyed Foley with suspicion. Their looks however, didn't concern Foley. He was married to the woman he had always loved, and no matter what anyone said, everyone, including the trappers, would have to accept it.

"Foley, can you bring the bread please?" Sarah said coming back to the table carrying her new tin pot steaming with chicken stew. Without hesitation, Foley stood up and went to the kitchen. When he came back with a plate piled high with thick slices of freshly baked bread, Joe raised his eyebrows and smirked. Sarah spoke and Foley jumped. At least to Joe, this was a good sign.

Regardless of his threat, Foley figured people were talking, and he didn't want the trappers to hear rumours or innuendos from anyone. He wanted Joe especially to know the truth about him, Maria and Sarah. After Sarah served the stew, and while everyone ate, Foley spoke at length, and the men listened without interruption. While everyone's attention was on Foley, Sarah sat quietly beside Lizzy helping her with her meal. Foley told the truth about the baby not being his and how Sarah knew about it. He told how he treated Sarah after he found out she knew, and how he locked her out of the farmhouse with Lizzy still inside. Not happy with

Foley putting Sarah through such pain after what she had already been through, at that point, Joe sat back and pursed his lips. Foley apologized profusely for his behaviour, then looked seriously at Joe.

"I have loved Sarah a long time Joe, I think you know that already, and I will love her for a long time to come." Reaching for Sarah's hand, he took it in his and gave it a gentle squeeze to reassure her he meant what he said. But Joe didn't congratulate them on being married. He already decided to wait to see how things were between them. Sarah appeared happy, but everyone knew Foley was a serious man. Joe couldn't recall a single time where he saw him laugh, and he knew all about Foley and Brady witnessing the fire where they lost both their parents and sister. There was the scar on his face he bore as a permanent reminder from the time he had been whipped on account of Sarah too. Joe knew how many years Foley proposed to her because he kept count, and he never once had cause to warn him against it, not like he had other men. He had believed Frank was the right man for Sarah, but soon realized his mistake when Frank met his end on the mountain. Christian too should have ended his promise when he married her, and it shocked Joe to his very core to learn he was gone. But now, with Sarah marrying Foley, he felt he needed proof Foley was the right man to break his promise. Joe couldn't relax, he never would, not where Sarah was concerned.

After the meal, everyone congregated around the fire. With the green winged chair pulled aside to allow Foley and the other men to sit on chairs beside them, Sarah and Joe sat beside each other on the couch. While they talked at length about trapping and goings on in town, Lizzy sat on the rug in front of the fire playing with her rag doll. Sarah explained how land had opened up on the other side of the river behind the pier where row boats were moored, and how several new houses had already been built. She mentioned how Christian always said the town would end up spreading out over the other side of the river, and how she laughed at him for how silly a suggestion it was. When Sarah left Foley talking with the men while she put Lizzy to bed, Foley let Joe know she wanted to go back to the mountain.

"Sarah has made her decision Joe, she isn't happy here in town," he ended quietly. Joe nodded in agreement to his statement.

191

"What about you Foley? What do you say to that?" Joe thought Foley might want Sarah to stay in Cedar Creek like she had with Christian and studied him for his answer.

"I've agreed to take her back, it's what she wants." Foley thought it should have been obvious that he would agree to take Sarah home, and gazed into the fire when he spoke, but his words didn't convince Joe. Joe needed Foley to be committed to Sarah as well as Lizzy.

"Yes, but you are sheriff here, it's important work, and it pays well, and there's your farm, are they not important to you?" Foley didn't have to think long before he answered.

"Sarah asked me the same Joe, she hasn't been happy since Christian died and I didn't help, she means everything to me, and if she is happy, then I am happy, the mountain is where she is happy." Foley knew he was being grilled as to his commitment to Sarah. He loved her and that was all that mattered to him, but he wanted Joe and the other men to trust him. "Being sheriff isn't what I want to do for the rest of my life, and Brady is already taking care of our farm." After putting Lizzy to bed and Sarah came back downstairs, the men stood up.

"I think we might go Sarah, it has been a pretty big few days, you know how it is?" After the long trek off the mountain, Will was dead on his feet and needed to lay his head down without the worry of wolves chasing him, and feeling the same as Will, Garrett and Fergus thanked Sarah for dinner and bid her and Foley goodnight. Sarah hugged each man in turn then said she would see them around town now they were back. Before leaving, Joe wanted to talk to Sarah some more, so the three men retired to the Ferguson House without him. Foley left Sarah and Joe sitting in front of the fire drinking coffee and went to bed.

Needing to know what Joe thought about her marrying Foley, while he sat deep in thought, Sarah studied him.

"What are you thinking Joe?" she asked.

"I'm thinking about you and Foley Sarah, what else?" Joe answered.

"Talk to me Joe, say what you want to say." Sarah looked down at her mug.

If Joe was going to tell her she was a fool to have married Foley she would be disappointed, but he couldn't change her feelings for Foley, she was in love with him, somewhere deep inside, she knew she always had been.

"I think Foley may be alright Sarah, he's no fool, what happened with Maria was a terrible tragedy, but he loves you, he always has, hasn't he?" Joe smiled awkwardly at her and went on.

"What if you had married Foley when he proposed to you that first time? You may have had a dozen children by now, and you know, if he had married you, he wouldn't have married Maria, and you wouldn't have married Christian... and Lizzy..." He stopped talking and sitting back suddenly, pursed his lips. He loved Lizzy, she was so much like Sarah was at her age, and it got him thinking. 'If things had worked out the way they should have before Sarah was born, then maybe Thomas would have been his grandson, and if things had turned out, then Lizzy would be his granddaughter. But what if Thomas and Lizzy are my grandchildren? That would mean Sarah...' While so many what if's and maybe's went coursing through Joe's mind, Sarah didn't mention the fact Foley didn't want children, and changed the subject.

"We are going back to the mountain Joe," she said bringing him back to reality.

"Yeah, Foley told me," he answered as Sarah poured them another mug of coffee.

"I've missed it Joe... I want to go home."

Joe gave considerable thought to that before he spoke. "Are you happy to take Foley up there Sarah? Is he going to be like Frank?"

Sarah was taken aback by what he said. "No! Foley is nothing like Frank! he is strong willed, he isn't the type to take things lightly!" she snapped.

Raising his eyebrows Joe nodded in agreement. "What about Lizzy? You prepared to take her to a place she has never seen before? It's as wild as it ever was up there."

"I remember what it's like Joe, Lizzy will learn, she has me to teach her, and you will help, won't you?" Sarah said looking him in

193

the eye. When she smiled coyly, Joe looked at her from under his brow and leant back against the back of the couch.

"I'm not as young as I once was Sarah, I can't promise you anything," he answered.

"I'm not asking you to promise me Joe, just be around, that's all," she replied, resting her hand on his arm.

"Well, you needn't worry about that darlin, because I plan on being around a long time," Joe said patting her hand, and sounding tired, stood up to go.

Having said goodnight to each other out on the porch, Joe kissed Sarah on her cheek, and after kissing him back, she watched him walk along the street to the Ferguson House before going back inside. When she went upstairs to her room, Foley was still awake. After watching her get undressed, he lifted the covers for her to slip in beside him, and pulling her into his arms, caressed her gently before they both fell asleep.

As Joe walked back to the Ferguson House, he smiled to himself. He was a happy man, because come spring, Sarah would be going back to the mountain where she belonged. Joe felt this winter in Cedar Creek was going to be the best one he ever had.

Chapter Sixteen

Winter came and went in Cedar Creek. Sarah and Foley along with Lizzy, enjoyed their time spent with the trappers. Joe had the best time of all, and when Sarah held a last Christmas dinner party, the lodge was packed with happy smiling people. Joe thought Sarah might miss her friends when she went back to the mountain, but he didn't care, she was going back with him, that was the important thing. Joe was exceedingly glad when this winter drew to an end.

The two packhorses were heavily laden with supplies they would need for the entire year. Foley was to lead one, Sarah the other, and for added safety, Lizzy was to ride sitting in front of Sarah. Sarah packed some of her belongings from the lodge onto the horses to take with her. She thought having these things at the cabin would keep her from missing the lodge while she and Foley made their home on the mountain.

Her locket and a few pieces of her mother's jewellery were placed in the little jewel box the trappers had given her for her first Christmas she spent with them after her father died. The rest was stored in her bank box at Morley's bank. The shawl Joe gave her that first year she spent with the trappers was folded and packed. One silver candlestick was put into a bag along with cutlery and linen then strapped to her packhorse. All her beautiful dresses she wouldn't need on the mountain were left hanging in her closet. The portrait of her mother remained hanging in pride of place above the fireplace in the huge expanse of the living area. The piece of board Christian saved from the shack that had Frank's declaration of love for her carved in it was left sitting on the mantel below her mother's portrait. Other items she didn't want to take to her cabin were packed away and locked up in the attic. Now Mountain View Lodge was open to let, Sarah was anxious to get going.

Brady and Ellen with their children Matthew and Charlotte, Ham and Patrice with their daughters Sissy and Lilly, Doc Harris and Gerda, along with Martha and Dave were all there standing with a throng of people seeing Sarah and Foley off. The men shook hands with Foley, and hugged and kissed Sarah and Lizzy, and the women cried when they said goodbye. Sarah's few friends were going to miss her and Lizzy terribly.

Happy to be going to the mountain with the woman he loved, before heading to the corrals where Sarah was waiting, Foley stopped by the Sheriff's Office where he unpinned the star off his shirt and handed it to Smith, then after shaking both deputy's hands and bidding them farewell, he walked out.

Taking the lead to his packhorse, he climbed into his saddle and looked at Sarah. Sarah looked lovingly back at him. He hadn't argued with her over her decision to return to the mountain, which made her feel she made the right decision in marrying him. He said anywhere she wanted to go, he would go with her. All she wanted was to go home to her cabin, that was as far as she wanted him to go.

Joe and Fergus led the trappers over the bridge and out of town. With Lizzy sitting in front of her, Sarah led her packhorse over the bridge behind them. Before falling in line behind Foley, Will looked back and waved goodbye to Sissy. Sissy waved back as he and Garrett moved off. The rest of the trappers fell in behind them.

Spring brought with it warm sunny days. No-one was in a hurry to get back to the mountain except Sarah, but she soon settled down and relaxed as they made the trek slowly along the trail. By the end of their first day they were only halfway to the place they called 'The Wells.' That first night they camped out on the prairie, Foley kept Sarah and Lizzy close for their protection.

Their second night proved much the same. After making camp, Sarah squatted at the fire getting Foley and Lizzy a plate each of rabbit stew. Joe crouched beside her getting himself a plate of food too.

"You told Foley about tomorrow?" he asked her quietly.

"Not yet," Sarah answered as she spooned stew onto the plates.

"You tell him Sarah, get him prepared!" Joe said sternly. "What about Lizzy? She can't be sitting in front of you like she is now when the wolves come." Sarah looked over at Foley and Lizzy busy working together laying out their bedrolls while they waited for her to return with their food.

"So long as you keep us in the middle where we won't have to ride hard, Foley will be prepared, and Lizzy will be safe strapped to me… you just keep the wolves away from us." When Sarah finished scooping stew on the tin plates and stood up, Joe got to his feet with her.

"You put a lot of responsibility on me Sarah," he laughed halfheartedly.

"You were the one that made a promise Joe," Sarah laughed back at him.

"Just make sure Foley is ready!" Joe said turning serious before going back to his bedroll. Taking the food to Foley and Lizzy, then after returning to the fire to get herself a plate, Sarah sat beside Foley on her bedroll and let Lizzy sit in front of them.

"What were you and Joe talking about Sarah?" Foley asked quietly. Watching Sarah and Joe with their heads together, he wanted to know if what they were talking about was him and wasn't prepared for the conversation that followed.

A long time had passed since Sarah had been to the mountain. Joe told her wolves still hunted around the base, but had become scarce high up near the High Ridge Camp. The men were having to travel further to trap them. Sarah began eating her meal before answering.

"Tomorrow, when we get to the mountain, we will come up against wolves, we need to be prepared for them."

"How do we prepare?" Foley questioned.

"You need to check your rifle and make sure it's loaded, check your handgun too, if there is trouble, keep extra bullets handy so you can reload fast." Foley watched Sarah intently while they ate.

"We won't see any wolves until we get close to the mountain," Sarah said, wiping the corners of her mouth with her finger. "But we need to be ready for them when we leave here." She went on to tell him Lizzy would be tied to her, so it was up to him and the rest of the men to keep the wolves away from them. Having finished his meal, Foley waited for Lizzy who was slowly getting through her food to finish hers.

After finishing eating, Lizzy shoved her empty plate toward Foley. "Mommy, I want to sit with uncle Will," she said, not waiting for Sarah to give her permission to go. Sarah and Foley watched her push through the throng of men standing around the fire smiling as they moved to get out of her way so she could get to where Will was sitting on a log on the far side of the camp. Smiling at Lizzy, Will scooped her into his arms and sat her on his knee. Watching Garrett and Fergus seated either side of Will laughing and talking to Lizzy, Foley could see if anything were to happen to Sarah, or him, the men would go out of their way to protect Sarah's little girl. After spending time talking and giggling with Lizzy, Will carried her back to Sarah.

"She's getting sleepy Sarah," he said handing her back.

While Sarah nursed Lizzy on her lap, Foley lifted Lizzy's legs across his and covered them with his blanket. With Sarah's head resting against his chest, her hair brushed his face allowing him to breathe in the fresh scent of flower blossoms in each soft strand. "I love you Sarah," he whispered before closing his eyes. When Sarah didn't reply, he settled back and fell asleep.

As Joe looked across the fire at the three huddled together, his eyes remained on Foley. There had been plenty of opportunities during winter for him to see how Foley treated Sarah. All four men had been invited to eat with them at the lodge on many occasions and Sarah had her special dinner party that she always held close to Christmas. It had been a fun time for all with Lizzy getting lots of gifts, and they laughed a lot, and when the men were breaking horses and Sarah took Lizzy to the corrals to watch the men at work, Foley went with them. After her fall the year before, Lizzy wasn't allowed to sit on top of the fence, making Joe satisfied Foley was capable of taking care of both Sarah and her. But it didn't stop him worrying about Foley going to the mountain. If Foley could stick out the freezing conditions like he and Calahan had done those first years they were on the mountain, maybe he would prove himself a worthy man to be there. Even though Frank proved himself a good trapper, Joe hoped and prayed Foley could handle the mountain better than Frank had.

At sun up next morning, everyone checked their guns. Sarah checked her rifle and pistol. Frank's heavy black colt .44 was loaded and stowed in her rucksack. Foley loaded his handgun and shoved it back in its holster at his hip. Bullets were fastened in his gun-belt where he could reach them quickly. He loaded his rifle and filled his jacket pockets with bullets for that. Sarah climbed into her saddle, and when Foley lifted Lizzy up to sit in front of her, he took note as to how Sarah secured her by wrapping a length of cloth crosswise around Lizzy then around herself. When the horses start to run, soil and rocks would fly in all directions, and not wanting Lizzy getting hurt, Sarah put on her fur coat to protect her from dust and flying debris. Pulling the coat around her and Lizzy, she fastened it with a length of rope in the same manner she carried Thomas to and from the mountain until he was old enough to ride on his own. Lizzy gripped the saddle-horn, just like her Ma taught her.

Letting the trappers lead the way, Sarah and Foley fell in behind and rode alongside each other. When they saw Joe stop ahead of them, they caught up to him.

"Sarah, Foley, from here on, you stay in the middle of the group and keep your rifles ready," he ordered.

Taking his rifle from its holster, and not wanting it going off and accidently shooting either Sarah or Lizzy who would be riding beside him surrounded by men all holding rifles at the ready, Foley rested his rifle on his leg so its barrel pointed upwards.

When Joe gave the signal, everyone rode at a gallop. Never having gone this fast before, when the cloth keeping her secured between Sarah's arms pulled tight, Lizzy became frightened. Gripping the saddle-horn as tight as she could, her knuckles turned white and tears filled her eyes when men and horses went racing by ever so quickly. Looking at men and packhorses racing along beside him, Foley lowered his gun and kicked his horse hard to keep up.

When a shot rang out giving the signal to open fire Garrett yelled, "here they come!"

With wolves bursting from the forest amidst a hail of gun fire, and running in close to the galloping horses, Foley couldn't get a clear target. Trying to get off a shot, but surrounded by men and horses, he watched Sarah concentrating on holding Lizzy while keeping her horses racing between horses running alongside her. Hearing a shot, he saw a wolf that seemed to come from nowhere run toward Sarah's horse, and watched it fall and roll to a stop.

"Foley!" Sarah screamed, managing a quick glance over at him. "Look out!"

Hearing her warning, Foley turned to look at where he was and found himself out in the open. Having been forced to separate, the trappers fell back giving him a clear view of a wolf charging toward him. Gripping his reins in his hand, he lifted his rifle to his shoulder and fired. As his horse carried him toward the mountain, he looked back to see the wolf lying unmoving where it fell. Glancing over at Sarah still racing along beside him, they nodded to each other to show their satisfaction at keeping the wolves at bay. With every skin counting toward winning the pot at the end of the year, no man was going to leave a skin behind. When the attack ended and rifle shots faded, Foley and Sarah kept their horses clear while the men set to work.

"Rest up, then we'll head up the trail to the caves, we should be there in plenty of time to set up camp before it gets dark," Joe announced when the trappers gathered around. "Everyone alright?" he asked. Although Lizzy was crying, everyone agreed they were fine.

"Hey Lizzy! that was real good riding!" Samuels reassured her with a smile. With Samuels praising her, Lizzy gulped back her sobs, and wiping her eyes with her hands stopped crying. "I want a wee mommy," she said up to Sarah. Quickly unwrapping her from her coat and the cloth harness, Sarah passed her down to Foley. Taking this as an opportunity to get off their horses and stretch their legs, Fergus and Will set about making a fire and brewing coffee. Lizzy however couldn't wait to go. Running past Samuels standing near where Fergus was making the fire, she headed toward the trees before anyone could stop her. Sensing something wasn't right, Sarah watched her approaching a thicket. A wolf, hidden from view, lay in wait to seize its opportunity to take the smallest of prey. As Lizzy approached, the wolf sprang from the thicket, and seeing it Sarah screamed, "*Lizzy!*" and startled everyone into action.

Being the closest to Lizzy, Samuels turned in an instant, and grabbing her, knocked her to the ground under him. Deciding any prey was better than none, the wolf turned its attack on Samuels. Not wanting to risk shooting Lizzy or Samuels, when the wolf clamped its jaw around Samuels arm, Joe raised his rifle by the barrel and rushed headlong into the fray.

Swinging his rifle wildly through the air, Joe gave the wolf a savage blow to its head and sent it reeling. Letting go of Samuels, the wolf growled viciously and turned on Joe, but failed to carry out its attack when a loud report rang out. With the bullet slamming into it, the wolf howled in pain. Saliva poured from its mouth as it stumbled trying to get away until another shot finished it. Looking around to see who took the wolf down, Joe was satisfied when he saw both Foley and Garrett with their rifles pointing to where the wolf lay. Stooping down, he helped Samuels get to his feet. Samuels was a big man and worried he may have hurt Lizzy when he fell on top of her. With Lizzy clinging to him, he checked to see if she was alright. Along with Joe and the rest of the men, Sarah was grateful for his quick thinking.

"She's alright, I didn't hurt her!" Samuels said trying to reassure everyone Lizzy was fine.

"Samuels, did the wolf bite you?" Sarah asked while taking Lizzy from him. Samuels checked himself first and seeing no wounds checked his coat. Having had his coat a very long time, it was well-worn so he wasn't concerned by the damage the wolf did.

"No, but goddamn it! it tore my best goddamn coat! just look at that!" he said pulling at the tear. "Goddamn it! I love this coat! this is the best goddamn thing a man could ever own," he exclaimed winking at Sarah. Hearing him making light of his old coat being shredded in several places, everyone laughed.

"Lizzy darlin, you can't go running around on your own, you got to stay with mommy," Samuels said hoping she understood his warning. But all Lizzy wanted was relief. "I need to go, mommy!"

After giving her a hug Sarah put her down, then when they saw Lizzy jiggling in desperation, the men turned their backs so Sarah could help her go where she was.

"You alright Sarah?" Joe asked when she finished with Lizzy.

"Yes, I'm fine, and thankfully so is Lizzy."

Relieved Lizzy wasn't hurt, Foley gave her a quick hug, then embracing Sarah, rubbed his hands up and down her back to comfort her.

"Thanks for shooting that wolf Foley," Joe said to him. Foley nodded and said it was nothing.

"So!... who do you suppose should have this skin?" Samuels asked, kicking the dead wolf.

"Why don't you have it?" Joe answered.

"Can't!" Samuels replied. "That be against the rules Joe, you hit it, and Foley and Garrett there shot it!... that makes it not a clean skin." According to the rules of the mountain set up by Joe and Calahan, Joe had to concede that to be the case, and nodded in agreement. While everyone stood there looking at the wolf and wondering what to do with it, Sarah pulled her knife from its sheath. "Hell," she said. "I'll make a coat and hat for Lizzy out of it!"

Watching her knife move swiftly, the men grinned at each other as she took the skin for herself. Glad Sarah hadn't lost her touch, Joe glanced at Foley watching Sarah work, and wondered what he was thinking. Foley was in awe of Sarah's ability, and it reflected in his stance. Just in case there was another wolf lurking about, when everyone went to the fire to get themselves coffee, Lizzy stayed close to Sarah.

Allowing the men to get skins and have refreshments took time. The day was getting away from them. If they were to get to the caves before dark, Joe needed to get them moving.

Coming on the entrances to three caves, Foley was again in awe as they split into groups and took their horses inside where they were tethered to makeshift hitching lines. The cavern he and Sarah were sharing with Joe's group and three other trappers was enormous. Stacked well away from a large stone firepit built in the middle of the dirt covered floor that had room enough around it for everyone to spread out their bedrolls, was a huge pile of dry wood. There were makeshift wooden benches housing pots and pans and tins of food. Foley perused the tins containing beans and sugar, coffee and flour. Joe told Foley they always replenished the wood and replaced any food they used on the way up the mountain in readiness for the winter trek back to Cedar Creek. Foley was amazed at how well organized the trappers outfit was, and feeling at ease, while Lizzy slept in her own bedroll beside them, he settled down with Sarah for the night.

It was another full day's ride up the mountain to the Low Ridge Camp and Sarah's cabin. As they rode along, Joe let Sarah know he and the other three men used her cabin whenever they came that way to hunt, and after saying they stayed there before leaving the mountain each winter, Sarah replied she didn't mind, and said it was better they use it rather than let it fall down.

Coming off the trail and into a clearing, Sarah's lean-to was the first thing Foley saw, then her old dirt floor cabin. As they moved further into the clearing, he hoped the old cabin, which appeared to be falling down, wasn't what they were going to be living in. The outhouse was next to be spotted. It stood in the open on its own for good reason.

"When you use the outhouse," Joe explained. "You have a good view of the whole area around it in case wolves are lurking about… never go to the outhouse without your rifle," he warned.

Moving further into the clearing, Foley felt especially relieved when another cabin came into view. This cabin, sitting on a gentle slope, looked well-built and much larger than the old cabin he first saw. The ground behind it, leading back onto the forest was open and grassed. A little way from the front was a clearing where the ground was barren of grass and shrubs. Several large logs placed around a fire pit were obviously used for seating. On one side of the cabin was a huge stone chimney and along the front windows with shutters that had been closed for the winter. Six wooden steps led up to a covered porch that looked over the clearing to an outcrop of boulders. Seeing a trail leading from the clearing, Foley wondered where it would take him.

Watching Sarah and Foley for their reaction to the cabin's still pristine condition, the four trappers pulled their horses into the clearing and began setting up camp. Leaving Lizzy sitting on her packhorse, Sarah shoved the reins at Foley and left him to hold all four horses, then racing up the steps, pushed the front door open and disappeared inside. Foley stood at the foot of the steps watching for her to come back out. When she did, she stood on the porch looking over him at the men.

"It's the same as it always has been Joe!" she called happily.

"We kept it in good order for you Sarah, we figured you would come back one day," Joe smiled up at her, and with a smile still on his face, he glanced over at Foley looking stony faced back at him. Joe always knew Sarah would return to the mountain she loved. How could she not? The mountain was in her blood.

Racing down the steps to Foley and their horses, Sarah lifted Lizzy down then turned to Foley. "Come on Lizzy, come take a look at your new home, you too Foley!" she said grabbing his hand. When Sarah pulled him excitedly toward the cabin, he let go of the horses and after quickly getting the shutters open to allow light to stream in, all three went inside.

Glancing about, Foley saw the cabin was bigger than his and Brady's farmhouse. The living and eating room consisted of one large room that had a stove for cooking built into a stone wall next to an open fireplace that would keep the cabin warm when the weather turned foul. A wooden table and four chairs sat in front of the stove and a couch faced the open fire. There were two doorways off to one side leading to bedrooms and another to a washroom where a large tub for bathing and a copper washstand for heating water stood. A large walk-in cupboard built into one wall looked capable of storing all their supplies. Sitting in an alcove, above a wooden trunk with four large cushions on top, was a small shelf housing an oil lamp, making the spot a comfortable place to sit and perhaps read. Going through the washroom, Foley found another door leading outside to a path that led to the outhouse in the grassed clearing. Foley thought the clearing behind the cabin where they would be able to see wolves lurking about, would be a good place for a garden and for Lizzy to play.

204

Joe and Fergus, standing by the cooking stove with Sarah, watched Lizzy going from room to room, looking in corners and behind doors.

"What are you looking for Lizzy?" Joe asked her.

"I can't find them!" Lizzy said holding her hands up in puzzlement and frowning.

Watching Lizzy open the supply cupboard door and look inside, Sarah watched her bottom lip quiver.

"What is wrong honey?" she asked seeing her dismay.

"I can't find the stairs mommy!" Lizzy said with her eyes brimming with tears.

When everyone realized Lizzy was expecting her new home to have stairs to another level just like the lodge where she was born, everyone laughed, and because everyone was laughing, when Sarah picked her up, Lizzy buried her head against her shoulder.

"Oh! sweety, there aren't any stairs for you to worry about," Sarah assured her. Feeling better when her Ma explained she didn't have to climb stairs every time she went to bed, she hugged her tight. While Sarah showed Lizzy her room, the men relieved the packhorses of their loads.

That night, using fresh vegetables and dried pieces of meat she brought with her in her supplies, Sarah cooked a large meal and invited the four trappers to eat inside with her and Foley. Not long after finishing with coffee, the four men retired to their camp in the clearing and Sarah put Lizzy to bed in her new room. With their first night drawing to a close, Sarah and Foley retired to their room where they undressed, and because both were too tired from the long trek and unpacking to make love, they simply lay in each other's arms and fell straight to sleep.

When daylight streamed through their bedroom window Foley came awake, and looking around at where he was, found it wasn't such a bad room. A tallboy standing against the far wall, had a dresser beside it. A small table beside the bed housed their oil lamp, and a wooden chair with their discarded clothes thrown over it sat in a corner. Sarah's bed was a comfortable iron framed bed, and on the whole, Foley thought Sarah's cabin wasn't bad at all. Sensing him awake, Sarah lay quietly in his arms, but when she slid her hand across his stomach, he turned his body to face her. They hadn't made love since leaving Cedar Creek and anxious they settle in to their new way of life, Foley brushed his hand through Sarah's hair and kissed her lightly, then moving his hand gently down her body, brought his fingers between her legs. Keeping her arm about his waist, Sarah lifted her leg over his hip to allow him to bring himself against her. With Lizzy's room being close to theirs, Foley didn't want her hearing their grunts and groans as their thrusting became heated, so with their bodies pressed together, they made love as quietly as they could so as not to wake her. Lizzy however woke up early too, and was excited to spend her first day exploring her new home. When she came bounding into Sarah's room just as they were about to climax, Sarah looked horrified at being caught out. Having their lovemaking come to an abrupt halt, Foley looked just as horrified as Sarah, and quickly moving away from her, groaned in agony at his peak being cut short.

"Lizzy, go out honey while we get dressed," Sarah said giggling at hearing Foley's groan beside her. Being ordered out of the room, Lizzy beat a hasty retreat to the table in the living area to wait for her Ma to get her breakfast.

With breakfast over, Foley and Lizzy were taken down the trail leading beyond the clearing where they stood at the edge of the river listening to the gentle babble as it flowed over boulders further down-stream where it meandered between tall trees on its way down the mountain. Where they stood was a wide body of water where, way out in the middle at its deepest point, Sarah said her horses swam. "I still can't swim very well Foley, so my horses swim freely," she let him know.

It was a beautiful spot around Sarah's cabin and Foley thought he would enjoy living there. On the opposite side of the river a forest of tall trees grew with shrubs of differing hues covering the ground beneath their trunks. Behind where they were standing were tall trees also, and a wall of boulders separating a narrow strip of grass that would make a nice spot to have a picnic. Taking Lizzy by the hand, Sarah began to go back up the trail. "That is where Thomas was born," she said nonchalantly pointing to an area beneath the wall. Aware Sarah gave birth to Thomas on the riverbank, but not knowing it had been right outside her cabin, Foley stopped to look at where she pointed.

When the four men left Sarah's cabin to meet up with other trappers at the High Ridge Camp, Sarah took Foley and Lizzy exploring further afield. Taking their rifles and walking along the river to the River Flats, Sarah showed Foley where Frank had his camp. There wasn't anything left now, the forest had overgrown the spot, but using familiar landmarks Sarah remembered where it had been. She took them to the ridge and showed him where she was attacked by a wolf and explained how she got her wound on her shoulder. Foley was familiar with that part of Sarah's life too but after seeing the place where it happened, he could relate it better to her scar. As the days warmed, they had picnics on the riverbank down from Sarah's cabin, and although remaining cautious, Sarah found the courage to venture into the water while Foley taught Lizzy how to swim.

The trappers had been on the High Ridge for some time. Now that Foley was taking care of Sarah, they didn't see the need to go to her cabin quite so often, which allowed them to hunt higher up on the mountain. Foley didn't want to hold back when making love to Sarah, but afraid of getting her pregnant, their first month on the mountain he was careful. This particular day however, he spent all day cutting wood and stacking it near the front steps of the cabin, and after dinner he sat on the couch in front of the fire with his eyes closed. After bathing Lizzy and putting her to bed, Sarah emptied the tub and refilled it, then approached Foley asleep on the couch. Feeling her take hold of his hand, he opened his eyes and blinking, tried focusing on her.

"Come on," Sarah said softly. "I've made you a bath."

Coming partially awake, Foley got up and let Sarah lead him to the washroom. After helping him out of his clothes, Sarah removed her clothes and stepped into the tub with him. Now wide awake, when Foley rubbed soap over Sarah and she did the same to him, their gentle lathering caused both of them to become aroused. With the intention of taking her to their bedroom where he could make love to her in their bed, Foley lifted Sarah out of the tub. But just like the day Sarah hit Pike over the head with a tin pot when they never made it to their bedroom at the lodge, they never made it to their bedroom in Sarah's cabin.

Lying on the washroom floor amidst suds and water, they came together in a frenzy, their grunts and groans so loud, when they pushed their bodies against each other, they worried they would wake Lizzy, but neither stopped. As Foley's body gave in to his desire, Sarah tightened her legs around him trying to prolong the moment of completion until, with their juices flowing, they came together. Breathing heavily and feeling spent from their physical workout, when they were done, they retired to bed where all they could do was hold each other. The next morning, when Foley helped Lizzy by taking her to the outhouse, Sarah had a moment alone. Quickly finding a pencil and paper, and to remind her of the night they made love on the washroom floor, she began marking off days with a cross, then each day, she hid the paper in her tallboy amongst night dresses she never bothered wearing.

After that night of frenzied lovemaking, Sarah couldn't help notice when Foley made love to her, he returned to his way of leaving her wanting more. She felt frustrated at his seeming to think by withdrawing early he wouldn't get her pregnant. But Sarah felt his release when he came against her on the floor, and knew the precise moment she fell pregnant.

Although wildflowers still bloomed here and there, spring was drawing to an end, and each day Sarah and Lizzy filled the cabin with fresh blooms. The small vegetable garden Foley dug behind the cabin where Sarah and Lizzy planted bean seeds Brady had given Sarah before they left town, flourished with a thick crop. After picking the beans, as well as preserving them and putting them in stews, they ate them raw. When Lizzy was put to bed, Sarah and Foley enjoyed sitting outside watching the stars before going to bed themselves and making love.

After venturing to the River Flats where Sarah killed two wolves, Foley once again watched in awe as she skinned them. He never thought she was as skilled at skinning as the men, but watching her work, he held a new found respect for her. Other than shooting two wolves, they had no trouble from other wolves or any other wild animals, Sarah though was troubled. She wanted desperately to tell him about the baby she was expecting, but his constant reminding her he didn't want children left her worried that once he found out she was pregnant, he would leave her to go back to Cedar Creek and his old life. The only thing she could do she decided, was to keep having their baby to herself for as long as she could.

Foley was happy with life on the mountain. He felt it was the fresh mountain air that was making him feel relaxed, and being with Sarah made him happy, relieved too, when months passed and she didn't appear to be pregnant.

Chapter Seventeen

T he fire burning in the fireplace behind where Sarah and Foley sat facing each other across the table eating their evening meal made the cabin comfortable.

"It's time Foley," Sarah said pushing vegetables across Lizzy's plate so she could reach them with her fork.

"Time? Time for what?" Foley asked curious as to what Sarah meant by time. Was she telling him it was time for them to get serious about having children? If so, he was going to put a stop to that thought, Lizzy was proving a handful for him as it was.

"We have spent most of our time hunting along the river, it's time I set traps, and to do that I need to go higher up the mountain," Sarah said looking at him. Foley wasn't keen to go to the High Country where Frank met his end and thought if they stayed close to the cabin they would get by until winter.

"How far up do we need go?" he asked putting his knife and fork down and sitting back.

"As far as the middle ground, about four, maybe five hours walk," Sarah answered putting her knife and fork down then too.

"What about Lizzy? She struggled going along the river, and this will be uphill, she can't walk that far," Foley said looking at Lizzy. When Sarah reached over and brushed hair off Lizzy's face, Lizzy looked up at her and kept eating.

"We will take turns carrying her, but she will have to walk some of the way, we will be carrying traps and rucksacks, and our canteens and rifles." Foley studied Sarah across the table.

"You know we don't need to trap," he said picking up his knife and fork to finish eating.

"I need to trap," Sarah said resuming her meal. "We have to have an early night so we can get up at first light and get going." As far as she was concerned their discussion was ended, and not wanting to get into an argument with her now their lovemaking was everything he ever wanted, Foley resigned himself to the fact Sarah would always be a trapper first before she would ever consider what her family wanted.

The next day they walked three hours up the mountain to a spot Sarah was familiar with whilst out trapping with Thomas years before, but they hadn't yet arrived on middle ground. Four traps had been set and Sarah wanted to set another two higher up, but Lizzy's continual whining was making both her and Foley short-tempered with each other.

For some obscure reason Sarah couldn't fathom, Foley was wearing her fur coat. After telling him he didn't need it because the days were warm and they would be back at the cabin before nightfall, she shrugged her shoulders when he didn't comment and put it on. With his handgun strapped to his hip, his rifle on his back and two canteens filled with water hanging from his shoulder, and having already carried Lizzy part of the way he was feeling worn, and so was Sarah.

Getting rid of heavy traps by setting them made Sarah's load a lot less, but she was still carrying two, and even though her rucksack was only holding half of what she started out with, it was on her back, and with her rifle slung over her shoulder, she couldn't carry Lizzy as well.

Picking Lizzy up again, Foley carried her a little further before putting her down again. Lizzy managed to walk a short distance, but now everyone was feeling miserable.

"Come on Lizzy! you can walk!" Sarah said in a demanding tone.

"Don't yell at me mommy! I can't walk no more!" Lizzy grizzled.

"Yes, you can! I can't carry you, and Foley isn't going to carry you either!"

Foley was just as tired as Sarah, but Lizzy was little, and listening to Sarah berating her, he decided he could carry her further.

"Come on Lizzy, I will carry you," he said, walking toward Lizzy to pick her up.

"Let her walk Foley!" Sarah snapped.

"She is tired Sarah! and frankly, so am I!" he snapped back.

"When I was her age, I walked all over this goddamn mountain!" Sarah let him know firmly while looking at them standing further down the trail. Although Foley didn't like to argue with Sarah he had had enough.

"Lizzy isn't you!" he snapped again.

"She won't learn to walk the mountain if she doesn't walk a little of the way!" Sarah said trying to get him to see reason. But while Lizzy kept whining, Sarah and Foley kept arguing.

"I don't need this! I'm going back to the cabin!" he informed her heatedly. Figuring if he walked away Sarah would change her mind and follow him, he took the canteens off his shoulder, and dropping them, started down the trail.

"Don't you dare go Foley! we need to stay together!" Sarah urged, but Foley didn't heed her warning and kept walking.

"I'm going Sarah! you come back when you've finished!" Heading down the trail, he soon disappeared between trees and thick undergrowth. Seeing him go, Lizzy began to run after him.

"Wait for me Foley!" she cried, holding her arms up to ward off bushes when their branches brushed against her.

"Stop Foley! Lizzy damn it! come back! you need to stay with mommy!" Sarah called trying once more to get them to stay. Pursing her lips in anger, Sarah watched Lizzy and Foley disappear into the forest.

"We have to stay together!" she called loudly. But both ignored her and kept going.

"Goddamn it!" she cursed.

Seeing Lizzy coming behind him, Foley smiled and stopped to let her catch up. Lizzy wasn't going to walk another step with Sarah, but wasn't having any trouble running after him. "Come on Lizzy," he laughed. Picking her feet up high to get over twigs and small sticks, Lizzy bounded down the trail toward him. There wasn't much time for Foley to act before he caught a glimpse of something from the corner of his eye hiding in the bushes. When a huge grey wolf leapt towards Lizzy, he put himself between it and Lizzy as Samuels had done and lifted his rifle to shoot it, but as the wolf sprang toward them, he knocked Lizzy over in his panic.

Unable to get to its smaller prey, with saliva spewing from its mouth and savage guttural growls emanating from its throat, the wolf barreled headlong into Foley causing him to stumble backwards and drop his rifle. Trying to keep from being mauled as its powerful jaws tore into him, he went for his handgun, but in the ensuing struggle to get away, he dropped that too. Tearing savagely at Sarah's coat, the wolf sent him crashing backwards through the undergrowth as he tried desperately to draw it far enough from Lizzy to give her time to get back to Sarah.

"Run Lizzy, run back to mommy!" he yelled.

Picking herself up from where Foley knocked her over, and standing transfixed with fear while watching the wolf attacking him, Lizzy wanted her mother, so closing her eyes and opening her mouth, she screamed at the top of her lungs.

It was only a matter of minutes after looking up the trail where she wanted to set her last two traps, then looking down the trail in the direction Lizzy and Foley had gone, that Sarah heard the high-pitched ear shattering scream that sent a spine-chilling shudder running through her.

Dropping her traps, and gripping her rifle at the ready, she sprinted in the direction Lizzy and Foley had gone. Getting to where Lizzy was shaking with fear, she found Lizzy alone and crying hysterically. Dropping to her knees, Sarah hugged her, then looking around for Foley saw where undergrowth had been trampled, but Foley nowhere to be seen.

"*Foley!*" Sarah screamed.

Foley and the wolf continued their violent battle against each other, one for food, the other for its life. Growling savagely, the wolf clenched its jaw firmly around Foley's arm, and shaking its head violently from side to side tried to tear him apart. He felt some relief in that Sarah's coat, thick with fur, gave him some protection. While able to protect his hands from the wolf's fangs, his arm hurt, but that didn't matter, he had to keep drawing the wolf away.

When the wolf suddenly let go, Foley saw his chance to escape, and turning, rushed headlong through the forest. The wolf though wasn't about to let its prey get away. Slamming into Foley's back, it knocked him to the ground and began gnawing savagely at Sarah's coat. With its mouth filling with fur, it found itself unable to keep its grip, but the fight was far from over. While the wolf gagged, it gave Foley a chance to stagger to his feet. Crashing through tangled brush, he stumbled over vines and tree roots and came bursting from the forest above the river where his leg dropped suddenly over the edge of a rocky slope, causing his foot to slip on loose gravel. Unable to stop his fall, and with the wolf again on his tail, both went spiraling over the side. Twisting and turning, over and over as they fell, Foley's arms and legs flailed.

Smashing into a large boulder, the bone in his right leg snapped. Screaming in pain, he continued his uncontrollable spiral descent. Finding itself unable to keep its footing, the wolf tumbled down the slope behind him.

When he finally came to a stop, even though in intense pain, he looked for the wolf, and seeing it land not far from him, tried to stand to get away, but with his right leg unable to support him and his left arm torn from his shoulder, he began to shake uncontrollably.

Momentarily stunned, the wolf was not about to give up its attack. Getting to its feet, it shook the dust from its coat, then raced toward Foley.

Foley felt he was done, but he had no choice, he had to keep fighting. As the wolf tore into him, before going down in a heap, he pulled the hood on Sarah's coat over his head haphazardly and asked himself. 'Where in God's name is Sarah?'

While relieved nothing happened to Lizzy, Sarah worried something dreadful had happened to Foley.

"Where is he Lizzy?" she cried. "Where is Foley?" There was no sign of him anywhere, and Lizzy was too frightened to speak.

215

With her hand shaking, all she could do was point. Picking Lizzy up, Sarah headed swiftly to where she pointed.

Coming out on the ridge, Sarah's stomach dropped. Looking along the riverbank, she stared in horror at Foley lying in a heap with a wolf standing over him. Putting Lizzy down and taking her rifle off her back, she cocked it and raised it to her shoulder. From where she was standing, the wolf should be an easy kill, but she didn't want to hit Foley.

Lowering her rifle, she ran her tongue around her dry mouth and wiped a bead of sweat from her brow, then taking a deep breath, and raising it again took aim. The wolf stood in her sights. Holding her rifle steady, she closed one eye, and looking along the barrel, couldn't pull the trigger. If Foley wasn't dead already and she made a mistake, she would kill him. Quickly shaking off her rucksack, she threw it hard away from her and watched it sail through the air to hit the ground at the bottom of the slope.

"Come on Lizzy, let's get down there!" Squatting in front of Lizzy, Lizzy obediently hooked her hands around her neck and climbed on her back. "Hang on tight," Sarah ordered.

Gripping her rifle in one hand, she stepped over the edge, and keeping her feet working to stop herself sliding too fast and falling head first, they slid their way down the slope. Pushing her rifle ahead of her and letting it go, she watched it slide over loose stones to come to rest at the bottom of the slope. Almost at the bottom, she checked to see there were no more wolves about, then getting Lizzy off her back, stood up and ran the rest of the way down.

Satisfied it had its kill, the wolf standing over Foley growled low and didn't sense Sarah was there. Foley wasn't moving. With the coat covering his body now covering his head, Sarah was unable to tell if he was dead or alive. The wolf appeared to have won the battle, but Sarah wanted this wolf dead, so not wanting to scare it off with a gun-shot, she pulled her knife from its sheath and got ready. "Stay behind me Lizzy," she said quietly back to Lizzy.

Holding the tip of her knife's blade and breaking into a run, she pulled her arm back and released it toward the wolf. If she missed, it wouldn't matter, Foley was probably dead anyway. But her knife flew straight and impaled itself deep in the wolf's side.

Howling in terror, the wolf let Foley go and while staggering away, tried to free itself from what hurt it. Coming to where Foley lay, Sarah pulled her pistol from her trousers, and stepping over him, put a bullet in the wolfs head, then without stopping, emptied her pistol into it.

Lizzy was frightened and didn't want her Ma getting too far away from her. Sliding down the slope behind her Ma, she could see Foley lying unmoving on the stones, and when she got to the bottom, she ran after her Ma running toward him and the wolf, but by then she was sobbing so much she didn't see her Ma's knife sailing through the air. When the wolf howled, her body shook with fright, then again at hearing gunshots as her Ma stepped quickly over Foley.

Lying on his back with his arms outstretched, his right leg broken, and his left arm numb, he was exhausted, but he heard through a haze of near unconsciousness Sarah emptying her pistol into the wolf before sinking into a quagmire of darkness and letting it engulf him.

"You alright sweetheart?" Sarah asked turning to Lizzy

"Yep!" Lizzy answered wiping tears from her eyes. "Mommy? Is Foley dead?" she sobbed as she flopped down beside him. Dropping her empty pistol beside the wolf, Sarah knelt opposite Lizzy and reaching over Foley, put her hand to the side of Lizzy's face.

"I don't know baby, I hope not," Sarah answered feeling despair rising in her.

"Foley?" she enquired of him while carefully removing the hood off his head so she could see what damage had been done. Not liking the bruises to his face, but relieved at finding him still breathing, after running her hands through his hair looking for signs of injury, she checked his body. Although his shirt was torn, there didn't appear to be wounds of any kind. Cupping his face in her hands, Sarah brought her mouth down on his and kissed him.

"Foley, please, wake up!" she begged.

When he didn't wake, her eyes began to well. "Foley! come on, wake up goddamn it!" she said almost sounding angry. "Open your eyes!" But Foley still didn't wake.

While he lay unconscious, Sarah thought of the two men she once loved and lost. Frank had been told she loved him all the time, but still he died alone in the High Country. She loved Christian and told him so every time they made love, only to have him shot dead by an outlaw still only a kid. But Foley had no idea she loved him because she vowed never to tell him, and here they were, he was going to die not knowing how she felt about him.

"I love you Foley, but you have to wake up!" She urged kissing him and shaking him.

Feeling himself rising from the dark bottomless pit he had descended into, Foley thought he heard Sarah saying she loved him, and if she said those words, it would be the first time she had ever spoken them, but he thought because he wanted to hear them so much, he might already be dead and was just imagining them. Opening his eyes and focusing on where he was, he found he wasn't dead after all. Leaning over him was the woman he loved. His left arm lay useless, and although his right arm hurt, he lifted it around her and pulled her toward him.

"I want to hear you say you love me Sarah," he whispered in pain.

"I love you Foley," she said, brushing a tear from his cheek where it fell before gripping the front of the ragged coat in both hands and kissing him again. But they couldn't stay out in the open where they could fall prey to wild animals on the hunt. Scanning the area around them, Sarah decided the ridge they came down would do for cover.

"How bad are you?" she asked needing to get him on his feet.

Foley's body ached from the violent attack and being twisted when he fell, and even though he didn't want Sarah worrying, he had to tell her the truth about how hurt he was.

"I hit something on the way down the slope, my right leg is broken for sure, my left arm… I don't think it's broken, but it hurts like it's come away from my shoulder." Looking around for prowling wolves and seeing none, and to avoid putting more fear into Lizzy, Sarah kept her voice steady when she spoke.

"We have to stay here tonight, but we can't stay out in the open for fear of attack, tomorrow, I will get you back to the cabin… it isn't far." They weren't far from the cabin if Foley could walk unaided, but with his broken leg, they were a long way from the cabin.

Unable to ignore his pain, he let Sarah lift him into a sitting position. Hooking her arm around his back, she lifted his good arm over her shoulder and helped him to his feet. Standing up, he mistakenly put weight on his leg which caused him great pain, and he let out a curse, but he had to do what Sarah wanted, she was right, they couldn't stay out in the open. Using her as a crutch, and hobbling precariously over to the ridge, he sat with his back against the wall and let her help him out of her coat.

While Foley rested, Sarah got busy. Racing back to where she threw her rucksack and rifle, she quickly carried them to Foley, then retrieving her knife from the dead wolf, she picked up her pistol, reloaded it and shoved it down her pants. Using her knife, she cut Foley's trouser leg and found the break. While Foley groaned in agony, she did her best to stop him moving his leg by wrapping sticks either side with the long piece of cloth she carried in her rucksack. To make a fire, Lizzy helped her collect deadwood from off the riverbank and pile it up in front of Foley. Squatting beside him for a moment Sarah took the time to think what to do next. When Lizzy knelt on the other side, Sarah and Foley looked at each other.

"Come on Lizzy, let's get you cleaned up," Sarah said looking sadly at her. Lizzy's bottom lip quivered and her eyes filled with tears. "I'm sorry mommy, I was scared."

Foley didn't want Lizzy to be embarrassed about soiling herself, after all, she was a little girl who had been confronted by such a terrible scene of someone, especially her new Pa, being attacked by a wolf, and it scared her. "It's alright darlin," he said through his pain while trying to make light of her predicament. "I was scared too, and very nearly did the same thing."

"Keep an eye out for wolves," Sarah said, handing her pistol to him. "If you see any close by, fire off a warning... come on Lizzy." Putting her rifle over her shoulder, she took Lizzy by the hand and led her to the river. Pursing his lips in anger at his own stupidity for leaving Sarah like he did, Foley was glad at least, that he could still use one hand to use Sarah's pistol. Holding it against his body with his finger on the trigger and taking in Sarah and Lizzy at the water's edge, he scanned the river up one way then down the other.

Laying her rifle beside her, Sarah undressed Lizzy then sat her in shallow water at the river's edge. The sun was going down, the water was cold, and feeling chilled, Lizzy clenched her hands in front of her chest and shivered. Seeing her shiver, Sarah quickly washed her and her clothes, then lifted her onto the riverbank. Meanwhile, Foley scanned the surrounding area until Sarah removed her vest then her shirt. Unable to take his eyes off her, he kept watching while she put her shirt on Lizzy and tied a knot in the front to give Lizzy room to move her legs. He kept watching while Sarah rolled up the sleeves and rubbed Lizzy to warm her. As Sarah put her vest back on and secured it in place, he tore his gaze away from her when he spied movement on the opposite side of the river.

A lone wolf coming out of the forest paced back and forth on the riverbank where it picked up Sarah and Lizzy's scent.

"Sarah!" Foley called, but the sound of the fast-moving current hindered Sarah hearing him. When he raised the pistol in the air and pulled the trigger, Sarah immediately grabbed her rifle and standing up, looked to where he was waving her pistol at her.

"Sarah!" he called again, and pointing in her direction. Turning to look across the river, Sarah cursed. The wolf paced back and forth in a clearing she thought must be down wind of her because she hadn't picked up its scent. Cocking her rifle, she raised it to her shoulder, and taking aim, held it in her sights. One shot, that's all it would take for Sarah to end the wolfs life.

Raising its head, the wolf gave the air a sniff, then lowering it, looked for a way across the raging torrent. Taking her eyes off the wolf, Sarah glanced at the swift current sending a torrent of turbulent water rushing over submerged boulders too, making it difficult for man or beast to cross, and figured if the wolf tried, it would be swept down-stream in the rapids and end up smashed to pieces against the boulders. Looking back at the wolf, Sarah un-cocked her rifle and hung it over her shoulder. The wolf was in luck, it would live until another day, a day when Sarah thought she would get to take its skin. Stooping down, she lifted Lizzy into her arms and carrying her and her wet clothes, headed back to Foley.

Looking over Sarah's shoulder, Lizzy searched for the wolf. "It's gone mommy," she said when she couldn't see it. Turning to see for herself, Sarah was satisfied the wolf had disappeared back into the forest.

"Why didn't you shoot it?" Foley asked as she put Lizzy down beside him.

"Why waste a bullet when it was too far away to get its skin? There will come a day when I will get it," she said, digging in her rucksack looking for her small flower-patterned tin.

'Yeah,' Foley thought, looking at the dead wolf lying not far from them. 'I'll be grateful when that day comes.'

Having planned for them to be back at the cabin in plenty of time for dinner, Sarah pursed her lips in disgust at herself for not remembering unexpected things happen on the mountain. When she and Thomas left the cabin to go hunting, she always made sure not to leave without sufficient supplies in case something went wrong and they were forced to stay out overnight. They knew never to become separated. When Foley and Lizzy began to walk off, she should have gone with them, instead she chose to stay behind so she could set her traps. Feeling she had been away from the mountain far too long, she was aware she made what could have been a fatal mistake. Not counting on anything going wrong, when she opened the tin, she found there were only four cookies left, and now those cookies would have to do in place of their evening meal. Handing Foley and Lizzy a cookie each, Sarah asked Foley if he wanted the last one, when he said no, she handed it to Lizzy.

As the sun went down Sarah lit the fire, then all three huddled together under her shredded coat, Foley with his battered and bruised good arm around her, and Lizzy sitting on her lap where she soon fell asleep with her legs across Foley. Sarah had to admit he was right to bring her coat. Even though the days were warm, the nights were cool and having it over them gave them extra warmth. Before finally settling down for the night, Sarah loaded the fire with more wood.

"We have to keep watch Foley, wolves are out there, and we could come under attack when we least expect it," Sarah whispered, keeping her hand on her rifle lying on the ground beside her. Foley didn't answer, instead, he brought Sarah in close to rest in the crook of his arm. It wasn't long in the stillness of the night and the warmth from the fire that all three fell asleep. The fire began to burn low.

Sensing sudden movement further along the riverbank, Sarah woke with a start. Something was out there in the dark recesses of the forest, and using the glow from the fire, she scanned the riverbank to see what appeared to be a rather large shadow moving about in the distance. Perhaps it was a bear, not uncommon in the Rockies that may have wandered this far south. Narrowing her eyes to get a better look, she watched as the shadow broke apart to create smaller shadows. Instead of a bear, Sarah thought perhaps they were a wolf pack coming to investigate the fire. Picking up a piece of wood, she threw it on the fire and sent sparks shooting upward in the dark to dance like dragonflies before disappearing into thin air, then bringing her rifle toward her, she rested her finger on the trigger, and waited for the shadows to come to her.

As they drew closer it became evident these shadows were not wolves. While Sarah kept watching, each shadow took on shapes she recognized. Breathing a sigh of relief as they approached, she took her finger off the trigger, and lay her rifle back down.

"Hello Joe!" she greeted, looking up at the four men. When Fergus stepped up to the fire and stood next to Joe, Will and Garrett approached and looked over the fire at Sarah and Foley huddled together, and could just see the top of Lizzy's head under the coat.

"Hello Sarah, what in tarnation are you doing here?" Joe asked, and squatting on the other side of Foley, pulled Sarah's coat down a little and uncovered Lizzy. Seeing her fast asleep, he covered her back up and looked at Foley's outstretched bandaged leg. As Fergus threw pieces of wood on the fire to keep it burning, Will and Garrett walked off to bring back more.

When Sarah moved beside him, Foley woke to see shadows coming toward them for himself, and hoping they were trappers coming to their aid, he waited anxiously before becoming relieved when seeing it was Joe and his men.

"Had a bit of a tangle with a wolf Joe, legs broken." Even though in excruciating pain, Foley laughed halfheartedly at his predicament. Seeing their dilemma, Fergus got busy unpacking his rucksack to make coffee and prepare food. Will and Garrett came back with their arms loaded with enough wood to see them through the night.

"What are you doing here Joe?" Sarah asked.

"We were just about to set up camp, up there on the ridge, saw the fire and wanted to see which trappers were here, didn't expect it to be you three." Joe studied Sarah across Foley.

"How did he get in trouble with a wolf Sarah?" he asked becoming serious.

"I was setting traps up there on the trail, Foley was heading down the trail when…" Sarah began to explain when Joe interrupted her.

"Why was he heading down the trail?" he asked, narrowing his eyes. Foley felt Sarah tense when she didn't answer Joe's question. Ignoring that she didn't answer him, Joe went on. "Where was Lizzy?" he asked.

"She was with Foley," Sarah answered quickly.

"Why weren't they with you?"

Knowing she was being tested, and knowing Joe would be able to tell if she were lying, Sarah answered truthfully. "Lizzy got tired of walking, so they were heading back…"

"Why didn't you go with them?" Again, Joe interrupted before she could explain fully what happened. Sarah knew she made a mistake, but still tried justifying why she made it.

"I had traps to set and I got mad! I tried to get them to stay with me!" In all their years of knowing each other Joe never raised his voice to Sarah, but he always managed to make her feel bad when she did something wrong.

"You didn't try hard enough Sarah! and why would you get mad at Lizzy? Look at her! she's just a baby!" Sarah didn't have to look at Lizzy, she knew she was a baby, her baby.

"I walked all over this mountain when I was just like her," she said trying to justify making Lizzy walk. But Joe scoffed at her explanation

"You did not! your father or we four carried you everywhere you went!… you keep Lizzy close Sarah! if you can't trap and keep her

223

with you, then don't trap!... how come you didn't know the wolf was there?" Listening to Joe grilling Sarah, and to show he supported her decision to stay behind, Foley tightened his arm around her, but kept quiet.

"It was down wind of me," Sarah answered casting her eyes down.

"How far down wind?"

"Far enough for me not to know it was there." Sarah was near to tears, her voice cracked when she answered, but Joe wasn't satisfied.

"It wasn't was it? You made a mistake, didn't you? You should have known it was there," he said lowering his voice so as not to wake Lizzy. "Your mistake could have cost Foley and Lizzy their lives Sarah!" Even though Joe's voice was steady it told everyone he was angry.

"I've been away a long time Joe!" Sarah snapped suddenly.

Able to tell Sarah was upset at Joe's continual questioning her decisions, Foley wanted his grilling to end. "Wait a minute Joe! what happened was not Sarah's fault, it was…!" but Joe ignored him and continued with Sarah.

"You own what happened Sarah, a mistake like you made could have cost you dearly." He was glad she was back living on the mountain, but she had to remember all she had been taught from trapping years before, not remembering could cost her, her life, or that of her family. Joe reprimanding her without hostility was his way of reminding her to be diligent with the way things worked on the mountain. Looking at Sarah's downcast face, he was satisfied she knew she made a mistake.

"Yes Joe," Sarah answered.

Foley didn't understand how things worked on the mountain, and felt Joe had gone too far. Sarah was a woman, not a child to be scolded. "Don't go blaming Sarah for any of this Joe! I was the one that got angry and walked off! it wasn't the other way round!" he snapped.

"You know this fucking mountain do you Foley?" Joe answered suddenly and jabbing his finger at Foley. Baulking at Joe turning on him, Foley stopped to think.

"No! I fucking don't! but I'm learning... fast!" he snarled. Almost getting killed because of his ignorance of what happens on the mountain, he felt pleased with his reply and returned Joe's profanity. But he wasn't prepared for Joe's savage tirade aimed back at him.

"Sarah knows this fucking mountain better than all of us!... she was born to it! it's her mountain! and you better fucking listen to everything she has to say about it! you do everything she fucking tells you! don't you fucking question it, because this mountain will fucking kill you if you fucking let it!" Joe was talking to his equal. Not once did he curse or raise his voice in anger when berating Sarah for her mistake. Remembering Lizzy was with them, Joe quietened. He wasn't happy he berated Foley. All he wanted was for him not to make the same mistake Frank made when he got himself killed. "We'll set your leg in the morning, then get you back to Sarah's cabin, get some food into you and get some sleep."

Foley didn't like that he was being scolded either, but didn't say any more, instead thought it best to tell Joe what else was wrong with him.

"I can't move my arm Joe, I think the wolf pulled it from my shoulder." Sympathetic to Foley's injuries, after saying they would try to put his arm back in as well, Joe settled down on his bedroll for the night.

After placing his gear next to Foley, Will went to lift Lizzy out of Sarah's coat to lay her on his bedroll, only Sarah held the fur tight to keep him from seeing how she was dressed.

"I'm not exactly dressed proper Will," she informed him. Looking across the fire and seeing Lizzy's clothes spread out on scrubby bushes to dry, Will looked back at Sarah.

"She's wearing my shirt," Sarah said showing him a bare arm. Hearing what Sarah said, Fergus rummaged around in his rucksack, and coming round the fire, stood opposite while holding up what looked like a piece of rag.

"Here Sarah lass, yee wear this, it should do until yee get Lizzy's clothes dry." Shaking out the piece of rag, Sarah could see it was a well-worn shirt, and took it from him.

"Thanks Fergus, now turn around." When all four men turned their backs to the fire, Sarah sat on her knees in front of Foley and quickly removed her vest.

While watching her push her arms into the sleeves and pull the shirt closed over her breasts, Foley checked the men to make sure they had their backs turned, then smiling at Sarah watching him watching her, he winked. While doing up the buttons, Sarah felt thankful he tried backing her when Joe berated her for her mistake, and she smiled back and leant toward him.

"I love you, Mister Andrews," she whispered just loud enough for him to hear, and leaning further forward until their faces came together, kissed him.

"I love you, Misses Andrews," he returned softly when they stopped kissing. Peering over his shoulder to see what was taking Sarah so long getting the shirt on, Joe saw what they were doing, and turning back to face the river, smiled in satisfaction.

"You can turn around now," Sarah said once she finished buttoning the shirt. When the men turned, Sarah was putting her vest on.

Having worn herself out from walking the mountain and being frightened badly by the wolf attack, Lizzy didn't wake up when Will moved her to lay on his bedroll. Treating Lizzy as he would his own, Will would do everything in his power to keep her safe. After covering her with his blanket, he took off his coat and covered her with that too, then sat beside her to eat food Fergus had prepared.

Daybreak next morning, Lizzy woke to find Will sleeping on bare ground beside her, and looking around the camp at the fire still burning, she found Fergus and Garrett asleep and her Ma and Foley asleep in each other's arms. Joe was sitting by the fire keeping watch when Lizzy got out of Wills bedroll and scurried around to him. After wrapping her in his arms and giving her a hug, he got busy getting her food and preparing some for everyone.

When all had woken and eaten and Sarah dressed Lizzy in her own clothes, it was time for the men to get Foley sorted so they could get him to Sarah's cabin.

"Let's take a look at that shoulder first," Joe demanded. While groaning in pain, Foley let Sarah and Joe help him out of his shirt. Trying not to hurt him any more than he already was, when Sarah carefully pushed his shirt over his dislocated shoulder and Joe helped get it down his arms, they were shocked at seeing his body covered in bruises. Joe felt no animosity toward Foley from their disagreement the night before, in fact, he felt sorry for berating him at all.

"Shit Foley, you must have put up one hell of a fight, you sure your arms not broken?" he asked sounding concerned.

"That damn wolf had a good go at me Joe, but I'm pretty sure it slipped out, that's all, can you put it back?" Foley was putting on a brave face, his arm hurt like hell and his body ached in places he didn't know he had, but he didn't want any of them worrying, especially Sarah.

"We'll give it a bloody good try... Sarah, take Lizzy and go for a walk, Will you go with them, Fergus, you and Garrett can help me." Joe took control as he always did, and the other men followed his orders without question.

With Lizzy walking between them holding their hands, Sarah and Will walked to the waters-edge where they sat side by side watching Lizzy standing in front of them throwing pebbles into the water.

"It was awful to watch Will, when I saw him lying there with that wolf standing over him, I was sure he was dead," Sarah commented, wrapping her arms about her legs while keeping her eyes on Lizzy.

"Yeah, but he's pretty tough Sarah, he wasn't going without a fight."

Hearing a pain-filled cry coming from the camp as the men put Foley's arm back in place, Will and Sarah turned to look. Lizzy hurried back to them with her bottom lip sticking out in a pout.

"Mommy, are they hurting Foley?" she asked in dismay as Sarah wrapped her in her arms.

"They have to hurt him a little to help him Lizzy," Will offered before Sarah could answer. Satisfied with what Will told her, Lizzy went back to throwing pebbles.

"What Foley went through, was that what happened to Frank?" Sarah asked when Lizzy was out of earshot.

"Frank was already dead Sarah, he didn't feel anything." Remembering Frank shot himself before the wolves could get at him, Will put his arm around Sarah's shoulders to comfort her.

"I'm sorry I had to put it that way," he said quietly.

While Fergus held him down and Joe lined up his shinbone, Foley bit down on the stick Garrett put in his mouth and tried not to scream. After two reasonably straight pieces of wood were placed either side of his leg to form a splint, his leg was wrapped tight with Sarah's strip of cloth. When they were done, Fergus waved his arm in Sarah and Will's direction indicating for them to come back.

Foley seemed much more at ease now his arm stopped hurting and his leg was in a splint. While he rested, Will and Garrett took a walk back to where Sarah set her traps, and scouring the area where Foley had been attacked by the wolf, they found his rifle, his hat, and the two canteens where he quickly discarded them. They located Sarah's two traps where she threw them when she heard Lizzy's scream. Sarah dragged the dead wolf to the river where she skinned it then pushed the carcass into the water and watched the river carry it away.

After fashioning a stretcher out of tree branches and one of their blankets, the men lifted Foley onto it and carried him back to Sarah's cabin.

Chapter Eighteen

aving left Foley in bed to recuperate, the four trappers camped at Sarah's cabin for several days, cutting wood and helping out with other chores, but since then they made the arduous journey back to their camp on the High Ridge. Hearing Sarah moving about in the living area while speaking softly with Lizzy, Foley wondered what she was up to.

After loading her rucksack for the trek back to the place she set her traps, Sarah went to the room where Foley lay to let him know she was going. Foley stared at her shoving her pistol down the front of her pants as she came through the door, and wasn't happy.

"Where are you going?" he asked, worried she may be going hunting and would be leaving him on his own.

"I have to check my traps," she said casually.

"What the hell for? What about Lizzy? You leaving her with me? And what about me Sarah? You know I can't do anything without your help!" Joe fashioned a crutch for Foley to use once he could get up and hobble about, but Foley felt he wasn't ready to get out of bed unaided.

"You can get to the washroom, I put a bucket in there for you, and I will leave you some food," Sarah said picking her sheath up off the tallboy.

"Goddamn it Sarah! your traps are not important! we don't need the skins, and you know it!" he snapped in anger. Foley had seen her book at Morley's bank filled with deposits and knew she didn't need money, Sarah though, was unaware of how much she had because no one had reason to tell her.

Standing in the doorway dressed and ready to go too, Lizzy watched Sarah tighten the strap holding her hunting knife around her waist. "I can walk, Foley," she let him know.

Fearful they would come under attack from wolves, and ignoring what Lizzy said, Foley urged them not to go. "It's a six hour walk up and back Sarah!" he stressed. "You won't get back before dark!"

"We'll get back well before then," Sarah replied turning her back on him and leaving the room. A few minutes later she returned carrying a covered tray which she placed on the chair beside the bed. "There's bread and cheese and a bowl of preserved fruit, water is in the jug and there's a mug, you'll be alright until I get back." Foley clearly was not going to win this argument no matter how hard he tried.

"Goddamn it, Sarah! I'm going to lie here worrying until you get back!" he said feeling useless. "Be careful," was all he could muster. When Sarah bent down and kissed him, he wrapped his arms around her and held her. "I love you!" he said sternly before letting her leave.

"I love you too." Sarah answered, pulling away and leaving the room.

Sarah and Lizzy made good time. They only stopped twice on the way to where Sarah's traps were set. Once for them to relieve themselves, the other to have a bite to eat. Sarah's traps were easily found by searching the canopy of trees above them where she tied red rope markers. Telling Lizzy to stay beside her, she checked four traps lying in a wide arc at the edge of a clearing. Two traps held a wolf each. Another had been set off by a smaller animal walking over it. The smell of rotting flesh permeated the air. The fourth trap was still set and lay empty so Sarah left it where it was.

After skinning the wolves, and cleaning the rotting animal out of her trap, she reset the traps, then rolling the skins up and tying them to her rucksack, she and Lizzy set off back to her cabin. Along the way Lizzy walked slowly and closed her eyes, but she wasn't complaining, she didn't want a wolf attacking them like when Foley was attacked. When Lizzy began to stagger, Sarah could see how tired she was becoming.

"Come on Lizzy, I will carry you a little of the way." Putting her rifle over her shoulder, she picked Lizzy up and kept going. It wasn't long before Lizzy put her head down and fell asleep, making Sarah carry her all the way home.

Dragging himself out of bed, and using the crutch Joe made him, Foley made his way to the washroom and the bucket. Trying not to put weight on his leg, he hobbled back to bed where he continued to worry. He was missing Sarah badly. The cabin was far too quiet. He had become used to Lizzy making noise and missed her constant banter. After eating the food Sarah left and sleeping fitfully, he thought how he had been careful not to get Sarah pregnant. He still didn't want her pregnant but made up his mind the next time they made love, he wouldn't be so careful, of course he would need to wait until his leg mended before he could do anything, but he vowed he would make up for how he was leaving Sarah and himself unfulfilled.

When Sarah called out to him to let him know she and Lizzy were back, a feeling of relief washed over him. After putting Lizzy to bed, Sarah went to the bedroom to see him. When she dropped her rucksack on the floor just inside the door and sat heavily on the side of the bed with her hair disheveled and her face red from exertion, he saw the skins she had trapped.

"How did you cope?" she asked, reaching out to brush a strand of hair from his brow.

"I didn't," he said, grabbing her and pulling her against him before she could protest.

"Foley!" Sarah exclaimed in surprise after he kissed her with passion. Smiling when he let her go, she stood up and picked up her rucksack.

"I have to go back in a couple of days," she said taking the rucksack outside where she untied the two skins and took them to her old cabin for storage until winter when she would take them to Cedar Creek. Hearing what she said, and having hoped she wouldn't reset her traps so she wouldn't need to go out again, Foley leant back on the pillows in frustration.

While Lizzy slept and Foley rested, Sarah busied herself making dinner and tidying the cabin. She felt tired but had to keep going. Foley needed her and so did Lizzy. After emptying the bucket from the washroom, she washed her face and hands, changed into clean shirt and trousers, then brushed her hair and tied it back in a tail.

When dinner was ready, she took Foley's meal to the bedroom for him where he could see by her eyes, she was tired. "I can come to the table Sarah, I've been up once already," he said not wanting to be a burden.

"You stay where you are!" Sarah scolded lightheartedly. Going back to the table where Lizzy was sitting having her meal, Sarah said something to her that Foley couldn't hear. When Lizzy and Sarah entered the bedroom carrying their dinner plates, his eyes widened in surprise.

"Hold this for me!" Lizzy said shoving her plate at Foley and giving him no choice but to take it. Careful not to touch his broken leg, she climbed over him, and once seated cross-legged with her back against the wall, Foley handed her plate back to her. "Thank you, Foley," she drawled in her sweetest voice, and crinkling her eyes in a smile, tucked into her food.

Looking from Lizzy to Sarah sitting on top of the covers with her legs outstretched and leaning back on their pillows, he smiled. Smiling back, Sarah stuck her fork into her vegetables and began to eat. While Foley ate, he was filled with happiness. Sarah and Lizzy had returned safely. The two most important people in his life were sitting right there on the bed beside him.

Two days later Sarah prepared to go out to check her traps again, and while she and Lizzy were gone, Foley worried. He only hoped the day would go as it had before.

When they came upon Sarah's traps, Lizzy was talking incessantly, telling Sarah about the birds she had seen and the tiny bush mice she saw scurrying about in the undergrowth. Sarah felt pleased Lizzy spotted the animals. It seemed she was beginning to get a true feeling for life on the mountain.

The four trappers were hunting above that part of the mountain they called the Middle Ground when they came upon Reece and Samuels. The six men greeted each other amicably.

"Where you headed Reece?" Joe asked as he looked from one to the other.

"Heading back to the high ridge, been hunting here for a few weeks now, had enough, wolves have gone... cause we might have scared them off with our catch!" Reece answered grinning and pointing to his horse. Joe could see both men had a good many skin's strapped to their packhorses. Joe's group didn't have their horses with them this time around. Leaving their horses to be taken care of at the High Ridge Camp meant they could move through the dense forest much more quickly and stealthily, letting them come upon wolves without their sensing they were there. Reece and Samuels could see Joe and his men were all carrying a lot of skins on their backs. The two men were especially in awe of Joe. He was the best at trapping. Every year he never failed to win the pot, but this last winter, when Samuels beat him by one skin, Samuels hoped to beat him again this year, but he could never tell how many skins Joe got.

"Where you headed Joe?" Reece asked returning the question.

"Thought we might hunt along the river for a while," Joe said looking around at where they were. "Got a few skins ourselves not far from here!" he said inclining his head toward the forest where they came from.

"Passed Logan and Reeves some time ago, hunting a bit further along, weren't having much luck though." Knowing Joe liked to keep track of where trappers were trapping, Samuels thought it important to offer up information about Logan's whereabouts. When he said Logan was nearby, Joe immediately became suspicious.

"Where did you say they were headed?" Joe asked.

"I didn't say Joe, but they were heading for the low ridge, seems they hang about down there quite a bit." Telling Joe where Logan and Reeves were going, caused Samuels to frown at the look that crossed Joe's face. The Low Ridge covered a wide area, taking in the River Flats, Sarah's cabin and the pass, and to get there, one had to traverse the Middle Ground.

"Did Logan say exactly where he might do his hunting?" Joe questioned further. Samuels could see Joe getting agitated and nodded. "Yeah! not far from Sarah's cabin, if that helps any." Joe cursed out aloud. When it came to Sarah, he didn't trust Logan as far as he could spit.

"How long ago did you see them?" he asked.

"One… maybe two, hours ago!" Samuels answered.

"Let's go!" Joe said turning sharply toward Fergus, and rushing past Will and Garrett, set off at a cracking pace.

"See you Joe!" Samuels called. Joe didn't look back. Heading in the direction of the Low Ridge, he simply raised his arm in acknowledgement and while keeping on going, the other three men followed him.

"What do you make of that?" Reece asked Samuels as they watched the four men getting further away.

"Don't know, trouble with Logan maybe, you know Logan!" Samuels answered scratching his head in wonder.

"Yeah! I know him alright!" Reece said rubbing his hand over his jaw. 'All too fucking well!' he said under his breath. Turning toward the forest, the two men pulled their packhorses behind them and loped off in the opposite direction to the four trappers.

Fergus trotted along beside Joe. "You think Logan may be going to try something Joe?" he asked trying to keep up.

"You know I don't trust Logan, he shouldn't be anywhere near Sarah's cabin, I warned the men to stay away from the low ridge… especially Sarah's cabin." Joe was walking fast, Garrett and Will were almost running to keep up with both him and Fergus.

As they hurried on, Joe told the men if Sarah was out hunting while Foley was laid up, then she could be in serious trouble if Logan and Reeves came across her by herself. Even if she could hide her tracks, Logan knew the mountain as well as any of them, and Joe didn't trust him not to find her. Except for a few derogatory remarks, Sarah hadn't had trouble from Logan since Joe beat him senseless when he tried taking her for himself all those years ago. Every trapper took Logan's beating as a warning as to what they could be in for if they tried anything where she was concerned. They knew all too well if Joe didn't punish them, there was Fergus, and both Garrett and Will to contend with.

Being part of the family of trappers, the men respected Sarah, and while she was raising Thomas, they left her to hunt and trap wherever she wanted, and most times she only ventured as far as the River Flats, but occasionally she chose to trap along the Middle Ground, and that was where she was setting traps when a wolf attacked Foley. Joe worried things were going to get out of hand now all the trappers knew Foley was laid up with a broken leg and couldn't go hunting with her.

There was another thing the four trappers were deeply concerned about, and that was if Sarah took Lizzy with her, then Lizzy would be in danger too, and the men had no doubt Lizzy would be with Sarah. All four men pushed their way quickly through the forest as they picked up their pace.

Chapter Nineteen

Sarah was disappointed to see only one wolf caught in her traps this time. Before removing its skin completely, the scent of something that wasn't wolf tickled her senses. A distinct smell of a trapper nearby wafted in the air. She had to hurry, trappers were coming. Putting her head down, she got busy getting the skin from the carcass.

"Mommy, look?" Lizzy called seeing movement in the forest. Glancing up at Lizzy seated on a log close by, and seeing her pointing to a stand of trees, Sarah ceased skinning the wolf and stood up when she saw two men coming her way.

"Howdy Misses Andrews!" Logan greeted with a sly grin as Reeves came sauntering along behind him. Knowing what Logan thought of her, Sarah wasn't taking any chances. As the two men approached, she checked her pistol was still firmly tucked into her trousers where she could get at it easily.

"Howdy Logan... Reeves," she greeted with a nod, then immediately Reeves walked past her and sat on the log next to Lizzy, she knew she was in trouble. Gripping her knife tight, she felt the hilt pressing into her palm.

"Get away from her Reeves," Sarah warned.

"I'm just takin' a rest Misses Andrews," Reeves grinned slyly. When Logan grinned too and turned to look at their surroundings, Sarah shifted her grip on her knife to get a better hold.

Turning back suddenly, and using the back of his hand, Logan struck Sarah on the side of her head catching her by surprise, and stunning her with the sudden blow, caused her to stagger sideways and fall. Seeing her Ma get hit, Lizzy let out a shrill cry, but before she could run to where she had fallen, Reeves pounced. Struggling when he grabbed her, Lizzy screamed and pounded him with her tiny fists. Although dazed, Sarah heard Lizzy's cry and seeing Reeves take hold of her, was not going to let them hurt her daughter, but before she could get to her feet, Logan sat heavily on top of her and pinned her down.

Hoping he hadn't seen her knife, she gripped the hilt firmly, then swung her hand toward his face. Catching a glimpse of Sarah's knife coming toward him, Logan raised his arm to protect himself. Sarah's knife, as sharp as it was, sliced easily through the sleeve of his coat cutting his arm. As blood spurted from the wound, Logan yelled savagely and balling his hand into a fist, punched Sarah hard across her face almost knocking her out, then forcing her hand open, prized her knife out of her hand.

"You fucking bitch!" he cursed, and throwing the knife aside, pulled her pistol out of her trousers. "You won't be needing this!" he snarled while tossing the gun away.

Although dazed, Sarah began to fight, not for her life, but for Lizzy's. Twisting her body trying to get out from under Logan was impossible, but reaching up, and digging her fingers into his face, she dragged them downwards and tore his skin before grabbing his beard and pulling it as hard as she could. Not expecting her to fight back as much as she was, Logan snarled as her fingernails drew blood. After punching her viciously, he tore at her shirt angrily trying to expose her. Continuing to fight, Sarah tried to cover herself as best as she could, but her blows had little effect. Pushing her hands easily out of his way, Logan tugged at her trousers and got them open.

"Mommy!" Lizzy sobbed before Reeves clamped his hand over her mouth. "It's alright darlin, he's just having some fun with mommy, it'll all be over soon," he sneered.

"Reeves! goddamn it! Joe will kill you!... Logan! I'm pregnant!" Thinking if she told them she was having a baby they might let her go, Sarah did something no trapper would ever do, and that was resort to begging.

"Reeves! help me, please!... Logan, please, I beg you, stop!" she cried, but her pleas made no difference to either man. Fighting valiantly while crying hysterically, Sarah tried desperately to stop Logan getting her trousers down where he could get himself on top of her.

"I've paid you good money for what I'm going to do to you, bitch! it's time I collect what's owed me!" Logan sneered.

Sarah didn't understand what Logan meant by paying her money, she couldn't remember there ever being a time when he gave her money. Seeing an opportunity to get away from him when he let go of her to undo his trousers, she dug her fingers into the earth either side of her, and grabbing a handful of rocks mixed with dirt and grass, suddenly brought both hands up, and letting go of the soil, watched it hit Logan in his eyes and mouth. While spitting dirt and gagging, Logan lashed out, and punched Sarah hard across her face.

Hearing Sarah say she was pregnant, for a moment Reeves thought maybe they should let her go, but wanting to see how far his partner could get, instead of helping her, he decided not to do anything. While Sarah lay dazed, Reeves starred over the top of Logan when he thought he saw movement amongst the trees. Getting to his feet, he let Lizzy go when he recognized Garrett and Will with their rifles at the ready running at a fast pace towards them.

Busy readying himself to take Sarah, Logan didn't notice the men were upon them. Even if Logan hadn't got to Sarah, Reeves understood if he didn't do something to stop Logan, both he and Logan were dead men. When a shot rang out, and Reeves felt a bullet whizz by close to his head, he rushed at Logan, who by this time had lowered his trousers over his hips to reveal a grubby pair of long-johns. Striking out with his foot, Reeves smashed his boot into the side of Logan's head, and knocked him off Sarah.

"Get off her you son-of-a-bitch!" he yelled, but only for Garrett and Will's benefit.

Thinking it would stand in his stead if he went against Logan, he swung his foot again. Lying dazed and bloodied on the ground, Logan wondered why the boot from his partner of many years suddenly connected with his head.

When Sarah felt Logan's weight shift, she came around, and although dazed, managed to sit up. Her face hurt, her cheek burned with pain where Logan punched her, her nose bled and her lip was cut, she could taste the sweet pungent taste of her own blood. Seeing Garrett and Will run past, she pulled her trousers closed and scrambled to do up her shirt. Most of the buttons had been torn off leaving her shirt gaping down the front, but she hastily pulled it across her body and tucked it roughly into her trousers. Free of Reeves clutches, Lizzy could be heard sobbing loudly as she ran to Sarah. Throwing herself into Sarah's outstretched arms, they both kept crying as they clung to each other.

As Will rushed toward him, Reeves scrambled to get out of his way. But before Reeves could escape, Will hit him a hard blow to the side of his head with the butt of his rifle, and sent him crashing to the ground in an unconscious heap beside Logan. Coming out of the trees behind Garrett and Will, Joe rushed to where Sarah and Lizzy were, and kneeling beside them, took them in his arms. While Will kept his rifle aimed at Reeves waiting for him to come round, Garrett and Fergus lifted Logan roughly to his feet. After helping Sarah to a log, Joe sat her down, and taking in her torn clothes and bruised and bloodied face, didn't like what he was seeing.

"Are you alright Sarah? Did he get to you?" he asked sounding concerned. Keeping Lizzy, who was still sobbing turned from Logan so she couldn't see him with his trousers down, Sarah looked into Joe's face and could see the disgust he was feeling, and wondered if it was for her, or for Logan.

"He tried Joe, but all he got was a look," she answered with little feeling. This was the second time Logan tried forcing himself on her, and Sarah was thoroughly disgusted with him. The men looked at Logan's head, and could see where it bled when she scratched him and from Reeves boot connecting with it, but Sarah couldn't bring herself to look at him.

Holding her while kissing her on her forehead convinced Sarah Joe's disgust was for Logan. Leaving her and Lizzy together, Joe rushed over to Logan, and clenching his hands into fists while glaring angrily into his face, wanted to kill him right there for what he had done. But Joe wasn't a killer and wouldn't go against the law, but he was going to make damn sure Logan, and Reeves paid dearly for this day. With Fergus and Garrett holding Logan firmly in their grasp, Joe pummeled him until they could no longer hold him up. Hearing Reeves moaning as he came round, the two men stood him up just as roughly as Logan so he could meet his punishment head on.

"I tried to stop him Joe," Reeves said when seeing the punishment these men were going to mete out. Joe's punishing blows on Logan the first time he tried taking Sarah should have been enough to scare Reeves, but he went along with Logan simply because he was his partner.

"Reeves held Lizzy Joe! he didn't try to stop Logan! not until you came along!" Sarah didn't care that Reeves got Logan off her. She didn't hesitate to let the men know what they would have done once Logan violated her. "They wouldn't have ended with me Joe!"

That thought left all four men feeling sick to their stomach and Joe lashed out, landing punishing blows on Reeves body until he collapsed to the ground beside Logan. Picking up one of the men's rifles, and standing beside a tree, Joe held it by its barrel and swinging it furiously at the trunk, broke it in two. Without stopping to draw breath, he picked up the other and did the same. While Fergus stayed with Sarah and Lizzy, Garrett and Will built a fire.

"What were you doing back here Joe?" Sarah asked when he went back to her. Squatting in front of her, and feeling sickened at seeing her eyes already turning black near her bloodied nose, Joe wet a cloth from his canteen and carefully cleaned her face.

"We heard Logan was hunting down this way, thought we would take a look as to why he was here when he should have been on the high ridge, sorry we weren't sooner Sarah, are you sure you're alright?" Joe worried Sarah may have been violated before they could get to her.

"I'm alright Joe," Sarah replied knowing what he was asking. "He didn't get to me, if he had, I would put my gun to my head and end it," she said sadly. Tears welled as she thought of what Logan said. "Joe, Logan… he said he… he paid me for… for, you know… what he was going to do to me… and that it was time for him to collect… what did he mean Joe?"

Studying her bruised face and understanding what she was asking, Joe pursed his lips trying to decide whether he should tell her or not the reason for what Logan threatened.

"I'll be back in a moment," he said handing her the cloth.

Sarah watched Joe go to where the men were huddled watching over the fire, and watched them talking animatedly while keeping their voices down until Joe squatted back in front of her. The secret, not only these four but all the trappers had been keeping, no longer needed to be kept secret. Before speaking to Sarah, Joe bowed his head in thought for a moment.

"The trappers have been putting money in your book Sarah," he said looking up at her and thinking his few words should explain everything, but Sarah looked aghast at his declaration.

"What do you mean, putting money in my book? What money? What for Joe?" Sarah was confused and angry and wanted Joe to explain fully what he meant.

"Part of the money the men make from trapping has been going to you to help you out," he answered. As tears swum in her eyes, Sarah looked away.

"Why Joe? Why would they want to help me?" Sarah asked turning back to face him. When Joe started to explain, he waved the men over where they crowded around to listen.

"When your Pa died, you were left with nothing. That first year you trapped on your own you didn't do so well, so we decided to give you some of our money to help you for when your trapping wasn't doing so good, you were always on the bottom of the board Sarah, and we just wanted to help. Then when Thomas came along, the money was there to help you raise him, and you did raise him, all on your own, you did a damn fine job with that boy, and we are proud of how he has turned out." The other men nodded in agreement.

"All of you?" she asked softly looking around at the men.

"Not only us but all the trappers," Joe said, and because he was proud the men had done what he asked and had kept it secret all these years, he smiled faintly.

"I never used any money other than what I made from my skinning Joe!" Sarah stressed.

"I'm afraid you did Sarah, you think you sent Thomas off to college with what little money you had? That took more than what Christian left you and what you made from skinning a few wolves." When Joe smiled up at the men, it got Sarah thinking.

"But Joe, do all the men think the same as Logan? Do they think I owe them for what he wanted? Is that why they proposed to me all the time?" As a tear ran down Sarah's bruised cheek, all four men gasped at what she said.

"No, goddamn it! that is not why!" Joe's shocked response and disgust for Logan showed in his voice as he got to his feet. "Goddamn it Sarah, they wouldn't dare! besides, Logan is just an asshole! I should have dealt with him a long time ago!"

"The money has to go back to the men Joe! when I go back to town, I will see to it!" Sarah said. Watching her stand on shaky legs, each man gave thought to her statement.

"I don't want my money Sarah." It was Will who spoke first, then Garrett, then Fergus. None of them would ever consider taking back the money they gave her.

"None of the other men will take it either Sarah, I can guarantee that," Joe said while thinking he would make sure they wouldn't.

Sarah felt ill, but taking Lizzy by the hand, had to make her way back to the cabin to try and explain to Foley the state she was in. "I don't want Logan's money in my account Joe!" she said bursting into tears. As she swayed as if to faint, Joe grabbed her and held her in his arms.

"It's alright sweetheart, you can get rid of his money, maybe give it to the school, or the church for charity." Sarah leant against Joe for him to comfort her. "You know I don't give charity Joe," she said lifting her face and looking up at him. "But I guess, I can make an exception, just this once." When Joe laughed and hugged her, Sarah tried laughing then too, but her face hurt and she refrained.

"Come on, let's get you back to your cabin," Joe said letting the men gather her gear.

243

While Sarah walked beside Joe, Fergus carried her rucksack and canteen, and Garrett her rifle. Will scooped Lizzy up and carried her on his shoulders.

"Joe!" Sarah said, letting the other men get a little further ahead of her before stopping Joe on the trail. Looking into her bruised and battered face, Joe stood facing her waiting for her to speak, and was saddened by what damage had been done. Needing to tell him something, but wanting him to keep it to himself, at least for now, Sarah looked him squarely in his eyes, and spoke so the other men couldn't hear.

"Joe, I'm having another baby."

Suddenly realizing with Sarah being pregnant how the situation with Logan could have been much worse, Joe's eyes immediately softened, and reaching out, pulled her toward him. "Jesus Sarah," he uttered sounding dismayed and holding her.

"Don't tell Foley Joe, he doesn't know."

Visions of Christian learning she was pregnant moments before she fell off the cliff and into the river flowing below Cedar Creek flashed before Joe's eyes.

"Why haven't you told him?" he asked frowning.

"After what happened with Maria," Sarah stated sadly. "He doesn't want children, I have to tell him in my own good time, please don't say anything!"

After agreeing not to say anything, he said he thought she was making a huge mistake keeping it from Foley, after all, he was her husband and a good man, he deserved to know she was carrying his child. When the men stopped to wait for them further down the trail, Joe and Sarah caught up. Seeming to have forgotten the traumatic events that just happened, Lizzy talked to the men incessantly, bringing a smile to each man's face. Watching Sarah walking with Will and Garrett either side of her, Joe wished they could go back to an earlier time, a time before his friend Calahan, had died, a time before things started happening to Sarah.

Before arriving at the cabin, the four trappers agreed they would give up hunting for a few days. Joe told Sarah she was not to go trapping at all, she was to stay at the cabin while Foley continued to recover. Sarah agreed she would. What happened with Logan and Reeves frightened her enough to make her do as he bid. Foley felt relieved when he heard Sarah and Lizzy come back earlier than they had two days before, but frowned when hearing other voices with them. Lizzy's giggling and talking nonstop to the other men when Joe stepped into the bedroom, gave Foley no reason to think anything was wrong. "Didn't expect to see you back so soon Joe," he said smiling at Joe standing in the doorway.

When Sarah stepped into the room behind Joe, Foley's smile disappeared, his eyes widened and his heart went to his throat at seeing the condition of her face. Taking in her swollen cut lip and black eyes, he stared at her torn shirt pulled haphazardly across the front of her. "Sarah! what the bloody hell has happened?" he asked as his heart raced.

Having already asked Joe to explain what happened, Sarah tried not to look at Foley while she went straight to the tallboy where she pulled open a drawer and took out a fresh shirt and pair of trousers.

"Sarah! did a wolf do that?" Foley asked thinking she met with a wolf the same has he.

"Goddamn it! how did you get those fucking bruises?" Feeling anger rising in him at not getting answers, he thumped his fists on the bed as Sarah made to leave the room.

"Sarah!" he snapped sharply when she ignored him and glanced at Joe.

"Goddamn it Joe! tell me what the fucking hell is going on!?" He demanded after she disappeared into the washroom.

"She met up with Logan," Joe said keeping his voice calm.

Well aware Logan wanted Sarah for himself, Foley stared wide eyed at Joe and felt his stomach drop at the feeling of dread overcoming him from the possibility Sarah may have been violated. Hearing Foley's anguished pleas coming from the bedroom, the other men kept Lizzy occupied in the living area while leaving Joe to explain the events as they happened.

The more Joe talked while sitting on a chair next to the bed, the more furious Foley became, and feeling helpless lying in bed unable to get about, he cursed out aloud to think Logan tried taking his wife, and was angry at himself for having a broken leg that stopped him being with her to protect her from men such as Logan. Clenching his hands into fists, he gripped the bedclothes tight until his knuckles turned white with fury. "I will fucking kill him Joe! I will kill that fucking son-of-a-bitch with my bare hands!"

"You don't have to worry about Logan, or Reeves, they are dead men!" Joe said leaning forward and looking at the floor. He didn't like doing what he had done, but he wouldn't let anyone hurt Sarah, especially the way Logan was going to, both men deserved the punishment he gave them.

Foley wondered what Joe meant by saying Logan and Reeves were dead men. Knowing the four men made a promise to keep Sarah safe, he wanted to know if their promise meant they would kill to do it.

"What do you mean they are dead men Joe?" he asked.

"We stripped them of everything, burnt their clothes, and what was left of their guns. The only weapon they have to defend themselves with is one small knife, they won't survive long out there without guns." Having thought he explained enough, Joe got up and left the room.

With no weapons to defend themselves against wild animals that took a fancy to fresh meat, after being attacked by a wolf himself, Foley could imagine what it would be like for Logan and Reeves to be on the mountain as naked as the day they were born. The two men had no way of trapping food and wouldn't last long on a mountain that could sometimes be beautiful, but most of the time was deadly.

Struggling out of bed to relieve himself, but instead of going back to bed, Foley stood beside Sarah at the fire while she poured them coffee. He wasn't convinced by what Joe told him, and with the thought of what Logan may have done to Sarah eating him up inside, he had to ask the question gnawing at him.

"Did he rape you Sarah?" he asked almost inaudibly. But Sarah heard, and looking at him, frowned when she didn't understand his question.

"Rape?... I don't understand what you mean." Sarah knew what Joe meant when he asked her if Logan had 'got to her,' and she knew of another unsavoury word to describe taking a woman. She was almost at an age some folks considered old, and no-one had ever mentioned the word rape to her, Foley was the first. Frowning solemnly at Sarah not understanding what he meant, he put his question another, more straightforward way.

"You know what I mean, did he… fuck you?" When he used that somewhat distasteful word for sex, Sarah stopped pouring their coffee and looked knowingly up at him.

"He tore my shirt and pulled my trousers down, he got a good look at most things and I fought as hard as I could to stop him, I was lucky Garrett and Will came along when they did, I wouldn't have been able to fight him off if they hadn't come along." Sarah handed Foley his mug.

Although satisfied with her answer, Foley hoped Logan and Reeves died a slow death. If the mountain didn't kill them, then he would. No man while ever he drew breath was going to disrespect Sarah, she was his wife, he loved her, but he was thinking maybe now it was best if he didn't touch her, at least for a time.

"You best sleep in with Lizzy," he said feeling despondent. Shocked by his telling her to sleep in the other room with Lizzy, Sarah stared wide-eyed up at him.

"Why?" she asked feeling confused. They had been sleeping together ever since they married. Even while his leg healed, they managed to get by with fondling and falling asleep in each other's arms.

"After what Logan did, you won't want me touching you." Foley wanted to keep making love to her, but he wouldn't, not unless she gave him permission. Sarah was adamant she was not going to sleep with Lizzy.

"Logan did nothing!" she replied putting the coffee pot down rather heavily. "I tell you the same as I told Joe… if he had got to me, I would take my gun and shoot myself! you are my husband and I love you! and damn it, Mister Andrews! I won't be having you not making love to me!" Taking their mugs, she sat them on the table and wrapped her arms about him. Foley reciprocated by wrapping his arms around her and holding her tight. Since being attacked by a wolf she started telling him she loved him, and he liked hearing it, she was telling him all the time now, and he was happy to hold her in his arms and caress her while his leg healed.

While Foley continued to recuperate, the four trappers remained camped outside Sarah's cabin. They stacked firewood, filled the water barrels to overflowing and checked the roof of the cabin for leaks. They took her horses to the river and swam them. The four men kept Lizzy entertained with games. They also taught her how to throw a small knife at a block of wood until Sarah told them to stop. Joe wasn't put off by her demand, saying it wouldn't hurt Lizzy to carry a knife when she went out with her to check her traps. Sarah didn't argue with Joe, but she put the knife in the wooden trunk until she thought Lizzy would be old enough to use it.

Before leaving Sarah's cabin to head back to the High Ridge Camp, Joe told Sarah and Foley he would spread the word about what they did to Logan and Reeves as a warning to any other man having thoughts about getting with Sarah.

Chapter Twenty

Several weeks passed since Joe and the other three men helped Sarah after Logan attacked her. Sarah still hadn't told Foley he was going to be a father, and Foley didn't seem to notice her belly swelling a little more each day when they made love.

The four trappers were hunting above the High Ridge Camp, but it was slow going. Joe couldn't explain it, the wolves seemed to have moved on, so he decided it was time they headed back to Sarah's cabin to see how Foley's leg was healing. When they got there, Foley was up and about using the crutch Joe made to keep the weight off his leg. He even managed to cut some wood and stack it near the front steps of the cabin. Joe was pleased Foley's leg healed so quickly.

The men had just finished eating the rabbit stew Sarah made and were bedding down in the clearing for the night when Sarah carried her coffee pot from the cabin down to them. It was a clear night, stars filled the sky and the air was still, but Foley decided to stay indoors with Lizzy and let Sarah spend time with the men. All four men settling around the campfire held their mugs up for Sarah to pour them the hot brew. When she finished, she sat beside Joe on a log in front of the fire. She had something she wanted to ask him, but feeling unsure if he would refuse her request, she clasped her hands together to stop them shaking.

"Joe, I want to ask you something," she began.

Thinking Sarah might be going to ask him what he thought of Foley, Joe had an answer ready. At dinner that night at the lodge, when Sarah told him Foley and she were married, he had been taken aback by the news, but in a way happy she married him. Foley asked Sarah to marry him many times before she married Christian, in fact, he was more surprised when Sarah and Christian, who was a complete stranger to her got together. When he could see Sarah was happy being Christian's wife, he thought because Foley married Maria, he had lost all interest in Sarah and he put Foley's proposals out of his mind. He still didn't give it a thought that they might get together after Sarah lost Christian and Foley Maria, and was more than a little suspicious about their union, but now he couldn't be more pleased. Sarah was pregnant again, and although she hadn't yet told Foley, she appeared to be happy once again.

Before going on, Sarah took a deep breath, and tried to get what she wanted to ask Joe right without him getting cross with her, but because she was nervous, she said what she wanted to say without much thought.

"I want to go to the high country to see Frank's grave, and I want you to take me there!" Her heart rate rose rapidly and her hands shook as she thought how she told the four men to go to hell after Frank died, making them back off so she was forced to take care of herself, but when Thomas was taken and Joe tried not to interfere, he stepped in anyway and helped get him back, and when Millicent Crawley tried to kill her, she and Joe made peace with each other, and just recently the four men saved her from being attacked by Logan. Joe never turned her down when she asked him for anything, so why would he say no to her now?

"No!" Joe answered sternly, putting his mug to his mouth. As far as he was concerned that was the end of their conversation.

"Joe please, I have to see…" Sarah began.

"I am not taking you up there Sarah! it is no place for you… not now!" he interrupted lowering his voice. "Not now you are pregnant! you can't go up there!" Putting his mug to his mouth again, he lowered it without taking a drink. "Besides, you can't be thinking of taking little Lizzy up there!" he added getting to his feet.

Staying seated on the log, Sarah's eyes welled at his refusal, but she didn't care that she was pregnant, it had nothing to do with what she wanted to do, and the men would keep Lizzy safe. "Please Joe, I have to say goodbye, I got to say goodbye to Christian."

Joe tipped his left-over coffee out and turned to her. "Leave it alone Sarah, you are not going up there," he whispered.

Getting to her feet, Sarah put her hand on his arm. "I can't leave it Joe, I need to see where Frank is so I can move on with Foley."

Joe saw the sadness in her eyes. "What about Foley? What does he say about you going up there?"

Sarah let his arm go. "He doesn't know, I will tell him when you agree to take me… Joe, you can get all the men to go with us, it will be a lot safer if all of us go."

Joe looked incredulous at Sarah. Frank said the same thing, then went up the mountain on his own and got himself killed. But Joe was adamant he was not taking Sarah up there. "Just like you haven't told him about, you know what!" he whispered sternly then sighing. He was tired of keeping the news Sarah was having another baby from the other men.

"When I was with Christian, I never thought about Frank, and now I'm back here I think about him all the time, I love Foley Joe, but it doesn't feel right when my thoughts are with Frank, I need to let him go." When Joe didn't answer, Sarah went back to the cabin with her shoulders slumped in disappointment.

Standing in front of the fire, Joe watched her go up the steps and across the porch, and after going inside, he watched her close the door quietly behind her. "Fuck!" he cursed, then turning to the men, told them what Sarah had demanded of him.

After putting Lizzy to bed, Sarah went to the washroom to ready herself for bed. Hearing a knock at the cabin door, Foley opened it and Joe stepped inside. Coming out of the washroom, Sarah stopped in the living area looking at Joe as he looked across the room at her.

"You get yourself ready Sarah, the men have agreed to take you to the high country, we leave first thing in the morning!" Before stepping back outside, Joe glanced at Foley. Foley knew about the area called the High Country. He also knew it was where Frank died, and knowing it was a dangerous place, wasn't keen on going up there.

After closing the door behind Joe, Foley followed Sarah back to the washroom where he confronted her with what Joe said. "What

251

did he mean Sarah?" About to undress when he entered, her trousers sat open and low on her hips where she pushed them.

"He's taking me to the high country," she answered nonchalantly.

"I gathered that, but why?" Foley asked standing beside her.

"I need to see it Foley, I've never been up there, and I need to see it for myself." When she saw the questioning look in his eyes, she tried moving around him.

"You need to see what?" Foley asked staying where he was so she couldn't get past.

"You need to see where Frank is buried, is that it? Is that what you need to see?" he demanded. Looking him squarely in his eyes, Sarah didn't hesitate to answer.

"Yes, I need to see where Frank is buried." Then seeing anger on his face, she decided not to bother washing. Pulling her trousers up, she fastened them, then pushed past him.

"Why do you need to see his grave now? You know he is buried up there, seeing his grave isn't going to achieve anything," Foley said following her to the living area.

"I need to say goodbye," Sarah said seriously. Thinking it ridiculous for her to want to say goodbye to Frank after so many years had passed, Foley laughed.

"If you love me Sarah you won't go up there," he said turning serious.

"I love you but I'm going," she answered honestly.

"You can't be thinking of taking Lizzy up there, she had trouble going to where you set traps, the high country is too far for her to walk and far too dangerous." Keeping their voices low so as not to wake Lizzy or let the men hear their discussion, they continued trying to justify their reasons for and against going.

"Lizzy will be safe Foley, the trappers will see she gets there," Sarah said making her way across the room to their bedroom.

"There are four men out there Sarah that have agreed to take you, not all of them!" When Foley suddenly sounded angry, Sarah turned to face him.

"Joe will get the other men to go with us," she answered. Foley looked bewildered at her. As far as she was concerned, she had all the answers.

"Well I'm not going," he ended matter-of-factly.

"Fine! stay here," Sarah answered sullenly disappearing through the bedroom doorway. Pursing his lips in frustration, Foley remained in front of the fire for a moment to think, then following Sarah into their room saw she had removed her shirt. When she saw him come in behind her, she held her shirt in front of her as if he had never seen her naked before.

Tilting her head to the side, she looked at him. "Let me ask you something Foley... do you honestly love me?"

Her question took Foley by surprise. "After all the years I've been in love with you, you need to ask me that?"

But Sarah wasn't going to give in, not this time, she wanted to bring up the fact he sometimes never ended their lovemaking. "They are words Foley, words can be spoken without meaning." Foley's mouth dropped open in astonishment at her thinking his words meant nothing.

"I mean what I say!" he retaliated angrily.

"Do you?" Sarah's voice rose when she questioned him.

"Yes! goddamn it!" By asking him if he loved her, she was making him angrier. She had to know full well he loved her. But it wasn't so much how he felt about her that was bothering Sarah, it was how he made her feel when he made love to her.

"Then why don't you love me like you should? Why do you keep leaving me feeling unfulfilled when we make love?" Tears sprang to Sarah's eyes when she went on. "Why don't you finish with me instead of leaving me wanting more? You say you love me, when all I want is for you to show me!" her voice broke in a sob.

Not wanting the trappers to know they were fighting, Foley lowered his voice. "You know I don't want to go through with you what I went through with Maria, I won't risk getting you pregnant, we don't need more children for us to be happy!"

Wanting to tell him it was too late, Sarah bit her tongue then glared at him. "I'm not Maria! besides, Maria was not having your child!" she reminded him. She wanted to add, 'I am' but stopped herself. She wanted desperately to tell him she was having his baby, but he hated the very thought, which made her dilemma far worse. Fighting back tears, she was at a loss as to know how she was going to explain it to him.

Before Sarah could burst into tears, Foley cupped her face and pushed his hands into her hair, and lifting her face to his, kissed her passionately.

"You don't have to remind me about Maria Sarah, but I will not risk losing you, it has taken me far too long to get you to accept me." Removing her shirt from in front of her, he slid his arms around her and pulled her into his embrace. Feeling his warmth, Sarah put her arms around him as a tear ran down her cheek. Now wasn't the time to tell him she was pregnant. As Foley held Sarah's warm body against his, he gave in.

"We best get to bed if we want to get up early and get on the trail." Letting Sarah go with a kiss, he wiped his finger across her tear stained face. "I love you," he whispered. "Let me show you how much."

Sitting on the side of the bed, he removed his boots and drew Sarah in to stand between his legs. After helping him remove his shirt, Sarah wrapped her arms about his neck and brought him against her. Cupping her breasts, then taking a nipple in his mouth, he moved his tongue gently over the nodule and brought it to its fullness. When he stopped suckling and their kissing turned to fervent wanting, the rest of their clothes were removed in wild abandonment. Quickly lifting Sarah onto the bed, Foley pushed himself between her legs. As their bodies became sensitive to the sensation each of them was creating, Sarah lifted her legs to give him better access, and tightened them around him. With their bodies pressed together, and their thrusting gaining momentum, Sarah's womanhood swelled as Foley's moment neared completion. With a moan of satisfaction escaping him, he buried his face in her hair, and bringing his mouth close to her ear whispered. "Oh lord, Sarah."

Keeping her feet pressed against his buttocks, and moving in time with him, Sarah forced her body up under his, and helped keep their momentum going. With their bodies now melded together in heated passion, Sarah pushed her fingers through Foleys hair and felt the moment he came. As her own climax reached its peak, she slid her feet down his legs and hung on. "I love you," she gasped audibly as her thrusting continued uncontrollably. Again, a deep, guttural moan of satisfaction escaped Foley.

Having satisfied their desire for each other, they lay entwined in each other's embrace, and after kissing, withdrew into their own thoughts.

Foley remembered, making love to Sarah like this on their wedding night, and on the rug in front of the fireplace at the lodge. Here too, in the washroom amidst suds and water where it had been frenzied lovemaking like now. After that night in the washroom, he went back to being careful. Now though, he couldn't help himself, he wanted Sarah to know he did love her, so stayed until he finished. Before falling asleep however, he prayed he hadn't got her pregnant.

Although wanting desperately to tell Foley she was pregnant so he could share in her joy of having their child, but figuring, because her pregnancy was in its early stage, she still had plenty of time to tell him, Sarah decided to wait until they came back from visiting Frank's grave.

Chapter Twenty-one

It was a good two hours before daylight when Sarah woke. She had a lot to do. There were rucksacks to pack with enough food to last them until they got to the High Ridge Camp where they could replenish their supplies. The rucksacks had to hold enough bullets to keep wolves at bay and rifles had to be loaded. But first she needed to wash before getting dressed. After washing her face and hands in a dish of cold water, she lathered a washcloth, then wiping it over her breasts and under her arms, wiped between her legs and washed her and Foley's lovemaking away. Once dressed, she didn't bother with breakfast. She could get a lot done without Lizzy underfoot, so leaving Lizzy and Foley asleep, she got busy packing the rucksacks.

It was only when she was loading her rifle Foley woke and came out to see what Sarah was doing. Wiping sleep from his eyes, he stared at seeing her dressed in clean trousers with her hunting knife hanging from her waist, and her pistol down the front of her pants. Her fur vest she usually wore, she had on over her tight-fitting shirt. Her hair was already braided down her back, and on her head, she wore the old raggedy hat with its split brim.

"Have you eaten already Sarah?" he asked unable to smell coffee brewing or anything cooking on the stove.

"Not yet, I thought I would wait until you and Lizzy were up," Sarah answered loading a bullet into her rifle.

"You should have woken me," Foley yawned before heading to the washroom. As he grabbed his rifle and headed out the side door to the outhouse, Sarah thought at least he didn't sound angry. Some mornings she woke feeling angry with him, especially when he didn't finish their lovemaking. This morning she didn't feel any anger toward him at all. In fact, she felt in love with him more now than at any other time, because last night he made her feel wonderful. She turned sullen however, when thinking one day she was going to spoil what they had just experienced by telling him she was going to have his baby.

They were eating breakfast when Joe knocked and came in. When all three occupants appeared dressed and ready to go, Joe looked at their rifles standing next to their rucksacks fully packed and looking heavy leaning against the wall.

"Everyone ready?" he asked looking from Sarah to Foley and back again.

"Just about Joe, got to do Lizzy's hair, check the cabin and then we can go," Sarah answered for them.

Foley thought Joe didn't sound too pleased when he said, "I'll see you outside then." Then nodded before leaving them to finish getting ready. When Sarah helped Foley get a rucksack on his back, he staggered under its weight and thought perhaps his bad leg wouldn't carry it.

"Hell Sarah! what have you got in here, rocks?" he asked adjusting the load.

"Everything we need for the journey up the mountain," she said adjusting its straps.

She wasn't about to go through the items she packed with him, she wanted to get on the trail, but there were bullets, coffee, beans, cookies and flour, dried milk powder and sugar to make hotcakes. Hopefully rabbits would be caught, but dried pieces of meat were packed for adding to stews. A new fur coat was rolled and tied to the rucksack on top of Foley's bedroll. Sarah's rucksack packed with a little less, was still full. Lizzy's coat was stowed in Sarah's rucksack and her old coat she mended was fastened on top the same as Foley's. Lifting her rucksack onto her back, unlike Foley, she didn't baulk when adjusting its weight.

By the time they came out of the cabin, Foley had washed the breakfast dishes and put out the fire while Sarah brushed Lizzy's hair and braided it. Two braids with dark blue ribbons tied on their ends hung over her shoulders. Dressed in trousers and a check shirt, she wore a small hat on her head that matched her brown boots. Lizzy looked just like Sarah did at that age, and Joe, watching her bounding down the steps, felt a pang at the memory. When Lizzy ran over to him, he smiled and scooped her into his arms.

Everyone followed Joe along the trail, but Lizzy slowed them down somewhat so once again Will took charge by carrying her most of the way. Lifting her onto his shoulders, everyone laughed when she put her hands over his eyes so he couldn't see where he was going, and again when she placed her hands under his chin and grasped his newly grown beard to stop herself falling. Garrett showed her plants along the way, and pointed out different small animals and birds, even naming them so she knew what they were. When she walked beside Fergus holding his hand, he sang lilting Irish songs that had everyone walking along in silence. Listening to everyone's banter, Foley was learning about the mountain too. Good ground was covered that first day. Their first night out they made camp without any trouble from wolves.

The second day proved much the same as the first, but as far as Foley was concerned, his rucksack was still too heavy. When the group stopped to rest on an outcrop of boulders on the edge of the mountain, everyone peered over dense forested valleys of green to mountain ranges stretching as far as the eye could see. Foley wondered at the mountains beauty, but they weren't yet half way to the top. The High Ridge Camp was still another two days trek away. When they made camp that night, Foley's leg ached from walking so far.

During their third night out, talk came around to wolves and why they hadn't encountered any. "Sometimes they move to different hunting grounds, maybe this year they are on the other side of the mountain," Garrett was saying.

"Maybe they are up in the high country," Fergus offered, causing everyone to go quiet. Joe hoped Fergus's statement wasn't the case and became pensive. While Lizzy slept cocooned between Will and Fergus where she was safe, Joe watched Sarah sleeping in the crook of Foley's arm with their bodies pressed together, and was very much aware Sarah still hadn't told Foley she was pregnant. Joe closed his eyes to get some much-needed sleep while Garrett took the first watch. Fergus and Will would both take guard duty before his turn at the early morning watch.

The fourth day, as they approached the High Ridge Camp, trappers came out of their shacks to greet them. On seeing Lizzy, they became curious to find out why they were there, and gathered around whispering amongst each other.

"We are taking Sarah to see Frank's grave, any of you willing to come with us?" Joe announced. An uproar of disbelief came over the camp when hearing where they were going.

"You must be a damn fool to think we would go up there just to see a grave!" One of the men said to Sarah, but Sarah didn't reply, she preferred it if Joe talked to the men, he had to be the one to convince them to go with them.

"You men want to keep hunting around here for nothing? You all know the wolves have moved on, we didn't see a single one on our way up here!" Joe glanced from man to man then addressed one of them.

"Doyle! you trapped anything lately?"

"Nothing lately Joe, got less than a dozen skins since coming back," Doyle replied looking at Joe. Joe nodded in satisfaction to what he said then turned to the other men.

"The wolves have moved to higher ground! come with us, help Sarah get to the top of the mountain, I guarantee you will have your skins!" He waited silently for several minutes for someone to volunteer. As he pursed his lips in disappointment at the lack of response, a voice from the back answered, "I'll go Joe." When several other men put up their hands, Joe accepted their offer, but felt disgusted at the lack of response from others.

"Alright! get settled in for the night, we'll leave at first light tomorrow." Joe had hoped he would have at least a dozen extra men to go with them, as it were, he settled for the six he got. At this rate he thought, it wasn't going to be an easy trek.

Taking Sarah with Foley and Lizzy to one of the shacks, Joe stepped aside and let them go inside. "You sleep in here, stow your things and we'll get something to eat, over there," he said pointing to where men were busy at a pot hanging over a fire. Stepping into the shack, a sudden chill ran up Sarah's spine.

"This is where Frank stayed, isn't it?" she said turning to Joe. Feeling it uncanny how she knew Frank had stayed in this particular shack, Joe stared at her.

"Yeah, he built that," he said, nodding toward the stone fireplace. Reaching out, Sarah touched the stones, then quickly pulled her hand back as she glanced at Foley. Seeing a look of sadness cross her face, Foley wondered what she was going to be like when she saw Frank's grave. Quickly stowing their rucksacks in a corner, they set up their bedrolls and the trio followed Joe back outside to the firepit.

Having retired for the night, Foley cuddled up to Sarah's back, and Sarah, feeling comforted that Foley had his arm around her, slept with her arm over Lizzy holding her close. The next morning when they came out of the shack, a large group of men were standing around the firepit with their rifles and rucksacks. Will, Garrett and Fergus, getting themselves food, moved aside to let the trio get to the fire. Joe winked at Sarah from the other side of the pit.

"They are all coming with us Sarah," he grinned with satisfaction.

Joe was pleased his berating the men for their lack of sympathy toward Sarah the night before convinced the men to volunteer their time. Thirteen men, besides his group of five, stood ready and waiting, making it an excellent sized group to escort Sarah to the High Country.

Sarah was pleased with the turnout too. While she helped Lizzy with hotcakes, Joe sidled up to stand beside her. Straightening up, Sarah licked treacle off her fingers.

"You told Foley what he has to do?" he asked her.

"Not yet, I will give them to him before we leave."

Joe nodded and went to get coffee. Standing on the other side of Lizzy, Foley overheard their exchange.

"What do you have to give me Sarah?"

"Hold out your hand," Sarah ordered while digging her hand in her shirt pocket.

Keeping his eyes on Sarah, Foley did as she asked, and when she dropped three bullets into his open palm, he looked puzzled at them.

"Why are you giving me these? I've already loaded my gun."

"You need to carry them in your pocket… if we run into wolves, which I'm sure we will, and we happen to run out of bullets, you will need to use them… on us!" Sarah said haltingly.

"I'm carrying the same," she said, patting her pocket. "If something happens and you can't do it, then I will have to!" Sarah kept her eyes on Foley to see if he understood what she was saying.

Foley understood perfectly what Sarah was telling him, but was horrified to think he may have to kill Sarah and Lizzy, let alone himself. He didn't come to the mountain to have to end up killing the two people he held dear to him. When he suddenly grabbed Sarah and kissed her, every man around the fire gaped. Mugs were suspended midway to their mouth's, hotcakes were held in hands, treacle dripped off fingers. Sarah kissed him back, then when he let her go, he looked at the men then back at Sarah whose face had turned pink from noticing every man watching them. "Nothing had better happen to make either of us have to use these bullets!" Foley said loud and clear for everyone to hear.

They made good time their first day out from the High Ridge Camp. By the time they set up camp that night the men were mystified as to why they hadn't encountered any wolves. Dividing equal time between four groups of men, fires were hurriedly lit and guard duty quickly set up. Foley, Sarah and Lizzy were made to bed down in the middle of a ring of fires where they could be protected.

On their second day, as they climbed higher than ever before, the entire mountain range could be seen through tall trees. Far distant escarpments jutted upwards from gorges and green valleys. The air grew thin, and cold. Everyone hastily put on their coats. It was too far and too high for Lizzy to walk so she was carried on the shoulders of the men. Sarah sometimes felt dizzy and struggled too, but it wasn't the mountain air making her feel that way. Foley held her hand as they walked through dense forests. Joe didn't let them stop to rest for too long. He had to get them to the top of the ranges before it became too dark to make camp.

It was dusk when they reached a plateau. Walls of stone stood behind them, in front, open valleys and escarpments stretched out in the quickly fading light. Fires were lit in the dark, food was prepared, everyone was busy doing something. Lizzy was helping Will spread out bedrolls. Foley was busy helping Joe gather firewood. No-one noticed Sarah standing stock still.

There was something unusual about this place, Sarah could feel it. When a sudden sadness overwhelmed her, her chest became tight, tears she couldn't control ran down her cheeks and dripped off her chin. She glanced about at the men, at the darkness all around her, but didn't make to move.

Dropping wood next to the fire, Foley glanced over at Sarah and his mouth dropped open. Nudging Joe to get his attention, Joe looked over at Sarah too, and saw she had her eyes closed with her hands clasped against her chest.

"Shit!" he muttered, then he and Foley rushed to where she was standing. Foley reached out to grab her, but before he could, Joe put his hand up and stopped him.

"Sarah what is it?" Joe asked while not attempting to touch her.

There was an eerie stillness in the air making the men nervous. There were no sounds, not a breeze, nor wolves baying in the distance. Everyone stopped what they were doing and were watching Sarah when a sudden unexplained gust of wind blew in across the plateau from off the valley floor. It blew around the men and the campfire, sending flames and sparks high into the air before dying down to a gentle breeze as it swirled around Sarah. Joe felt it, so did Foley.

"Mommy?" Lizzy's bottom lip curled in sadness as the breeze swirled gently around her. Feeling a shiver run up his spine, Will scooped Lizzy into his arms and held her tight. Sarah opened her eyes.

"This is it Joe, this is where Frank is, isn't it?" she asked.

Joe couldn't believe what he just witnessed. Had Sarah felt Frank's presence? Or was it because she was pregnant?

"Yes Sarah, he is here," he answered softly. As Sarah's legs buckled, Foley moved quickly and picked her up.

"Bring her over here," Joe said indicating a bedroll close to the fires. Putting Sarah down, Foley sat with her in his arms while Lizzy squirmed her way out of Will's grasp and ran to her side. When Joe wiped Sarah's brow with a damp cloth, she opened her eyes and looked at him.

"I'm alright Joe, I just felt tired all of a sudden, is there food?" Puzzled by her seeming to brush off her fainting spell, Foley glanced at Joe but Joe seemed indifferent to what happened.

"You three stay here, I'll be right back!" Joe hurried away to bring them food.

"That was strange Sarah, what made you think Frank was here?" Foley asked when he was gone.

"I felt sad Foley, like something happened here, I just felt... sad!"

"Mommy, that wind, it tickled me," Lizzy said feeling puzzled.

Suspecting it was the baby she was expecting making her feel the way she was, but unable to be sure, Sarah put her arms around Lizzy and drew her into her embrace.

The first watch had started. Although Sarah said she was fine, Joe sat on his bedroll next to her and Foley while they ate.

"Get some sleep if you can, I want you up at daylight Sarah, you too Foley," he said settling himself for the night. With the other three men surrounding them on their bedrolls, Lizzy was put down between Sarah and Foley. After wrapping his arms around Sarah and Lizzy, Foley thought if something untoward was going to happen, he would protect them with his life. He wasn't afraid of the mountain, nothing was going to take Sarah and Lizzy away from him.

The night had been uneventful, but the men remained uneasy. When the four trappers took the last watch, some of the men commented on the lack of wolves. Wolves had always been present on the mountain. Their constant howls of warning were always there for the men to hear, they had become used to them, not hearing them was more unusual, more unnerving.

When Joe tapped Foley to wake him, daylight was fast approaching. As soon as Foley felt Joe's hand on his shoulder he woke. "Get up Foley, don't wake Lizzy, let her sleep." Reaching over him, he tapped Sarah. Other trappers had woken and were busy getting themselves coffee and hotcakes. When Sarah woke and looked up at Joe, he put his finger to his mouth indicating not to wake Lizzy. Sarah and Foley helped themselves to food Fergus was making while Garrett and Will remained on watch.

"The sun will be up in about an hour," Joe said pointing to the distant mountains. "It will come up over there." Holding her mug with both hands, Sarah let its warmth comfort her, and listening carefully to Joe, looked to where he was pointing.

"When it moves across the face of the mountain Sarah, you need to follow it as it comes toward us." But Sarah didn't understand what Joe meant by following the sun. Finishing her coffee quickly and getting rid of her mug, she stood between Joe and Foley to watch the sunrise. When Lizzy woke unexpectedly, Sarah hurried over to help her. After quickly straightening her up, she hurried Lizzy to the fire to get her something to eat so she wouldn't miss the early dawn.

"I'll take care of her Sarah, you need to see the sunrise," Will offered taking Lizzy's hand.

Still puzzled at not knowing what was so important about seeing the sun come up, she nodded to Will, and leaving Lizzy with him, hurried back to Joe and Foley. Joe took her hand in his and squeezing it, waited for the suns golden rays to appear from behind the mountain range.

As the sun slowly ascended into the sky, everyone stood still and watched it cause shadows to slowly ebb away as the mountain became basked in brilliant golds and yellows. Its golden glow moved ever so slowly across the face of the escarpments, inching its way toward the plateau where Sarah and the men stood enthralled by the beauty of the valleys and mountains coming alive with the new day. As the sun's rays moved across the plateau to shine on the rock-face behind where they stood, Joe let go of Sarah's hand as they turned. When the wall behind them lit up in brilliant sunlight, Sarah's breath escaped her as she took in the magnificent wall of stone. Foley stared open mouthed. The trappers turned as one to stare at what was behind them. Some had been here before, others had not. Joe wasn't surprised, nor Fergus or Will and Garrett. They each had seen it when they followed Joe to this very spot many years before.

It was Will who fashioned the cross, and Garrett who carved Frank's name on it and the date they found him. The cross stood like it had been placed there yesterday. The mound of rocks covering Frank's body so wolves couldn't dig him up were still heaped in a neat pile. But it wasn't the cross, or the pile of stones that had Sarah gasping or causing Foley to open his mouth in awe. It wasn't Frank's grave that had everyone staring.

Sarah wept openly when she saw it. Lizzy could see it too, but even though she had started school, she didn't know what it meant.

The letters, roughly carved above Frank's resting place read 'Frank Mason Loves Sarah Cole,' carved by a hand shaking with fear just before Frank used his spare bullet on himself. Sarah wiped tears from her eyes as she took in the words so she could see them better. Frank had carved their names in the mountain for all eternity, for high up on the mountain, sheltered from the weather, it would be an eternity before their names would disappear.

Foley knew Frank loved Sarah, but didn't know how much until this moment. Moving away from him and Joe, Sarah knelt at Frank's grave and wept as she spoke to the pile of stones. After allowing her time to say goodbye, Joe went to her with his gear loaded on his back and his rifle slung over his shoulder.

"We have to go Sarah, we want to be well away from here for our first nights camp," he said standing by her side.

Sarah stood up to go. "Goodbye Frank," she whispered.

Picking a leafy twig from a shrub, Lizzy carried it to Frank's grave and laying it on the stones, slipped her hand in Sarah's and squeezed it gently.

"I'm ready to go now Joe," Sarah said walking away from Frank's grave. Sarah didn't look back, Foley was waiting for her by the trail, and when she looked at him, her heart swelled with love. "I love you Foley," she whispered, putting her arms around him.

Foley told her he loved her and held her for a moment, then lifting Lizzy up to sit on his shoulders, they headed down the trail together.

As they made their way down the mountain a wolf was heard howling in the distance, then another, and another. The men stopped to listen, then smiled broadly to each other in satisfaction. Around their campfires, talk revolved around how each of them believed Frank knew Sarah was coming to visit him. The men agreed it was Frank that made the wolves give Sarah safe passage to the top of the mountain. It was Frank in that gust of wind they said, coming to say hello to Sarah, and they firmly believed, once she said goodbye, Frank let the wolves come back.

Chapter Twenty-two

The mountain was crawling with wolves, but the men weren't complaining, skinning had resumed, so after making the trek back to Sarah's cabin, the trappers immediately returned to the High Ridge Camp. Meanwhile at the cabin, several days passed with no sign of trouble.

Wanting to get a good stack of wood prepared so he wouldn't have to spend so much time at the chopping block, Foley was at the woodpile cutting wood and had worked up quite a sweat. With a stack of wood lying scattered at his feet, he sat another piece of wood on the block, and lifting his axe above his head, brought it down hard. The sound from the axe as the wood split in two echoed across the mountain. While Sarah was kept busy filling water barrels, Lizzy lay on the porch on her stomach with her feet swinging in the air and her slate in front of her trying to draw.

Having already made several trips back and forth from the river to the barrel on the porch, Sarah made her way back up the incline, but this bucket she was carrying felt heavier than all the others. Coming on level ground near the clearing, water slopped over the rim wetting her trousers. It seemed an awful long way to her cabin, and besides feeling hot, her eyes had developed spots in front of them. She could barely see Foley at the woodpile, and was unable to see Lizzy on the porch at all. Blinking rapidly, she tried bringing her into focus but instead, brought on a feeling of dizziness. Glancing toward Foley, he and the cabin suddenly tilted sideways and her vision disappeared altogether, making her drop the bucket when everything went black.

Scribbling on her slate and humming to herself, Lizzy looked up for a moment, then looking back down, brought her eyes up quickly when she saw Sarah lying on the ground near the clearing. "Mommy?" she questioned sounding confused and getting to her feet.

"*Mommy!*" she screamed when realizing Sarah had fallen. Throwing her chalk aside, she came down the steps quickly and ran toward her.

Foley had his axe poised ready to strike another piece of wood when he heard Lizzy's cry. Puzzled, he looked first at her, then to the clearing where Sarah lay. "*Sarah!*" he called and dropping the axe, ran to her. Falling on his knees beside her, he turned her on her back and could see the side of her face and front of her clothes covered in dirt where she lay in wet soil. When Lizzy began to whimper, he picked Sarah up, and hurried toward the cabin.

"Lizzy, go open the door," he beckoned as he ran. Running back to the steps and climbing them as fast as she could, Lizzy raced across the porch and held the door open. When Foley carried Sarah inside and hurried with her to their room, Lizzy followed. "Lizzy get a wet a cloth so I can wipe mommy's face, and be quick," Foley ordered laying Sarah on the bed. While he got busy getting Sarah out of her dirty clothes, Lizzy ran to the washroom.

As he removed Sarah's boots and worked her trousers off, Lizzy could be heard pulling a chair over to the washstand. The sound of water being slopped from the jug into the dish was audible. After quickly removing Sarah's shirt, and before covering her with blankets, Foley noticed how her stomach seemed to be distended. Frowning at this new development, he rested his hand on her stomach and felt the small bump.

When Lizzy hurried through the door with the wet cloth dripping all over the floor, Foley thanked her as he took it and wrung water out of it. Feeling the cold cloth on her face, Sarah opened her eyes and blinking, focused on Foley's stern look. He hadn't noticed anything different about Sarah when they made love, but had a pretty good idea what caused her to faint, and knowing that look, Sarah could see he knew what caused it, but still she tried making light of her sudden fainting spell by smiling at him. "I must have overdone it with the buckets," she said dismally. While Sarah held his gaze, Foley studied her for the truth.

"Are you pregnant?" he asked without wavering. Sarah didn't have to answer. When her hand moved instinctively to her stomach, and her eyes filled with tears, Foley had his answer.

"When were you going to tell me?" he asked keeping his voice steady, but just like she kept Maria's deceit from him, he felt angry with her for keeping her pregnancy to herself. Sarah swallowed back tears.

"I wanted to tell you, but how could I? You have made it plain you don't want children."

Foleys mind raged in turmoil. 'Had Sarah lied when she said Logan hadn't got to her? Could Logan have fathered this child?' he was thinking.

"How far along are you?" he asked. When Sarah didn't answer right away, he kept his eyes fixed on her while ordering Lizzy out of the room.

"Lizzy, go sit at the table while mommy and I talk." Understanding Foley's stern demand, Lizzy went out without hesitation.

"I've missed my times," Sarah answered when Lizzy had gone.

"How many?" Foley asked knowing what Sarah meant by times.

"Three I think, in the top drawer there's a piece of paper, I mark each day I have missed, I have been marking it ever since the night we made love in the washroom… you remember?"

Sarah looked at him sadly while thinking surely, he must remember that night.

Foley remembered, but ignored her reminding him of it. Going to the tallboy, he pulled out the top drawer, and after rummaging through her neatly folded unworn nightgowns, found the piece of paper. Instead of sitting back on the bed, he remained standing, and unfolding the paper saw a lot of crosses and nothing else.

"Foley," Sarah whispered.

When she said his name, Foley glanced at Sarah then back at the paper, and quickly counting the crosses, figured Sarah was right in that she had missed three times.

"Foley, this is our baby," Sarah said hoping he wouldn't reject her and their baby and leave her.

Recounting her crosses, Foley figured if the crosses were correct, then she had become pregnant the night they made love on the washroom floor. They had not made love in there since. Since then he had been attacked by a wolf, Sarah had been attacked by Logan, and they had been to the High Country and back. They had made love many times, and some of those times were more passionate than others, but that night was pure unadulterated frenzied sex and he had enjoyed it. Figuring Sarah was well into her pregnancy, he left the room and closed the door quietly behind him.

When he walked out without saying a word, Sarah was of the opinion he didn't want anything to do with her or his child. Turning her back to the door, she pulled the covers over her head, and pushing her face into her pillow, sobbed. This was exactly what she expected.

Lizzy was sitting at the table when Foley came out of the bedroom. "Mommy all good?" she asked with a pout.

"She's all good Lizzy, mommy is having a baby," he answered while focusing on Sarah's piece of paper. Telling Lizzy what caused Sarah's fainting spell, he didn't see her eyes widen when she heard his news. Sitting up straight in her chair, she sucked in her breath.

"Huh!... now?" she asked in surprise. Lifting his gaze, he suddenly smiled at her thinking Sarah was having their baby right then. "Not now Lizzy, when we are back in Cedar Creek, maybe for Christmas," he explained. This statement made Lizzy even more surprised.

"We are having a baby, for Christmas!" she exclaimed, and climbing excitedly off her chair, made to run to the bedroom to inform Sarah they were going to have a baby for Christmas, but before she could, Foley grabbed her and stopped her. He reminded Sarah time and time again he didn't want her becoming pregnant, but conceding it was too late to do anything about it, he decided he wasn't going back in to comfort her.

Kneeling in front of Lizzy, he held her at arm's length. "Mommy is upset right now, when you go to her, stay there, and tell mommy you love her," he demanded softly. Thinking Foley didn't know she loved her Ma, Lizzy whispered, "I do love mommy." Prodding her gently through the bedroom door, Foley closed the door behind her, and went outside where he sat on the porch to think.

Sitting in the sun with his feet on the top step, he grasped Sarah's piece of paper firmly in his hands. He had struggled to keep his love for Sarah hidden for a very long time, and now they were together he felt consumed with so many questions and doubts about how she got pregnant.

He had been careful when making love to her, and Joe said the four of them got to her in time to stop Logan violating her, but could he trust Joe's word? Joe was a man who lived by his word, he would never lie to cover a thing like this up, and neither would the other men, he answered for himself. Sarah was already pregnant when she had been attacked by Logan. According to Sarah's crosses it was not Logan's baby, it was his. Accepting the baby was his gave Foley another reason to want to kill Logan, if he wasn't dead already! The afternoon sun shone on the porch warming him, and leaning back against the railing, he closed his eyes and smiled. Sarah was having his baby, was that so bad? If everything went well, he would be a father after all. But could he allow himself to be happy about it?

He couldn't, not this time, not like he had when Maria told him she was having his baby. Oh, she was having a baby alright! just not his! Maria turned out to be a conniving liar, letting him believe he was going to be a father, then destroyed any hopes he had of becoming one. For seven month's he had been on top of the world only to have his life turned upside down.

When doubts about Sarah's pregnancy seeped into his thoughts again, he went over what he knew about her and looked at the paper he was holding. 'Sarah could have written these crosses simply to cover up when she fell pregnant, couldn't she? But she would never lie, would she? She wasn't raised to be a liar, she never lied about anything. He knew from experience she always said things as they were. She wasn't an educated woman, and wouldn't knowingly falsify crosses on a piece of paper. She marked honestly one cross for each day that passed, and she said she loved him, and that was not a lie.' Foley closed his eyes and felt satisfied Sarah would never deceive him, but still he felt he had a dilemma.

Climbing over Sarah, Lizzy shimmied down inside the blankets next to her and put her arm around her. "I love you mommy," she whispered. Putting her arm around Lizzy, Sarah held her close. "I love you too Lizzy," she answered with a sob breaking from her throat.

"Mommy, we are having a baby." Lizzy didn't know if her Ma knew they were having a baby, so she kept her voice low when she told her.

"Oh Lizzy, yes, we are having Foley's baby!" When Sarah burst into sobs, Lizzy, all of five, held her while she cried.

It was dark when Sarah got out of bed and dressed in clean clothes. Lizzy got up too and going to the living area, they found Foley had prepared their evening meal. After setting the table, Foley sat waiting on the couch in front of the fire for Sarah and Lizzy to come from the bedroom. Sarah looked at him then at the table before hurrying to the washroom to freshen up.

There was nothing she could say. He had shown he wasn't interested in her having his child. Standing in the washroom, she tried not to think of his attitude toward her now he knew she was expecting. Except she couldn't let it go. Bursting into tears again and hearing her, Foley went to the washroom to find her sobbing into a cloth she was holding to her face.

"Sarah," he said softly. "There is nothing I can say to make you feel better, I will not get excited about your condition, not after what Maria went through, but I…" He was going to say 'I accept we are having a baby' but Sarah interrupted him.

"I am not Maria! and don't go making it sound like I have a disease! having a baby is not a condition!" she snapped angrily, throwing the wet cloth in the dish and storming past him.

"I'm sorry, it's just…" He said following her to the table. Wanting to tell her he loved her very much and was scared to death of losing her, he again didn't get a chance to explain when he reached out to comfort her, and she pulled away.

"Don't touch me!" she answered sternly.

Stunned by her rebuttal, he tried justifying the way he was feeling. "I never wanted to risk your wellbeing by getting you pregnant Sarah, I won't relax, I can't, not until this baby is born and I know both of you are fine, isn't that enough?"

Sarah looked up at him dismally. "If you feel that is enough, then, I guess that is all I can expect." She couldn't understand why he felt the way he did and her eyes dimmed. What happened to Maria was behind them. They were husband and wife, there was no good reason why they couldn't enjoy having a family together, after all she was perfectly healthy. After Sarah served up their evening meal, dinner was eaten in silence.

Chapter Twenty-three

Sarah rose at dawn as usual and had the table set before Foley came out of the bedroom. Rubbing his eyes, he stared at her standing in front of the stove busily preparing breakfast and wearing one of his shirts which the top of her long legs disappeared under. They hadn't made love last night, instead they argued for the umpteenth time about the impending birth of their baby. Foley argued he didn't want to witness Sarah giving birth, saying he would not watch her go through what Maria had gone through and he would not be happy until it was all over. Sarah argued again she wasn't Maria, and if he didn't want to be there then fine, she would have their baby on her own, after all, it wouldn't be the first time she had a baby on her own, she had Thomas on the riverbank, by herself, she reminded him. Foley turned his back on Sarah and Sarah turned her back on him, then quietly cried herself to sleep.

Lizzy woke and desperately needed to go to the outhouse, so did Foley. "Mommy, I need to go," she said jiggling from one leg to the other. Sarah looked at both Lizzy and Foley as if to say, 'well, what do you want me to do about it?'

"I'll take her," Foley offered, not wanting to get into another argument with Sarah so early in the morning. Leaving her to return to her cooking, he picked up his rifle, and he and Lizzy headed through the washroom where Lizzy waited behind him while he opened the side door and looked out. After checking up and down outside the cabin as far as he could see, then peering over at the lean-to, he glanced at the old cabin and lastly checked the area around the outhouse. Satisfied no wolves were lurking about, he stepped outside and let Lizzy run on ahead of him. Not wanting her to get too far ahead, he reached back, and pulling the door closed, quickly followed her along the path to the outhouse. To be sure nothing was hiding in the outhouse when they got there, he opened the door and checked inside. When everything appeared as it should, he lifted Lizzy in.

At the precise moment Foley lifted Lizzy into the outhouse, an ear shattering scream and crashing noises like furniture being thrown about could be heard coming from inside the cabin. Turning his head sharply to look back at the cabin, and seeing the side door standing open, he turned back to Lizzy with a shocked look on his face. "Lizzy! stay here until I come back for you!" he called, then slamming the door closed, ran as fast as he could back along the path.

Sarah was concentrating on cooking hotcakes. Several batches were already sitting on a plate on the table. After lifting another batch out of the pan, she set about frying thick slices of bread, then cracked four large wild hen's eggs into the same pan. While watching the eggs and bread frying, she thought about her and Foley's argument. At least now he accepted she was having his baby, but she remained disappointed that he didn't want to be present at the birth.

The wolf raised its head, and sniffing at the distinct smell of food, slinked around the side of the cabin and stood hidden by the side of the stone chimney. When it saw two two-legged animals, one large, one small come out of the cabin and hurry away, it came out from hiding and saw a door slightly ajar. The smell of food was stronger here, so, while running its tongue hungrily around its mouth, it pushed its nose against the door and made it swing open.

Feeling hunger pulling at its stomach, it crept gingerly through the washroom, passing by the cast iron bathtub and the washstand until it came through the doorway into the open living area where it stopped in its tracks when it saw another two-legged animal standing in front of a fire with its arms working as it flipped food it was frying.

Sarah hadn't sensed the wolf was there, she was far too busy. The smell of hotcakes, frying eggs and burnt bread dulled her senses to other smells. But she could not mistake hearing a low guttural growl.

As carefully as she could, she stopped flipping the bread and slowly turned her head to see a mangy looking grey wolf standing in her cabin. The wolf was young but looked starved, which didn't make it any less dangerous. Sarah's stomach lurched, her eyes widened with fear. If she were to move now the wolf would strike. Sizing up her situation, she tried to figure out a way to escape the imminent attack she knew was coming. Her rifle standing against the wall beside the front door was too far away to get at, she wouldn't reach it before the wolf would be upon her. If she could turn them to her advantage, the table and couch would be her best defense. The hot pan she held in one hand and the flip she held in the other would have to be her weapons. The wolf put its head down, and baring its fangs, growled low and long.

Thinking a sharp noise might buy her time to escape, Sarah suddenly screamed, and flinging the hot pan, threw it straight at the wolf. Momentarily startled by Sarah's scream, the wolf flinched as the pan came hurtling towards it. When the pan crashed against the floor and bounced, fat splashed all over the wolf and the floor. Hot burnt bread hit it on the snout, fried eggs went flying between its legs causing it to jump as hot fat singed its fur and burnt its skin. As Sarah scrambled to get away, the wolf leapt toward her.

Grabbing the side of the table, she tipped it over and hoped it would block the wolf's path. Crockery and cutlery along with the plate of hotcakes went crashing in all directions. Taking hold of a wooden chair, she swung it up in front of her for protection then rushing toward the couch, dived over it. The couch tipped onto its back with a loud crash, causing Sarah to land heavily on the floor. Skidding over spilt fat, the wolf charging after her crashed against the wall beside the fire and slowed its attack until it could gain its footing. Holding the chair up in front of her and pushing herself backwards along the floor, she managed to keep its legs either side of the wolf's head as it tried getting at her. With her back against the wall, she kept the wolf at bay.

Snapping its jaw and baring its teeth sent saliva spraying from the wolfs mouth as it pushed viciously against the chair. Sarah had little time to think. The attack became a fight for hers and that of her unborn baby's life, but she didn't know how long she could keep up the fight. The wolf hadn't eaten for days and wasn't about to stop its attack until its belly was full.

Hoping Lizzy would stay in the outhouse until he came back, Foley hurtled back through the doorway, went barreling through the washroom, then into the living area where he slammed into the wall and came to a sudden stop. Seeing Sarah struggling to hold the wolf off, he straightened up and cocked his rifle. If he wanted to save Sarah and his child, there was no time to lose. Lifting his gun to his shoulder, he fired off a shot, and struck the leg of the chair. Splinters of wood scattered around the room as the wolf recoiled from being wounded.

Feeling the burning pain spreading through its body, the wolf forgot the two-legged animal on the floor and instead, turned its attention to the animal standing. There wasn't a moment to lose. Cocking his rifle again, Foley fired off a second shot, and watched the wolf drop at Sarah's feet.

With her breath coming in gasps, and her body shaking, Sarah dropped the chair, and pulling her legs in close, tried to get away from the scene in front of her. Stepping over the mess on the floor and around toppled furniture, Foley knelt beside Sarah where they both stared at the wolf lying in a spreading pool of blood.

A moment before passing out, Sarah gazed unseeing up at Foley. The realization that he could have lost Sarah and his baby hit Foley like a gale force wind. Putting down his rifle and placing one arm behind Sarah's back and the other under her knees, he lifted her, and carrying her to their bed, lay her gently amongst the pillows. While pulling the covers over her bare legs, he bent down and kissed her.

Lizzy was still in the outhouse when she heard gunshots coming from the cabin. When Foley slammed the door on her and told her to stay put, she did as she was told. Having relieved herself, she closed the lid on the seat over the pit, then stood behind the door where she could peek through a crack to see if Foley was coming back. When he didn't come back like he said he would, she began to worry. She could see the cabin, but now couldn't hear anything, so to attract attention, she did the only thing she knew best how to do. She took a deep breath, closed her eyes tight, opened her mouth really wide, and screamed really loud.

While Sarah lay oblivious to everything around her, Foley sat on the side of the bed brushing her hair off her face and kissed her again. He loved her so much, and in light of what happened, thinking her giving birth could not be any worse than losing her to a wolf, he decided he wanted to share in the happiness of having their baby. It was then he heard the ear-piercing scream coming from the outhouse.

Scrambling across the mess of food and broken crockery in the living area, he grabbed his rifle, and racing through the washroom and out the side door, he heard Lizzy screaming. While running back along the path to the outhouse, he listened to Lizzy screaming. As he jerked the door open and reached in, Lizzy kept her eyes shut tight and continued to scream. Feeling herself being lifted, and fearing a wolf had her, she screamed louder. After forcing herself to open her eyes and finding it was Foley holding her and not the wolf, she stopped screaming. Then throwing her arms about his neck, she hugged him and cried, "Papa!" Holding her tight in his arms, Foley carried her back to the cabin.

As he took Lizzy straight through to his and Sarah's room, Lizzy looked at the upturned table and couch, at the wooden chairs lying on their sides amidst dented pots and pans, and at the broken dishes and ruined food scattered all over the floor, and seeing the dead wolf, her eyes went wide.

"Stay with mommy Lizzy, I have to clean up," Foley said putting her on the bed. Wriggling down inside the blankets, Lizzy snuggled up to Sarah, but Sarah didn't know she was there, she was still passed out from the shock of it all.

There was no-one else to blame except himself for what happened. When he took Lizzy to the outhouse, he could have sworn he closed the outside door, but obviously it hadn't caught. Taking hold of the wolf by its tail, and leaving a trail of blood on the floor, he dragged it outside where he stood looking down at it. It wasn't the first wolf he had ever encountered, but it was the mangiest. 'It doesn't seem too vicious now,' he thought, kicking it with his bare foot.

Determined Sarah would wake to a clean and tidy cabin just like she always kept it, after going back inside, he picked up the couch, and except for the one chair that now had a broken leg thanks to his shooting through it, he stood the table and chairs back up, swept up the broken crockery and ruined food and along with the wolf, buried it all in a deep hole away from the cabin. Getting a bucket of hot soapy water and getting down on his hands and knees, he scrubbed the floor clean of blood and leftover bits of food.

Sarah and Lizzy were sitting up in bed where Foley made them stay while he cooked a fresh breakfast for everyone. After carrying the tray with a plate of hotcakes covered in treacle, two mugs of coffee and a mug of warm milk for Lizzy to the bed, all three sat there eating.

Foley was being attentive, and Sarah could see through the doorway the cabin was back to how it was before the wolf came in. But Sarah felt she had to say something to show she was not happy with him leaving the door open.

"We have never had a wolf in our cabin... not ever!" she said trying to keep her voice from sounding angry. "What do you think would have happened if Lizzy, or you had been sitting at the table?" Sarah wasn't thinking of what almost happened to her. Her eyes brimmed with tears when he didn't answer. Being attacked by a wolf himself, Foley knew all too well what could have happened. He knew he had made a terrible mistake, one that could have cost him dearly. Life on the mountain was a precious thing. Danger lurked behind every bush and boulder. He was learning fast not to take anything for granted, and made a promise to himself he would not make the same mistake again. Bending forward, he kissed Sarah passionately and let her go on berating him. "You have to make sure the goddamn door is closed!" she ended.

Watching her Ma and new Pa kiss each other, Lizzy's eyes crinkled in a smile. Foley looked deep into Sarah's eyes. "I love you Sarah, and I think... no, I don't think I know, I want to be with you when our baby is born."

Taking stock of what he said, a tear rolled down Sarah's cheek. "Oh Foley!" she said gasping back a sob, and because it took a wolf to make Foley realize he wanted to be included in the joy of having their baby, it was the first time ever, Sarah felt grateful to a wolf. Grasping the front of his shirt, she pulled him to her. "I love you too, so very much," she cried. While Lizzy ate the last of the hotcakes, Sarah and Foley held each other.

Several days passed since the wolf came into the cabin. Sarah woke at daylight as usual. Lizzy came out of her room rubbing her eyes trying to wake up, and finding her Ma in the washroom went to her. "Mommy, I need a wee." Sarah dried her face and hands and picked up her rifle leaning against the wall. "Me too Lizzy, come on, put your boots on."

Lizzy pushed her feet into her boots and Sarah opened the door. Not wanting what happened with Foley to happen again, before stepping outside, Sarah checked for signs of wolves. When she couldn't see or sense any, she opened the door wide, and after stepping out, made sure the door was closed behind her before starting for the outhouse.

"Come on Lizzy," she said taking Lizzy's hand. Lizzy stepped into the outhouse with Sarah, and when they were both done, Sarah opened the door and looked about. Seeing it was safe, they stepped out and headed back toward the cabin. Before getting very far along the path, Foley came out of the cabin dressed only in his trousers, his feet were bare, the ground was damp and the morning air was cool, and he came striding toward them looking half asleep. Sarah looked him up and down.

"Where is your rifle?" she asked him as he drew level.

"I don't need mine when you have yours!" he drawled sleepily. As he stretched his arms and flexed his muscles, Sarah felt a wanting sweep over her. They made love last night but seeing him now with just his trousers on, she wanted to go back to bed and have him make love to her again. Sarah and Lizzy both stopped walking.

"I'm not waiting for you!" Sarah said brushing aside the feeling that had come over her. Foley stopped in front of the outhouse door.

"I won't be long Sarah, wait for me," he replied stepping inside and closing the door. While Sarah and Lizzy stood on the path and waited, Lizzy looked up at Sarah and started to giggle. Foley's morning cadence was loud and Lizzy giggled some more at the sounds coming from the outhouse. Sarah looked at the door, then trying to be serious, looked down at Lizzy and started to laugh when the noises continued.

"Mommy, Foley farted!" Lizzy's giggling was now full-blown laughter. Sarah couldn't help it either, she burst out laughing loudly. Foley stepped out of the outhouse to see two females in fits of laughter and stopped to face them.

"What?" he asked looking from one to the other.

"You farted Foley!" Lizzy said between giggles. Lizzy's laugh was infectious and Sarah tried to stop laughing but couldn't. When Foley walked indignantly past them, Sarah and Lizzy started to follow him back to the cabin.

"I suppose you two don't fart!" he said over his shoulder.

"Not loud like that we don't!" Sarah giggled. Foley stopped walking and turned to face her and Lizzy. When he looked seriously at them, they both stopped laughing.

"But you do fart?" he asked. When Sarah didn't comment, Foley's face broke into a grin making Lizzy giggle when he crossed his eyes at her. After the three of them broke into fits of laughter, they went inside, and Foley closed the door securely.

Over the next few months, Foley watched Sarah's belly grow, and with Sarah already expecting, when they made love he didn't hold back. After waiting for Lizzy to fall asleep, they made frenzied love to each other in the washroom, on the couch and floor in the living area, and in their bed where they reached their peaks together. Foley told Sarah he loved her every chance he got and Sarah told him she loved him in return. On the outside they were getting along fine. But on the inside, there was still one thing giving Foley a dilemma, and that was the baby's imminent birth. Recurring bad dreams woke him when he dreamt of their baby being wrenched from Sarah's body, and Sarah, soaking wet and covered in blood, disappearing in a shroud of rain like mist. Not wanting Sarah to worry, he kept his dreams to himself.

After going to the top of the mountain with the trappers, Sarah wanted Foley to see how beautiful the mountain was, so while walking the trails Foley watched Sarah closely, and seeing she appeared fit and healthy, he thought perhaps he was worrying needlessly. The three of them spent glorious days exploring the area near their cabin. Packing a rucksack filled with food to eat along the way, and carrying their rifles in case they should come across wolves, Sarah took him and Lizzy along the river in both directions. Sarah slipped her hand in Foley's as they walked, and not wanting to let her go, he grasped her hand tight in his. Foley was happy, his love for Sarah never waned, they were going to have a baby, and Lizzy started calling him Papa.

Chapter Twenty-four

While Joe was above them on the ridge setting the remainder of his traps in the dense forest, the other three men stayed by the river taking skins they caught along with him. After leaning his rifle against a tree, Joe got busy setting his next trap. Having some difficulty getting the old trap to stay set, he forced the jaws apart and while cursing, carefully let it go. Standing up and stepping back, he looked at the trap and hoped it would stay open long enough to catch one of the wolves he had seen wandering through the forest. Reaching back for his rifle, he stopped when he saw it wasn't where he left it.

The sound of a gun's hammer being pulled was unmistakable. When Joe heard the click behind him, he knew it came from his gun. Turning slowly, he came face to face with the very man he thought he would never see again.

"Fucking stupid mistake on your part Jones, you should have killed me when you had the chance," Logan smirked while keeping Joe's rifle aimed at him.

"How the fuck did you manage to survive? You piece of shit!" Joe sneered back.

"You think you're the only one can survive this fuckin' mountain? I been trappin' here almost as long as you!... me! I got camps all over the fuckin' place! all I had to do was get to one of em!" Logan sneered while keeping his finger poised against the trigger.

With his handgun in its holster at his waist, and his knife in its sheath alongside it, Joe was thinking if he could get his hand to either one before Logan got off a shot, he might be able to disarm him, but not wanting to startle Logan into doing something he might regret, Joe didn't make a move.

"Where's Reeves?" he asked, keeping his hands in the open where Logan could see them.

"A man can survive better when he ain't got no one slowin' him down!" Logan laughed. With Logan being the type who wouldn't hesitate to kill his own mother to better his chance of survival, his answer told Joe Reeves was dead.

Joe made to take a step toward Logan, but Logan saw him move, and keeping Joe's rifle pointed at him, took a quick step back. "Don't try anything stupid Jones," he said nervously. Logan didn't trust Joe not to do something cunning. Joe might be a trapper now, but he had been a cavalry man adept at fighting hand to hand against his enemies. Joe took a step forward.

"I said don't fuckin' move!" Logan snarled taking another step back.

"I should have killed you the first fucking time!" Joe said while thinking of Logan forcing himself on Sarah in Cedar Creek with her four-year old son Thomas sleeping alongside her. Thomas being there was something which made no difference to scum like Logan. Logan helped himself to whatever he wanted, and be damned if anyone got in the way of stopping him.

"I should have fucked that bitch when I had the chance! you ever fuck her Jones? she would be a good fuck wouldn't she? Maybe worth dyin' for!" Logan goaded, flicking his tongue over his broken yellow teeth that Joe had been responsible for breaking. Joe treated Sarah like a daughter. Logan asking if he had bedded her had him feeling disgusted. When Logan went on describing certain parts of Sarah's body, it ate at Joe, and unable to hold back he lunged forward.

Fergus had almost finished taking the skin from the carcass of the last wolf he caught and was squatting with his head down not far from where Garrett and Will were busy taking theirs.

"Wonder what's keeping Joe?" he asked, looking over his shoulder towards the ridge. Garrett didn't look up. "He'll be along, you know it takes Joe a bit longer to set his traps these days!" he answered. All three men heard the echo of a shot coming from the ridge.

"Sounds like he's got something," Fergus grinned, taking a quick look around at where they were.

When Joe suddenly lunged toward Logan, Logan lifted his foot and took another step back. "Stay back Jones or I'll shoot you dead, you son-of-a...!" Joe's trap sprang shut, cutting Logan's curse short. As the powerful jaws bit into his leg, Logan screamed as pain shot upward through him causing him to pull the rifles trigger. Trying to jump out of the way of the shot, but being too slow, Joe felt the bullet strike him in his side where it smashed into his hip and almost brought him to a standstill. As pain tore through him, and before Logan had a chance to pull the trigger a second time, he pulled his hunting knife from its sheath and flung it toward him.

Sailing through the air on a straight course, Joe's knife embedded itself in Logan's chest, cutting bone on its way through his lungs and heart, and only came to a stop when the knifes tip jutted from his back. Caught like a wild animal in Joe's trap, with his hands still gripping Joe's rifle, Logan was dead before his body hit the ground.

Holding his hand to his side to stem the flow of blood pouring from the gaping wound, Joe staggered toward the ridge trying to get to his friends, but his side hurt like hell, and he found he couldn't make it. Sitting with his back against a tree for support, he lifted his handgun from its holster, and holding it up in his blood-covered hand, fired three shots in quick succession. Taught this signal in the cavalry to let their company know when they were in trouble, it hadn't been used in a long time, and Joe hoped his friends remembered it and would come running.

Hearing three distinct shots, the men stopped skinning, and slowly rising to their feet, looked toward the ridge where the shots came from. For a moment each man felt bewildered by the reports, but then suddenly remembering his time in the cavalry and what these shots signified, Garrett picked up his rifle and started to run.

"*Joe's in trouble!... come on!*" he yelled back to the others. Thinking Joe was having trouble with a wolf, Will hastily picked up his rifle, Fergus did the same, and leaving their skins where they were, ran after Garrett. When they came on Joe leaning against a tree on the ridge, they found him in a bad way. Seeing blood saturating his clothes, Fergus dropped to his knees beside him. "Saint's be fuckin' praised Joe! what happened?" he asked furrowing his brow in concern.

"Logan..." Joe managed with his breathing coming in short bursts while inclining his head in the direction Logan lay. "Over there."

Going to where Logan lay staring blankly up at the sky, it wasn't difficult for Will to see he was dead. Taking hold of Joe's knife, he pulled it from Logan's chest, then went back to the men. "He's dead," he informed them without feeling.

Joe knew he was dying, but there was something important he had to tell Sarah, and he needed to stay alive long enough to speak to her.

"Get me to Sarah's cabin?" he begged the men.

"It's too far Joe, yee'll never make it!" Fergus implored.

"I'll make it... but if I don't... take me there anyway... bury me next to Elizabeth!" Joe closed his eyes against the pain overtaking him. Not knowing how much time Joe had left, Will and Garrett hurriedly fashioning a stretcher, then carefully lifted Joe onto it. As the men carried him along the trail, Joe thought back to a day and time before Sarah was born.

This particular day, Joe came from his cabin on the High Ridge to visit with Calahan and Elizabeth, whom Calahan had just brought back from Philadelphia as his new bride. Trapping along the High Ridge wasn't doing Joe much good at the time, so he decided to move down to the Low Ridge to visit his friend and give hunting a try along the river. It was late afternoon when, after following the watercourse, he came to Calahan's cabin.

When Joe saw smoke billowing from the chimney, he thought Calahan was there, so putting his gear in the clearing nearby, he made his way up the steps and onto the porch. Thinking Calahan would hear him and come to the door to see who was lingering about, he knocked loudly, and when the door opened, he got a shock to see Elizabeth standing there with neither gun nor knife for protection.

Elizabeth knew Joe and Calahan were friends, and after telling him Calahan was not there, he made to leave, but before he could, Elizabeth said his company would be welcome, and invited him in for coffee. Thinking Calahan may not like it if he came along and found him alone with his wife, Joe stood there trying to decide whether he should go or stay, but Elizabeth begged him to stay, and for a moment he took in her beauty before making up his mind to enter the cabin.

Taking off his coat, Elizabeth hung it behind the door, then after pouring them coffee they sat on the couch together in front of the open fire talking. Elizabeth said Calahan was somewhere on the mountain, she didn't know where, she didn't know the mountain at all well. After finishing his coffee, he said he should be going, but Elizabeth smiled and invited him to stay for dinner. She had already prepared enough food she said, hoping Calahan would be back to eat with her. Joe could see the pot steaming on the stove. Elizabeth said it was only proper that she invite him to eat with her, after all, he had come all that way down the mountain to visit his friend, and she would not let him go before he had eaten, so he stayed for dinner.

During the meal their talk was amicable. Elizabeth was pleased she had company, and smiled sweetly at him across the table. Joe was enjoying her company too, and thought perhaps he was enjoying it a little too much.

They were standing together in front of the fire in the living area when he said he should be going, but when Elizabeth rested her hand on his chest and looked into his eyes, her beauty overpowered him and he felt himself overcome by her deep blue eyes gazing into his. Elizabeth begged him to stay, she didn't want to be on her own she said, she was afraid of the nights she spent alone when Calahan was away trapping, the noise of the forest frightened her. She begged him to stay the night, in the cabin. Joe told her, with Calahan not being there it would not be proper, but Elizabeth insisted, saying she could make up a bed for him in the spare room, or if he preferred, on the couch. When she kept gazing longingly at him, he gave in and said he would sleep on the couch.

When Elizabeth retired for the night, Joe took off his boots and made himself comfortable. The fire in the open fireplace warmed the cabin, and he had been lying quietly watching the wood burn low when he heard Elizabeth's faint sobbing. Getting up, he went to her door just to ask if she was alright, and was there anything he could get her. When her door opened, Elizabeth said she was fine, she said she cried a lot when Calahan wasn't with her.

They were both awake, so he took her out to the living area and sat her on the couch. Elizabeth told him about her fears, of why the mountain frightened her. He put his arm around her to comfort her while telling her Calahan would not be gone long, that he would not leave her if he thought she would be in danger. Elizabeth was comforted by his words, and when she kissed him lightly on his mouth, he returned her kiss.

It was then he took Elizabeth back to her room, and her bed, where he helped her remove her nightgown. After helping him remove his shirt and trousers, he lifted her into his arms and lay her on the bed. Their lovemaking was gentle. Joe had never made love to a woman such as Elizabeth before, she was delicate, and had to be treated with care. Looking at her lying naked beside him, he saw how the soft glow of the lamp made her appear even more delicate. When Elizabeth held him to her and they caressed each other in ways that made him want more, he stayed until the early hours of the next day.

While getting dressed, Elizabeth made him promise he would never mention what they had done to anyone, especially not to any of the other trappers. Elizabeth said she didn't regret having slept with him, but she told him she loved her husband more than she could ever love any other man, and she didn't want him finding out she had been unfaithful. Promises made on the mountain could never be broken, and living by his word, Joe promised Elizabeth he would never divulge what they had done.

When Calahan came home, Joe was sitting at the table eating breakfast Elizabeth cooked. When Elizabeth rushed into Calahan's arms and they kissed passionately, Joe could see she was in love with him, and he with her. Surprised to see Joe in his cabin, Calahan asked why he was there. Elizabeth explained he had not long arrived and that she had insisted he stay to have breakfast to allow him to wait his return. Calahan seemed to accept what Elizabeth was telling him, and Joe and he shook hands in friendship before Joe left to return to the High Ridge Camp.

When he returned to Calahan's cabin a few months later, an unexpected surprise was awaiting him. By then he had become partners with James Fergus, and they had been trapping along the river where they met up with Brent Garrett and Will Sloan. The two young men had not long arrived on the mountain and all four men stopped at Calahan's cabin where they made camp in the clearing for the first time as a group. Calahan welcomed the men, and after their evening meal he and Elizabeth joined them at their fire. It was there Calahan announced proudly, Elizabeth was pregnant.

Knowing the mountain trails well, with Garrett carrying one end of the stretcher, and Will and Fergus the other, the men walked fast

"Hurry!" Joe whispered, catching his breath. The men picked up their pace, but they were still a long way from Sarah's cabin and didn't think Joe, being gut shot would make it. When Joe went quiet, the men put the stretcher down to check if he was still breathing.

"Are yee still with us Joe?" Fergus asked getting up close to his face. Hearing him, Joe's eyes fluttered then opened.

"Why the fuck did you stop? Keep going!" he barked then coughed. Lifting the stretcher, the men walked almost at a run. Trying to conserve his strength and determined not to die until he said what it was that was important to Sarah, Joe pressed his hands over his wound and held them there. Coming out of the forest near Sarah's cabin and into the clearing the men slowed.

"*Sarah!*" Will called urgently as they put Joe down. "*Sarah!*" he called again.

"We've made it Joe, we've made it to Sarah's cabin." Fergus's voice held a note of concern as he knelt beside Joe. Hearing Sarah's name being called, the cabin door opened, and Foley with his rifle in his hands, stepped out to see who was approaching.

"Where is Sarah?" Garrett asked looked up at him standing on the porch.

"She's dressing Lizzy!" Foley answered with a frown as Garrett came bounding up the steps. Seeing the three men and what appeared to be Joe lying on the ground, Foley knew something had happened but stayed where he was.

"Get out of my way!" Garrett said shoving past him.

"What's happened to Joe?" Foley asked as Garrett crossed the porch.

"He's been shot!" Garrett said through gritted teeth and going inside. "*Sarah!*" he called. Sensing someone coming along the trail, then hearing both Will and Garrett's agitated voices calling her, Sarah came out of the bedroom where she had been brushing Lizzy's hair.

"It's bad Sarah, Joe's been shot," Garrett announced when he saw her.

"*Joe!*" she screamed, and tossing the hairbrush aside, it hit the wall, bounced off and crashed to the floor as she rushed past both Foley and Garrett and down the steps. Holding her hand against her bulging belly, she ran to the clearing and fell on her knees beside Joe. "Joe!" she cried. "Oh Joe?" Putting his rifle aside and with Lizzy, Foley followed Garrett to the clearing.

Blood covered Joe's stomach, his clothes were saturated. Lifting his bloody hand up to Sarah, Sarah took it and Joe felt her firm grip in his. She was a strong woman, with a lot of strength in her, and all because four trappers made a promise to look out for her.

"I... I should have killed him Sarah... the first time he tried... Logan... he got me good." When Sarah began to cry, Joe closed his eyes, but he had no time to waste. "I have to tell you something sweetheart... before I go."

"No, Joe, no, you're not going anywhere," she said looking up at the grim faces of the men surrounding them. Then looking back at Joe, waited for him to make his peace.

Joe began by telling Sarah why he made a promise to take care of her all those years ago when five men sat around a campfire on what became known as Sarah's Mountain. Telling her revealed the relationship he had with her mother Elizabeth. "I loved her Sarah... when Calahan brought her to the mountain, I fell in love with her."

"A lot of men loved Ma Joe," she replied clasping his hand tight while thinking his statement just an endearing comment.

"Not like I did, or Calahan... you see, Calahan and I never trapped together after Elizabeth came along. He trapped along the river flats and the middle ground so he could be near her... I kept to the high ridge so they could be alone. That first month she was here, I came down to visit... I could look at her all day... I never tired of looking at her... she was a beautiful woman." Joe paused then went on. "Calahan was away trapping the day Elizabeth and I..." He paused again, this time to catch his breath. "I loved her Sarah, what I mean when I say I loved her is, she didn't say no when I took her to bed... she said she loved me too, but she loved Calahan more." Joe's memory of Elizabeth was as clear as the day he met her. Although a city woman Elizabeth soon learnt how rugged life was on the mountain, but still retained her beauty and eloquence. Making love to her was a wonderful moment in Joe's otherwise mundane life.

Around the campfire that night, when Calahan told the men Elizabeth was pregnant, Elizabeth blushed profusely, and for a fleeting moment her eyes met Joe's across the campfire. While trying to work out just how far along she was, Joe stared back at Elizabeth and came to the conclusion he was the father of the child she was expecting. When Calahan went to the cabin to bring a bottle of whiskey to the fire to celebrate their good news with the men, Joe sat quietly contemplating what should be his and Elizabeth's celebration, not Calahan's.

Two nights they stayed camped in the clearing at the cabin. Joe would not leave until he asked Elizabeth about the baby she was carrying, but he had to wait for an opportunity to be alone with her so he could talk to her.

When she stood on the porch one night to watch stars twinkling in the sky before retiring, he got his chance. Standing beside her and keeping his voice low, he asked her if the baby was his. Elizabeth was not shocked by his asking her, but was adamant she was having Calahan's baby when saying she was already pregnant before he spent the night with her. But Joe was not convinced, so pressing her to tell him the truth, Elizabeth through her tears, confessed it was possible he could be the baby's father.

In saying she loved him, Elizabeth begged him not to say anything to Calahan because Calahan was her husband, and she loved him the most, and because of her confusion as to which man was responsible for getting her pregnant, Calahan was chosen as the child's father. Then, while standing on the porch together and holding her hand to her stomach, Elizabeth said if he loved her as much as she knew he did, he would promise her he would keep their affair secret, and she begged, if anything should happen to her, he was to promise to help Calahan raise 'their' child. Not wanting to hurt Elizabeth or his good friend, the night Joe made his promise to Elizabeth, he gave up his love for her and the right to claim the child he believed was his.

"After learning Elizabeth was pregnant, I could see Calahan was excited at becoming a father, and so I would not... could not... take that away from him." With pain etching his face, Joe looked up at Sarah. "I promise you Sarah, I had only ever been with your Ma once." Although shocked by Joe's admission, the men remained silent. Tears trickled down Sarah's face as she wept. "Please Joe, don't say any more," she begged.

"I'm dying sweetheart." Before his time ran out, Joe wanted to finish what he began.

"Elizabeth begged me to promise I wouldn't say anything, so I promised her... and I kept my promise because I loved her... when Calahan asked me to make him a promise, he asked me to promise not to make you my own, and it hurt me to make that promise, but I did... then he straight away took me aside and asked me if I had ever been with Elizabeth."

Until that moment Joe believed Calahan was unaware he had slept with his wife, but keeping her affair secret got the better of Elizabeth, and she confessed her sin to her husband. Hurt by her indiscretion but deeply in love with Elizabeth, Calahan forgave her, but was the child his? After Elizabeth died, and Sarah was three years old, that question gnawed at Calahan until the night he asked the men to make him their promise.

As his voice broke, Joe took a deep breath. "Goddamn it! it tore me apart when Elizabeth passed, Calahan could see how it affected me... we were friends, I couldn't lie Sarah, but I broke my promise

I made to Elizabeth when I confessed, I had been with her. Calahan wasn't angry with me, he said the two of us shared responsibility for taking care of Elizabeth's daughter... perhaps you are mine, perhaps you are his... we both loved you as a father would... I would never have taken you away from him." Joe had to hurry, it was becoming difficult for him to speak.

"Like Elizabeth, Calahan asked me to promise never to speak about our union, and I promised him I wouldn't breathe a word until the day I die... I'm so sorry sweetheart." Holding Joe's hand in hers, Sarah sobbed at hearing the truth why Joe cared for her as much as he did.

Feeling tired all of a sudden, Joe felt his time had come. "Don't cry Sarah, we both loved you... you remember that," he said taking a deep breath.

Seeing Sarah's dismay, Foley handed Lizzy to Will, and kneeling beside her held her. Joe looked up at him. "Foley, promise me you will take care of Sarah, and little Lizzy... and... he knows doesn't he Sarah?" Sarah couldn't answer, her sobbing was such she couldn't speak, but Foley knew what he was asking. "I know Joe, and I promise I will take care of Sarah and Lizzy, and our baby, for you." Feeling their own dismay, Fergus, Garrett and Will stood witness to Foley making his binding promise to Joe on Sarah's mountain.

Joe closed his eyes then opened them. He had always understood the love Major Hardy held for Elizabeth long after she passed. Having been betrothed to Elizabeth before she married Calahan, Major Hardy was unable to let her go, and Joe had been the same. Staring up at Sarah leaning over him sobbing, he lifted his bloodied hand up to her face, and as the light in his eyes began to dim, he saw Elizabeth's angelic face gazing lovingly down on him.

"Elizabeth," he whispered looking longingly at Sarah. Covering his hand with hers, Sarah held it to her cheek.

"I'm here Joe... it's time now, come... come to me Joe," she whispered in a voice he remembered so well, and looking up into what he believed were Elizabeth's beautiful dark blue eyes, a tear ran down the side of his face as he took his last breath.

Joe was buried beside Elizabeth beyond the cabin in a clearing close to the forest. Will fashioned the cross and Garrett carved Joe's name. 'Joseph Beauford Jones' and at Sarah's request, he carved the following. 'Beloved father also of Sarah' and the year '1879.'

It took a lot of tender love and care from Foley to get Sarah over her loss. Fergus, Garrett and Will missed Joe's camaraderie, but continued to trap the mountain until winter that year. When they passed the word along about what happened to Joe, every trapper came by Sarah's cabin to pay their respects. It had been Joe that kept the men together with his knowledge and friendship. Now with his passing, some of the men were no longer willing to keep on trapping.

Chapter Twenty-five

Things changed on the mountain after Joe's passing. Trapping lost its appeal for both Fergus and Will. When winter came around, Sarah and Foley along with the rest of the trappers made plans to travel back to Cedar Creek. This year they would be led off the mountain by Fergus.

Snow was already thick on the ground when the trappers, with packhorses loaded for the long trek back down the mountain gathered at Sarah's cabin. Fergus, Garrett and Will, all stood on Sarah's porch stomping snow off their boots while Foley, Sarah and Lizzy were inside keeping warm. When Fergus knocked on their door, Foley opened it and greeted them with handshakes. Now heavily pregnant, Sarah had slowed down some, and hadn't been out trapping for several months. Not wanting to leave Sarah alone for too long, when Foley took over trapping for her, he set his traps close by.

The trappers hadn't been back to Sarah's cabin since burying Joe. They knew she was expecting, but hadn't known how far along she was. Once Foley made his promise to look out for her, none of them gave her much thought now the need for them to keep their promise had ended, but like Joe, the three men didn't like to back away from their responsibility. If Joe were alive, he would want them to carry on with their promise once more, and so the men agreed they would see Sarah safely back to Cedar Creek for the birth of her and Foley's baby.

When the men came in out of the cold, Sarah was standing outside the washroom with Lizzy. As soon as she saw the men, Lizzy bounded across the room toward them and of course it was Will who scooped her into his arms to greet her. Fergus stared at Sarah in surprise.

"Saints be praised Sarah lass!... are yee about to drop?" he remarked trying to smile while worrying her condition may hinder their going down the mountain.

"Soon Fergus, Foley figures about a week after Christmas." That! Fergus quickly worked out, was barely two months away. Waddling over to him, she gave him a hug, then after hugging the other men, waddled back to the fire and stood next to Foley. Sarah missed Joe, especially right then. He was their leader, and always led them safely down the mountain. Fergus shook hands vigorously with Foley again.

"Congratulations an' all Foley if I have nay told yee before," he drawled in his thick Irish brogue. "But we have to get crackin', the bloody snow is still fallin' and we won't make it through the pass lest we go now, are yee packed?" Having stepped up to take charge, it was up to him to see they all got to Cedar Creek safely.

"Horses are ready, we just need to get Sarah sorted, how is she going to ride like she is?" Foley asked worried she couldn't ride as big as she was. Sarah worried about her size too, and not wanting to be a burden, looked questioning at the men. Garrett and Will also wondered if Sarah would be able to make the journey. Putting their heads together with Foley and Fergus, after much debate they all agreed if they pulled Sarah's stirrups up high, she could sit her horse in a squat which would take the strain off her legs and make her seat level.

After Garrett adjusted the stirrups and Foley helped Sarah into the saddle, everyone set off for the pass. Finding her ride comfortable for about an hour before her bottom began to ache, Sarah brought everyone to a stop to let Garrett put a blanket on top of her saddle to cushion her seat. The blanket helped a little, but not knowing how far she could ride sitting like she was, she told the men she would go as far as she could before having to stop again. Showing his concern, Foley told Sarah to let him know when she needed to get down, he would help her, after all, she was his wife he said, and his responsibility. After the wolf got into the cabin, he finally got used to the idea of her having his baby, but he wouldn't allow himself to relax until they were safely off the mountain and their baby delivered. Sarah worried about being able to outrun wolves lying in wait at the bottom of the mountain.

With Fergus leading the way, Sarah came next, then Foley. Garrett and Will rode behind them with the rest of the trappers. When they got to the pass, Fergus searched the trees looking for Joe's rope markers. Joe had no problem following the markers he set, but over the years they had deteriorated from weathering making it difficult for Fergus to locate. Fergus made a mental note to himself that when, or if he came back to the mountain, he would replace Joe's markers with his own.

Making their way safely through the pass to the caves just on nightfall, they split into groups and quickly set up camp. Foley made Sarah and Lizzy comfortable on their bedrolls, then got their meals and Sarah her coffee. When Garrett asked Sarah how her ride was, she said her ride was comfortable, but explained when they got to the base of the mountain, she wouldn't be able to ride fast sitting the way she was. After much discussion, it was agreed her stirrups would be lowered to enable her to ride that leg of the journey with her legs down as usual. The men would bunch up around her and Foley for the race through where the wolves congregated, allowing Sarah the chance to race along without her horse throwing her. The next morning Sarah herself lowered her stirrups.

Walking their horses cautiously along the trail at the bottom of the mountain, everyone watched for signs of wolves. When they spotted them surging from both sides of the forest, Fergus quickly reminded everyone to stay bunched up, then kicking their horses hard, they began galloping ahead of the pack.

Although trying their best to keep bunched up, the wolves forced everyone to separate. Hearing shots ringing out all around as she raced along, Sarah found it difficult to keep her horse in the middle of the bunch.

Spotting a wolf weaving between the horses and running in close to Sarah, with Lizzy sitting in front of him, Foley couldn't get off a clear shot. When Sarah's horse bucked suddenly while trying to ward off the wolf, she lifted out of her saddle, came down heavily, and had trouble holding on. Fearing a wolf would bring her horse down, she ignored the sharp pain she felt against the inside of her leg as she landed and kept her horse going.

Watching on in horror as Sarah was thrown about in her saddle, Foley rode swiftly along behind her trying to catch up. As shots rang out in the distance, their horses took them further ahead of the others When they were clear of wolves and the sounds of shots became less frequent, Foley slowed his horse, but Sarah didn't stop. Kicking his horse hard, he gave chase, but unable to catch her, he watched helplessly until two trappers suddenly appeared from behind to overtake him.

Thinking wolves were still chasing her, Sarah kicked her horse to get it to go faster. With its breath coming in gasps the horse was lathering, but knowing the danger it was in, it kept going. Sarah couldn't see where Foley and Lizzy were, not until Samuels and Garrett came alongside and pulled her horse to a stop. Getting her off her horse quickly, they sat her on a log and waited for Foley to catch up. Coming to where Sarah was, he removed his coat quickly, then untying the harness holding Lizzy, passed her down to Garrett. After dismounting, he knelt in front of Sarah and cupped her face in his hands.

"Are you hurt?" he asked with concern evident in his voice, but before Sarah could answer, he stood back up. "Her horse almost threw her!... *you!*" he yelled pointing angrily at the two men. "You were supposed to keep those fucking wolves from getting between us!"

"We couldn't stop them Foley, there were too many!" Garrett answered. Worried they might have injured Sarah and her unborn baby, he put Lizzy down, and knelt beside Sarah.

"I'm sorry Sarah, are you alright?" he asked equally as concerned as Foley.

"I think so... yes, I'm... I'm fine." Not wanting to alarm anyone, Sarah didn't mention the pinch to her leg. Before putting her back on her horse and heading to their next camp, the men let her rest until the other trappers finished skinning their kill.

Once everyone arrived at the wells, Sarah and Lizzy relieved themselves while the men set about making camp. Coming from behind dense shrubs, Sarah beckoned Foley to her.

"I'm bleeding," she informed him while keeping her voice low so the other men couldn't hear. Foley stared at her in disbelief. This was not good, visions of Maria covered in blood as she lay dying sprang to mind.

"How bad is it?" he asked while cursing inwardly and embracing her.

"It's not too bad, I don't think it's the baby, I think it may be something else, but I need to check," Sarah answered while leaning against him for comfort.

Remembering when they had been chased by wolves when Samuels fell on her, and her new Pa had been attacked, and the wolf getting in the cabin, Lizzy clung to Foley and Sarah while they talked.

"What do you want me to do?" Foley asked rubbing his hands over Sarah's back.

"Get Garrett and Fergus, and maybe Will to hold blankets up so you can take a look?" Foley stopped rubbing. "You want me to take a look... here?" he answered, looking over Sarah's head at all the men milling about.

"I can't very well look at myself Foley, I can't bend over that far," Sarah laughed, then stopped because her situation was serious. "I don't want to worry you, but if I am bleeding from you know where, then it is the baby, but if it's just a cut because I felt a pinch when I hit my saddle, then it will be nothing, but you have to look so you can tell me where the blood is coming from." After Foley explained Sarah's situation to the trappers as best as he could. The three men brought their blankets over to Sarah.

"How do you want to do this Sarah?" Garrett asked.

"We need light, can we do it over there?" Sarah asked pointing to the fire. Without being told how Foley was going to inspect Sarah's injury, while the other trappers kept their backs turned, the men formed an enclosure around her. After helping Sarah out of her trousers, and laying her on his bedroll, Foley studied her for a time, but unable to tell where she was hurt, helped her back into her trousers and smiled. "I don't think I've ever seen you looking more beautiful," he said leaning in close and feeling relieved the blood didn't appear to be anything. When Sarah hit him hard on his arm he flinched, then holding her face in his hands, he kissed her. After getting to his feet, he told the other men they could come back to the fire.

"Are you feeling alright?" Foley asked Sarah as they were settling down for the night.

"I feel fine, but I don't know that I should get back on my horse in case it is the baby." Foley agreed to that, and went to discuss Sarah's situation with the three trappers. "Now what do we do?" he asked when he finished explaining.

Joe would have known what to do, but Fergus was at a loss. Sarah couldn't very well walk all the way to Cedar Creek, it was another full day's ride to their next camp on the prairie and then another to town. They put their predicament to the other men.

It was Samuels who came up with the only solution that made sense. He suggested he and Reece ride to Cedar Creek and bring a buckboard back so Sarah could get to Doc Harris in comfort. The men argued, saying Sarah and Foley would have to stay camped at the wells too long, which could be a worry if her problem was the baby. Samuels suggested if they left now, they could cross the prairie in the dead of night and get into town early next morning allowing them to turn around and come straight back. If it was the baby, they all agreed, there was nothing they could do about it anyway, but they wouldn't let her get back on her horse. Foley and Sarah agreed Samuels suggestion was the only way.

The trek across the prairie took Samuels and Reece longer in the dark than anticipated. Riding all night, they made it to Cedar Creek late afternoon the next day. After explaining to Ham why they rode in without their skins, the two men procured a buckboard from his livery, then before leaving, Samuels came up with another idea.

Along with Foley and Sarah, the three trappers watched Samuels and Reece appear along the trail first, and stood with their mouths open when they spied a buckboard with Doc Harris in control trundling along at speed behind the two men. As the buckboard came to a dusty stop, Sarah and Foley smiled at each other then rushed to the buckboard to greet the newcomer.

"Doc! what are you doing here?" Sarah asked sounding surprised.

Pleased that Samuels and Reece made it safely back, the three trappers welcomed them with slaps on their backs. The two men were used to going without sleep for days at a time for fear of attack from wolves, but still they looked worn. Having not had any sleep since leaving the caves, Samuels strode over to Sarah and Foley and greeted them with a wide grin.

"We figured instead of bringing the wagon and taking you to Doc, we would bring Doc to you." When Sarah unexpectantly hugged him, Samuels eagerly put his arms about her and hugged her back. Overjoyed to see the men, Foley shook their hands vigorously and nodded to Doc to acknowledge his presence before shaking his hand. When Fergus handed Reece a canteen, he took a long drink and let water spill down the front of his coat before wiping his hand across his beard and grinning in satisfaction at Samuels.

Although weary from having driven the buckboard through the night and all that day, Doc climbed from the buckboard and he and Sarah hugged each other. He hadn't been asked to go to the mountain when Sarah's mother fell ill with fever, and at the time was saddened to learn of her passing. The moment Samuels and Reece informed him Sarah was expecting and may be injured, he didn't hesitate to come and see for himself how badly hurt she was. Doc studied Sarah, and although she appeared in good health, he worried she might be losing her baby.

"I can check you now if you like," he said sounding tired but concerned.

Sarah had rested while waiting for the men to return, and felt her injury may not be as bad as first thought. "It's alright Doc, the bleeding has stopped, but I still need you to check me, have some coffee and a rest, then we can take a look." Sarah ushered him to the fire where she got him a mug of freshly brewed coffee.

While leaning back on her elbows inside a screen set up by the fire where Doc was preparing to examine her, she filled him in on what happened and used this time to study his face. His was a kind face. His hair and moustache were as white as snow, his back stooped, but his eyes, showing creases at the corners, were still full of life.

Spotting the injury causing Sarah concern, Doc smiled up at her, and feeling her face turning bright red, Sarah quickly looked away. Foley had seen her plenty of times when they made love, and Doc was familiar with her bodily functions, but this was proving all a bit much.

"There is nothing for you to be concerned about Sarah," Doc said, unconcerned with her embarrassment. He delivered her into the world and had seen all of her when he helped deliver Lizzy. Checking Sarah's belly with his listening device, and finding her baby's heart beating strong, Doc called Foley over. Having already suffered enough through Maria's deceit, Foley didn't want to hear anything bad and approached nervously.

"Take a look," Doc said, indicating for him to get inside the screen. When Doc told him to look between Sarah's legs, Foley glanced sheepishly at him. He had already done that, and his face turned pink with embarrassment.

"I don't need to look Doc, just tell me... is it serious?" Doc laughed at Foley's seemingly bashful manner. As a gunfighter, Foley was a man not afraid to stand up to any badman that came his way, but to look at his wife intimately in front of another man, even if that man was a doctor, that was something else entirely. Sarah told Doc Foley already looked to see if she hurt herself, so with a shrug, Doc let his refusal to look pass.

"No," Doc said in answer to Foley's concern. "It's a small cut high up on the inside of her leg, near her groin, she said she felt a pinch when she hit her saddle and that is what happened, she pinched her leg making a small cut which bled a lot, the baby's heart is strong, Sarah is healthy, she looks good, going to town in the buckboard will help too, everything is as it should be." Doc smiled at Sarah with satisfaction. Lying back quietly, Sarah watched the two men discussing her wellbeing. Foley didn't appear to be showing any regret about them having a baby, and Doc seemed to take looking at her in his stride.

Sarah was relieved to hear everything was fine, not so Foley. He believed Doc when he said Maria was fine, when in the end she wasn't. With a feeling of doubt still in his mind, Foley left Sarah with Doc and went back to Lizzy and the men at the fire. Sarah returned to watching Doc kneeling between her legs as he rummaged around in his bag.

"You know Doc, you are the only other man I would ever let look at me there." Sarah blushed some more when Doc laughed as he secured the cut on her leg with bandages.

"Well, don't you go telling anyone, but I've seen a lot of these, and believe me when I say, when you have seen one..." he helped Sarah put her trousers back on and get to her feet. "You're not surprised when you see others," he whispered with a smile and a wink. Sarah giggled at what he said, and putting her arms around him, hugged him.

The morning after the night Samuels and Reece left to get the buckboard, the rest of the trappers broke camp and travelled on ahead of Sarah and Foley's group. When it was decided the now smaller group would spend one last night camped out on the prairie, then take a leisurely day to reach town, everyone relaxed and settled down for the night.

Sarah and Doc sat beside each other on a log talking while Foley squatted beside Lizzy at the fire where they were engrossed with each other as he dished food onto a plate for her. "He's not happy about me being pregnant Doc," Sarah said watching them.

"He's scared Sarah... when Maria died, he witnessed something no man should ever have to see," Doc answered watching Foley and Lizzy too. "It wasn't just that Maria had a bad heart, when she drew her last breath, I thought the baby might stand a chance if I got to it quickly, I haven't told anyone this, nor should I, but you need to know why Foley is afraid to let you have his children... even though Maria said she wasn't having his child, how could she be certain it wasn't his?"

Sarah turned to look at Doc and pursed her lips. "A woman knows who she has been with at the time of... of getting pregnant! who else knows better who the father of her child is?" she snapped sharply, but then thought of both Calahan and Joe not knowing which of them fathered her. Her mother was not certain either, and here she was thinking Maria should have known who the father of her baby was. She put her head down in disgust at what she said.

307

"Perhaps," Doc replied. "But I think it was more what I did that frightened Foley the most, oh, it has been done before, in cities, but it was the first time I ever did it, and it scared the hell out of me." He let out a sigh before going on. "Foley didn't deserve to see what I did, you see..." Doc looked off into the dark, then looking back at Sarah watching him, drew his finger across his stomach. "I cut Maria severely... here, but it all went horribly wrong, and well, Foley had to have been in shock after seeing that."

Sarah watched Foley give Lizzy a gentle nudge to send her on her way. Carrying her plate carefully so as not to spill her food, Lizzy came walking toward Sarah and Doc. Hearing Doc relate what happened the night Maria died, Sarah understood Foley's lingering concern for her, and her eyes welled. She felt sorry she had been nasty to him when they argued about her being pregnant. She hadn't understood at all what he went through at the time. When Foley brought her and Doc a plate of food each, Sarah reached up to take her plate and seeing her tears, Foley frowned but didn't ask what could be making her upset, instead, he turned and went back to the fire to get food for himself. When Sarah swiped a tear off her cheek and sniffled, Doc heard it.

"I'm sorry Sarah, maybe I shouldn't have told you," he said spooning food into his mouth. "I'm glad you told me," Sarah said doing the same while watching Foley come back to sit beside her.

That night, when everyone was asleep in their bedrolls, Sarah and Foley lay in each other's arms.

"I'm so sorry," Sarah whispered.

"What have you got to be sorry about?" Foley asked, not understanding her apology.

"I'm sorry I didn't understand what you went through... with Maria."

Figuring it was Doc who said something that got Sarah upset, Foley pursed his lips. "Just what the hell did Doc tell you?" he asked sounding stern.

"He told me what he did to Maria the night she died, I'm so sorry," Sarah repeated drawing back a sob.

"Goddamn it!" Foley said angrily. "He should have kept that to himself, didn't he swear an oath to keep quiet, goddamn it?" he repeated. As Sarah wept a little harder, he brought her closer. "Foley Andrews, you know I love you, and I will do my utmost best to deliver you our child," she sobbed while lifting her head and kissing him passionately.

"I know you will," he whispered returning her kiss. But knowing there was nothing he or Doc could do if something were to go wrong, Foley remained worried about the birth.

At sun up the next morning, everyone and their horses were rearing to go. Garrett and Foley got busy freeing Sarah's packhorse of her skins and spreading them out in the back of the buckboard. When her horses were tethered to the wagon, Doc steered it with Sarah sitting beside him while Lizzy travelled comfortably in the back where she got to enjoy the scenery and giggle at Will and Garrett making faces at her while riding along with Samuels and Reece. Foley took the lead beside Fergus with his packhorse in tow.

For their last night, they made camp out on the prairie before heading into town. After leaving Samuels and Reece to unhitch all the horses from the buckboard and tether them to a rope hitching line, Garrett and Will got a fire going and the men shared the chore of preparing food. Later that night, Sarah and Foley, with Lizzy sleeping in front of them, slept together in the back of the buckboard wrapped snugly in wolf furs and blankets.

"I think next spring, when we head for your mountain, this is the way we will go," Foley whispered lovingly in Sarah's ear as he slipped his hand inside her shirt. Feeling her warmth against his hand, he moaned softly as he massaged her breast, making Sarah smile in the dark.

"What will we do with the wagon when we get it to the mountain? There's no way to get it through the pass," she whispered back. As her nipple hardened, Foley got to thinking.

"We could leave it at the bottom of the mountain and use it each time we come to town, but we would have to cover it to protect it from the weather." Foley thought that a good idea. Sarah thought so too. "Or maybe we could build a shelter to keep it in," she whispered, letting Foley's fondling warm her.

After reaching Cedar Creek, Foley took Sarah and Lizzy to the lodge where he saw them settled. He kissed Sarah lovingly then went to the Ferguson House to let the rest of the trappers know everything was fine with her. Once the men said they were relieved to hear the news, he left the house and headed to the Trading Post where he put Sarah's skins in and collected the chits to take to the bank. Sarah wasn't written up on the board for the pot. She couldn't take part in winning the thousand-dollar prize because Foley and Garrett helped unload her skins into the buckboard. Even so, she had a good number of skins which netted her a tidy sum. Ham's buckboard they borrowed to get Sarah to town was returned to him at the livery.

Chapter Twenty-six

Foley wouldn't let Sarah risk her or their unborn baby's health by letting her take their buckboard anywhere now she was so close to delivering their baby. He stipulated forcefully their buckboard was to stay in the shelter at the lodge where it had been sitting unused since last winter when they married. Just like with Maria, he put his foot down and demanded Sarah do as he bid. He informed Brady and Ellen, if they wanted to see Sarah and Lizzy, they were to visit them at the lodge. He became overprotective by going with her every time she visited friends around town. Taking orders from Foley, or anyone for that matter was difficult for Sarah, but she went along with him so he wouldn't worry so much. Their nights they spent making love, or just holding each other in their big four poster canopied bed while they slept.

To give them a clear indication as to when their baby would be born, Sarah kept writing her crosses on her piece of paper. If Sarah marked her time right, Foley was certain their baby would be born one week after Christmas.

Lizzy was excited to be back at the lodge where she was born. Her first night home she ran up and down the stairs so much it wore her out, causing her to fall asleep at the dinner table. Foley carried her upstairs and Sarah put her to bed. The very next day Lizzy recommended school two days a week.

The trappers secured work with Major Hardy out at his ranch. Steers were branded and horses were brought to the corrals to be broken. Major Hardy had buyers waiting and was desperate to get his stock to Moreton. A drive was organized the first week the trappers were in town.

It wasn't long after being back Sarah collected her very first letter from Thomas. His letter carried good news. While still attending college, he had secured work as a cadet reporter at the 'Philadelphia Gazette.' To start with, he informed Sarah, he would be working on a casual basis, and later, after completing college, he would have an opportunity to become full time. Thomas wrote he was enjoying reporting on social happenings around the city, however, he still liked writing about Cedar Creek and Sarah's mountain in his journals and asked Sarah for every bit of information she could give him. He also wrote to the Hammonds and they, being pleased that he was interested in the goings on in their town, wrote back with their own pieces of news.

After reading Thomas's letter, Sarah immediately wrote back. This letter Sarah wrote, told of good news about her expecting Foley's baby, and it carried with it bad news about what happened to Joe. Becoming upset as she tried to write, Sarah broke into tears and ended up having to enlist Foley to help finish her letter.

Wanting to be in Cedar Creek to spend Christmas with his family, Thomas didn't find out Sarah was expecting, nor did he learn about Joe. He had already left Philadelphia before Sarah's letter arrived.

Four days before Christmas, Cedar Creek lay under a thick blanket of snow. The road from Moreton was heavily covered, however, six supply wagons bringing much needed supplies managed to push through. Items town folk couldn't get from Henry's Emporium they ordered from Henry's catalogues arrived just in time for Christmas. People were busy bustling about getting themselves organized for the holiday. Sarah's annual Christmas Dinner Party was to be held two days out from Christmas and they needed to stock up on food, so Sarah took Foley and Lizzy to the store to do their shopping. Christmas this year would be a solemn affair. Sarah felt miserable, Joe was no longer with them and of course, Thomas would remain in Philadelphia. She missed Thomas and Joe immensely, but kept her feeling of sadness hidden because she was happy at least that Fergus, along with Will and Garrett, would attend her dinner as they did every year. Foley's family of Brady and Ellen, and their twins Matthew and Charlotte were amongst Sarah's guests. Lizzy loved playing with the twins. Having told everyone she was having a baby too, and knowing full well what she meant, everyone laughed at her innocent comment.

While Sarah and Foley were at the counter with Henry, telling him what supplies they needed for their party, Lizzy strolled around looking at all the pretty things and spied a doll dressed in a white dress with tiny sequins stitched to it, making it look like a princess. Lizzy knew all about princesses. She listened intently when Tilly O'Rourke read stories about them. The doll had rosy red cheeks and red painted lips, and dark curly hair topped her pretty porcelain face, and Lizzy thought her the most beautiful thing she had ever seen. The only doll she owned was a rag doll she took to bed with her and played with all the time. She loved her rag doll, but had never seen a more beautiful doll than this one. After being put to bed that night and before going to sleep, Lizzy thought about that doll. It was still a few days until Christmas, and she prayed she would receive a dolly just like the one in Henry's store.

There was such a lot to do, and wanting to take some of the stress off Sarah, both Martha and Patrice arrived early to help her prepare the festive dinner. Having felt they owed Samuels and Reece for their help in getting Doc to Sarah, the two men were invited to dine with them, so along with the three trappers, Samuels and Reece got ready at the Ferguson House.

Doc Harris, his wife Gerda, Dave Henderson, and Ham Hammond with his daughter's Sissy and Lilly, and the five trappers, all arrived at the lodge at the same time. Seating was arranged at the table so Will had no choice but to sit beside Sissy.

The merriment around the table was in full swing when Sarah stopped eating and looked toward the dining room door. Foley stopped laughing at something one of the trappers said and looked at Sarah. With her eyes focused on the door and her brow furrowed in a frown, she seemed oblivious to the noise around her.

"Sarah?" Concerned by the immensely serious look on Sarah's face, Foley reached over and covered her hand with his.

"Someone is coming Foley," she whispered. Foley squeezed her hand.

"I'll go take a look," he answered, getting up and leaving the room. With the exception of Martha and Dave watching Foley leave, the guests kept talking. Sensing there were people at her door but unable to tell who they were, Sarah waited quietly for Foley to return.

As Foley walked across the living area passing the open fireplace, he heard a knock on the front door, and glancing over at the fire, felt its warmth emanating throughout the room making it comfortable, then before opening the door to possible strangers, he reached for his gun where it hung in his gun-belt on a stand alongside his hat and coat. Holding his gun firmly with his finger on the trigger, he gingerly opened the door.

Two people, their features hidden from Foley by darkness, and with their thick coats wrapped snuggly around them, stood on the porch in the cold. Holding his gun up, he aimed it squarely at the silhouette standing closest to him.

"Hello Foley," the silhouette greeted. Thinking he recognized the voice, Foley's heart gave off a sudden thump.

"Thomas?" he asked in surprise.

When Thomas stepped into the light and smiled broadly at him, Foley opened the door wider and lowered his gun, then wrapping their arms around each other, they greeted each other with welcoming slaps to their backs.

"My god Thomas! is Sarah going to be surprised to see you? When did you get in?" Foley asked moving Thomas and his companion further into the room so he could see them better.

"Just now, on the coach," Thomas said removing his coat, and after handing it to Foley turned to the person standing beside him. "Foley, this is Gabrielle," he said introducing the young woman with him. Foley looked surprised, first at Thomas then at Gabrielle.

Sarah was wondering what could be taking Foley so long when Foley stepped back into the room with a somewhat serious look on his face and looked down the length of the table where she was sitting. "Sarah, there is someone here to see you!" he announced trying to keep from smiling. Everyone around the table stopped talking and turned to look at the door. When Thomas strolled in casually with a wide grin on his face and stepped around Foley, Sarah's heart almost stopped beating.

"Thomas!" she cried, getting out of her chair a little too quickly. "Oh! Thomas," she said grabbing the side of the table to steady herself. Thomas hurried toward her but stopped when he saw her condition. "Ma!... you're expecting!" he exclaimed.

Ignoring his exclamation at her appearance, Sarah held her arms out and burst into tears as, with her bulging stomach getting in their way, they embraced each other as best as they could. Knowing Thomas would make Sarah cry the minute she saw him, Foley stood beside her while mother and son clung to each other.

"Ma! I want you to meet someone," Thomas said smiling, then letting Sarah go, went back to the door. What Thomas was about to say may come as a shock to Sarah and Foley wasn't going to take any chances with her and his baby, so putting his arm around her, he gave her a gentle squeeze and held her. While everyone watched in silence, Thomas drew Gabrielle into the room and helped her out of her thick woolen coat.

"Ma, this is Gabrielle, and Ma... Gabrielle is my wife," he announced smiling proudly. Surprised by his statement, everyone turned to look at Sarah to see how she would react to this news and Gabrielle's obvious appearance. Sarah already knew a little about Gabrielle, Thomas had written about her in his letter. But Thomas failed to mention they were married and were expecting a baby.

Knowing Sarah's past when dealing with strangers, the three trappers watched with bated breath as Sarah moved away from Foley and went and stood in front of Gabrielle. Both Thomas and Gabrielle waited silently for Sarah to say something.

"Welcome to my home Gabrielle, just how far along are you?" Sarah's eyes didn't give anything away, and her voice didn't waver. Thomas warned Gabrielle his Ma was suspicious of anyone she didn't know, so keeping her eyes firmly fixed on Sarah she replied, "I'm all of five months Misses Andrews, and you?" and then waited for Sarah's response.

A smile suddenly broke out on Sarah's face, and putting her arm around Gabrielle's shoulders she led her to the table. "I'm just about ready to drop, you must be tired after your long journey, are you hungry? come," she said not waiting for an answer. "Sit, Fergus, Garrett, make room for our guests!" With everyone sighing with relief, they hastily shuffled along and made room around the table for the newcomers.

Once again, after Sarah sat down with Thomas and Gabrielle seated beside her, the room became noisy. Spying Lizzy sitting between Will and Samuels, Thomas rushed around the table, and picking her up, made her go bashful. Holding her up high, Lizzy cried and giggled at the same time, then put her arms around his neck and hugged him.

There was more noise around the table than before when Sarah heard a second knock on the front door. No-one else heard the knock above the din, and while amazed at Sarah's uncanny ability to know someone was there, Foley went to investigate.

"Hello Foley," Billy Henderson said shivering on the porch. Equally pleased to see Billy, Foley greeted him the same as he did Thomas.

"Your folks are inside," he said laughing along with Billy.

"I thought they would be, I went home but the house was in darkness, I figured it was time for Sarah to have her dinner party." Foley couldn't believe how much Thomas and Billy had matured since leaving town. When he led Billy to the dining room, Martha and Dave almost fell off their chairs when Billy entered. Both cried when welcoming him, then laughed when they asked where his wife was and he told them he was too busy with the law firm he secured a job with to get married just yet. Even so, he informed everyone, there was a girl he was seeing.

"Where is Joe Ma?" Thomas asked innocently while looking around the table. When conversations died away and the trappers bowed their heads, Thomas looked confused from one to the other, then to Sarah.

"I wrote you Thomas, I guess you didn't get my letter," she replied sadly.

"Joe is no longer with us Thomas." It was Foley who gave him the sad news, but it was Fergus and Garrett informing him and the rest of Sarah's guests how Joe's death occurred that left Thomas stunned. By the time they finished speaking, his eyes brimmed with tears, and Sarah had her face buried against Foley's chest while she cried.

"I'm sorry Ma, I didn't mean to spoil your party," he managed while swallowing the lump in his throat. Sarah sat up suddenly and everyone saw her face wet from crying.

"No! oh no, Thomas! I'm happy to have you home... Foley!" she said holding her hand out to Foley. Used to Sarah bursting into tears at any given time, Foley handed her his handkerchief. Doc said it was due to her emotional state, with her being pregnant it was to be expected, so Foley took to carrying a handkerchief in his pocket for just such an event. Sarah dried her eyes and put her hand over Thomas's. "We'll talk later." Foley squeezed Sarah's other hand to reassure her everything would be alright. Then when Thomas announced he had a gift he wanted to give his Ma, the party mood resumed.

Rushing out to the porch, a few minutes later he was back standing at the end of the table with a large box sitting in front of him. When Gabrielle smiled lovingly at Thomas, Sarah was in no doubt she was very much in love with her son and thought given time, she may like her. Watching Gabrielle waver, Sarah got up and hurried around the table.

"Thomas, whatever that is, it can wait, Gabrielle needs rest, come, let me show you to your room, Thomas you come too, tomorrow is soon enough for us to see what is in that box and for us to get to know each other," Sarah said looking at Gabrielle and waiting for her to get up from her chair, but Gabrielle remained seated.

"I'm fine Misses Andrews, please, let Thomas give you his gift." With Gabrielle saying she was fine, Sarah sat down and let Thomas proceed in telling everyone what his surprise was.

"In here is something I have treasured all my life, and now Ma, I want you to have it." Reaching inside the box, for a moment Thomas left his hand there. "I'm sorry Joe isn't here to see this," he said saddened by the thought Joe was gone. "But Ma, I found someone as interested in my journals as much as I am."

The moment Thomas lifted a book out of the box, Gabrielle settled her eyes on Sarah. She knew the book Thomas was about to give her. Unable to put it down, she had read it with great gusto right to the very last page. Billy sat quietly alongside his parents knowing what Thomas was giving Sarah too. Sarah wondered what a book had to do with Thomas's journals.

"This book is everything I have ever written about the mountain," Thomas said smiling down the length of the table to where Sarah sat looking back at him expectantly. "Your mountain Ma, and you," he added going around the table and getting down on one knee beside Sarah's chair. While everyone watched, he handed the book to Sarah who took it and studied the cover.

A girl looking very much like a young Sarah sitting astride a horse with a white star in the middle of its forehead graced the cover, reminding Sarah of Star. A raggedy hat sits atop her head, and she wears an oversized coat made of wolf skins. Appearing to be racing from pursuing wolves, her long braid swings behind her. The rugged face of a man, his hair and beard grey, shaded under a hat trimmed with fur, Sarah recognized as Joe, fronts a snow-covered mountain in the background. As Sarah read the title her eyes brimmed with tears.

"You wrote a book… about me?" she asked, holding Thomas's hand.

"Not only one Ma, but three! I've been writing about you and the trappers all my life, they are all in here, you too Foley." As well as Fergus, Garrett and Will sitting opposite Sarah were overwhelmed that Thomas wrote about them. Thomas smiled at the look that crossed Foley's face when he looked surprised at getting a mention.

"This book," Thomas said going back to the box and extracting a second book. "Is all about Cedar Creek, and just about everyone in town gets a mention." Glancing around the table, he held the book up so everyone could see it, then passed it to Billy who showed it to Martha who looked at it and passed it on. While the second book went around the table, Thomas withdrew the third and kept speaking.

"This is the first" he said tapping the cover. "It tells of a promise, a promise made by four men," he swallowed when thinking of Joe. "Men who have never forgotten they made it."

When the first book got to Fergus, Fergus held it so Garrett and Will could see it. Reaching into his pocket for a handkerchief, Fergus blew his nose loudly. "Looks like we got some reading to do," he said with tears in his eyes.

"We'll be sure and let you know if what you wrote is true Thomas," Will said, appearing serious. But Will's comment made everyone laugh.

"Everyone is reading Thomas's books Misses Andrews," Gabrielle told Sarah softly.

"Everyone?" Sarah questioned.

"Yes, Thomas's writing is very popular in Philadelphia," Gabrielle said proudly of her husband's achievements. Going back to Sarah, Thomas squatted beside her and looked up at her.

"A lot of people know about you and your mountain Ma."

Sarah wasn't sure if she wanted people to know about the way she lived. Resting her hand against Thomas's cheek, a tear trickled down her face. "I missed you so much Thomas." Thomas hugged her. "I missed you too Ma," he whispered, and with everyone saying they couldn't wait to start reading Thomas's books, the atmosphere in the room returned to one of celebration.

It was late when the dinner party came to an end. When all her guests were gone, Sarah tucked Lizzy in bed and Thomas helped Gabrielle retire to what used to be his room. Foley kissed Sarah longingly and retired to his and Sarah's room leaving her with Thomas sitting on the couch in front of the open fire in the large living area.

"You want coffee Thomas?" Sarah asked.

"Is there enough in the pot for two?" he asked smiling, and because they both knew it was how she greeted Foley out on the prairie all those years ago where he used to propose to her, they both laughed.

While drinking their coffee, Sarah and Thomas talked and cried for Joe. When she told Thomas about Joe's secret, he was not at all surprised, saying Joe had always been there for her just like a father would be, and she was so much like him. Sarah talked about how

319

much she loved Foley, and how stupid she had been for not knowing all along how she felt about him. Even though she loved Christian, she said her and Foley's love was different. When Thomas talked about Gabrielle, Sarah could see he was very much in love with her. It was late when they retired to their respective rooms. After undressing as quietly as she could so as not to disturb Foley and slipping quietly into bed beside him, she found he wasn't asleep. Reaching for her, he brought her against him to lie in his arms.

The very next morning Thomas informed Sarah, he and Gabrielle would be staying in town for when Sarah gave birth to her baby. Those next weeks would give Sarah plenty of time to get acquainted with Gabrielle.

Sarah and Gabrielle were in Henry's store. As well as finding something unique for Thomas she couldn't find in Philadelphia, Gabrielle wanted to buy gifts for Sarah, Foley and Lizzy. Gerda loved having Lizzy spend time with her, so didn't mind when she was left with her while the two women went off together. Foley used the women's shopping as an excuse for him to go to Brady's farm to see how his brother was handling things on his own. Thomas spent his time at Jonathon O'Rourke's presenting him with a copy of each of his books for the school. Sarah and Gabrielle were busy looking at different items as potential gifts, and had already chosen Lizzy's when they heard a gunshot outside on the street.

As shots echoed through the air, Sarah rushed to the window to look out and saw several men with their guns drawn arguing loudly. Gabrielle was standing beside Sarah trying to see what was happening when a bullet smashed through the store window and whizzed between their heads. Sarah instinctively grabbed her, and taking cover, pulled her out of harm's way. Keeping himself low, Henry rushed the two women to safety behind the counter, but Sarah couldn't help herself. Standing up to see what was going on, she peered out the shattered window, and saw a man she recognized as Clint Sharp standing in the middle of the street with a gun in his hand.

Clint Sharp had a wife and family of six children. He worked long hours at the lumberyard to provide for his family, and had never been in any kind of trouble before now. When the shooting started and town folk outside dived for cover, Sarah couldn't see Sheriff Smith standing further along the street, and after almost being injured by flying glass from the shattered window, Sarah was furious. The bullet came dangerously close to her and Gabrielle.

Gabrielle's eyes widened as Sarah, almost full term with her pregnancy, reached into the folds of her dress, and pulling out her pistol, rushed out the door and stood on the boardwalk facing Clint Sharp.

Snow began falling and it was freezing outside. "You son-of-a-bitch Sharp!" Sarah called, holding her pistol up in readiness. "You could have killed me, or my son's wife! If you want a goddamn bullet in your stupid goddamn head for Christmas, I can oblige you!" she said in anger. Sharps eyes went wide when he turned to see Sarah holding her gun on him.

"I don't want no trouble from you Misses Andrews!" he called.

"Oh, but you've already got it, damn you! I'll give you one goddamn minute to get home to your family and stop being so goddamn stupid!" Sarah called back. Standing beside Henry with her mouth open, Gabrielle listened to Sarah confront Sharp. When Sheriff Smith, who had been holding his gun on Sharp saw Sarah come out of Henry's store to join the fracas, he stared open mouthed and wide eyed at the risk she was taking in regard to her and her baby's safety.

Having gotten into an argument with Sharp, Deputy Taylor and Sharp drew their guns on each other, which resulted in Taylor getting wounded when he tried to take Sharp to the jailhouse to cool off. Taylor was now standing in the street holding his arm trying to stop blood dripping off his fingers.

"Think about it Sharp!" Sheriff Smith called waiting for Sharp to decide what he was going to do. All three, Sheriff Smith, Clint Sharp and Sarah, waited with their guns in readiness for one of them to make the first move. Sharp kept his gun aimed squarely at Sheriff Smith.

Seeing a heavily pregnant Sarah and Sheriff Smith holding their guns on Sharp, men came out of hiding to gather along the boardwalk and outside the saloon. Clearly outnumbered, Sharp didn't stand a chance, so bets were quickly taken on whether Smith or Sarah would shoot him, then everyone waited in anticipation for something to happen.

When Sharp appeared to have given up and lowered his gun, Sheriff Smith lowered his and started to walk toward Sharp. Thinking it was all over, Sarah lowered her pistol, but Sharp was still angry about losing his job at the lumberyard. There was no money to keep him from losing his farm or provide his family with food for a meal, let alone buy his children gifts for Christmas. Feeling an overwhelming sense of failure overtaking him, he raised his gun and fired at Sheriff Smith. Anticipating his move Smith dived sideways, and fired back. At the same time as both men pulled their triggers and missed their targets, Sarah raised her pistol and got off a shot. Her bullet hit Sharp's gun-hand, causing him to drop his gun.

When Sarah's gun went off, Gabrielle jumped in shock and covered her face with her hands. Knowing it was typical of Sarah to get herself involved, Henry shook his head from side to side and tut-tutted. Sheriff Smith led Sharp off to the jailhouse to spend the night, and before Doc went to the jailhouse to fix Sharp's hand, Taylor went to Doc to get his arm patched up. The men who bet on Sarah shooting Sharp collected their winnings and disappeared into the saloon to buy a round of drinks. After shoving her pistol inside her dress, Sarah went back inside Henry's store to help Gabrielle finish her shopping. Then, after locking Sharp in one of the cells, Sheriff Smith hurried across to Henry's store to catch Sarah before she left.

"Thanks," he said. "But I could have handled Sharp, you took a hell of a risk doing what you did, you know he could have shot you." Shrugging off Smith's remark about getting shot, Sarah asked him what the trouble was about.

"Sharp lost his job at the lumberyard, I guess he's angry because he doesn't know how he's going to take care of his family." Smith ended with saying he would let Sharp go home once he cooled down and apologized for shooting Taylor. After tipping his hat to Sarah and Gabrielle and wishing them a merry Christmas, he went back to the Sheriff's Office.

Immediately after Smith left, Sarah got Henry to make up a stock of supplies for Sharp to give to his family and enlisted Gabrielle to select gifts for Sharp's children. Sarah insisted Henry was to see to the delivery, saying if Sharp happened to ask, Henry was to say the gift was from the whole town. Sarah would not see someone in her town go without, especially children. Gabrielle was amazed at Sarah's kindness, and stared at her in awe. When they carried their packages back to the lodge, Sarah asked Gabrielle not to say anything to Foley about what happened.

Gabrielle didn't mention it, she didn't have to, word soon travelled all over town that Sarah, almost ready to drop her baby, shot Clint Sharp and wounded him when he tried to shoot their sheriff. When word got back to Foley, he was furious at Sarah for risking her and their baby's lives. Thomas and Gabrielle stood in the kitchen listening to Foley berating Sarah and Sarah putting up a pretty good argument back at Foley as to why she stepped in to stop Sharp from getting himself killed right on Christmas. 'What would Sharp's family do without a father?' she was heard saying. Foley argued right back at her by saying, 'what would I do without you and my baby if you were to get yourself shot?' Foley and Sarah thought they couldn't be heard when they were alone in the living area. When it suddenly went quiet, Thomas and Gabrielle poked their heads through the doorway to see what was happening. Smiles broke out on their faces as they stared at Foley and Sarah standing in front of the open fire in each other's embrace, and kissing each other passionately.

Chapter Twenty-seven

When Henry delivered the supplies and gifts to Sharp's family, Sharp knew full well it had been Sarah who organized for them to have something for Christmas. While delivering her gift, Henry offered Sharp work at his store. Henry said he could no longer handle all the work he was getting now Cedar Creek was on the stagecoach line. An enormous amount of business was coming his way, and he desperately needed help, so Sharp would work in the storeroom packing and unpacking bulk supplies. He would also be responsible for delivering those supplies to customers around the county. Sharp eagerly accepted Henry's offer, and would start straight after Christmas. Sharp went to the lodge to thank Sarah for giving his family a second chance.

When Sarah opened the door, she noticed Sharp's hand wrapped in a bandage from where she shot his gun out of his hand. She noticed too how he looked more than a little nervous. After what happened while Sarah was at the store with Gabrielle, Foley stood on the porch with Sarah in case Sharp decided to do her harm.

Gripping his hat tight, Sharp swallowed before proceeding with what he wanted to say. "I'm right sorry about the shooting ma'am, and just so as you know, I don't accept charity easy, but I came here to thank you on account of my children, they will have a good Christmas because of you." Holding his bandaged hand up in a gesture of thanks, he turned to leave.

Trying to deny what she had done, Sarah grasped her hands in front of her as she stood defiantly next to Foley. "I didn't have anything to do with your children Sharp, but merry Christmas to you and your family all the same."

Until that moment Foley hadn't known Sarah organized for Sharp's family to receive supplies and gifts for his children, all he and Sarah argued over was her getting involved in the shootout.

Ignoring Sarah saying she had nothing to do with his families good fortune, Sharp stopped on the steps and looked back at her and Foley.

"I got work too on account of you, at Henry's Emporium," he said smiling at Sarah. "Merry Christmas to you and yours Misses Andrews." Putting his hat back on, and leaving Sarah and Foley watching after him, he proceeded down the steps.

"I didn't know you gave them charity," Foley said putting his arm around Sarah.

"It wasn't charity Foley, you know I don't give charity to anyone." Knowing from experience Sarah didn't tolerate trouble from adults but had a soft heart when it came to children, Foley turned to Sarah and hugging her, smiled over her head at Sharp walking off with his head held high.

Christmas day loomed early in the lodge. Lizzy was excited. Scrambling out of bed and racing downstairs to see what gifts had been left, she spied bulging stockings hanging from the mantel and parcels stacked around the bottom of the tree. Racing back upstairs, she pushed open the door to Sarah's room and ran to where Sarah and Foley were asleep in each other's arms.

"Mommy come on! come and look!" she cried excitedly as she climbed on the bed and tried sitting on Sarah. Having become used to Lizzy jumping into bed with them, Foley moved out of her way, but because most nights he and Sarah slept naked, he still didn't like her doing it.

"Careful Lizzy, mommy doesn't need you sitting on her belly," he said cursing silently, and reaching for her, put her between himself and Sarah. Lizzy squirmed her way inside the blankets and when Foley rolled his eyes at her, she giggled and hunkered down in the warmth Sarah and he had created.

After dressing, everyone went downstairs to open their gifts. While Sarah and Gabrielle sat on the couch in front of the fire keeping warm, Thomas helped Foley get breakfast. When Foley went out and brought back an armload of firewood, he let everyone know it was snowing heavily outside.

Having eaten a hearty breakfast of bacon and eggs that Foley cooked, and hotcakes drowned in treacle that Thomas made, everyone crowded around the fire and watched Lizzy open her gifts. Amongst candy and hair ribbons was chalk for her slate. There were boots and underwear, trousers and shirts, but Lizzy didn't want any of those, she wanted a dolly. Dropping her bottom lip in a pout, she climbed on the couch next to Sarah.

"What is it honey? Don't you like your gifts?" Sarah asked.

"I wanted a dolly mommy," Lizzy answered putting her head on Sarah's shoulder. She prayed for three nights for a doll just like the beautiful one in Henry's store, and now she thought she didn't pray hard enough. "Never mind Lizzy," Foley soothed. "Maybe next year you will get a dolly." But Lizzy felt miserable as she sat watching the adults exchange their gifts.

Gabrielle received a silk shawl from Sarah, similar to the one Joe gave her for her first Christmas she spent with the trappers in the Ferguson House after her Pa was killed. That shawl brought her happiness at the time and she cherished it, and still had it safely tucked away in her dresser upstairs in her room. Gabrielle said the shawl was beautiful and thanked Sarah and Foley for her gift. The leather-bound journal Sarah and Foley chose for Thomas was perfect. Thomas said he couldn't wait to write more stories about the mountain and Cedar Creek in it. He received an exquisitely beaded money pouch crafted by native Indians from Gabrielle, which she said was something none of their friends had back in the city.

When Foley received a pipe carved from ivory from Sarah, he turned it over in his hand to study it. He wasn't angry about the gift, he just didn't think it appropriate now he didn't smoke.

"Why did you give me this?" he asked Sarah curiously. "You know I gave up smoking when you said you could smell me all the way across the river! which I thought at the time you were right, so I gave it up, you remember? You were snaring rabbits and shared your coffee with me, I lit a smoke and you said I stunk." He smiled at the memory, and putting his arm around Sarah's shoulder, pulled her to him and kissed her. "I have never tasted better either, have I?" he winked. Watching him kiss Sarah again, Thomas and Gabrielle laughed.

"I remember Foley, I don't mind the smell of pipe tobacco, it's better than those cheroots all you men like smoking." Getting up and going to a dresser, Sarah opened a drawer and coming back, handed Foley a pouch of tobacco. When Foley filled the pipe and lit it, then put it to his mouth, he thought maybe it wouldn't be so bad if he took up smoking again, after all, it was a beautiful pipe.

When Foley handed Sarah the smallest gift of the day, for a moment she looked puzzled at its size, then, before unwrapping it she kissed him and thanked him for it. Her gift consisted of a small black box which, when she lifted the lid, revealed a silver diamond and ruby encrusted brooch in the shape of a fan shimmering on its bed of black velvet. When she looked back at Foley, her eyes glowed. "This is beautiful," she said turning the box around so Gabrielle and Thomas could see. Gabrielle jokingly asked Thomas why he hadn't bought her something as beautiful as Sarah's brooch, however, she added quickly, she loved the silver engraved mirror, hairbrush and comb set he gave her. After Foley pinned the brooch to Sarah's dress, to show she was pleased with her gift, she kissed him again.

It appeared all the gifts had been opened and Lizzy had given up on getting her doll, but there was still one box under the tree. Pulling out the long box bound with a pink ribbon, and already knowing what it contained, Thomas smiled up at Sarah and Gabrielle.

"Gee, I think this might be for Lizzy," he said with a wink. Getting off the couch, Lizzy sat on her knees in front of the box, and her eyes again filled with tears. When Thomas helped her pull the ribbon free and lifted the lid to show the curly haired doll with the white sequined princess dress and the red ruby lips smiling up at her, a smile spread across her face.

"Is she really mine?" she asked Thomas softly as she brushed her tears away.

"She is yours Lizzy," Thomas smiled. Figuring she had been a good girl after all and her prayers had been answered, Lizzy lifted the doll carefully out of the box and held her tenderly in her arms.

At dinner that night her doll sat beside her on her chair while she ate, and when she fell asleep, her doll went to bed with her.

Christmas day ended well, Sarah was happy, Thomas had come home and brought his wife with him. Fergus, Garrett and Will, celebrated the day with Sarah and her family. After the guests left and Lizzy had been put to bed, Thomas made sure Gabrielle was comfortable in their room before coming back downstairs to sit with Sarah at the fire. Knowing Sarah and Thomas had more to talk about, Foley once again retired alone.

While sitting on the couch together, Thomas brought up the time he put dead rats in Jamie Finch and Daniel Connells beds after they broke Billy's arm and Sarah got the blame for it. He mentioned how she went picking berries and he and Christian found her injured in the cavern at The Falls and the fact he gave Christian permission to cuddle her that night. Christian had cuddled her, he said smiling, because they had taken their clothes off to do it. Sarah blushed when she remembered, and then laughed at the memory. Thomas went on telling her he met Gabrielle in the same class he was attending at college, and that when he smiled at her across the room and she smiled back, he knew instantly she was the one for him. He explained the reason he brought up the dead rats was because, as a young boy, he hadn't fully understood the meaning of love, but having met Gabrielle, he remembered the way Christian and Sarah had been together that night at the cavern, and after taking Gabrielle to bed for the first time, he came to realize, the love two people experienced together was something special.

"I love Foley," Sarah said unexpectedly and looking down at her hands.

"I know you do Ma, I see it when you look at him," Thomas answered, putting his hand over Sarah's and holding it there.

"It's different to how I loved your father, and it's different to how I loved Christian." Sarah looked toward the staircase. "He is a serious man, more so than Frank and Christian ever were, he wasn't happy to learn about me having his baby." Then looking sadly at Thomas, she explained what happened between Foley, Maria and herself, and their argument on the mountain when he found out she was expecting. She told him about the wolf getting into the cabin, and how it frightened them, and that being when Foley accepted her being pregnant, but he didn't say he was happy about it. "I think he may not be happy still." Sarah added, her eyes dimming as she rested her hand on her belly.

"He's scared Ma, scared he will lose you like Maria, I'm scared too, scared for you, scared for Gabby, but we have to let these things take place and hope everything goes well." Thomas's answer reassured Sarah as to how Foley must be feeling.

"And Ma! What great stories to put in my next book!" After both laughing about that, they let his comment bring their night to an end. Thomas had matured since leaving Cedar Creek and Sarah could see how much of a man he had become. A man who would himself, soon take on the responsibility of a father.

When Sarah got to her feet, Thomas stood too. "It's late Thomas, I better go up and you better get some sleep, it's been a big day." Walking upstairs together, they kissed each other outside Sarah's door and said goodnight.

Sarah undressed, and when Foley felt her slip under the covers beside him, he turned to face her. Putting his arm around her, he rubbed his other warm hand over her belly. "I love you Sarah," he whispered leaning over and kissing her softly before lying back down. "I love you too Foley," Sarah whispered as she snuggled against him and closed her eyes.

Chapter Twenty-eight

Thinking how wrong she must have been with her baby's birth date, two weeks after Christmas Sarah was still waiting for its arrival. With Sarah being overdue, Foley worried the baby wasn't his after all, and so fearing she could have lied about Logan when he attacked her, he rode to the farm to talk to Brady. Brady tried reassuring him Sarah was having his child by saying Sarah would never lie to him, besides he said, wasn't Sarah pregnant before Logan's attack? Foley remembered being told that, but still felt uneasy that if Sarah went any longer, he wouldn't be able to cope. Brady laughed and put his arm around his shoulders.

"That's all part of having children Foley, what do you think I went through when Ellen gave birth to two babies? Hell, my heart nearly stopped beating let me tell you! everything will be fine, besides, Sarah's already had two children, what could possibly go wrong?" Foley reluctantly agreed with what Brady was saying. Surely Sarah having his baby wouldn't be anything like when Maria had her baby.

Sarah knew Foley was worried about their baby's overdue birth. She couldn't have been wrong about it. Their baby had been conceived on the washroom floor in her cabin, she was sure of it, which meant she should have delivered it by now.

Everyone was off doing something, even Lizzy. During the winter months, Lizzy spent two days a week with Tilly O'Rourke learning to read, and today was one of those days. Thomas and Gabrielle were spending the day at Billy Henderson's. Foley was out at the farm helping Brady sow a field of bean seeds, which meant Sarah was alone at the lodge. But just because she was expecting, didn't mean she had to stay at home on her own while everyone else was off having fun, so while waiting for everyone to return, instead of doing mundane housework, she decided she would take the buckboard to the farm to visit Ellen and the twins, and that would enable Foley to come back to town with her.

The first thing she had to do, was get one of her horses from the livery and hitch it to her buckboard. When she got there, Ham was working at his forge, Patrice was inside their residence with Lilly. Now they were seeing each other regularly while Will was in town, Sissy was off somewhere with him. Preferring to head straight to Brady's farm, Sarah didn't stop to talk.

"Howdy Sarah," Ham said smiling as she came waddling through the door. "You here to visit the women?"

"Howdy Ham," Sarah answered matter-of-factly. "Not today, just getting my horse, heading to the farm to meet up with Foley," she answered going to where her horse was stalled.

"I gave him a run yesterday, he shouldn't be too frisky for you to handle," Ham said helping her put the bridle on.

"Thanks for that... see you later," Sarah called leading the horse outside.

"Yeah, see you later," Ham called before she disappeared down the alley.

Sitting idle in the shelter at the lodge was the buckboard that had been used to take Foley and Brady to Sarah and Foley's wedding. On returning to town this winter, Foley insisted Sarah not use it in her late stages of pregnancy, but she was a good horsewoman and felt she could handle a buckboard no matter what her condition.

After hitching her horse to the buckboard, Sarah climbed up and made herself comfortable on the seat, then tapping the reins across the horses back, got the horse to start off easily, and trotting along at a steady pace, made their way past the Trading Post and out along the road heading for Foley and Brady's farm.

It had stopped snowing and with snow now mixed with mud, the road turned to slush making the road slippery. As she took the road steadily, Sarah looked at the sky and could see dark clouds forming across the river. Maybe, she thought as she went along, she would get caught in a shower of rain before she got to the farm, so tapping the reins on the horses back a little harder, made her horse pick up its pace. As the wagon trundled along at speed, it bounced over rough ground. To Sarah, the road seemed much worse than she remembered.

She was travelling along quite quickly when one of the buckboard's wheels hit something in the road, making the wagon pitch to one side, and forcing Sarah to hold the reins tight in one hand and the back of the seat with the other. When the wheel came loose, then came adrift altogether, it rolled into a ditch along the side of the road, causing the buckboard to suddenly tip and the back to drag along the ground through the mud, and scaring her horse so much it shied. Bolting in fright, the horse dragged the lopsided wagon towards the steep edge of the roadway. As the wagon slewed dangerously back across the road, it was all Sarah could do to hang on.

Having no control over where the wagon was headed, the wagon careened over the edge and sent Sarah falling across the seat. Finding herself being flung through the air, she screamed before landing heavily in a ditch where she became embedded in thick mud. Stumbling into the muddy hole and while trying to gain its footing, but unable to gain traction because of the slippery slope, the horses head slammed into the bank at the side of the ditch where it ended up lying with its neck broken. For one quick instant, Sarah was thinking how lucky she was because she hadn't been hurt when the buckboard, still on its downward spiral, toppled over and landed across her legs pinning her down. As the wagon settled in the mud, Sarah screamed in pain.

As the day wore on, the sky grew dark. Lightning streaked the sky, thunder when it rumbled shook the ground, bringing with it freezing rain mixed with sleet. When the clouds unleashed their wrath, Sarah lay in the ditch wondering how to get herself out.

Lying with her legs pinned under the wagon, she figured the wagon must be the one Foley and Brady had their accident in on their way to the lodge for her and Foley's wedding. Having swapped her wagon for theirs so Brady and Ellen could get home safely, it had been left in her shelter since last winter and its back wheel had never been fixed. When the ditch began to fill with water, Sarah began to panic. Trying desperately to get a grip on the wagon to lift it off her legs, she managed to free one leg by pushing her foot back and forth in the mud and making a small channel for her leg to slip out of. At least now she could turn on her side, but with her other foot held fast on hard ground, she was still in danger.

Foley was on his way back to town when the storm broke. As more rain fell heavily, he thought of Sarah at home waiting for him, and not wanting to be caught out in the storm, put his head down and spurred his horse to go faster.

At the schoolhouse, children had been collected by their parents, all except Lizzy. Remembering being told she wasn't allowed to leave with anyone but her Ma, Lizzy sat in the classroom with Tilly and Jonathon and waited for her to come and get her. Thomas and Gabrielle decided to wait at Billy's until the storm blew itself out.

It was dark when Foley arrived back at the lodge. Securing his horse to the hitching rail, he rushed up the steps and went inside to be greeted by an empty house. The house was cold, the fires were out, making him wonder where everyone could be. Heading back into the rain, and thinking where Sarah might be waiting for the storm to abate, he ran up the street to Doc's practice where Doc informed him, he hadn't seen Sarah all day. After standing outside with his hands on his hips trying to think where else she might have gone, he raced back around the corner and into the street, and coming to the lodge, straight away noticed the buckboard was missing. Standing in the shelter already soaking wet, he looked at the empty space and thought maybe Thomas and Gabrielle took Sarah somewhere, and to do that they would have to get a horse, so running to the livery, he raced inside to see Ham packing up his forge for the day.

"Hey Foley, where you off to in this god-awful weather?" Ham asked removing his apron. When he saw the worried look on Foley's face he frowned. Ignoring Ham's question, Foley asked. "Did Thomas come here to get a horse?"

"No, but Sarah did, said she was going out to your farm... to meet up with you," Ham said and frowning wondered why he was here and not at the farm. Feeling the hairs on the back of his neck stand up, and cursing, Foley didn't hang about for Ham to say more.

"*Foley!*" Someone called above the storm. Hearing his name being called, Foley stopped running when he saw Jonathon waving to him from the steps of the schoolhouse.

"Sarah hasn't come for Lizzy, she's still inside," Jonathon said trying to be heard above the storm as Foley came toward him and stood in the rain.

"Goddamn it, Sarah isn't home! she must have headed to the farm!" Foley said wiping his hand over his wet face. 'So why hadn't he passed her along the road?' he thought. Becoming concerned for her safety, with the promise he made to Joe suddenly springing to mind, Foley cursed sharply. "Fuck!" It seemed he was failing to keep that promise. 'If she didn't go to the farm, where could she be?' he asked himself while cursing again. Before he could look for Sarah though, he had to get Lizzy sorted.

Seeing Foley hurrying toward her, Lizzy straightened up. He was her new Pa, and she was pleased to see him, but her Ma told her she was never to leave school with anyone but her.

"Lizzy come on honey, come and stay with Gerda while I find mommy," Foley urged. But Lizzy wasn't about to go. When Foley went to pick her up, she bellowed and fought him. Foley didn't have time for Lizzy's tantrum. Grabbing hold of her, he lifted her screaming into his arms and raced outside and into the storm.

Foley was asking Gerda to take care of Lizzy so he could look for Sarah when it suddenly dawned on him the buckboard Sarah had taken, was the one he remembered losing a wheel off on the way to the lodge the day he married her. After the wedding, none of their guests gave a thought to Brady's damaged wagon, and because he was too taken with playing happy husband to Sarah, neither had he. Nor had Brady, who became busy ploughing fields and planting crops to worry about wagons. Knowing Sarah had unwittingly taken the damaged buckboard, Foley was now in a panic. If the buckboard threw him and Brady into a ditch, then Sarah must be lying somewhere along the road to the farm, hurt, or worse still, dead. A shiver ran up Foley's spine as his heart sank to the bottom of his stomach.

335

Leaving Lizzy with Gerda, he sprinted to the Ferguson House and was glad to find most of the trappers were there. After telling them what he thought must have happened to Sarah, the men filed out quickly and mounted their horses, and with lit torches, headed along the road in search of her. One of the men having the presence of mind, rushed to the saloon to tell the men there Sarah was missing. Without hesitation, the men left their drinks where they were and racing outside, commandeered a buckboard to take them out searching. While riders searched further along the road, others walked both sides close to town. Burning torches were held aloft to assist with scouring ditches. Ice mixed with rain continued falling heavily as they searched, drenching everyone through to their bones.

When the rain stopped suddenly and the storm passed, clouds dissipated and stars came out. Stormwater washing along gullies created a river like effect, sending muddy water cascading along the sides of the road and running from ditch to ditch in a torrent. The ditch where Sarah lay for what seemed to her like hours, quickly began to fill. While trying not to think too much about her predicament, her first contraction started. Now she had the added worry she was going to have her baby there in the ditch, and if she didn't get rescued soon, her baby, if it survived the birth, would drown in a mud filled waterhole beside the road. Thinking she heard someone calling her, she called back for help, but no-one came.

Valuable time passed, Sarah's leg where it was caught became numb and she could no longer feel her stomach. Fearing her baby may already be dead, she thought of Foley not wanting her to have a baby in the first place, and now having accepted she was, she would give him a dead baby like Maria had. Foley would once again be devastated, and all because she made a stupid decision not to do as he asked and stay at the lodge.

Shivering, and trying again to pull her foot free from under the buckboard, she screamed in anger when she couldn't. After surviving being shot and attacked by a wolf, and almost drowning in the river on the mountain, then surviving falling off the cliff with Millicent Crawley and landing in the raging river above the waterfall, her and her baby were going to die in a mud filled ditch. But Sarah wasn't going to have any of it. If she could survive almost drowning twice, then she could survive this. Surely someone would miss her and come looking. Groaning with pain, she pushed her hands into the mud and forced her head and shoulders out of the water.

Meanwhile men were spreading out along the road. Some riding ahead searched closer to Brady's farm, while others walked toward town holding their torches high to enable them to see clearly in the dark. Along with Fergus and Garrett and Will, Foley began his search where he thought he and Brady lost the wheel off the buckboard. As he walked, a feeling of dread overwhelmed him when he thought he was going to lose Sarah and his baby after all. The men spread out, calling for Sarah as their torches eerily lit up the stretch of road for a long way. As the night wore on, the search continued.

Keeping her hands buried deep in the mud trying to hold herself up from the rising water, Sarah shivered, her body was numb, she could no longer feel a thing.

Clint Sharp had been drinking in the saloon when the call came out that Sarah was missing. Feeling he owed her a debt of gratitude for giving his family a good Christmas and for getting him work at Henry's Emporium, he didn't hesitate to join the search. He was enjoying the work, more so than when he worked at the lumberyard. Sharp was walking in the direction of Brady's farm when he noticed broken and flattened bushes and something in the water filled ditch where he was searching. Straining to see in the dark, he wiped water out of his eyes to get a better look, and stepping cautiously down from the road, held his torch away from him and saw what appeared to be an upturned wagon. Recognizing what he was looking at, he yelled as loud as he could. *"Here!... she's here!... I've found her!"*

Scrambling into the ditch, he could see a dead horse lying where it fell and the wagon lying upside down in a hole almost full of muddy water. Hearing his call, men came running from all directions. *"She's down here!"* Sharp called again, then wading through the slush and coming around the buckboard, he found Sarah with her head just above the still rising water. Throwing his torch away, he slid in beside her, but not knowing she was pinned down, tried lifting her only to have her scream in agony at being moved. "It's alright Misses Andrews, it's me, Sharp, I've got you!" All Sharp could do now was hold her up until help arrived.

Upon seeing she had been found, Sarah gave up her fight to stay awake. When word she had been found passed quickly down the line, Foley and the three trappers raced along the road passing men huddled in a group on the roadside. As men jumped into the ditch and spread out along one side of the wagon, Foley threw away his torch, leapt into the ditch and scrambled to Sarah. Becoming free when the wagon was lifted, Foley and Sharp carried her up to the buckboard where Foley climbed in and held her in his arms. Sarah didn't look good. Her body was cold and limp, her skin grey, she looked like death had already taken her.

They were half way between the lodge and Brady's farm, and wanting Doc to attend her straight away, a decision had to be made where best to take her.

"*Get her to the lodge... now!*" Foley called at the top of his lungs. Leaving the rest of the men to make their own way back to town, after the three trappers clambered in alongside Foley, the buckboard was quickly turned, and raced away.

Careening around the corner at the Ferguson House, the buckboard came to an abrupt stop in front of the lodge, then leaving Garrett and Fergus to help Foley get Sarah out of the wagon, Will jumped out and raced to get Doc. Not needing help carrying Sarah, Foley hurriedly climbed the steps, and carrying her inside, headed toward the staircase.

When they returned from spending their day with Billy and his folks, Thomas and Gabrielle were in high spirits. Finding no-one home, Thomas assumed Sarah had gone to the farm with Foley, so he and Gabrielle busied themselves with getting dinner ready for when they returned. Fires Thomas lit soon had warmth emanating throughout the lodge.

When Foley came barging through the door carrying Sarah, the sight left Thomas shaken. In a state of panic at seeing the condition his Ma was in, Thomas left Gabrielle downstairs and followed Foley upstairs. Gabrielle too was shocked by what she saw. Sarah did not look good, and Gabrielle felt she should stay out of everyone's way while they attended her. When Doc and Gerda came hurrying in with Lizzy, Gabrielle told them to go straight upstairs while she took Lizzy and kept her with her. Doc and Gerda raced to Sarah's side. When they came inside out of the weather, Garrett, Fergus and Will removed their hats and coats and took off their muddy boots. They would not dirty up Sarah's clean house with their wet mud-caked gear. Sarah was meticulously clean, even on the mountain. All they could do now was wait with Gabrielle and Lizzy while everyone else was upstairs with Sarah. To ease the situation while they waited, Gabrielle made them a large pot of coffee.

Foley was helping Gerda get Sarah out of her wet clothes when Sarah woke for a brief moment. "I'm so cold," she managed, her voice almost inaudible. Using warm towels, Foley and Gerda rubbed her briskly to warm her, then Foley lifted her into bed. Keeping his back to them while they worked on his Ma, Thomas stoked the fire in the fireplace, and soon had it blazing.

While Thomas stayed busy at the fire, Doc checked Sarah. Even though her skin felt cold, she had a sound heart. When a contraction overtook her, her face contorted in pain, forcing her to pull her legs up suddenly. Needing to check how close to giving birth she was, Doc pushed Foley out of his way. "Foley, the baby," Sarah called feebly, causing Foley to experience a sudden bout of having been in this situation before. Maria told him before she died, she wasn't having his baby. 'Was this what Sarah was telling him?' he asked himself.

"Foley!" she called more urgently. Their baby was about to enter the world. Still in wet clothes, Foley knelt beside the bed and took Sarah's hand in his. But when Gerda came scurrying in with a bucket full of hot rocks to warm Sarah, Foley again was pushed aside to allow her to place the rocks under the blankets.

Sarah didn't feel cold anymore, in fact she felt euphoric when feeling grateful for the thick mud that saved her. The only part of her that was injured when the wagon fell on her was her right foot. Now she just wanted to concentrate on having her and Foley's baby. When Sarah looked up into Foley's worried face, her contractions were much closer.

"Our baby Foley, our baby is coming, help me have our baby." Hearing Sarah say 'our baby' and understanding what she was asking, Foley's eyes welled, and swallowing the lump in his throat while brushing her hair off her face, he kissed her lightly, then standing up, began removing his sodden clothes.

They had just made love in Sarah's cabin, and afterwards Sarah had lain between his outstretched legs. As she leant back against him, she commented on how comfortable she felt, and how this would be a nice way to have their baby. Holding her lovingly between his arms at the time, and feeling her warm body pressed against his, he agreed.

"What on earth are you doing Foley?" Doc asked in amazement as he watched Foley take off his gun-belt and begin to strip. "You heard what Sarah said, she needs my help to have our baby."

Doc thought helping Sarah have her baby didn't mean for Foley to take his clothes off, so quickly pulling out a drawer in their dressing-table, he extracted a clean pair of trousers.

"Here, put these on," he said throwing them at Foley then ushering Thomas and Gerda out of the room.

"There isn't time Doc," Foley said hearing Sarah moan in agony. Leaving everything on the floor, he climbed in behind Sarah and lifting her into his arms, stretched his bare legs either side of her. Sarah was in pain but she quickly warmed to his feeling of intimacy.

"It's alright Sarah, we are having our baby right now… together," Foley whispered in her ear. Spreading her fingers out on top of his bare legs, Sarah prepared herself for birthing.

Having gone downstairs, Thomas let everyone know there what was happening upstairs. With Foley decently covered by blankets, Doc called for Gerda to come back in. When Gerda saw Foley sitting behind Sarah, she wasn't the least bit surprised, in fact she thought it rather romantic that Foley should want to take part in their baby's birth that way.

As Sarah's pains were no longer apart, Gerda quickly removed the rocks from under the covers and covered Sarah and Foley with extra blankets. Sarah had lain in a ditch feeling so cold she was unaware of her contractions, but now she had become warm, she was feeling every ache and pain coursing through her, and she let everyone in the house know it.

Lizzy wasn't going to wait, she wanted to see her mommy, so before anyone could stop her, she raced up the stairs and rushed into the room. Not wanting to miss out, Thomas grabbed Gabrielle by her hand and raced with her upstairs behind Lizzy. Standing in front of the fireplace keeping warm, the three trappers looked at each other in silence. They didn't want to wait downstairs on their own either, they wanted to see what was happening upstairs.

"Fuck this!" Garrett cursed suddenly, and all three scrambled up the stairs two at a time to get to Sarah's room.

Thomas stood alongside Lizzy squeezing Gabrielle's hand as they waited just inside the door watching for the baby to appear. Gabrielle's heart was racing, this was what she had to look forward to, and she wondered when she gave birth to their baby if Thomas would be with her like Foley was with Sarah. Crowded in behind them, the three trappers watched on in amazement at seeing Foley sitting behind Sarah. "I love you so much." They heard him say. Feeling intense pain coming on, Sarah gripped his legs tight.

"Come on sweetheart, we can do this," Foley whispered. As Sarah pushed on his command, her face turned pink, and pushing with every bit of strength she could muster, let go of his legs and grabbed his hands. With their cheeks pressed together, Foley gripped her hands in his and felt her body go limp. "I love you Sarah, please, darling, don't leave me," he whimpered.

Recalling Maria going limp before she could deliver her baby, Foley studied Doc for reassurance that Sarah would be alright, but Doc was too busy to notice. When the baby slipped into his hands, he leapt into action. Cutting the cord, he slapped the baby gently, but got no response. He slapped it again, this time a little harder. Feeling Sarah come awake, Foley's heart lurched and he let out a breath, but he felt no relief because his baby hadn't yet taken a breath.

Excited to know what sex his Ma and Foley's baby was, Thomas gripped Gabrielle's hand more firmly. He was there when Lizzy was born but this moment was different. This time Foley helped his Ma deliver their baby. Thomas could almost feel their love as they waited to hear their baby's cry. Hearing Lizzy weeping softly for her Ma, Thomas let Gabrielle's hand go, and squatting, wrapped his arms around Lizzy to reassure her everything would be alright.

When a loud bellow suddenly broke the silence that had descended over the room, everyone including Foley yelled in surprise. The three trappers, while cheering loudly, slapped each other on the back and hugged each other. Sarah cried with relief. Having descended into hell while lying under the upturned wagon, she had all but given up hope of being found, but she and her baby had pulled through. With a huge smile on his face, Doc held the baby up so everyone could see, Foley had a son.

Holding Sarah lovingly, Foley cried with joy. "He's beautiful Sarah," he said, kissing her cheek. Lizzy saw the tiny baby lifted from between her Ma's legs and wondered where it came from. Before Gerda could whisk the tiny boy away to bathe him, he was placed on Sarah's chest so they could spend a moment with him. Sarah called to her children. "Come on Lizzy, Thomas, come and meet your brother."

While Foley got dressed, Gerda ushered everyone out of the room and stood with them in the hall. As soon as Doc finished with Sarah, he made way for Gerda to come back in. Once Sarah was sorted, Foley covered her with warm blankets, then kissing her passionately again, told her how much he loved her and how scared he was when he thought he lost her.

"I love you Foley Andrews, so don't you go thinking I will leave you that easy," Sarah returned, and then kissed him with her own passionate kiss.

After congratulating Sarah and Foley on their baby's birth, the trappers raced back to the Ferguson House and told the men waiting there Sarah had survived her ordeal and delivered a healthy boy. On hearing good news, the men gleefully broke out bottles of whiskey and drank to Sarah and Foley, and their baby's health.

Clint Sharp made his way back to his family. He was soaked through and cold but managed to tell his wife and children what happened with Sarah and that it was him that found her. He told them about Sarah giving birth to a boy baby, and what with Doc and Gerda looking after them, both Sarah and her new son were in good hands. He slept peacefully knowing he had repaid his debt to Sarah for the kindness she showed his family.

Later that night when the house was quiet and everyone was asleep, even though worn from her ordeal, Sarah and Foley held each other lovingly and talked at length about the accident and how close she came to losing her life. Foley voiced his anger at everyone including himself for forgetting about the buckboard. Sarah didn't blame anyone for her accident because, as she told Foley, she had forgotten it too. Foley made her promise she would stay away from water when she had their next baby. Smiling, Sarah said she hoped they had another, and she promised she would do as he asked.

"What shall we name him?" Sarah asked as they lay in each other's arms.

"I don't know, I haven't been thinking clearly about our baby Sarah." Foley felt ashamed that he had been too afraid before the birth to be happy. Thinking family names were the way to go Sarah asked, "what was your Pa's name?"

"My Pa's name? It was David, everyone knew him as Dave... Dave Andrews." Foley studied his son for a moment. "So, tell me, why do you want to know that?" he asked sheepishly.

"I think David is a lovely name," she answered watching him with his arm resting over her. Foley was happy Sarah had survived her ordeal and at becoming a father. Sarah too was happy. Closing her eyes, she fell asleep, comforted in a loving embrace.

When Major Hardy heard about Sarah's accident, he presented her with a new buckboard. Even though they were getting along fine, Sarah still didn't trust him completely, so before accepting the Majors gift, she made Foley make sure the wheels were secure. After giving the wagon a thorough going over, Foley assured her the wheels, and the rest of the wagon were in perfect working order, and said she could take Lizzy, and David, to visit Brady and Ellen or anyone else she was so inclined to visit any time she liked, she would be fine.

Chapter Twenty-nine

*I*t took two weeks after David's birth for Sarah to get on her feet, but in the mean time she wasn't going to spend her days cooped up in her bedroom. Each day at her insistence, Foley carried her downstairs to sit on the couch in front of the open fire where she sat quietly nursing David while he got their meals. Once upon a time Foley may have been a hired gun, but as it turned out, he wasn't such a bad cook. Occasionally he carried Sarah to the back porch where he sat with her in dappled shade, drinking coffee he made, then while his son slept and Lizzy played with her princess doll at their feet, they talked about people from town and about the farm, and each night he carried Sarah and his son upstairs where he and Sarah slept contented in each other's arms.

Proud that he had a son, Foley beamed when he talked about his family with the men from Major Hardy's ranch at the saloon. Sarah though wasn't keen on him going there. She worried a saloon girl would turn his head, especially while she was unable to fulfill her role as a lover to him. But Sarah needn't have worried, Foley didn't need anyone else satisfying him. It took a long time for him to get Sarah to love him, and he was happy to give her time to get over the birth of their son before making love to her again.

This winter, after Joe died, while sitting in one of the old armchairs in front of the fire in the Ferguson House, Fergus gave trapping a lot of thought. Major Hardy's men ran in a lot more horses this time around and having to rise early, the other trappers had retired to their rooms. Fergus felt he was too old to be thrown about on the backs of wild horses, but he loved the mountain. After travelling all the way from Ireland to take part in Indian wars, he trapped there a lot of years. There were conflicts in Ireland too, but as a young man, he wanted to explore the Americas, and to get there he boarded a ship, and after spending many grueling months at sea, it was only a few hours after arriving, that he became friends with Calahan and Joe.

They were in New York recruiting men to join the cavalry when he met them, in of all places, an Irish Inn not far from where he came ashore. When they plied this, redhaired bearded man they had never seen the likes of before with drinks to welcome him to their country, he liked the two men straight away, but saints be praised if he didn't know what they were playing at. After filling him with liquor, the next thing he knew, he was wearing the blue uniform of a cavalry man and had signed up for several years. The three of them had a lot of fun serving together, but suffered countless heartache when men they came to know were killed in battle.

When Calahan and Joe left the cavalry to take up trapping, he joined them on their trek to the Rockies, where they formed a deeper friendship that has withstood the test of time. He misses Calahan and Joe's company immensely, but still holds dear his friendship with Brent Garrett and Will Sloan.

Having come across Garrett and Will by accident while hunting along the river, he was proud to learn they served in the same cavalry unit he once served in. The two both very young, and very scared men, didn't know the first thing about trapping, so taking them on as partners, he taught them all he knew, and over the years the two lads became sons to him, Now grown men, Garrett and Will are as good at trapping as he. Fergus's thoughts however, lay with Sarah.

Like the other three men, he made a promise not to make her his own, and had never once considered her for a wife, however, he found it hard not to consider her a daughter, because as a child, Sarah was sweet and kind when with the men, and they all saw how beautiful a woman she would become, but as she grew, she showed them all she was no gentle girl when it came to hunting and trapping wolf.

Closing his eyes, Fergus remembered having long talks with Sarah as a girl and as a young woman, sitting beside each other on logs or boulders up on the mountain. She would ask him something about his country, and he would talk about his homeland with passion.

Smiling to himself, he thought of Sarah asking him about his home just so she could hear him speak his Irish brogue. His mind quickly turned to a time when Sarah was a young woman of fifteen years.

The night his friend Calahan Cole risked everything he owned on a game of poker and lost Mountain View Lodge and all his money, he witnessed Calahan throwing a punch at Benjamin Crawley and missing, causing him to fall and hit his head, which shocked not only him but the other men when they saw Calahan was dead. None of them thought Crawley killed Calahan or cheated at cards because Joe checked the deck and found nothing to prove Crawley cheated, so they let it go until many years later when Jonathon O'Rourke instilled the idea into their heads that Crawley was a cheat and a murderer. Sarah knew that mangy coyote killed Calahan and was stealing bits and pieces of her belongings from the lodge while she and Thomas camped in the cold on the riverbank below town. Whenever she went to Crawley's store for supplies, she and Crawley could never see eye to eye and Fergus figured that was the reason. Fergus felt glad Crawley was dead. When the lodge was returned to Sarah, that was a good day.

When Fergus's thoughts jumped to Thomas as a baby being taken from Sarah and given to his grandfather, he remembered it being a bitter blow for Sarah and a gut-wrenching time for them, because it was then Sarah's attitude to everyone changed. In a constant rage, she fired her rifle at anything about town and threatened anyone that stood in her way of getting Thomas back, resulting in her being locked in a cell a number of times. Fergus sniggered though when he remembered what she did in the church. He had never seen Sarah reduced to savagery before, but he figured that was when she grew up. Thomas belonged with his mother, not with Major Hardy, and he hadn't wanted her suffering any more than she had already, but Joe reminded him and the other men they promised not to interfere. Then when Joe finally agreed they had to help Sarah get him back, it was Foley who showed them where to find the longhorn bull that resulted in Thomas's return. How could Foley not help them? He was in love with Sarah even then.

Sitting in his chair in front of the fire, Fergus nodded in agreement to his own statement, then letting his thoughts return to what they did in Major Hardy's nice new barn, he laughed out loud, and startling himself, looked around in case someone heard, but no-one did.

It was a grand day the day Sarah got Thomas back. Pursing his lips, and feeling the warmth from the fire, he rubbed his hands together and let his thoughts turn to the year Sarah married Christian.

It was bitterly cold that winter and they were glad to come off the mountain, but because Sarah wanted to beat Joe for the pot, she and Thomas stayed behind chasing two white wolves. Fergus smiled, she beat Joe alright, and Joe wasn't happy about it, nor about her staying too long on the mountain. The day Sarah and Thomas rode in and she clashed with Christian, Joe said she was going to be trouble again, and she proved him right. Holding his hand over his heart, he thought of Sarah and her clash with Millicent Crawley.

He hadn't known until then that Christian taught Sarah how to swim, and he felt grateful for him teaching her. How could he or the other men not have promised to teach Sarah how to swim, or for that matter read and write? Reading and writing may have seemed unimportant to them, but they should have taught her. They promised to teach her how to hunt, and how to ride! and they promised to make her happy! They kept their promise by making her a good shot with her rifle. She could handle horses and knew how to pick a good one. As cavalry men, when coming under attack, their lives depended on taking cover as quickly as possible. Jumping from their horse while it was still in motion, and running for cover was something they all learnt to do, and do well. Shaking his head from side to side, he remembered he helped teach Sarah that dismount, and was still amazed at how quickly she picked it up. Calahan may have taught her how to set a trap, but it was they four that honed her skill at skinning that made her good with her knife, but damn it! trapping was mostly carried out along the river, Sarah should have been taught to swim.

Fergus had been shocked to learn Christian had been shot by a kid no older than Thomas. As a bounty hunter Christian had been fast with a gun, but no-one, not even Christian could have known how fast the kid was. Some said it had been pure luck the kid killed Christian that day, but Fergus has learnt since, the kid has killed other men and has become an outlaw.

There were times when their promise was at its best, like when Sarah returned to the mountain each spring for the next years trapping. It was then, while trapping along with the men, she was truly happy and she could forget everything that happened in Cedar Creek. She liked walking the mountain, and she loved the thrill of the hunt. Sometimes, when she made fun of hiding her tracks from the trappers, searching for her took them long hours to locate her. It was during those times the mountain became known as Sarah's Mountain.

Turning his thoughts back to Foley, Fergus wasn't sure exactly when he took an interest in Sarah. He thought it may have been the night Major Hardy caught her and Frank at the shack, the night Foley and Brady turned up at the Ferguson House with Sarah wrapped in blankets and Foley's face cut from the whiplash meant for her. But if the truth be known, it was when Sarah was twelve years old and they bumped into each other in the street in Cedar Creek. Since marrying her, and before making his promise to Joe the day Joe died, Foley proved himself to be the right man for Sarah, and Fergus has no doubt he would keep his promise.

Closing his eyes to the warmth of the fire, Fergus dreamt of Ireland. Of walking the hills of Kilkenny, and strolling through green meadows once more. He wants to meet family he has never had the chance to meet before his time runs out. There are five brothers and three sisters younger than him, and all would probably have children, perhaps even grandchildren. He could be a great uncle to many an Irish lass or lad. Oh! how he longs to be back there now, and feeling Sarah no longer needs him, he went to bed that night with his mind made up. It was time for him to leave Sarah's mountain and go home.

Waking at daylight, he made a batch of hotcakes for the men, then told them his news. The men were stunned. "Who will lead us off Sarah's mountain if you go Fergus?" Samuels wanted to know. "Yee all know your own bloody way off that mountain, yee have all been going up and down it long enough to bloody know." When he felt his ire rising, Fergus's rich Irish brogue never failed him. The men felt bad enough Joe was gone, so when Fergus admonished them, all they could do was stare at him. Wanting to be the one to tell Sarah he was leaving, he ordered them all to keep their mouths shut. But when was the right time to tell her? Watching her broken-hearted sobbing when Joe died, and having just come through a bad accident which could have killed her and her baby, she was still getting over the trauma of it all, and he didn't want to upset her again. There was Foley too, doting over Sarah and his new son to consider. Foley had never been a man to smile much, but when he held Sarah's hand and carried his son wherever they went so he could show him off to anyone passing by, his face was never without a smile. Making up his mind, Fergus decided he would wait until the trappers were ready to go back to the mountain to tell Sarah his news. Having become reliant on Joe and Fergus's guidance to see them through their years of trapping, the trappers didn't want Fergus to go and left the house with heavy hearts.

Sarah joined a large crowd of trappers and town folk saying goodbye to Thomas and Gabrielle as they boarded the stage for Moreton where they would catch the first of many coaches and trains that would take them back to Philadelphia. Foley held David in one arm, and because Sarah was upset once again at seeing her son going away, he held her with the other. When Thomas and Gabrielle invited Sarah and Foley to go to Philadelphia to visit them, Sarah didn't say she wouldn't visit, but felt she would never see the city. Fergus stood alongside Sarah saying goodbye to Thomas and Billy, but he still hadn't the nerve to tell her he was leaving.

When the stage finally rolled out of town, Fergus decided to tell Sarah his news before she found out from some loud-mouthed trapper. Taking a deep breath and without telling her the reason, he turned to her and invited her to visit him at the Ferguson House the next day.

Spring was still a little way off and the days carried a blast of cold air from the snow-covered mountains. The river was running high, and along with her family and the trappers, Sarah would soon return to the mountain and her cabin. Carrying David wrapped warmly in rugs against the chill of the days cold breeze, Sarah stepped onto the porch at the Ferguson House and knocked lightly on the door.

Regardless of the weather, there were wild horses needing to be broken. When the stage returned in three weeks, it would head back to Moreton with a fresh team straight from Major Hardy's herd. The men were ready to head to the corrals when Samuels let Sarah in, and as Fergus ushered her over to the fire where she sat in an armchair nursing David, the men filed out.

Bringing mugs filled with coffee to Sarah, Fergus sat opposite her in another old chair as she took her mug and lifted it to her mouth. Taking a sip of the hot brew, she tasted how smooth it was, and liked how it was the same as she makes it. It had been Fergus who taught her when she was around nine years old how to make a good pot, and she smiled at the memory. Both sat silent for a few minutes while drinking their coffee and watching David sleeping on her lap.

"I'm leaving Sarah, I'm going back to Ireland," Fergus announced suddenly deciding there was no easy way to tell her. Sarah's shoulders slumped at hearing the news.

"Fergus," she said softly. "Why?" she asked.

"I canna stay any longer lass, I miss Joe, I miss the old times, it's nay the same as it used to be," he answered looking sadly at her.

"But we are your family, there's Will, and Garrett, and me... and... and all the other men," Sarah stammered, not wanting him to go.

"I know lass, but there be family back in Ireland too, brothers and sisters I have nay seen nigh on forty years, yee have Foley now, and he's taking good care of yee and the little ones." When Fergus smiled sadly, Sarah looked back at him equally as sad.

"When will you be going?" she asked as the lump in her throat threatened to burst.

"I sent word before Christmas that I would be coming home, I'm booked on the coach, I'll be away in three weeks, then it will be a long journey across the ocean to meet with my clan, and yee know? I will probably get there before my letter arrives," he said jokingly with a tear in his eye. Feeling her eyes welling Sarah stood up, and carefully laying David on the chair, turned to Fergus. Fergus stood when she did and faced her.

"Oh, Fergus," she wept, wrapping her arms around him. "I will miss you so."

Holding each other for the longest time, Fergus wept too. Even though Sarah didn't want it to, their time on the mountain and in Cedar Creek had come to an end. She would miss him terribly, but thought it best if he went home while he still had time to enjoy his family. She would be happy at least to know he was there walking the hill's and green meadows he often spoke about.

"Will you write to me Fergus? I would love to hear of your family, to receive a letter all the way from Ireland would be wonderful."

"I promise yee lass, I will write yee."

Holding each other at arm's length, they looked into each other's eyes. Fergus was an old man now, but Sarah loved him dearly. He was still a young man when he taught her how to ride like the wind and jump from her horse like a cavalry man. He taught her how to appreciate what she had and never had a cross word with her whenever she made a mistake. Next to Calahan and Joe, Fergus was the closest to being a father to her.

In tears again, Sarah left Fergus at the Ferguson House and went back to the lodge where Foley found her sitting on the couch in front of the open fire crying. Sitting beside her, he pulled her into his arms and held her close while between sobs she told him Fergus was leaving.

Having grown to like the four trappers when he first came to Cedar Creek, Foley was saddened to hear the news. The men had always been kind to him and Brady. They never questioned why Brady couldn't talk, letting Foley take his time to tell them it was because of what happened to their parents and sister. When he and Brady became Major Hardy's gun-hands, the men were less than impressed, but after they helped Sarah the night Frank was whipped, the trappers felt differently about them. Neither man went outside the law when dealing with out of hand cowhands, or trappers alike, and it had been proven both he and Brady were men to be trusted, and not one of the four ever warned him to stay away from Sarah when he proposed to her, not like they had Sarah's other suitors. Wherever Joe was, Fergus was always there alongside, giving advice or support. Later that night, knowing he would miss Fergus too, after he and Sarah retired to bed early, Foley showed Sarah how much he needed her.

An unassuming man, Fergus never caused a great deal of trouble during the years he spent in Cedar Creek. Although everyone had an idea it was him, along with the other three men that were involved in what happened to Major Hardy's bull, no-one questioned it. The four trappers were always in some sort of carry on where Sarah was concerned. What Fergus did to that bull was probably the worst thing he did while staying in town, so when Major Hardy got word Fergus was leaving, he organized a farewell party at the town hall.

After ordering one of his steers be provided for the feast, the whole town turned out to celebrate, and the next day, when Major Hardy and his cowhands came to see Fergus off, the town again took on a carnival atmosphere. Along with a large crowd of town folk standing outside Henry's Emporium, the trappers were there to the last man. Before Fergus climbed aboard the stage, he said his goodbyes. While clinging to Sarah for what seemed like an eternity, Sarah clung to him not wanting him to go, and as usual wept, causing Foley to hand David to Gerda who held him like he was her own. When the stage carrying Fergus rumbled out of town, everyone went quiet except Sarah who had her head buried against Foley's chest sobbing loudly.

For a time after Fergus left, town folk got around looking as though they were mourning a death in their family. But things needed to be done, so Ham got on with working his forge and fixing shoes to horses and repairing wagons. Doc kept up his practice seeing to gunshot wounds and illnesses. Horses continued to be broken and cattle branded. Life gradually got back to normal as cowhands after getting paid, went to town and drank their fill until their drunken fights ended with Sheriff Smith and Deputy Taylor kept busy carting them off to spend a night in the jailhouse. To help Sarah over her loss, Foley took her, Lizzy and David out to the farm twice a week, where the adults sat on the porch in the afternoon sun watching and laughing at Lizzy and the twins chasing geese in the backyard. Will and Sissy's relationship became serious.

Chapter Thirty

*F*ergus had been gone a month when the dinner party Sarah organized for the last time that winter came to an end. Lizzy and David were safely tucked in their beds upstairs sound asleep. Foley had his arm around Sarah's waist holding her close while they stood on the porch saying goodbye to her guests and watching one particular group making their way along the street. Ham and Patrice walked on ahead with their youngest daughter Lilly while Will and Sissy walked slowly along behind them. By the time the group got to the end of the street, Will and Sissy were holding hands.

"I think there is going to be a wedding," Sarah said smiling up at Foley. Foley squeezed his hand resting against Sarah's waist and smiled back.

"Oh! what makes you think that?" he asked jokingly, because it was obvious on seeing Will and Sissy together during the dinner party, Sarah was right.

The years Will spent on the mountain, he developed feelings for Sarah, but she found love with Frank, then fell in love with Christian, now she was in love again and happily married to Foley. Will would always love Sarah, but he didn't want to think of her in a manner that stopped him having a relationship with another woman.

Will started taking notice of Sissy one winter when he saw her standing with Ham and Patrice watching the men with their packhorses in tow ride over the bridge and into town. Having matured into a fine-looking woman, Sissy wasn't hard to pick out in a crowd. When she smiled up at him and gave him a wave of welcome, he raised his hand in response and smiled back. As he got further down the street, he turned in his saddle, and picking her out of the crowd straight away, found her still watching him. Then when he turned to face the way he was headed, he smiled broadly to himself and proceeded on to the Trading Post.

During the months that followed, Will and Sissy started spending time together. Between breaking Major Hardy's horses and branding cattle, when the men were given Sundays to have to themselves, he and Sissy managed to get out of town in a buckboard to enjoy picnics, and he had been invited to dine with her and her family many times at their residence. Those times Sissy prepared the meal, which more than satisfied Will, making him impressed with her cooking, and they attended the winter dance at the Town Hall where they danced together all night. When other men tried cutting in on them, Will told them in no uncertain words where to go, and ended with saying Sissy was his partner for the night, not theirs. Over the course of their first winter together, Will developed romantic feelings for Sissy.

As a man of twenty-two, when Will made his promise to look out for Sarah, he could not have known twelve years later, when Sarah was a mere slip of a girl at fifteen, he would fall in love with her. According to his promise he was unable to make her his, but he held out hope Sarah herself would choose him as her husband. Their friendship developed on the mountain and in Cedar Creek, but it was never easy to have Sarah to himself. Trappers were always around wherever he was, particularly the other three, so his and Sarah's friendship remained just that, a friendship. While teaching her to track animals and men alike, he taught her how to use her hunting knife to defend herself from attack. If she happened to be knocked to the ground, she was shown how to pull her knife quickly from its sheath, giving her the chance to use it defensively, and she used what she learnt to defend herself against Christian the day she met him, then promptly fell in love with him, leaving Will and every other man who thought they were in love with her out in the cold. Over time, Will became like a brother to Sarah, and the one time he proposed to her, when she said she loved him only as a sister could and could not marry him for that reason, he didn't like it but accepted what she said.

Sissy was two years younger than Sarah with olive skin and dark hair. Unlike Sarah who was always in trouble, Sissy was quietly spoken and liked to keep to herself by not getting involved in gossip. Over many years Will had his fair share of trouble trying to keep Sarah out of harm's way. Thinking his problems with Sarah had ended after she married Christian, when he returned to town and found Christian gone, he straight away took back responsibility for looking out for her. Knowing Will had a promise to keep, Sissy kept her distance, allowing him to spend his time making Sarah happy, and Will was pleased Sissy was so understanding.

After so many years of Foley proposing to Sarah and then losing Maria, Will was surprised to learn Sarah had married him, but he accepted it was only natural for them to get together. With Will's promise he made pushed to the back of his mind, when Foley had been attacked by a wolf and laid up with a broken leg, Will knew Sarah would need his help again, and he agreed along with the other men to stay close by. Sarah did need their help, but not in the way the men thought she would.

Their decision not to go back to the High Ridge Camp came as a relief when they saved both Sarah and Lizzy from Logan and Reeves. Hoping one day to have children of his own, Will wasn't about to let anything happen to Lizzy. As he charged through the trees toward Reeves, he could see the hold Reeves had on her and how it was making her frightened. His hatred for Reeves right then was greater than he had ever felt before, and he would have killed him, if only Joe had let him. "Don't kill him Will, just let them know we're here!" He remembered Joe calling. Even though he was a crack shot and could have killed Reeves easily, he did as Joe bid and aimed his rifle just close enough to Reeves' head to allow his bullet to fly by with little room to spare. What followed made Will wish he had disobeyed Joe's order.

Finding Joe lying wounded where he set his traps, Will did not know who was more surprised, Fergus, Garrett, or himself when learning Logan had survived the mountain. With Sarah being so like Joe, it didn't surprise any of them when Joe confessed to bedding Sarah's mother Elizabeth and could be her father. Having cleared his conscience of his long-kept secret, and having made two promises, it was a bitter blow to the men when Joe died outside

Sarah's cabin. Joe had become their leader, not by vote, but from respect. A strong-willed man, Joe wielded a sense of power over every trapper, and every trapper willingly followed him.

Will knew the mountain would never be the same once Joe was gone. Fergus knew too. After coming off the mountain this winter, Fergus didn't want to stay, and Will didn't blame him.

Both Joe and Fergus treated Will as their equal, and he considered them far better men than his father had ever been. A cruel man, his father's only thought was to treat him with contempt, and his body still bore the brunt from floggings his father gave him with whatever he had in his hand at the time. He was never happier than when he was sent off to join the cavalry, because even though his time there wasn't always good, he made a friend in Brent Garrett.

It was there they heard stories about the bravery of the Indian guide Calahan Cole and his captain, Joseph Beauford Jones. One tale told of how they saved a battalion of men when they came under attack from an Indian war party by leading them over rugged terrain along the Missouri river and back to the safety of Fort Chester. By the time he and Garrett joined the cavalry, Calahan and Joe had already left, and having heard the stories, as soon as his and Garrett's enlistment was up, they headed for Wyoming and the mountains where they met up with James Fergus. Having become friends with those four men, Will knew his life had changed for the better, and even though he couldn't make Sarah his wife because of his promise, there was no promise made where he couldn't treat Lizzy as his daughter, and that was what he did, but wanting children of his own, when he began seeing Sissy and they became lovers, he and Sissy both agreed they wanted large families.

Will was about to ask Sissy for her hand in marriage, but instead of asking her to live on the mountain like Sarah, he was thinking about trying his hand at farming, and besides, if he lived in Cedar Creek he could still go to Sarah's mountain whenever he wanted, because as Joe used to say, 'the mountain would always be there.' There was another thing Will considered too. Brady Andrews owned a farm and hired people to pick his crops, and this year his beans were ready to harvest, and Will thought if Brady could farm and do well, then he could produce just as good a crop as he, but first he needed to see what farms were available for purchase.

The bank manager Lewis Morley, held the deeds to many of the farms dotted around Cedar Creek, and had a list of ranches as well as land that was for sale. Morley carried out all transactions, writing up deeds as well as overseeing the exchange of money. Morley was secluded in his office when Will paid him a visit, so after Morley's teller Michael knocked loudly on his door and ushered Will in, Will was shown to a seat in front of his desk.

"What can I do for you Will?" Morley smiled as he took in Wills appearance and shaking the hand Will offered. Except for a thick moustache covering his top lip, Will was clean shaven. His hair, once light brown and hanging over his collar, now had streaks of grey running through it. The cowhide jacket he was wearing had a fringe around the bottom and along the sleeves. His hunting knife hanging from his waist and gun-belt strapped to his hips looked menacing.

Morley had known Will a long time and wasn't put off by his appearance. All four trappers were amicable when doing business with him, and on odd occasions he sat and had a drink with them in the saloon. Morley was well aware the men could hold their own when trouble reared its ugly head. They had proven it many times over the years, especially when dealing with trouble Sarah created.

"I was wondering..." Will started nervously, and sitting up straight in his chair, rubbed his hands along the tops of his legs. "If you have any farms for sale, and if so, can you tell me the best ones to look at?" Without hesitation Morley got up and went to a cupboard, and pulling out a drawer, lifted out a folder. Sitting back down, he opened it and extracted a sheet of paper.

"Here is a list of farms and ranches for sale, now, depending on what you want to do with it Will, the best farm would be..." As Morley paused to peruse the list, Will leant forward to hear better what he had to say. "The Rankin farm, Bert Rankin didn't do much with it when he had it, when it came to growing crops, or running stock, he was a lazy man, and he got behind in payments, however... if you put aside what happened out there, I can recommend it as the best farm out of all the others." Aware Bert Rankin killed his wife in the house and himself in the barn, Will asked Morley if he could take a look at it before making a final decision.

The ride into the farm was a pleasant one. The road was wide enough for a buckboard to travel along easily. Pulling his horse up at the front of the farmhouse, Will stepped onto the porch where he stopped to gaze around before going inside. Although a lot smaller than other farms it consisted of level ground, and Will thought if he owned it, along with growing crops he could run a few horses and some cattle as well. He opened the front door and went inside.

Since their demise, almost nothing of the Rankin's had been touched. After walking through to the kitchen, he went back along the hall to the bedrooms. Standing outside the main room wondering what he might find inside, he slowly pushed the door open, and looking in, cringed when he saw blood still staining the wall behind where the bed stood. The bed itself had been removed, and he didn't know who would have done that but he didn't care, it was gone and that was the important thing. Stepping up to the wall, he studied the stains, and decided the wall could be scrubbed and painted to cover any remaining marks.

After going from room to room and deciding he liked the look of the house, he made his way across the yard to the barn. The barn was a huge building where once inside, he found a wagon still in pristine condition sitting in the middle of the floor. Making his way around the wagon, and walking between stalls on either side, he stopped at the last stall and looked in before turning to go back, and as he did, he noticed the stain on the back wall. This was where Bert Rankin blew his brains out. Will didn't dwell too long on what happened in the barn, or in the house. Putting his hat on, he left the farm and went straight to the bank. When he left the bank, Morley had placed a hold on the Rankin Farm. Will still had to propose to Sissy.

The following day, Will rose early, had something to eat, then made his way to the livery where he found Ham busy working his forge.

"Howdy Will," Ham greeted when he stopped striking the hot metal horse-shoe he held in a clamp. "You're out early this morning, got work, have you?"

360

"Not today Ham, I wanted to speak with you." Again, Will felt nervous. He was a lot older than Sissy and didn't know what Ham thought of him, but hell, he was thinking, if Ham refused to let him marry Sissy, he would be sorely disappointed but would go back to trapping.

Expecting Will to ask him if he could marry his daughter one day, Ham thought maybe today would be that day, and yesterday he heard Will had been out looking at the Rankin farm with the idea of buying it, and because Sissy told him she was in love with Will and said she was happiest when she was with him, Sissy demanded if Will were to ask him for her hand, he was to say yes. Ham didn't care if Will was so much older than Sissy, besides, he liked Will, Will had never given him any trouble. "What is it you want to speak to me about Will?" he asked.

Taking off his hat Will shuffled it nervously in his hands. "I've been looking at farms, the Rankin farm in particular, thought I might buy it, and I wanted to ask if you wouldn't mind if I take Sissy out to look at it." Will didn't ask for Sissy's hand right then, because if she didn't like the farm he chose, he would choose another one, one she liked. All he knew was, he wanted to marry her and have a family with her.

"Well now Will, why would you want Sissy to look at a farm you are thinking of buying? What has Sissy got to do with it?" Ham asked with a twinkle in his eye.

Will looked at his feet. "I was thinking, maybe I should ask Sissy to marry me." Then keeping a serious look on his face, looked up at Ham. "But I want to ask her out at the farm, maybe she will accept me and the farm, maybe she won't." Ham didn't answer, instead looked beyond Will standing in front of him.

"Maybe if you ask me to marry you Will Sloan I might accept!" Sissy said from behind him and carrying a tray with a coffee pot and mug on it for her father. When he heard Sissy's voice, Will turned to face her. Ham smiled broadly as Sissy sat the tray down and walked over to Will. "Well, you going to ask?" Sissy said looking into his eyes.

"Not here in the livery Sissy, it has to be somewhere special, come with me to the farm and take a look, if you like it, that's where we are having our family," Will replied smiling sheepishly. Sissy raised her eyebrows at him and smiled back. They had already come together on several of their picnics, and she couldn't wait to marry him.

After taking the buckboard out to the farm, Will stood back and watched while Sissy went through the house. It was perfect, she said standing on the back porch, and while looking beyond the barn to the fields, said they could paint the walls and remove all of the furniture and replace it with their own. Then when Will asked Sissy to marry him and Sissy answered yes, he scooped her up in his arms and after carrying her inside, they made the farm their own.

Their wedding was the rowdiest of affairs. The ceremony itself went off smoothly. All except Joe and Fergus, the trappers were there to a man crowding into the hall. There was an abundance of food and too much alcohol. The hall bounced from the many feet stomping its floorboards to Fess's fiddle and the piano player belting out a tune. Drinks flowed, and men got wilder as the night wore on. The celebration came to an end when a fight broke out with Sheriff Smith and Deputy Taylor having to take several of the trappers and Major Hardy's cowhands off to the jailhouse to sleep off their drunkenness.

Chapter Thirty-one

The town was still abuzz days after Will and Sissy's wedding, and now it was almost time for the trappers to head back to the mountain, but before Sarah could leave, there was something important she wanted to do first. After giving a lot of thought to what it was that she wanted to do, she still hadn't discussed it with Foley, after all, it had nothing to do with him, they belonged to Sarah, they were hers to do with whatever she liked.

When Sarah carried David up the street and into the alleyway near Ham's Livery and Stables, Foley was out at the farm helping Brady pick beans. Hoping she had come to the right decision, she was deep in thought as she made her way to collect Lizzy who was spending one of her last days at school with Tilly O'Rourke. Deciding to wait until school was finished for the day so she could talk to Jonathon alone, Sarah sat nursing David on the long seat under the tree outside the schoolhouse watching folk going about their business. She didn't have long to wait before children came charging out the door making excited noise as they scattered for home.

While Lizzy stayed seated at one of the desks as usual waiting for Sarah to collect her, Jonathon had his back to the door cleaning the board of the days lessons when Sarah entered.

"Hello Jonathon," she announced standing in the aisle between the desks. Jonathon and Lizzy both turned when they heard her voice.

"Hello Sarah," Jonathon greeted putting his duster down. Ready for her Ma to take her home, Lizzy got off her chair eagerly and held out her hand.

"Jonathon, would you and Tilly come to the lodge please?" Sarah asked taking hold of Lizzy's hand. Thinking Sarah was asking him and Tilly to come for dinner, Jonathon smiled at her invitation. "What time would you like us?" he asked.

Inwardly Sarah was shaking. Maybe she was making a huge mistake, and maybe everyone would think her a fool for her decision, so wanting to get what she wanted to do over with as quickly as possible before she changed her mind, her answer was abrupt. "Now!" she said turning sharply, and with Lizzy in tow, disappeared out the door.

Watching Sarah's back as she hurried out, Jonathon frowned. They hadn't got off to a good start when they first met. Coming straight from Philadelphia to a teaching job in a town he thought was going to be as big as Moreton, he found it to be a small isolated town where fur trappers came once a year to frighten the life out of unsuspecting town folk. After proudly presenting a bell to the town, Sarah shot the rope off the bell and almost frightened him to death when she threatened to send him to Mexico to get her runaway horses.

Going to the other classroom, he informed Tilly of Sarah's invitation and that it didn't sound much like an invitation to dinner. By the time they discussed what possible reason Sarah could have for asking them to the lodge, Sarah was back there waiting for them.

To let her know they had arrived, Jonathon raised his hand to knock, only Sarah knew he and Tilly were there and opened the door before he could do so. "Come in Jonathon, hello Tilly," she said closing the door behind them when they stepped inside. "Hello Sarah," Tilly greeted feeling nervous at having no clue as to what Sarah's intentions were for asking them to her home. As all three stared at each other, Sarah broke the tension with a smile.

"Well, I guess you are wondering why I asked you here?" she said clasping her hands nervously in front of her.

"We are a little confused to say the least," Jonathon answered nervously back at her.

"This won't take long," Sarah said turning and pushing open a set of double doors.

"Come in," she said over her shoulder.

Jonathon and Tilly had enjoyed many of Sarah's Christmas dinner parties, but like most people, had never been invited to look through her grand home. While letting them look around, Sarah remained silent. "Wow!" was all Jonathon could muster as he gazed in awe at the walls lined from floor to ceiling with bookshelves, and every one stacked with books. He knew from Thomas that Sarah had books, but he didn't know exactly how many she owned. Before coming to Cedar Creek, he had visited libraries all along the east coast, and this room was nowhere near as big as those libraries, even so, there were a lot of books in Sarah's study. Standing with her mouth agape while looking around, Tilly thought. 'Oh, if only we had these books, how they would help us teach the children!'

"What do you think Jonathon?" Sarah asked.

"What do I think? I'm thinking… how come as a young girl you never learnt to read? You have your very own library!" Jonathon thought back to the day Sarah asked him to teach her to read. When he refused her request, it caused her to become angry, and at the time, it frightened him to think she might use the large knife she carried on him, but having come to an arrangement that suited both of them, he set about teaching her the fundamentals of reading and writing.

When Jonathon asked her about learning to read, Sarah thought about the years she spent trapping before coming to live in town. She loved being with the trappers, so why at the end of each day when she was worn out from hunting, would she pick up a book? besides, it never bothered the trappers that she couldn't read.

"There was never time Jonathon, besides, books didn't interest me, there were far too many better things to do," she answered.

Jonathon looked again at the size of the study. In the middle of the room stood a black leather couch and behind it a mahogany desk and leather chair. Imagining Thomas and Billy spending many hours here, Jonathon was in no doubt why they had become the scholars they proved to be, and felt proud of both his former pupils.

"I want you to have my books Jonathon," Sarah said keeping her hands clenched together. Presenting him with her gift rendered

Jonathon speechless, and he stared wide eyed at her. "Take all of them, use them to make your own library, or something," she said. On hearing Sarah's generous offer, and expecting Jonathon to accept her gift, Tilly clasped her hands together in glee. "Oh Sarah, thank you so much," she said feeling breathless.

"I cannot possibly take your books, Sarah!" Jonathon replied, taking his eyes off Sarah and glaring at Tilly. Feeling crestfallen, Tilly looked at Jonathon dismally.

"They need to be read Jonathon," Sarah insisted. "They are useless just sitting here, please, take them." Jonathon conceded he could use every book, but needed to be sure Sarah wouldn't come back years later to demand she have them back.

"Are you absolutely certain you want me to have them? And if I do take them, you won't come off your mountain and take to me with that knife of yours?" he laughed, trying to make light of what happened previously. Sarah remembered the time he was referring too. "I would not have hurt you then," she replied softly, looking down at her hands. "And I would never now."

The sincerity in Sarah's voice, convinced Jonathon what she said was true. Reaching out suddenly, he hugged her, leaving her no choice but to hug him back. "I will gladly accept your gift Sarah, Cedar Creek will have its very own library," he said after letting her go.

"You can have everything in this room," Sarah said indicating the furnishings.

"But what will you do with an empty study?" he asked. Sarah hadn't considered what she would do with an empty room, so while thinking of an answer to his question, Jonathon studied her thoughtfully. She was a beautiful woman and he had come to admire her for her strength.

"I suppose, I could make it into a… a bedroom! that way, I won't have to trap as much if my lodge is let to folk coming to town." Pleased with that idea, Sarah decided Foley would be told of her decision to give away her books as soon as he came back from the farm. Tilly clapped her hands with glee, gave Sarah a hug, and it was settled. Jonathon would take Sarah's books after she had gone back to her mountain. First thing he needed do, he informed both women before leaving the lodge, was write to the government to ask for funds to build the library.

Exactly two weeks after Will and Sissy married, the trappers rode out of Cedar Creek with a year's supply of goods loaded on their packhorses. Lizzy sat holding tight to the saddle-horn in front of the man she called Pa, and smiled at her Ma. David lay strapped to Sarah's chest for comfort and safety. Heading back to the mountain with an extra child was going to prove a task for Sarah. Glancing over at Foley sitting tall in his saddle, Sarah smiled. He was a handsome man and she admired him. When she informed him about giving Jonathon her books as well as the furnishings from the study, he hadn't so much as disagreed with her decision. When she said she planned on converting the room to a bedroom, he said it was a clever use of the room, more so than the study had ever been because the books were just collecting dust. Then seeing her disparaging look at assuming she didn't do any cleaning, he added quickly, 'it wasn't so much dust, it was with Thomas leaving, they just weren't being read.' Foley was a loving husband and father, Sarah could not ask for anything more than what she had right then. With the men stopping occasionally to let Sarah and her children rest along the way, they still made good time to each of their camps.

On the mountain, trapping resumed in earnest, but back in Cedar Creek, months passed by ever so slowly. Jonathon wrote to the government and finally secured his grant to build his library. The lumberyard was grateful for the contract to supply the timber. Men sitting idle were glad to build the building. The library sat on newly acquired ground beside the school and was larger than the schoolhouse, but smaller than both the Ferguson House and Mountain View Lodge. When the building was completed, wagons were commandeered, and with a group of men, Jonathon went to the lodge to remove the leather couch and desk and chair first. With help from women and children, the books were packed in wooden crates and taken to the new library. Tilly and Jonathon worked tirelessly, taking weeks to finish documenting all the books.

As the last of the books were removed, Jonathon closed the door but remained in the living area gazing up at the painting of Sarah's mother Elizabeth. Every time he visited Sarah's home, he stood in awe of the paintings likeness to Sarah. While standing there, Jonathon formed a plan, and hoped, when Sarah came back next winter, she wouldn't mind what he was about to do. Tilly was not happy with Jonathon's plan. Even though Sarah said she would never harm him, Tilley said she would be so angry she would not hesitate to use her knife on him. Jonathon shrugged off what Tilly said and put his plan into action.

Chapter Thirty-two

While Sarah sat on the porch of her cabin with her feet resting on the top step and nursing David, she scanned the area around the clearing where Lizzy was playing, and sensed she was safe from wolves on the prowl. Wanting to get down so he could play with Lizzy, David wriggled in Sarah's arms. When Thomas was a baby, he made Sarah laugh with his funny little antics, and David was now too. Since beginning to walk, he was getting into everything, making it hard once again for Sarah to go out trapping.

Foley meanwhile was busy at the woodpile cutting wood and had become overheated. Taking his shirt off, he threw it aside, then gripping the axe, he lifted his arms and taking a swing at a block of wood, caused his skin to glisten with sweat and his muscles to flex. Watching the axe split the wood in two, Sarah reflected not only on him, but the men that impacted her life.

Her happiest memories were of the four trappers and the times they roamed the mountain together, oblivious to the rest of the world, and of them teaching her to ride and to handle a rifle, and she considered herself as good a rider as any man, and a better shot than all of them. It was because Calahan believed he was her father, that he chose the men to make him a promise they would take care of her if anything should happen to him, and most of the time they kept their promise so she could experience life for herself.

Long before Joe confessed to possibly being her father, she adopted his way of doing things, and perhaps he had a right to his claim, but she had loved Calahan as a father too, and even though she would never know if it was him or Joe that produced her, as far as she was concerned it didn't matter, she was proud to be like both men.

Keeping her eyes on Foley at the woodpile, she remembered how she hated leaving the mountain to spend winter in Cedar Creek. Except for Mountain View Lodge, the town had nothing that appealed to her. The night Calahan died, her home had been taken from her by a man she still thinks of as a murdering, thieving, belly-crawling, rotten sidewinding snake. She had good reason for calling Benjamin Crawley those names, because while ever she was in his store and they were alone, he told her how he killed Calahan, and he knew she couldn't convince the trappers he did it, so he got away with it. Even though Crawley is dead, Sarah still bear's some hatred toward him.

While David continued to squirm, memories of the trappers filled Sarah's mind. Fergus was the kindest of all men, and she liked it when he called her lass. When he spoke of Ireland, she could see the land he loved as clear as if she were there. The green meadows and hills that stretched as far as the eye could see were like the mountains where she lived. In all the years she had known him, he never lost his way of speaking of it, and she liked it when, with his smile she came to love, he tried to explain something and got talking so fast it caused her to listen carefully to his every word. She missed him and his broad lilting accent terribly.

Once Joe was gone and Fergus said goodbye, the promise had truly been broken. Tears sprang to her eyes when she knew she would never see Fergus again. He was so far away. All the way across the land and the ocean, and having left Cedar Creek for the mountain soon after he departed, she was unable to receive a letter from him. Maybe there would be one waiting for her when she went back to Cedar Creek, she hoped so, and drawing back a sudden sob, wiped her hand across her eyes.

The quietest man she had ever known was Garrett. She couldn't think of a time when he raised his voice to her either. He taught her to love the mountain, and was always there beside the other men. When it came to trapping, all except Joe, Garrett was better than most.

Instead of being like an uncle to her, Will was more like a brother. But other than brotherly love, there was a time when she knew Will had feelings for her, but she felt pleased he married Sissy. Sarah felt certain they would have lots of children, and smiled because she was looking forward to visiting them when she and Foley return to town.

When Sarah looked back over her time spent with Frank, she remembered how it had been both a happy and sad part of her life. It was when he sat with her in the rain beside her then Pa's grave and tried to comfort her that they had become friends. It was soon after that, Frank gave her Star. Coming to the Ferguson House where she was staying with the trappers, he tried to make her feel better by bringing the colt with him to give to her as a gift. Star proved to be a reliable horse, and she missed him also.

It was at the old shack on Major Hardy's spread where she told Frank she was expecting Thomas that she remembered he had been excited at the thought of becoming a father. After carving their names in the timber wall, he asked her to marry him. Sarah smiled to herself because that piece of wall was sitting on the mantle above the open fireplace under her mother's portrait at the lodge where she constantly sees it. Sarah doesn't need a piece of wood to remind her of Frank, but is pleased Christian gave it to her.

Sarah does not wish to remember Frank's father threatening her with a whipping if she didn't stay away from Frank. She doesn't wish to remember the whipping Frank got in place of her, nor her ordeal at being caught naked by Major Hardy's men. She doesn't wish to remember being left all alone while a violent storm raged around her, but it is burnt into her memory and will stay with her forever. She will never forget it had been Foley, bearing the scar he received from Major Hardy's whip and Brady, appearing out of the storm that awful night, that wrapped her in blankets so they could get her back to town. Having told Foley on the ride she was expecting Frank's baby, he put his pain aside and while holding her close, he carried her back to the safety of the trappers. Sarah closed her eyes and remembered feeling safe in his arms then, and when he holds her now, he makes her feel safe.

When Frank died, she felt no reason to go on living. Blaming the four trappers for not taking care of him, she told them angrily to stay away from her, but the four men never broke their promise and didn't stay away. They merely stepped aside to allow her time to get over Frank's death and were there in an instant when she gave birth to Thomas.

After making the trek to the top of the mountain to see Frank's burial ground, she believed Frank was satisfied she had moved on, and that he approved of both Lizzy and Foley.

Her memories of Christian were the most recent. Oh! how she had loved Christian. They fell heavily for each other the instant they met, resulting in their first encounter becoming so steamy Christian made her pregnant with Lizzy. But they fought as hard as they loved. Being married didn't stop them having quarrels, but their love for each other grew stronger every day. Christian adored her and Lizzy both, and he loved Thomas as only a father could, and Thomas loved him equally. Sarah still couldn't believe the kid who killed Christian was faster at the draw than he.

Her life became one of turmoil after Christian's death. Had she known Maria's secret before Maria and Foley married, she would never have pushed him toward her. She hated that Foley tried punishing her for knowing, causing them to almost lose their friendship they forged over many years. Not once out on the prairie, where they met while she was snaring rabbits, did they have reason to quarrel. Before he came to her door that night, there were many lonely nights her thoughts turned to him. Afraid she would lose him like she had the others, she accepted his proposal of marriage before he asked her. 'Where was the harm in her saying yes before he proposed?' she asked herself. Foley proposed to her many times out on the prairie, and there was no other man in Cedar Creek, or on the mountain she would ever have considered marrying once Christian was gone.

Pulling her thoughts back to the present, she reminded herself of her and Foley's relationship, and how it began when she was twelve years old. Foley had not long arrived in town, and she was on her way to the corrals to watch the men break horses when she came hurrying around the corner from the lodge and barreled into him. She fobbed off the incident and went on her way, but that was the time Foley has since confessed, that he knew he would one day marry her. Sarah raised one eyebrow when she remembered him telling her that.

After their marriage, he confessed too that he spied on her while she was at the ponds bathing with Thomas as a baby, but insisted he kept seeing her to himself. He had been there the day Thomas was taken, when she tried her best to scare the town folk into giving Thomas back, but it was the incident with Major Hardy's bull that convinced her it had been him that showed the trappers where to find the bull that resulted in Thomas being returned to her.

Sarah would never forget Frank, or Christian, but has made a promise to herself she will love Foley until the day she dies. She hopes that day will be a long time coming.

Months passed where Sarah taught Foley trapping and made him her partner, and because of that her trapping was good. She would soon return to her winter home to once again hold dinner parties. As well as visiting her family of Brady and Ellen and their children, she liked visiting friends. But best of all, she loved living on the mountain. Even if it is a lonely life for Foley and her children, she loves being there where she can carry on with family traditions.

Looking at Foley working hard at getting firewood, her heart quickened. The pile was steadily growing. Nights on the mountain were growing cold, winter was approaching and they needed loads of wood to keep their cabin warm. Standing up, she carried David to the bottom of the steps where she put him down and watched him totter on shaky legs toward the clearing where Lizzy was scratching in the dirt. Seeing David tottering toward her, Lizzy dropped her stick, and running to him, helped him to the clearing where he plonked himself down. After picking up her stick and dragging it in the dirt, David watched in fits of giggles as she ran rings around him.

Going back to the porch where the water barrel stood, Sarah scooped water into a tin cup and took a drink. The water tasted good, fresh and cold. Scooping up another cupful, she carried it down the steps to Foley. Putting the axe down, Foley took the cup Sarah offered, and while he drank deeply, Sarah moved her eyes over his body. Hair on his chest glistened from sweat. His breasts stood firm. Reaching out, she traced her fingers over him gently. Having seen her watching him from the porch, Foley stopped drinking and looked lovingly at her. Then taking another drink, let water spill over the sides of the cup, where it ran through his neatly trimmed beard, trickled down his neck, then onto his chest. When Sarah instinctively wiped it away, he handed her the cup, then pushing his hand into her hair, brought her against him and kissed her passionately.

Foley has loved Sarah for more years than he can keep track of. They have been married less than two. If he could, he would love Sarah forever. He knows forever is not possible, but he will love her while ever he lives and breathes, and he hopes that will be a very long time.

Sarah knows she need not keep secrets from him anymore. As he looked longingly into her eyes, she looked lovingly into his. "Foley," she said softly. "I'm having another baby."

Chapter Thirty-three

Sheriff Smith was doing his usual nightly round of the town checking to make sure buildings were secure and town folk were safely tucked up in their homes. There were strangers in town now they had a stagecoach service and one could not be too careful. Smith checked the streets as he walked to see no-one was skulking about. Henry's Emporium was closed, as was the rest of the businesses along the main street. The eatery closed its doors soon after the last patron had finished eating their evening meal. The saloon was the only place still doing a trade.

As Smith made his way down the street toward the Trading Post, he passed by the saloon where he could hear the piano player belting out a tune. Voices raised in laughter drifted on the air. Smith planned to cross the road and go behind the Ferguson House which was locked up until the trappers came back at the end of the year. At the Trading Post, he walked around the back and checked the back door to see if it was locked. Satisfied the door was secure, he went around to the front and tried the front door. When everything looked as it should, he crossed the road to the Ferguson House and checked along the back of the building before walking around to the front where he climbed the steps to the porch. Taking hold of the door handle there, he rattled it to see if it was locked, and was pleased to find it was.

That was when he heard the distinct sound of breaking glass. To see where the sound was coming from, Smith looked both ways along the porch, but everything there seemed normal. Even so, he drew his gun from its holster and cocking it, turned back to the steps where he peered into the dark but saw nothing out of the ordinary until a flickering light coming from one of the upstairs windows of Mountain View Lodge caught his eye. Hurrying down the steps, Smith ran as fast as he could toward the lodge.

There was one guest registered as staying at the lodge. A gambling man who came on the stage from Moreton. Having heard about trappers and the money they made from skins, he thought it would be an easy gain gambling in Cedar Creeks saloon, except the gambler came to town at the wrong time. The trappers were still on the mountain. They wouldn't be back in Cedar Creek for months. Not until winter hit with all the viciousness it could throw at them.

The lodge was on fire. Sheriff Smith holstered his gun as he slowed his run outside the front. Upstairs, flames flared from the shattered window and raced up the outside of the grand building. Running onto the porch, Smith banged his fist on the door several times trying to rouse the occupant. When he got no response, he didn't hang about to watch the lodge burn.

Running back to the main street as fast as he could, he ran to the saloon where men were still drinking. Desperately needing their help to put the fire out, he tore through the swing doors yelling, *"the lodge is on fire!"* and everyone stopped what they were doing and stared at him. 'Did they hear him or not?' Smith wondered. *"Come on!"* he yelled before running back out.

They heard him alright. Leaving their drinks where they were, the men pushed their chairs back and jumping to their feet, hastily followed him outside.

Racing in a bunch around the street corner, they passed in front of the Ferguson House, and gathered in front of the lodge. Seeing thick smoke and flames billowing from every window upstairs, and unable to get to the river due to dense bush behind the building, buckets were hastily found and a bucket line going from a trough across the street and up the steps into the burning building was quickly formed. Passing buckets to each other, Smith being the last man, tossed water on the flames that were quickly engulfing the downstairs living area. Flames flowed across the ceiling like a quickly rising ocean tide lapping at the shoreline. The words 'Frank Mason loves Sarah Cole' carved in the board from the shack, disappeared when the wood became scorched and burst into flames. Intense heat forced every man back. Faced with having to evacuate the building to save their lives, men beat a hasty retreat across the street as flames consumed the last vestiges of the lodge. There was nothing anyone could do to save it. As timbers burnt away, Mountain View Lodge collapsed in on itself.

From the porch at his and Sissy's farm, Will saw the glow and wondered at the time what it was. When he realized it could only be one thing, he quickly mounted his horse and raced to town, but there was nothing he could do either. Standing across the street with the rest of the crowd that had swelled to everyone in town, he watched Sarah's winter home burn to the ground.

Out on the prairie, a lone wolf saw the glow lighting up the night sky, and running its tongue hungrily around its mouth, watched it for a moment before loping back into the dark.

The gambler could not be found. Being a heavy smoker and drinker, someone was heard saying he must have been the cause of the fire. The gambler never left town on the stage when it came to take traveler's back to Moreton. Sheriff Smith said when he saw flames coming from the upstairs window, he figured the gambler had gone to bed with a lit cheroot and fell asleep with the smoke still in his hand. According to Smith, the flames were so intense the body of the gambler must have been consumed by the heat of the fire.

The following day Will rode back to town to see if he could salvage any of Sarah's belongings, but except for the stone chimney from the living area, there was nothing left. Being on the mountain with Foley and their children, there was no way for Sarah to know her home, the grandest house in all the county was no more.

Will thought about the tragedy that had befallen Sarah once more. Having lost Frank to wolves and Christian to a gunslinger, and both Calahan and her lodge to his drinking and gambling, she had lost the lodge forever. He could imagine the loss Sarah would feel, because he was feeling it himself. Along with Calahan, and his three friends, he helped build the lodge for Elizabeth. Heavily pregnant with Sarah at the time, Elizabeth was still able to oversee the work, telling the men exactly how she wanted it built and they did it, for her, and for Calahan, and when Sarah came along, for her. Will's heart ached for their loss. Cedar Creek no longer had a grand house, and probably never would. No other house could ever be built that would come close to being as grand as Mountain View Lodge.

'Where would Sarah and Foley and their children live when they came to town now the lodge was gone?' Will asked himself. Of course, he would offer them a place to stay at his farm, or perhaps they would choose to stay with Brady and Ellen, after all, Brady was Foley's brother. It was a well-known fact the trappers over the years made sure Sarah would not go penniless. When Calahan died, and Joe asked them to bank a portion of the money they made from trapping into her book for her to be able to take care of herself, none of the trappers hesitated to do as he asked, and when Thomas came along, the money they hoped would help her raise him. They continued their practice in secret right up until Joe died, then only stopped because she found out what they had been doing.

Will knows Sarah doesn't need to trap, she is a wealthy woman with enough money in her account to build another lodge if she wished. He also knows a new lodge would never be the same as the old one. A new lodge could never give back the memories Sarah made there, nor the memories the trappers made spending time there with her. Will was despondent when he rode back to his farm. All he could do to find out what Sarah would decide, was wait for her return.

Chapter Thirty-four

Garrett had been to visit Sarah and Foley on the Low Ridge, and while there, after Lizzy and David were put to bed, they sat with him at his fire in the clearing and drank coffee Sarah brought from the cabin. They were having a nice time laughing about the good times they shared with the other three trappers when Sarah suddenly put her hand on Garrett's arm. "Will you keep trapping?" she asked him softly.

Asking if he would continue trapping caused Garrett's reverie to disappear, and when he saw a sadness creep into Sarah's eyes, it gave him the impression she was asking him if he too would be leaving her. Leaning forward and holding his mug in both hands, he stared into the fire and pondered what it meant for him to stay. His trapping was good, but he missed his three companions and knew Sarah did too, and if he were to leave, she would no longer have his friendship, nor the security of him watching over her.

Before coming to the mountain as a young man, his childhood spent in Boston was embedded in poverty and cruelty. As an only child, his mother was a loving mother, but down trodden by his father. His father was a very strict man who ruled his house with a firm hand. When it came to punishment, he showed no mercy. Garrett endured many beatings, more than twice a week, according to his father to teach him discipline and respect. The only escape he had from his father's cruel intent was to immerse himself in studying botany which he soon discovered a love for. When his father got tired of having him around and sent him off to join the cavalry, he used his escape as a way of documenting his love of the vast open land and variety of plants he encountered on his billets.

He didn't want to leave his mother, but after enduring years of brutality herself from his father, she begged him to go. Once gone, he was relieved to get out from under his father's rule. When after a few months had passed and he got word to say his mother had died at the hands of his father he cried for days, but then turned bitter and angry that she should have been the one to have suffered his father's wrath. Her insistence that he join the cavalry saved him from a life she herself had endured. After receiving word saying his father was hung at the gallows for her murder, he felt satisfied justice for his mother had been served.

Having come from a broken home just like Will, Garrett decided his time in the cavalry hadn't been all bad because he made a good friend in him. They shared the same sense of humour, and the two only two years apart in age, with Will being the younger. Remembering their fathers telling them the cavalry was a 'rite of passage to becoming a man,' Garrett huffed inwardly. It didn't take him long to find out the cavalry wasn't what he was cut out for, and he reckoned he didn't become a man until he made it to the mountain and killed his first wolf.

With his and Wills service coming to an end, even though neither had experience in trapping, they decided to give it a go, and anxious to meet up with Calahan and Joe, after riding the long and dusty trail to Cedar Creek to find the two men were already on the mountain, they lit out in search of them. By the time he and Will teamed up with Fergus, Calahan and Joe were well established. Calahan with his one room dirt floor cabin down on the Low Ridge, and Joe with his up on the High Ridge. After Both he and Will built their shacks next to Joe's, the High Ridge Camp came into being. It wasn't until Calahan took a year off from trapping to bring Elizabeth back as his wife, that Joe, Fergus, Will and himself joined up as a group.

Hating that Fergus left the mountain to return to Ireland, Garrett thought he would, right then, be somewhere in the middle of the ocean, on his way back to a land he hadn't seen in half his lifetime, and with Will marrying Sissy and buying a farm outside Cedar Creek, he was in no doubt by the time he returned to town next winter they would already have their first child, and Will would never return to trapping.

Garrett was no different to any other man that fell in love with Elizabeth. She was a breath of fresh air on a mountain that he grew to love. Her voice when she spoke was like a sweet melody drifting on a gentle mountain breeze, and he loved to hear it. When Calahan asked if he would help build a proper cabin for Elizabeth, like the other men he didn't hesitate, and he didn't hesitate to build Mountain View Lodge when asked either. Because Elizabeth was pregnant at the time, the men spent all winter getting the lodge finished so she could have her baby there, only to have her and Calahan return to their cabin because Calahan wanted their baby to come into the world, 'born of the mountain.'

With plants being his specialty, that cold winter night after Elizabeth died, when Calahan asked him to make his promise, he promised he would teach Sarah all about what made the mountain their home. Crossing paths with her and Calahan when they were out trapping, their breaks went from skinning their kill to sharing fires and eating with them, and teaching Sarah how to defend herself. Sarah learnt quickly how to throw her small knife, then when she took her father's heavy skinning knife as her own, she learnt all over again how to hold it and throw it until she could throw it well, and even though it was Calahan, before his hands became crippled who taught her how to remove a skin, it was they four who taught her how to take them off quickly.

He hadn't given any thought to Sarah in a romantic way, not until Calahan died and she came into the trappers care. Finding he had the same feelings for her as any man, but thinking himself far too old for a young girl such as Sarah to consider him as a husband, he kept his feelings to himself. Making his promise not to make her his didn't come easy, but he vowed to always keep that part of his promise. Even though he formed friendships with other women, he never found true love. They saw to his needs, and that was all he asked of them.

Learning Sarah had given herself willingly to Frank out of wedlock and was expecting his child disappointed him, and when she blamed them for Frank's death, her scathing words broke his heart. Joe especially was hurt with Sarah's attitude toward them. But they each put her wellbeing above everything else, including trapping as they tried their best to take care of her.

The night she gave birth to Thomas, was when Garrett felt the most love for her. Closing his eyes, he tried to forget what happened when Thomas was taken and given to Major Hardy, then sniggered to himself when he remembered what the four of them did to make the Major give Thomas back. Garrett knew as well as Joe had, Sarah would never forgive the Major for the things he did, and even though Sarah and the Major are on friendly terms now, he believes Sarah still doesn't trust him. He doesn't trust the Major either, and perhaps like Sarah, he never would.

There was a time, while drinking in the saloon in Cedar Creek minding his own business, that Garrett overheard Major Hardy's cowhands saying nasty things about Sarah being with the trappers, and he listened for a time, but a man can only listen to such talk for so long, and it made his anger rise in him. When the men kept sniggering out aloud, he leapt across the table, and grabbing the main offender by the throat, sent them both crashing to the floor amongst upturned tables and glasses. With every man joining in the fight, all Sheriff Clementine could do was stand back and wait until they sorted each other out.

After the fight ended, along with scattered money and torn playing cards, men lay holding their heads and moaning amidst broken tables and chairs, while others got drunkenly to their feet to stand in spilt drinks and broken glass, and because the saloon had been destroyed, Sheriff Clementine threatened to lock Garrett up for a week on account of the amount of damage he caused. Leaving the saloon in disgust, Garrett headed back to the Ferguson House, but instead of going inside, he went around the back and stood on the ridge above Sarah's camp where he could see Sarah and Thomas sitting by their fire having their evening meal, oblivious to what was going on at the saloon while talking and laughing at something they thought was funny. When Sarah ruffled Thomas's hair, and put her arm around his shoulders, Garrett reckoned the fight to defend her was worth the risk of being locked up, and at the time, he thought he would do it all again if he had to, and how right he was. There were plenty more times in the years that followed where he had to fight to defend Sarah's reputation.

Garrett had never before witnessed the sort of anger Joe displayed until such time as Sarah being attacked by Logan in her shelter, then again after she married Foley. Joe's beating Logan the first time should have taught him a lesson, but it had been when he attacked Sarah on the mountain that each man wanted to kill him. It was only Joe stopping them by saying they weren't killers that he watched Joe beat Logan within an inch of his life, then agreed to let him go. The sight of two men running away with their bare asses shining white against the stark green of the forest made him laugh inwardly, but he stopped laughing when he remembered what happened after that.

He didn't care that Reeves met his end from the knife Logan used on him. It was bad luck but nothing Garrett thought he didn't deserve. There were few days spent on the mountain he was not happy with, but when Logan ambushed Joe, seeing his friend he had known for the best part of his life dying before his eyes, was the worst day of his life.

As Garretts mind wandered back over time to where he and Sarah would sit and talk, and sometimes laugh about trapping, he tried putting his despair of losing Joe out of his mind by thinking of other men he had come to know.

Benjamin Crawley was no different to any other cowhand, rancher or trapper, he liked to drink and he liked to gamble. No-one believed Sarah when she said Crawley cheated at cards and killed Calahan. It wasn't until she became involved with Christian Morgan, that Crawley confessed he killed Calahan that they finally believed her.

Garrett liked Christian, even after finding out he once was a bounty hunter, but was disappointed in him when he had a disagreement with Sarah when she accused Crawley's daughter Millicent of stealing from her.

Garretts heart beat a little faster when remembering Millicent trying to dispose of Sarah because she wanted Christian for herself. Watching Sarah push herself and Millicent off the cliff above the waterfall to land in the river below town almost had his heart stopping. A shiver ran through him to think Sarah tried to sacrifice herself to stop Millicent shooting Christian, but that day was a good day when Sarah survived the fall and the rapids.

When Garrett's thoughts turned to Sarah and Christian's daughter Lizzy, he smiled. Lizzy is so much like Sarah was back when she was a child. Will adores her, and so does he, but he hopes Lizzy doesn't grow up with Sarah's temperament.

When Foley said he fell in love with Sarah long before Frank had, but said he was too young and too shy to approach her at the time because he felt clumsy and stupid whenever he was around her, and having said he was angry at Frank for beating him for her affection, he laughed along with the other men, but stopped when he realized Foley was serious.

Foley's promise made to Joe before Joe died was the same as four trappers making their promise. Foley knew that, and willingly became one of the family of trappers that hunted wolf, and the rules of the mountain set out by Joe and Calahan applied to him as much as anyone, and because Foley's love for Sarah was enduring, Garrett need not stay to make sure Foley would never break his promise. But he made a promise also, and because he was not one to go back on his word simply because Sarah was married, he would see it through to the end, just like Joe had.

Thinking about the promise he made, Garrett came to the realization that Calahan must have known when he asked him to make his promise, that it would be impossible for him not to make Sarah his own. Calahan knew the day would come where all four of them would become her family. Because that was why he asked them!

While waiting for Garrett's answer to her asking if he were staying, Sarah studied him. His beard had not yet grown too wild that it hid his features. His eyes were what impressed her the most. The light from the fire shone bright in them, and they still held the gleam she had come to know that told her he was full of life and ready for the hunt.

"I will have to give it some thought," Garrett finally said breaking from his thoughts.

That was not the answer Sarah was hoping for. Getting to her feet, she bid him goodnight, then not waiting for Foley, hurried to the cabin and went inside. Garrett and Foley stood when she did, then seeing her going, Foley nodded goodnight to Garrett and followed her.

On his way to the outhouse next morning, Foley stopped and looked at the clearing where Garrett had his camp. His fire was alight, his two horses were feeding, and his bedroll was still spread out on the ground, but Garrett was nowhere to be seen.

With rifle in hand, Foley glanced about and found him standing beyond the outhouse where a line of trees formed the forest. After making a hasty trip to the outhouse, he made his way to where Garrett was and coming to a standstill beside him, stood in silence as both gazed down at Joe's and Elizabeth's resting places.

"You staying or going?" Foley asked breaking the silence. Garrett already gave Sarah's asking if he would keep trapping a great deal of thought during the night, but for a moment pondered Foley's question. What happened with Sarah in the past was interesting, traumatic at times, but interesting. But the past was the past, and Sarah's future was where Garrett saw himself. "There's no other place I would rather be," he answered truthfully, then turning from Joe's grave, he nodded to Foley and started back toward the cabin. Both used their walking side by side to delve into their own thoughts. Garrett thinking the mountain was the only place he would ever call home, and Foley thinking Sarah would be able to stop crying once he told her Garrett was staying.

"You have a good woman in Sarah Foley," Garrett said stopping at the side door to the cabin.

"I can't disagree with you there," Foley answered smiling.

"You missed out on her younger years, but the ones to come will be her best," Garrett said before going on. "I made a promise the same as you, and it's up to us now to take care of Sarah, that includes her family," he ended, and watching Foley, waited for a reply. When Foley nodded and stuck out his hand, Garrett grasped it in his and they shook in agreement to his statement.

"Come on in and have breakfast with us," Foley said resting his hand on his shoulder. Garrett welcomed his invitation to eat with them, and followed Foley inside.

Before Garrett left to return to the High Ridge Camp, he gave Lizzy a hug, tweaked David's cheek and kissed Sarah on her forehead. Then after shaking hands with Foley again, Sarah and

Foley stood with their children and watched him head along the trail that would take him up the mountain to the Middle Ground, then on to the High Ridge.

Samuels was busy at the fire while Reece was scraping sinew from a skin stretched between two limbs of a tree when he looked up and saw Garrett coming toward them. Seeing the amount of skins Garrett had on his packhorse he cursed under his breath. Next to Joe, Garrett was an exceptional trapper, and Samuels would have to work hard if he wanted to beat him for the pot. Garrett could see each man had a reasonable amount of skins already and either one could be in with a chance to win the prize money.

"Where you headed?" Samuels asked Garrett curiously.

"Heading back to the high ridge," Garrett answered coming to a stop by their fire. "Mind if I rest a while?" he asked looking at both men.

"Nah! go ahead, we were about to eat, don't mind sharing if you don't," Samuels grinned.

"Thanks," Garrett replied tethering his horses to brush and getting his mug out of his saddlebag. Taking his rifle off his shoulder, he squatted by the fire and helped himself to coffee.

With the three men finished eating and relaxing around the fire drinking more coffee, Samuels and Reece became lost in their own thoughts. They had already discussed the fact if Garrett were to join them how much better their trapping would be, and both were thinking how lucky it was to have him come along. Except for Samuels beating Joe that one time at winning the pot, both he and Reece felt their trapping had become the worst they had ever done since coming to the mountain. As well as quality, there had to be a quantity of skins to keep up with demand, and with the High Country being out of bounds, if they partnered with Garrett, they could venture to parts of the mountain only he was familiar with. Unable to see any reason why Garrett wouldn't agree to joining them, Samuels put it to him. "How about joining up with us Garrett? I mean now your team has split, maybe you could give us a chance." Garrett stopped his mug halfway to his mouth to take a moment to think about what Samuels was asking, then seating himself on his bedroll he became engrossed in memories indelibly burnt into his mind.

When he first came to the mountain, except for his friend Will, he liked being alone, and trapping let him do that, until he met up with Fergus, then Joe.

His strict upbringing left him hating authority, and that meant he didn't like following orders, so while in the cavalry, he spent a lot of time in solitary confinement for his refusal to do what his superior officers ordered. Having met Joe after he started trapping and Joe tried telling him what to do, it had them getting into a fierce argument when he tried setting Joe straight by reminding him he wasn't in the cavalry anymore, and that he wasn't going to be ordered about by a no-good has-been captain, resulting in their verbal argument turning into a physical fight.

With Joe and he facing off and both bloodied and barely able to stand from the blows they rained on each other, it was Joe, extending his hand in friendship first that changed Garrett's way of thinking. With their group of four formed, when Garrett made his promise to Calahan, he was happy to let Joe be their leader, and their friendship spanned many years.

Looking over the fire at Samuels and Reece, Garrett could see they hadn't waited for his answer, and had bed down for the night. Watching flames licking at pieces of wood, Garrett let out an audible sigh. The peace and quiet of the mountain suited him, and just like Sarah, he hated when it snowed and he had to leave it. He hated being cold, but learnt to live with it because he loved his life, such as it was. He doesn't need partners. Samuels asking him to be their partner brought back his sometimes, painful memories.

He would like to continue trapping alone, but knowing how dangerous it can be on the mountain, he concludes it best to partner with someone, and who better to partner with than Samuels and Reece?

When Samuels woke to relieve Garrett from the first watch he was thinking, 'was he going to partner with them or not?' But Reece's continual snoring was loud enough to dispel any thoughts and keep any marauding wolves at bay, and both Garrett and Samuels laughed. Then slipping into his bedroll, Garrett decided morning was soon enough to let them know he was going to take them on. Pulling the blanket up, he closed his eyes, and because winter was approaching, he shivered, because once again he would have to leave Sarah's mountain.

Chapter Thirty-five

After Sarah told him she was pregnant again, Foley let the axe slide through his fingers, and when it fell to the ground, he wrapped his arms around her and kissed her lovingly. Standing together, they watched their children playing in the clearing, then letting each other go, Foley went back to stacking wood and Sarah gathered Lizzy and David and took them inside.

Months passed quickly, winter had arrived, and this time Sarah would only be a few months along when they returned to Cedar Creek, which would make their trek a whole lot easier and a lot less worrisome than last winter. Still, Foley would worry endlessly about Sarah until she delivered their next baby.

Snow lay deep on the ground and flakes falling heavily from the sky sat on the hats and shoulders of the trappers as they followed each other in a long line. Their trek down Sarah's mountain had been exhausting. Every one of them felt tired and most were feeling their moods could be better. Sarah being with child gave Foley good reason to make sure she didn't have any issues with wolves when they got to the base of the mountain. Although running from wolves and stopping to skin their kill took precious time, they made good time getting to their next camp. After spending their last night out on the prairie huddled together around a blazing fire, they rode at a leisurely pace toward town.

Mountain View Lodge, consisting of two floors with huge glass windows facing the mountains could always be seen on the approach into town. Seeing the lodge come into view, was the signal the trappers arduous journey was at an end. Coming behind the lead men, Sarah looked toward town and frowned. When horses began stopping and bunching up, Foley wondered what they were doing but kept his horse level with Sarah's. Unable to see the reflection of the sun bouncing off the upstairs windows at the back of the lodge, the men looked back at Sarah and waited for her to bring her horses to a stop alongside Garrett.

"What do you make of that Sarah?" Garrett asked as they kept looking toward town.

"I don't know!" Sarah answered kicking her horse suddenly and breaking into a gallop. As she headed toward the bridge, the trappers got their horses to follow. On drawing closer to town, everyone stared as the whole of the second floor of the lodge seemed to have disappeared. Even the trees that lined the riverbank behind the lodge weren't there anymore.

Seeing them approaching, town folk began lining the street in readiness to greet them, but after riding quickly over the bridge, instead of riding down the main street, Sarah turned her horse down the alley beside the livery, then rode into the street where the lodge should have been. As she got near to where the grand house once stood, she slowed her horse. When Foley rounded the bend from the alley behind her, he swallowed in dismay at the site before him. The rest of the trappers bunching up around them stared in disbelief.

At the spot where burnt timbers and ash lay piled on the ground, Sarah got off her horse, and standing with David still strapped to her chest, looked at what remained of her home. The only thing standing was the stone chimney from the open fireplace that once graced the huge living area, charred black from flames that had engulfed the building.

Throwing his leg over his saddle, Foley dismounted, and standing beside Sarah put his arm around her. "I'm so sorry," he said quietly. As Garrett and the other men stood silent, Sarah leant against Foley speechless. When Sheriff Smith pushed his way through the men to stand beside her, Sarah listened while he explained how the town had tried to save her home.

Everything was gone. Her mother's portrait that hung in pride of place above the mantle. The piece of board with Frank's declaration of love for her. Her mother's beautiful dresses she loved to wear at her dinner parties. The magnificent cedar dining table the trappers made and the high-backed tapestry chairs. Her comfortable red velvet canopied bed and the ugly green winged chair that stood in front of the open fire that her Pa Calahan and Christian had both come to love sitting in was gone, all of it, burnt to ash. All Sarah had left of her beautiful home were her memories. At least she thought, nothing could take those away from her.

The trappers were speechless, but none more so than Garrett. The grand house and all of Sarah's cherished things were no more. Lizzy looked at the pile of blackened timbers and ash, and wondering where the big house was, felt saddened, because now she didn't have any stairs she could run up and down.

After gathering herself, Sarah went with the trappers to the Trading Post and was glad to see Fess still there, but he looked much older than she remembered. Telling them the same as what Sheriff Smith told them, Fess ended by saying how sorry he was for the lodge burning down. Standing back, the men let Sarah put her skins in first. On account of Foley being her partner, she had a good amount of skins again this year, and although she didn't win the pot, her name was written up near the top of the board. The men tried to make the moment a happy one, but no-one felt like celebrating.

Before organizing to go to the farm to see if they could stay with Brady and Ellen, Sarah and Foley went to the bank to put Sarah's chits in her account. When they entered, Michael greeted them cautiously.

"Where is Morley?" Sarah asked looking around. The bank looked different, Michael had rearranged counters and furnishings to make the bank more open, giving customers room to move about once inside.

"He's gone Misses Andrews," Michael informed her.

"Gone? What do you mean, gone?" Sarah hoped Michael wasn't going to tell her Morley was dead, she couldn't stand any more bad news, her legs felt like giving way as it was.

"He's gone to live with his children, Esther passed away not long after you went back to the mountain, Morley felt he couldn't stay once she passed, he wants to spend his remaining days with his children and grandchildren." Michael seemed sad as he told Sarah the news.

Although relieved to hear Morley was still alive, Sarah was saddened to hear Esther was not. Sarah and Esther had been friends, and sitting on top of her chest of drawers in her cabin was the duchess set of doilies Esther had made and given her.

"I'm happy he has gone to be with his children, now, can we do business Michael?" Sarah asked him.

"Yes, we most certainly can, Misses Andrews." Michael hurried around the counter to get Sarah's book and the Fur Trading Company ledger.

"I'm Sarah, Michael, I see no reason for you to call me Misses Andrews if we are going to do business together." Michael looked amazed at Sarah giving him permission to call her Sarah.

"Well, thank you… Sarah," he said inclining his head toward her in acknowledgement, and smiling, got down to putting her chits in.

Glancing at the entries in Sarah's book, Michael could see she had a large sum of money held in his bank. The most recent deposit coming from Major Hardy, whom saddened by the destruction of Mountain View Lodge, requested his deposit remain secret. Sarah had loved his son and was the mother of his grandson Thomas, and he saw no reason just because she was married to Foley for her to go without the means to support herself, and because of Major Hardy's generosity, Sarah became a much wealthier woman.

While Michael entered Sarah's chit in her book, his face took on a flushed appearance, giving Sarah cause to study him, and for her to make up her mind he wasn't such a bad man after all. It was a long time ago that she frightened him with her knife so much she thought he was going to faint dead away. His arrogance surprised her when he thought he could call her Sarah, so pulling her knife from its sheath and pointing it toward him, she warned him of how she should be addressed, which left him not knowing what to call her, and most of the time when she came to the bank, he didn't call her anything. Sarah managed a faint smile as she remembered.

As Sarah and Foley made their way to the farm, Sarah began to cry. Reaching across the space between them as they rode side by side, Foley took her hand in his. Having experienced the same when he and Brady lost their family in the fire that destroyed their farm, there were no words he could say that would take away her pain of losing her home.

"I still have a few things at the cabin," Sarah sobbed. "I don't know why I took them with me, maybe I had a feeling something was going to happen." Sarah drew back her tears as Foley squeezed her hand. Along with silver cutlery and a silver candlestick, there were floor rugs, lace quilts and bed-clothes. She had the beautiful silk shawl Joe gave her. She even had a painting that would hang very nicely above the mantle in a new lodge, but Sarah wasn't giving any thought to rebuilding. Right now, everything seemed beyond her. She was expecting Foley's second child and her fourth, all she wanted was to get through this winter and return to her mountain and her cabin. She was determined to have this baby up there like she had Thomas. At least up there she was happy.

Chapter Thirty-six

Even though Brady and Ellen welcomed Sarah and Foley with open arms, with Lizzy and David having to share the same room as they, and as well as the twins scrambling about underfoot and throughout the rest of the house, Sarah and Foley were feeling the cramped living conditions. Desperate for freedom, Foley organized their first trip into town. After bathing, Sarah dressed in a white peasant blouse and black skirt Ellen let her borrow. Foley's best clothes burnt to ash along with Sarah's and Lizzy's beautiful dresses when the lodge burnt down, so he wore what he wore when he came from the mountain. While in town, Sarah planned to go shopping to get new clothes for all of them.

Stopping at the U S Mail Office first, Sarah was pleasantly surprised when she was handed two letters. One from Thomas in Philadelphia, the other from Fergus, all the way from Ireland. Eagerly tearing open Thomas's letter first, and with a little help from Foley reading over her shoulder, Sarah read Thomas's news. After learning she was a grandmother when the letter said Gabrielle had an easy birth and they welcomed a son, Sarah laughed and cried at the same time, and when Thomas asked if she didn't mind if they called their son Joseph Calahan Mason-Hardy, she was thrilled, and told Foley they would have to visit Philadelphia some-time in the near future so she could hold her grandson.

The other letter told her Fergus made it safely home, all be it over rough seas through horrendous weather to be greeted by family with a huge gathering of clans. But he wrote he missed her and his friends terribly, which convinced Sarah he was torn between his love for both countries. Happy at last to have good news, she folded her letters and put them in Foley's inside coat pocket for safe keeping. Then while spending time in Henry's Emporium choosing new clothes, Sarah sensed Henry was trying to hurry them along. Every time she put something on the counter, he asked her if that was all she wanted and if she was done. It was beginning to irk her and make her wonder just what he was up to.

Becoming perturbed by his manner, she took her time choosing two dresses for Lizzy along with petticoats and stockings to be worn with new boots and hair ribbons. She took her time helping Foley choose a new jacket. Then, after putting two pair of trousers on the counter and Henry asked her again if she was done, she glared at him and went and chose another pair simply because he was hurrying her up.

After Sarah and Foley left his store, Henry quickly locked up, and racing out the back, ran along the street behind all the buildings. There was somewhere important he had to be and he didn't want to be late lest he miss the surprise.

After coming from Henry's Emporium and loading their parcels in the buckboard, Sarah held Lizzy's hand and Foley carried David while they strolled arm in arm along the main street. As they walked, they both frowned when noticing the town seemed unusually quiet. It wasn't Sunday, the town should have been bustling. Rounding the bend in the street, they stopped and stared at all the folk gathered outside what appeared to be a newly constructed building standing next to the schoolhouse. Upon returning from the mountain, when Sarah and Foley rode in over the bridge, they were too engrossed in what happened to the lodge to notice anything different about the town. Seeing them come around the bend, Jonathon O'Rourke hurried toward them with a broad smile on his face. As he approached them, the crowd turned as one to watch.

"Sarah, hello, Foley, good to see you?" Jonathon said while greeting Foley with a handshake and Sarah with a kiss on her cheek.

Spying Brady and Ellen standing amongst everyone, and having no idea how they got to town before he and Sarah, Foley furrowed his brow further. They had been at the farm when he and Sarah left in Brady's buckboard.

"How did..." he started to ask but didn't finish as Jonathon ushered them quickly through the crowd. When Sarah spied

Henry standing amongst folk too, she thought this must be why he hurried them along. 'But why was there such a crowd here?' she wondered.

After Sarah and Foley left the farm to go to town, Brady and Ellen bundled the twins into their newly acquired surrey, and racing to Ellen's fathers farm he collected Otis, his wife Isabella and Ellen's sister Lara, then cut across farmland to Wills farm. Once there, Will, with Sissy nursing their first born in her arms, followed them in their buckboard to arrive in town before Sarah and Foley were halfway along the road. After Brady and Otis told everyone Sarah was on her way, they hurried to the Ferguson House and roused the trappers. It was no accident Major Hardy was in town looking over a herd of horses that had been brought to the corrals. He and his men stood with the rest of the town folk to watch the proceedings.

"Come on Sarah! you too Foley! I want to show you something!" Jonathon said excitedly taking Sarah by her hand. The crowd of eager onlookers watched what was about to unfold with interest as Sarah and Foley stood with Jonathon in front of the building where a large banner covered the façade. Jonathon turned to face everyone crowding in close.

"Folks!" he announced, holding his hands up for quiet.

"Sarah... I, and everyone here are very sorry for your loss, Mountain View Lodge was a grand building, without it the town seemed to be, well, less special." There were murmurs of agreement from the crowd.

"But now, because of your generous gift, this building, also grand I might add, will give much pleasure to all of us for many years to come... Sarah, allow me to present to you, Cedar Creek's, very own... library!"

With everyone staring up at the façade at what the banner covered, Jonathon handed the rope holding the banner to Sarah. Not sure what she should do with it, she pulled on the rope anyway, and watched as the banner fell away to reveal the buildings title, 'SARAH ELIZABETH COLE LIBRARY' which was followed by loud cheering and applause.

As Sarah read the words her eyes began to sting, but she still managed to look at Jonathon, who was smiling rather smugly back at her.

"The town took a vote as to which name of yours we should use, and we decided Cole was the best, no offence to you Foley," he said grinning at Foley. Pleased they chose Sarah's birth name, Foley smiled and embraced her. Embracing Foley in return, Sarah drew back a sob and taking David from him, went with Jonathon as he pushed open the two ornate entrance doors and ushered her, Foley and Lizzy inside to the huge expanse of the interior. Along with Major Hardy and others, Will and Garrett made their way in to look about and were amazed at how big the library was.

In the middle of the vast room stood Sarah's black leather couch. Her mahogany desk with its original glass lamp sitting in pride of place on top and leather chair stood behind the couch as it had done in the lodge. Shelves taken from the lodge lined all four walls, and each were filled with books.

"These are your books Sarah," Jonathon whispered, then feeling the lump in his throat rise when he saw Sarah's eyes settle on something on the far wall, he was glad he thought of what it was she was looking at. Taking David from Sarah and handing him back to Foley, he took Sarah's hand in his and led her around the couch and desk. As they drew near to the back of the room, Sarah couldn't take her eyes off the wall.

Between the bookshelves standing along that wall was a space, and in that space hung a portrait where the woman's angelic face smiled out at them. The tip of her long brown hair, curled over one of her bare shoulders, kissed the very edge of the white lace bordering the blue dress she was wearing. A gold chain and heart shaped locket, sitting just above her bust, hung about her slim neck. Sarah hadn't lost everything in the fire after all, and she could hardly see for tears welling in her eyes. Turning to look at Jonathon a tear slid down her cheek.

"I hope you don't mind Sarah, I looked at her, and for a moment thought your mother belongs here, watching over your books where folks can see how beautiful she was," he added.

398

"Oh Jonathon, they were her books, and I'm so happy you took her," Sarah answered tearfully, throwing her arms around him. Fighting the lump in his throat, Jonathon embraced her.

While her Ma and Pa and everyone else was sniffling, Lizzy hurried to a bookshelf, and pulling out a book, climbed on the leather couch where she sat and opened it. This was what a library was all about. With everyone borrowing books, it wouldn't be long before the library became the centre of town.

Taking Foley by the arm and Lizzy by the hand, Sarah left the library, and stepping into the street, was greeted by a crowd of men still milling about. There were ranchers and farmers, as well as cowhands and trappers, and timber cutters, all of whom she knew well, and all waiting for Beasley, the owner of the lumberyard to say his piece. Stepping forward nervously, Beasley cleared his throat.

"Misses Andrews, Sarah, if I may call you that?" He paused and waited to see if Sarah would object to his calling her Sarah, and when she didn't, he went on. "We here know how much Mountain View Lodge meant to you, and well..." He looked around at the men watching him with bated breath, and hoped they would back up what he was about to say. "We would like you to know, that if you decide to rebuild the lodge, every man here would be willing to help build it, and if it happens to be of interest to you, I still have the plans your father drew." When Beasley finished speaking, the men nodded in agreement.

Looking around at the men, Sarah took her time before answering, "I'm not thinking about it Beasley." Then pausing while letting her eyes rest on him she saw his disappointment, and thought she should at least consider it. "I will let you know," she said. Then hooking her arm in Foley's arm, and leaving the men staring after them, they walked down the street where they rounded the bend and headed back to their buckboard.

As they walked, Foley kept his eyes straight ahead. "That was a fine offer Beasley made you, you do know those men respect you, don't you Sarah? They will work for you for no pay." Foley wanted Sarah to rebuild so they could add to the memories forged in that house. She was happy there when entertaining her friends, and two of her three children had been born there.

"A new lodge would not be the same as the old one Foley," she said almost at a whisper as a kaleidoscope of memories swirled through her mind.

Stopping at the buckboard, Foley handed David to Sarah while he helped Lizzy up to sit on the seat. Turning to Sarah, he took David back off her, and with his free hand helped her into the buckboard. "We could make our memories in a new lodge," he said almost to himself as Sarah reached down and took David. After climbing up next to her, they returned to the farm in silence.

Once again Sarah and Foley found themselves crowded into the farmhouse with Brady and Ellen, and once again, with David and Lizzy and the twins running underfoot, the house became a nightmare to live in. Mealtimes were a free-for-all as everyone clambered over each other getting food. Sarah and Foley persevered with the living conditions for as long as they could, but it was getting Sarah down, and Foley was feeling agitated too. He and Sarah couldn't make love the way they did when they were alone in Sarah's cabin. What with Brady and Ellen sleeping in the room next to theirs, every time Foley tried to make love to Sarah, Brady and Ellen could be heard making love when their bedhead banged against the wall. Foley and Sarah tried getting in rhythm with them, but it only made them burst out laughing. Foley ended up feeling frustrated, and feeling the farm was not like her own home, giving her no freedom at all to move about in, Sarah gave it another week of suffering, until she felt she had had enough.

"Take me to town Foley!" she said seriously one morning when they were all crowded in the small kitchen. Foley didn't hesitate. Rushing to the barn to get the buckboard, he and Sarah along with their children went to town. As the buckboard trundled swiftly along the road, Foley kept glancing at Sarah clinging to the seat beside him with a look of determination on her face as she kept her eyes focused on the road ahead, making him wonder what she was up to.

"Stop the buckboard!" Sarah demanded as he brought the buckboard level with the bank.

Pulling back on the reins, he slowed the horse enough to allow the buckboard to come to a safe stop, but Sarah didn't wait for him to help her out of the wagon. Leaving Foley to lift the children out and follow, she climbed down and hurried into the bank ahead of everyone.

Looking up from his one customer he was serving when Sarah came in, Michael simply greeted her with a nod. When Sarah interrupted them by asking to do business with him, saying it was private, Michael quickly dispatched his customer and ushered Sarah's family to his office where he seated Sarah in front of his desk. Taking the chair next to Sarah, Foley sat David on his knee and let Lizzy stand beside him.

"Now, Sarah! tell me what 'private' business can I do for you?" Michael asked as he leant forward and clenched his hands together on top of his desk.

Hoping the answer to what she was about to ask would be satisfactory, Sarah kept her eyes fixed firmly on Michael, and felt her stomach quiver. Maybe it was nerves, but feeling it was more likely the new baby beginning to stir, she took a deep breath before speaking.

But would she be making the right decision? She had grown up in the lodge, it had been her winter home for fifteen years before Crawley took it away from her. It was there with her then father Calahan that she dressed in frilly dresses and later entertained friends with dinner parties. It was there, sitting at the table with her back straight like a lady, her silver knife and fork and china dinner service in front of her, that she learnt good manners. Her then father taught her to say please when she asked for something and thank you when receiving it. She had loved her parent's bedroom with its comfortable canopied bed and dresser with its three-sided mirror where she sat brushing her hair after it became hers when she married Christian, and again with Foley. Riding in and seeing Mountain View Lodge was no more made her feel she had suffered another death in her family, and she tried her best to move on from her loss, but events over the last few weeks were taking its toll. Although she loves her mountain home where she has taught Foley the art of trapping and skinning, and even though he has taken to it wholeheartedly, he has not yet become good at either, but what he said about making their own memories, and it being such a lovely thought had embedded itself in her mind, and so she has made up her mind.

Straightening up in her chair, she clasped her hands together in her lap and looked Michael in the eye.

"Is there..." she began, haltingly. "Do I..." she stopped and cleared her throat. "Is there, enough money, for me to rebuild the lodge?" she ended with a hint of nervousness.

Hearing Sarah's question, Foley's heart skipped a beat. Turning his head sharply to look at her, a feeling of satisfaction washed over him.

Having felt the strain of being cooped up in an overcrowded house, while standing in the middle of a newly ploughed field, Foley took the opportunity to speak with Brady, and they came up with a plan where Brady agreed to talk with the men around town, to ask them if they would be willing to help rebuild the lodge, for a small payment of course, and if they agreed, Foley planned to foot the bill. Brady came back a few days later and told Foley that when word got around about their plan, all the men agreed to pitch in, and they would gladly do it without payment, but only if Sarah would agree.

When Sarah told Beasley, she wasn't thinking of rebuilding, it almost threw Foley's plan into disarray, so he had to come up with some other way of getting Sarah to change her mind, and that was when he asked Brady and Ellen to let the children make as much noise and mess in their house as was possible to annoy Sarah, and it had worked. Sitting there in the bank, Foley made a mental note to himself that he must remember to thank both Brady and Ellen for helping him force Sarah into making her decision.

Standing up quickly, he shoved David across Michaels desk toward him. Having no other option, Michael stood up and reaching out, took him. As David and Michael studied each other, David's bottom lip quivered in a downward pout and Michael, hoping he wasn't about to cry, jiggled him up and down while Foley took both of Sarah's hands in his and lifted her to her feet. Then pushing his fingers through her hair and cupping her face, he gazed into her eyes.

"Misses Andrews! besides marrying me! that is the best darn decision you have ever made! and ever will!" He kissed her then, and while kissing him back, Sarah figured he had a hand in making her decide to rebuild Mountain View Lodge.

Winter passed at a more leisurely pace for Sarah and her family. After Foley and Brady organized a clean out of their barn, long tables and stools were set up so Sarah could hold a dinner party, and of course, Ellen's family were the first to be invited. Along with Garrett, other trappers attended too. There was Will and Sissy, who brought their baby with them and informed Sarah they were expecting another. Major Hardy was there with his two gun-hands, who came along to watch for trouble. Ham and Patrice, Doc Harris and Gerda, and Michael from the bank were only too pleased to attend. Others came too, like Henry from the store, who provided all the ingredients for the scrumptious food, and Fess who brought his fiddle so everyone could enjoy a dance or two. Although the party ended with drunken men firing their guns in the air outside to show their appreciation for being invited, Sarah was pleased with how her party went.

When winter drew to a close, work on rebuilding Mountain View Lodge began in earnest. Sarah did her utmost best to order furnishings from catalogues at Henry's Emporium similar to ones that had graced the lodge before the fire. If everything went according to plan, the lodge would be completed and furnished by the time the trappers returned the following winter.

Sarah and Foley had their buckboard packed ready for another year of trapping. When the trappers began heading over the bridge, they left Sarah and Foley with Beasley, going over plans for the new lodge. Excited to be overseeing the building work, Beasley was rushing headlong into it.

"There is no need to hurry," Sarah informed him. "I want everything to be perfect for when I return."

"You sure you want to have that baby on your mountain? Don't you want to have it here in the lodge?" Beasley asked looking not at Sarah but at Foley. Satisfied he and the trappers would be there for Sarah when she delivered their baby, Foley didn't offer up a reply. Assuming they were happy to have their baby on the mountain, Beasley shrugged and went on.

"Well, by the time you come back Misses Andrews, the lodge will be better than it ever was," he said rolling up the plans.

"I don't want it better, I want it to be the same as it was, just stick to the plans, and call me Sarah," Sarah said smiling and extending her hand. "Goodbye Beasley." Taking her hand in his, they held their grasp for a moment before Sarah turned to go.

"Goodbye, Sarah," Beasley replied as she made her way along the street to the bridge where a crowd was gathered and her buckboard sat waiting.

After saying goodbye to her friends, Sarah kissed Will and hugged him, then climbed onto the seat where she sat beside Foley. David slept comfortably nestled in Sarah's arms, while Lizzy sat perched amongst supplies in the back of the buckboard for their journey. Slapping the reins on the back of their horses Foley took the wagon over the bridge.

Once across the bridge, he stopped the wagon on the trail to allow Sarah to look back at the people standing at the bridge watching them leave. When everyone simultaneously raised their hands to her in farewell, Sarah raised her hand back, then turning to Foley, smiled.

"Let's go Foley," she said. "We'll see them all again next winter."

Epilogue

1901

$\mathcal{A}$ mere three hours walk up from Sarah's cabin, Lizzy's younger brothers David and Jonah were busy setting traps in the dense forest behind her while she stood on an outcrop of boulders looking over green forested valleys and escarpments of the mountain's they called home.

Dressed in tight fitting shirt and trousers, Lizzy also wears a vest made from wolf skins secured around her waist by a belt holding a sheath, that was handed down to her by her mother Sarah, which carries a large hunting knife that hangs to her knees. Shading her face from the hot noonday sun, is a sweat stained raggedy hat with a split brim that once belonged to her grandfather Calahan Cole. Slung over her shoulder is a long-barreled rifle that most times is used for hunting, but other times is used to ward off cowboys and farm-hands begging her to be their girl. Lizzy has a beau whom she loves very much, and one day she will marry him, but she still has a problem with those men that continually tell her she is pretty and keep proposing marriage to her, and so she is seriously thinking about getting her Ma to help her deal with them. Her long brown hair, thick with curls she wears fastened in a braid down her back just like Sarah wears hers. To look at Lizzy, one would think it was Sarah standing there.

Lizzy's porcelain doll had been put aside long ago. She loves the mountain where her mother Sarah and stepfather Foley have taught her and her brothers everything they know about trapping. David and Jonah are just like their father, which Lizzy knows pleases her mother immensely. But on account of three trappers, Garrett,

Samuels and Reece's influence, Lizzy is much like Sarah used to be, but unlike Sarah, she doesn't mind winter, because when they make the journey to Cedar Creek to spend Christmas in their grand home Mountain View Lodge, Lizzy gets to wear pretty dresses she doesn't get to wear on the mountain, and she gets to go dancing with her beau.

No longer the small town it used to be, Cedar Creek has become a city like Moreton with stores bigger than Henry's Emporium and numerous dance halls and gambling houses that have overtaken the saloon. There are paved streets and gas lamps, and someone mentioned there would soon be carriages running their streets that moved by themselves that would see horses no longer required to get around, which caused Sarah and her family to laugh at the hideous thought.

Having set their traps, David and Jonah bounded out of the forest to stand beside Lizzy where all three gazed silently in awe at the panoramic vista stretching out before them.

"You ready to go Lizzy?" David asked turning to face her.

"Yeah," Lizzy replied while scanning the escarpments for wolves.

"Come on then, I'll race you!" Jonah said smiling broadly.

Knowing their mother would be at their cabin waiting for them to return as she always did when they ventured out to hunt, Jonah turned swiftly, and leaping off the boulders, headed at a cracking pace back into the forest, making Lizzy and David run to catch up to him.

Sarah doesn't trap these days, nor does Foley. They prefer to take their rifles and go as far as the River Flats, or stay close to their cabin that Foley has extended to accommodate his family. If they happen to see a wolf, then good, but they don't go searching for them. Having imparted her knowledge of her mountain on to her children, Sarah still worries while they are away hunting. She won't permit herself to stop worrying, not until she sees all three coming along the trail toward her.

Standing beyond her cabin with Foley, Sarah held her hand to her brow to shade her face from the glaring afternoon sun and waited. When she spied shadows moving about amongst the forest, relief washed over her at seeing her children come bursting from the trail at a run, causing her to smile as her youngest son Jonah beat Lizzy and David to her side. Foley smiled too at seeing his children, and putting his arm around Sarah, gave her a gentle squeeze to reassure her everything was fine.

"How many wolves did you get?" Sarah asked frowning when noticing they weren't carrying any skins.

"None Ma," David answered.

"I think they are dying out," Lizzy said breathlessly.

"No... no, they are out there," Sarah replied softly while gazing off to the distant mountains before bringing her attention back to the moment.

"Come on," she said putting her arm around Foley. "Let's get you lot fed, you must be hungry by now."

"Starving," David answered for everyone, and laughing in agreeance to his reply, Sarah's children headed to the cabin ahead of her and Foley.

"Ma? While we are eating, can you tell us about the time you trapped two white wolves and beat Grandpa Joe for the pot?" Jonah asked.

"Goodness, Jonah! don't you ever get tired of hearing that old story?" Sarah exclaimed before smiling up at Foley and winking.

"Never!" All three children, and Foley chorused.

The End.